Human nature can be studied  the world too full of tragedy to allow a ⟨...⟩ gy suggests "that a person can be happy while confronting life realistically and while working productively to improve the conditions of existence" (Seligman & Csiksentmihaly, 2000)

QUEEN MARY

Sociology of the Common People

By Gregory Victor Snowden

CHAPTER ONE

TORTURED SOULS

It was the darkest night of my life. I ran frantically down a long, narrow road. It was pitch black. I couldn't see the moon. My blood was hot and my heart was racing. My heart was pumping with fear because I did not know what I was running from or why I was running at all. I could hardly see the road and I could barely make out that there was a low wooden fence along each side of the street. My hands and feet felt cold and the street sounded damp with pain underneath the pounding of my feet. I slipped, fell and caught my balance on the hard fence next to me. The force of the wood slamming into my side knocked the wind out of my lungs, yet made me aware of the short cut through the woods that would lead me to safety. At that moment I jumped the fence and continued running through the woods. I was alone and I could hardly see my own hands in front of me. I was trying to find something, anything to grab a hold on to in order to catch my balance while running through the thick brush. I could feel my shirt flutter with the speed and strength of the wind. It seemed to be trying to blow me backwards and had an evil sound of a ghostly wind that carried voices of lost souls. They howled and whispered words of despair, hate and revenge into my mind as a loud thunderous sound scorched the sky with wicked lightening that flickered down around me. Multiple bolts of lightning pierced the trees and set blazing fires to the branches.

 The fire burned the leaves and released a dark, greyish smoke that formed into a spiral of angry, black, spirits, which chased after me like a jet in the sky followed by its toxic fumes. Several of them caught up with me and I could feel them scratching at my back. I ran faster but they moved quickly in the wind that seemed to swirl around me and imprisoned my fear into hate.

 They stopped scratching and pulling at my clothes for a moment and then darted past me and formed this huge monstrous dark figure in front of me. I stopped in my tracks wanting to turn and run the other way but for some strange reason, I could not move. Something about it was familiar. Breathing heavily, I stared at it for a moment, just as it seemed to be analyzing me. Just for a few seconds, I was not afraid but curious. My heart rate slowed down and I was able to catch my breath. "Who are you?" "What do you want and why are you after me?" These were the questions I wondered but before I could speak them suddenly, the dark human figure of grey smoke let out an angry roar that blew back the skin on my face and smelled of death as if to say, "How dare you question me!"

At that moment I felt my body flinch to run, but it was too late. In one motion the spirits struck my chest and buried itself inside of me. I fell to the ground choking from the smell of the evil, wicked smoke that burned my throat and tightened its grip, surrounding my chest. I was laying there, on my back, gasping for air, and I couldn't get enough to fill my lungs. I thought I was dying, and then it began to rain. It came down hard and fast as if the rain was trying to punish me. The hard, fast, furious and cold rain seemed to be pushing me into the mud. I struggled to my feet and tried to make out my surroundings.

Confused, I wondered. "Where am I?" I wondered why this was happening to me?" The dark figure had struck me but I was still alive. I was soaking wet, tired and cold but now something was different. My heart felt just as cold as the storm and it was hardened with hate and revenge. I felt worthless, hopeless and rejected. I was furious and felt myself, clinch my hands together to form fists of war. I grinded my teeth together, jaws locked tight as my heart started to pump faster again. This time not from fear but from a place of hell that made me want to release the pain that I was feeling with just as much vengeful damage as I felt, inside my soul. Someone was going to get hurt.

No longer afraid of the dark night filled with spirits, fire, danger, a raging storm and evil, I ran deeper into the woods as I became one with it. I absorbed it and let the evil night feed my frustrations and turmoil that boiled in my stomach, burned my throat and poisoned my mind with false illusions. The power of it made me feel faster and stronger. It was like I had night vision. I had tunnel vision to a wicked place. I was running so fast now that the rain fell in slow motion around me. The wind was behind me and no tree or obstacle got in the way of my destination. I did not yet know where that destination was but I was approaching it fast with a furious grudge. My anger would not allow me to stop running until I reached the end of this horrible experience. I remember thinking how unworthy and how unloved I felt. I felt unwanted and only this evil night understood me. "What did I do to deserve this miserable existence?" I wondered. At that very moment of despair and feeling sorry for myself, my weakness caused me to lose my balance as I tripped over my feet and flew face first into the dirty, wet mud again.

I raised my head to breathe and catch my breath. It was a difficult task because the air was filled with a foul odor. The rain once again punished me and the night hated me. I didn't try to get up. I felt that I belonged there lying face down in this filthy sewage of black leaves, sharp sticks, dirty mud and a fowl, odor that was as dark as my soul. No one seemed to care about me anyway, so why should I give a damn? I broke down and cried feeling ashamed as a man. For so long I held on to my faith and now I was broken. I buried my face back in the mud, to drown my sorrows only to be startled by the sound of horrific laughter. I looked up and right in front of me stood a tombstone that wasn't there before. I could read it clearly as the rain washed away the splattered mud on the dark grey headstone. It was my father's name.

At that moment all the rage inside of me awakened again and I got to my knees and started frantically digging away the mud that covered his casket with my bare hands. I could feel the wet dirt harden underneath my nails as I pulled away tree roots and stones hidden in the mud. My arms were tired and my fingers were swollen and covered in blood but that didn't stop me at all. I quickly reached my destination. There it was, a casket that protected my sperm donor's body. I called him that because he was never there to guide me through the darkness of a cruel world. There was only one thing left to do and I could end this pain. I jumped on top of it and flung open the lid. Without a second thought I grabbed the remains of his body that was now an old, porous skeleton and pulled it up frantically in a half sitting position. I jumped to my feet, stood on the base of the casket and kicked in, what was once, his face over and over again. The rain was still coming down hard on my back. It punished me more and more as my anger allowed me to watch the bones of the skeleton's head break away into dust under the force of my Timberland boots. When there was nothing of him left I screamed. "You mutha, fuckaaa!" At that moment the rain slowed, my heart stopped beating so fast and I finally felt some form of relief.

I turned away to climb out of the hole, I had dug so ferociously. I could see a bit of light in the sky. Just before I reached the top, a black filled smoke slowly came out of my chest, I felt no pain. Then suddenly the smoke presented itself above me and forced me back into the grave. I fell back into the casket and what was once a resemblance of light in the sky was now a burning dark red frightening figure that raised all the wet mud slowly in the air and then swiftly willed it to cover me. The force of it took my breath away and then there was a deadly silence and cold feeling of nothing. Gasping for oxygen, I woke up in my bed confused, sweating and afraid I was losing my mind. It was just a dream but it felt so real. I was disturbed by the thoughts in my mind. Why did I have so much hate inside and why would I dream of such a horrible thing?

I searched for the remote underneath the pillow in my bed. I turned the T.V. on. Not surprising at all, there was more disturbing news that had occurred in my city. A prominent state representative in our community and his wife, was struck by a vehicle. He and his wife would walk each morning together for exercise and take the time to discuss community concerns and negotiations. They were both great at understanding the needs of the common people. He was sure to be the new mayor by popular belief in the community. Mr. Mark Wardlow and his wife were pronounced dead on arrival at the hospital. I rolled over and sat at the edge of the bed to gather my thoughts and cool down. My long dreadlocks often made me sweat around my neck when I would forget to tie them back before going to bed. But this time I had awakened fully drenched with perspiration of fear.

It was the hot scorching month of July, 2016 and the weather was the devil's breath. Sleeping with the assistance of cool air from the ceiling fan was a welcomed luxury, especially when I'd been drinking vodka straight on the rocks the night before. I pulled my dreadlocks back and let the fan cool the back of my neck while holding my head down in disappointment of the tragic news about Mr. Wardlow and his insightful wife.

I could see the sweat on my chest evaporate. I began to feel better from the cool breeze of the fan. I'm six feet tall and usually, I walk straight up, shoulders squared with pride but that morning I got out of bed and walked as if I was only two feet tall, head down and slouched my way to the dresser and turned up what was left of the bottle of vodka, I'd taken home from the night club my best friend owned. The liquor burned my throat, warmed my chest and hit the bottom of my empty stomach like a volcano. Breakfast of champions I thought to myself as I heard the voice of my brother Byron in the back of my mind say "Get yourself together Greg." He had always been my voice of reason when he was alive.

Byron loved listening to music. He wrote poetry and stood about six feet tall. He was the definition of tall, dark and handsome. He was very funny and he had an infectious laugh that made you want to laugh with him even if you didn't know what he was laughing about. He was physically fit and worked out early each morning. I would give anything to be a small boy again anxiously awaiting him to wake me up to go jogging with him again.

He and I had the same build with the exception that he was older and dark skinned whereas I was light skinned like my grandmother.. My brother Byron passed away in the month of April, 2016 from something called pancreatitis. We later found out that he knew his condition for years, but never told us. While serving in the United States Marine Corps, he learned of his condition. He served 10 years and received an honorable discharge. After that he continued to work on base in Albany GA, where his military friends called him captain even though he wasn't a captain at all.

He was a prideful leader and one of the most caring person, I've ever known so it didn't surprise me that he kept his condition a secret to protect us from worrying about him. He was that kind of man and had not only been a good brother to me but also cared and treated me as if he were my father whenever I needed it. He lived at home with us until I was about eight years old. After that he was home on leave occasionally during his time in the military but he still managed to be an influential role model in our life. He could make you laugh about anything and always told us stories and adventures of his life. Not to mention that he seemed to be mom's favorite son of the three of us boys.

Usually kids have a problem when they get a sense that one sibling is favored over the others but It didn't bother me. Well, hell, fuck it. Let's just say he was my favorite too. Larry was the oldest, I was the youngest and Byron was the middle son. My mother and her beloved son Byron passed away two weeks apart from one another in the same month of April, 2016. She gathered her wings on her birthday. Both mom and Byron were in the hospital fighting for their lives, therefore we couldn't tell them about the other one's situation in hopes that not knowing would increase their chances of survival. Sadly, they both passed away without knowing about the critical condition of each other's fate.

What was worse than that, my grand momma Valla, passed away from old age the following month of May, 2016. She was named Valla because she was born on February 14. She baked cakes constantly and gave all the money she made off of ice cream and cakes to the church she belonged to. She was known as the candy lady to all the kids in the projects because she sold sodas, ice-cream, pop-sickles, cookies and pies from her kitchen freezer.

She was 103 years old when she passed away and lived a blessed life. She was lucky enough to see a black president get elected and was better able to take care of herself due to President Obama's health care program that allowed people with pre-existing conditions to obtain health care benefits. Grandma had long black hair and smooth light skin. She often told us stories about how she would pass for white and get into the movies that black people were not allowed inside. Her father was white and her mother was a full blooded Indian. In her old age she was kind of heavy set with bad knees but still a beautiful lady with the ability to get around enough to always have a delicious dinner waiting for her loved ones and church every sunday.

Every time we visited her she was always sitting in the kitchen cooking and watching the kids play outside from her kitchen window. Her kitchen was always hot so she kept the kitchen window and back door open and allowed a cool breeze to come through the screen door. I never understood how she could be in there most of the day. The inside and outside of the project's walls were brick, and had small compacted rooms. From her seat at the kitchen table she could watch the food on the stove, go out the back door to hang clothes on the washing line or bring them in after they were dry. She knew that all the kids outside, including myself would wait until she hung her white sheets on the clothes line to run and play between them. So she watched carefully through the screen door while she baked cakes, to run away any kid caught running through her sheets.

The pantry connected to the kitchen is where she kept a long white, freezer, full of ice cream and frozen delights. The rest of the goodies were on shelves above the freezer. The pantry made it easy for her to sell candy and soda pops to the kids, knocking at her kitchen back door.. Of course we got goodies for free but we could only get one. "Don't get but one, that's how I get my money to give to the church baby," she would say.

I always sat on the freezer because it was cold and would make me feel better from being in her hot kitchen but she always thought I was waiting to steal more goodies than she was willing to give away free, so she would kick us outside. "Get on out there and play, I'm trying to cook"! Grandma, Valla didn't know about her daughter and grandson's death. Even if we had told her she probably wouldn't have remembered them. The last time I visited her in the hospital, she didn't recognize me at all. All three of them were hospitalized at the same time. My mother, my grandmother and my brother Byron were all in critical condition, so you can only imagine the kind of pain my family were going through.

Only a few months had gone by and now I was breaking down because I had lost the only three people in my life, which I knew for sure loved me all at once during the months of April and May of 2016. Hearing my brother's voice in my head would always allow me to gather the strength to move mountains. That particular morning the mountains were high and many. Their names were, mental anguish, divorce, death, and pain. To make my tortured soul even worse I was disgusted by my helpless feeling of seeing people of color being politically manipulated and victims of injustice and police brutality.

I walked into the bathroom, looked into the mirror and did not recognize the person looking back at me. My heart was heavy and my mind was a storm of sorrow, and self pity. Late night eating had become my companion in the middle of the night and alcohol had become the medicine that helped to ease my pain. Once physically fit, I had gained about twenty pounds in just a few short months after the passing of my loved ones. Ten pounds on my stomach, ten more pounds distributed in unknown places, but I could definitely feel them. The worry and stress on my face caused me to look sad most of the time. My smile was non-existent. My dreads were pulled back most of the time and needed re-twisting. There were times I had to motivate myself to shave, put on a fake smile in order to get through a normal work day and not reveal the torture inside.

Behind my smile, I wore a frown of an abused, neglected child. I was also saddened that I had reluctantly allowed myself to feel obligated to inform my father of my mother's illness before she passed away. It took him forever to come to the door and when he did, I wasn't invited inside his home. Not only did he insult me by talking to me on his porch as if I was a total stranger, he showed no emotion and didn't even attend my mother's funeral shortly afterwards. I wondered if that experience was the culprit of my evil dream. I honestly believed that he never visited her at the hospital. My mother was a strong independent, prideful woman. She never spoke one single bad word about him even though he was never there for us. She never asked for his help or attempted to seek financial assistance. "Why would she love a man like that," I painfully wondered. I knew I couldn't allow myself to think of him for long, so I shook my head as if to run away any feelings of weakness being the reason for a dream as dark as it felt in my soul.

Although, I couldn't understand his absence I knew my mother was a caring person, so perhaps one day I'd find a reason to accept him the way I wanted him to accept me. Unfortunately the older I got, I learned nothing more about him other than his cruelty and inconsideration. But mom had a heart of gold. She always said that she wouldn't force him to take care of his responsibilities. "Greg, no one will take care of you better than you'll take care of yourself," she would say. "As long as I got two hands, y'all will never want for anything". And that's exactly what she did. She worked her ass off at a factory, never missed a day and never took a vacation to take care of all six of us. Shaking my head in disappointment at the thought of how her dedication to a man so unworthy of her love, saddened her, I quickly adjusted my thoughts to my own despair.

I turned the cold water on, from the bathroom sink and splashed it all over my face as if it would take away this stranger in the mirror. I looked back in the mirror and still, stood this broken version of myself, as if to say 'I own your ass, you can't beat me!" I shook my head again and walked back into the bedroom looking for the rest of the black and mild to smoke. It was the last one. I needed it to calm my nerves, although I hated the smell and taste of it. It was another poison of self-medication I was destroying myself with. The lighter lit up the dim room as I put the flame to the tip. I pulled on it as if my life depended on it and exhaled. I sat in my old recliner by the window and I could hear the rain outside as it calmed me. The blinds were closed, so my bedroom was still dark even though it was early in the morning. There was a sound of slight thunder and I remember thinking that I must have heard the thunder in my sleep and perhaps that's why I was dreaming of a storm.

    I looked over at the picture of my mother on the nightstand next to the recliner and tried to concentrate on the happier times of my life together with my family. I rested my head back and remembered the good ole days. Ironically that time was long ago when we all lived in the projects. Oddly enough I thought it was strange to feel that my life in the projects as, a happier time in my life. Although I was thought to be successful by others, my heart ached and longed for the enjoyable experiences I had living in the projects. As a kid, we were unaware of the reality of the troubles to come and clueless to the world beyond. What you had or didn't have were non-factors in the mind of a child. A judgmental society, racism and economic statuses were not worries of a small child with a developing mind. Our unawareness and innocence was truly a blessing. We did not know and didn't care to know. My mother and every other single mother in our community united together to make sure all the kids were cared for and free to enjoy our innocence as long as possible.

    I most certainly did not know that as a young boy, living in the projects, once we moved away, it would be the last time, I would hear, my mother laugh so hard that tears of joy came falling from her face while sitting in that old, velvet looking gold chair. She talked on that red phone and laughed with her sister Louise for hours. Red was her favorite color so of course she always wore her red robe. The red banana shaped attachment she would speak into hanging on the kitchen wall, had a long red spiral cord connected to it that could be stretched damn near throughout two rooms at least, while she walked and talked on the phone. Most of the time, she would stretch the cord long enough to reach her gold chair in the living room.

She laughed on the phone with her sister most of the day when she wasn't cooking, washing clothes or headed to work. There I was in my own favorite recliner but I had no one to laugh with or talk to. My shoulders to lean on were now gone, my son was away and the possibility of divorce had me living alone. Remembering hood and my mother in her favorite recliner brought a temporary smile upon my face, it also came along with pain. It was also the beginning of the images of seeing people of color losing their innocence and turning into tortured souls while being victims of poverty and acquiring all the psychological mental effects that came along with it. As I got older I realized that as a child we didn't know we were so worthless in the eyes of human society and were conditioned to become consumers and workers for wealthy Americans who saw us as less than human beings in the first place.

It was kind of ironic that my happiest memories as a child were when we lived in the projects. I was still able to smile remembering all of us sleeping in the same bed as a fun and loving experience. One pair of shoes had to last all year. Those were your school shoes and soon as we came home, we had to take them off and wear our play shoes if we were going back outside to play. Play shoes were your old shoes from a year or two before.

There were no differences between the families in our community and we were unaware of the struggles our parents were going through in order to keep food on the table, clothes on our backs, pay the bills and protect us from the world that awaited us as we got older. My mother was a very hard worker and was taking care of all six kids by herself. "As long as I got two hands," I remembered her voice again and smiled. I didn't exactly understand her troubles at the time. I just thought it was kind of funny when she said it, stretching out her arms and shaking her hands as if they were magical. She did work up plenty of miracles for us. I admired her strength and work ethic. She made sure we had food, clothing and shelter. As children, we were not yet aware of our financial circumstances and how people from other economic, social groups viewed us and our place in society.

My mother had the first impact on my behavior, thinking and my value at home, with family and at school. She didn't try to force any bias, opinions about others on us, although, I'm sure she had them. She chose to allow us to experience as much happiness as she could and lead by example. Without saying it, our mother was preparing us to be strong in times of adversity, because she knew what was ahead of us as minorities in America. We were not taught that there were any differences in people in relation to skin color at home. She knew we would see it for ourselves and used the opportunity to advise us to remain confident and strong despite what others did or said. "Sticks and stones may break your bones but words can never hurt you." She would say.

My first experience as far as differences was that of an observation at school and outside of our community. We often walked to the corner stores and sometimes rode in the car with our mother to get groceries, visit family, or pay bills. I remember recognizing that outside of my community, white people were owners of the corner stores and in positions of authority, as teachers, at school. It didn't make me sad as a child but it did bother me enough to take the time and to flip through the channels on television, searching for more people who looked more like my family and friends in my community. This had a huge impact on me as a child. I didn't ask any questions about it, but I wondered why people like me, didn't exist in what was, my opinion then, magical people on T.V.

In order to turn the channel, we had to use wire pliers because the knob was missing. We were forbidden by mom to change the channel that way, but my curiosity of discovering our magical world on T.V. was too strong of a reward to resist. Suddenly I was stuck to the handle and the wire pliers. I couldn't move and felt a force of power take hold of me. A burst of rustic saliva was in my mouth as I felt electricity flowing through my chest and out of my other arm while the energy violently shook my free hand. As quickly as the power grabbed me, it threw me to the floor and I was free to feel the punishment of daring to think a magical world existed for us as well. I didn't die of course and I never told anyone of my brush with death. It seemed to me that the electric shock was a punishment from a super, natural force to remind me that decent humanity did not belong to minorities.

The second time I came to realize the validity human beings had given to differences, as a minority, was not discrimination from another race, but when I was about eight or nine years old, I was teased and bullied because I was a lighter skin, than those who attempted to bully me about it. I was confused and saddened to learn that my so-called friends saw me as different, and they felt that I didn't belong. Most of my immediate family was a darker, skin tone than myself. It was never a discussion in my home or an issue. My mother never mentioned or expressed skin color meaning anything to us, so I was greatly impacted by that experience.

That experience started my quest in proving myself strong and worthy. It increased my passion for equality and justice for all. For me, at that time, light skinned people were the most discriminated against people in the world. Not only did we have to face the same prejudice opinions and actions from being black, we also faced discrimination from our own race, for not being black enough. Ironically, I didn't learn about racism from a bad experience with another social group. I discovered it from negative people in my own community. As an adult I learned that it wasn't just the magical people on television and those around our community that validated the color of skin as a means of inequality, It was given power all over the world, regardless of the skin tone of each social group.

Sadly, because I had a lighter skin tone, I was so caught up in proving myself worthy and was abusing my body playing football or fighting. Making decent grades in school came easy for me and if I had known my potential then I would have flourished in school. But the peer pressure of fitting in caused me to choose being a tough guy over good grades. Ironically, I didn't notice my younger sister Angela's pain. She had become a victim of bias, opinions due to her brown skin and short kinky hair. She told me later in life as we got older that the girls at her school were mean to her and made accusations that she couldn't be my sister because I was light skin and popular in school. As beautiful as my brown skin sister was, she lost her self identity and suffered from self esteem issues due to what minorities learned from another race giving validity to the color of skin being a means of how a human being should be treated or worthy of in this world. We both learned of prejudice from our own social group in the beginning and the pain of not being accepted by our father. We were both taken by the surprise of it all as our innocence was deteriorating into the ugly awareness of a collapsing society. I deeply regretted, I didn't notice her suffering.

For me my first awareness of it was from observation, being light skinned and the television show "Roots," by Alex Haley. I remember how it made me feel and how upset my mother was. During that time I had never experienced any cruelty the way it was portrayed in the movie based on Haley's book. A little later at school, white teachers in history class, teaching minorities about slavery had adverse effects on us all. I remember thinking how screwed up the world was that even in times of prejudice actions towards differences in race, even within the same race, differences in appearance, thinking and behavior, caused discrimination among each other. How disrespectful to the human race, I remember thinking. Personally, I had no preference in skin color or viewed them differently. Especially since most of my family members were wonderful, dark skinned, people that I loved and admired. And I absolutely loved women of color. Chasing girls became one of my escapes. but it became both a blessing and a curse. We were all decent human beings hiding our dismay and victims of constructed poverty.

But society and the media, painted a different story about minorities, which allowed differences to be a tool for ignorant thinking and behavior. Today I know that my happiness in the projects came from being unaware and the appreciation for the simple things in life like family bonding, love, smiles, playing with friends or just eating jelly sandwiches in front of the only T.V. we had. As we got a little older, injustice, crime, scarcity, and the feeling of being black and poor meant that we were somehow not worthy of the magical things shown on television or what we saw outside of our communities like the huge, beautiful houses we saw on the way to school looking out the window of the school buses.

Today, people of color are mostly on the news, portrayed as angry criminals addicted to drugs and a life of crime. A handful are entertainers, actors, or professional sports players. It seems as though much has changed, yet so little has been done to support and protect the well-being and mental anguish of the common person of color. Conforming to the American society felt like an enormous giant, beating the hell out of hopes, dreams and opportunities of people that were not magical.

To escape the pain we would play games riding past their enormous homes. "That's going to be my house when I grow up, "one of us would say. "Look, that's going to be my house," another one would say, jumping at the chance to choose a bigger house or prettier car that the one someone picked before. As a child growing up in the projects, without realizing it, appreciation for what you had got slowly beaten out of you with the big ugly Billy club of awareness of the reality that you were somehow behind in life and those magical white people on T.V. and at school look at you as beneath them. Grades in school become the first divider of people along with peer groups. Color of skin is an added factor along with the quality of clothes, for kids in low-income communities. Innocence was lost and turmoil began.. Leaving a world of cultural indifference and going home to another culture became confusing to people of color and questions as to why were not addressed properly or hard to explain to a growing child in the hood. Living in, the hood and getting out most likely meant giving up culture and assimilating into a society that judges, color instead of ability and character. Being without for so long turned minorities into irrational buyers and renters.

Growing up poor as a child and as a young adult, had an indescribable feeling that we did not understand or even knew how to express. We did not even know how to inquire about it. Sometimes it felt like a ball of pressure inside of my chest that I couldn't get out. It was hard to breathe and relax. Other times it felt like an empty, cold, hole inside of my heart and slowly dying from the need of warm blood. It could not be filled and we would do anything to forget the pain or relieve the thirst for joy, happiness and peace of mind. There were other unexplainable feelings, and each one of them caused irrational, dangerous decisions. Even as adults, I saw those suppressed feelings come out in marriages, relationships and other undesirable forms of my friends. As victims of American society our connection with it was broken and our souls grew cold.

No one should've ever felt that way. Everyone wanted to feel loved, needed and accepted. Playing games as a kid, turned into teenage sub-groups, participating in sex, drugs, violence, or criminal behavior. Not because it was in our nature to do so, but because of the fear that someone would see the pain inside and the fear of death in our eyes. We hid behind our smile and acted out in ways to disguise our pain. We were all hurting from the beat down, and trying to keep the foot of society's opinions, restrictions and cruelty out of our asses. Our health

was always at risk due to limited resources, poor healthcare and low income.

I can still remember being given a fish sandwich by my blind aunt and was choking on a small fish bone. Unable to help me she sent me to the hospital in a cab. Calling 911 and obtaining an ambulance would've been costly, so my life was sacrificed in order to save what would be considered a few dollars to privileged Americans. Not able to describe or understand the feeling inside of making those types of sacrifices, expressing it to anyone would seem weak in the hood. Especially when everyone around you had that same look of fear, despair and stress in their eyes. Even our parents were in the lion's den, and to survive, meant to conform and accept a battle ground in your community, simply because of the socially constructed standards of the way a human being should be treated or receive justice and equality, due to economic status or color of skin. All we knew to do, at that age, was to just try and breathe, by any means necessary.

For my mother, getting out of the projects meant getting her kids away from violence. She wanted us to be safe, so after thirteen years, she was excited about renting a home on the eastside. Still in the hood but a home meant more space and a safer neighborhood. She never expected how hard it would be paying ridiculous rent as a single parent with kids would be. For thirteen years we lived as a family unit with togetherness, smiles, and laughter in the projects, although the occasional violence would remind us why we had to leave.

After getting out, the unity we once enjoyed rapidly disintegrated due to the stress of a single mother, paying enormous rent that lined the pockets of the magical people we saw on T.V. They came knocking each month with a nasty attitude and my mother cried and pleaded for more time. She wouldn't dare allow them to see her tears but we saw her pain once the door closed. Thirteen years we lived in the projects and we moved thirteen times from house to the next house, rent after higher rent each time before she died. Keeping us safe meant that much to her, but keeping a smile on her face was all we wanted to do. Crisis would prevail each and every time.

As I got older after seeing her go through so much for us started my interest in being a homeowner. No rent for me. I'd learned that it was cheaper to buy a home than it was to rent a home. At least the home would be mine and no one could put me or my family out. My plan was to move my mother in so that she could enjoy her life without any stress. If only I knew then what I know now, maybe I could have encouraged her to save money and build excellent credit before leaving the projects. With her incredible work ethics, buying a home would've put her in the position to rent a home and collect like the magical ones.

For me, buying a home meant that I would never allow my kids to go through the loss of family bonds, and prepare them to be property owners. Thirteen years of being put out of each home thirteen times until she died, had proven to be devastating to our family and the joy we once knew in the projects, as a family unit was forever strained. As a child in the projects, for the most part it's all a united thirst to connect and laugh as much as possible after slowly realizing as you get older how society views where you live and who you are because of it.

I learned through my mother's pain, that it's important to maintain family values and enjoy life's simple pleasures. It didn't cost us one cent to love each other, and allowing life's man made illusions of what happiness should look like, was detrimental to our well-being. Self-identity, unity and love rushed out the window. We lost a connection with each other, trying to connect with the judgmental world around us.

Criminals were not born, they were products', of society's failure to address poverty, indifference, and injustice properly. It is said that human virtues are taught at home, but in today's society, low-income communities are results of America's crimes against families of color. Most families in the hood were not blessed to have two parents at home and even the ones that did, suffered from an unhealthy structure in the home and unfortunately, parents themselves were suffering from improper coping skills or did not know how to protect their children from the indifferences of society. As a child, we were not aware of what was happening and as for me, my imagination and thirst for new adventures occupied most of my childhood in the projects.

After drinking heavily the night before, I remembered the day I was outside playing in the front yard with my toys and all of a sudden I became bored with them. Normally I could imagine for hours that I was a part of this imaginary world where I controlled my man action figures conversations and heroic activities. I guess you could call them boy dolls. By boy dolls, I mean I had toys like The Lone Ranger and The Six Million Dollar Man. I even had a Muhammed Ali and an O.J. Simpson action figure once. If only I'd taken care of them like my mother said they all would be a valuable collector's item today. To me, this was far better than what my older brother Byron chose to play with. He collected Coca-Cola bottle caps. In those days, mom would collect the original glass Coca-Cola bottles and return the empty bottles for extra money.

Byron always collected the tops of those bottles that twisted off and imagined them to be soldiers and played war with them. By the time I was born, my mother had a little better job so the youngest kids had the more realistic toys. Mom often got accused of treating the youngest siblings better than the older ones but that wasn't true at all.

Mom had a huge heart and gave everything she could to all six of us. The only difference was that she was a dedicated and hard worker. She would continue to get a better promotion or a better paying job. Although the youngest siblings enjoyed longer benefits of those promotions the older ones enjoyed her love and dedication in providing a better life for us all. As one of the youngest kids, I couldn't imagine what could be any better than we already had.

Playing outside in that small patch of yard we had, I noticed ants in the front yard. I was fascinated by them and watched them follow each other back and forth carrying food to their ant hill. I followed the trail they were on in order to see where the food was coming from. The trail of ants led me from the yard, up the two steps, onto our porch, up the brick wall and across to the window. There on the ledge of the window seal, was a half of a bologna sandwich someone placed or had forgotten about. The ants were having a feast. When I saw the sandwich, my first thought was, I wanted to know which brother or sister of mine didn't finish eating it and left the rest of it outside.

They were going to hear from me because I was hungry earlier and wanted some bologna but it was all gone. I had to eat a syrup sandwich. . If they were not going to eat all of it, I could have enjoyed that meal instead of watching these ants have a free all you can eat, meal with meat, while the inside of my stomach was still touching the back of my spine from eating a syrup, bread-poverty sandwich. I was hungry but momma was going to be furious when she discovered these ants coming from this half eaten sandwich left outside.. We couldn't afford to waste any food and she was going to be pissed. I started to go tell, but the ant's orderly and busy nature intrigued me and prevented me from doing so.

I went back into the small patch of yard we had and laid down beside the ants away from the sandwich because I wasn't going to be blamed for that one. Not today. I watched and admired them. They weren't bothered by me as long as I didn't disturb them. I was so focused on how orderly they worked together, I didn't notice my friend Lisa coming down the street. Before I knew it, she was right next to me and asked, "What are you doing Greg, playing with the ants?" I was embarrassed that she had caught me. Lisa was my little crush and she would surprise me with a little kiss every now and then.

We did like each other but we were too young for dating. "Nawh, I was just looking at them, "You wanna go inside and get some tea?" I was trying my best to distract her from the ants I was playing with. We were known to all the smaller kids for having sweet tea in the projects. Mom loved tea so we always had it in the fridge. "Come on, let's get some before mom wakes up." We went inside to drink a cup of tea that was always extremely sweet with too much sugar. We weren't allowed to drink out of moms favorite glasses, so we always had to use plastic cups. I poured Lisa a cup first, then mine. I watched her take a drink before I did to see if she liked it. Lisa never pulled the cup down once she started drinking it until it was all gone. I smiled and asked her, "Is it good?" She burped and smiled. "Yes, where is Angela?" We slipped into mom's bedroom and woke my sister Angela.. Angela was asleep, on the floor. Mom laid down carpet rug over the concrete floor so Angela would be more comfortable sleeping on the pallet. Angela normally would sleep in the bed with mom but she would be afraid of peeing in the bed and didn't want to get in trouble. She knew she was too old to still be wetting the bed.

We only had three bedrooms and sleeping arrangements were cramped since there were six of us. Lisa and I waited in the hallway for Angela to get dressed. Angela came out and went into the bathroom to brush her teeth. Lisa kissed me on the cheek right before Angela came out. I was happy because I knew I would get in trouble once momma found out most of her tea was gone. I would take the blame and the kiss from Lisa made it all worth it.

Angela came out of the bathroom and noticed the look of admiration for Lisa on my face and said, "Boy, what's wrong with you?" "Nothing, let's go outside" I said. Just then I noticed that I was still holding my cup of tea so I quickly drank it, put the cup in the sink and we all went outside to play, high off of life and sugar diabetes tea.

Walking out the front door, I quickly suggested that we go get Euhommie which was Lisa's brother and my best friend. We called him Homie. Before Lisa could remember about the ants I was playing with, Angela wanted to go to the corner store and get some jungle juice and now & later candy. We asked her if she had some money and she told us that she had slipped some change out of momma's purse after she got dressed. "How much did you get?" We asked. "One dollar and fifty cents' Angela said excitedly. In those days you could buy enough candy for everyone with a dollar. We all agreed that Angela and Lisa would walk to the store while I went to get Homie.

Before I reached their building, Homie was already coming out of the front door. He and I were not only good friends, he was the reason I became so competitive. They moved from Lincoln courts projects to the projects where I lived called Neff Circle in Memphis Tn. We lived in Neff Circle before Homie and his family moved in. The day I met Homie, I was walking outside, headed to the playground on a warm sunny day. At that time in the early 70's, I was slender with an afro that had turned reddish from the sun. In those days kids were always outside playing so it was common for hair to tint from swimming and too much sunlight.

I heard a group of boys on the porch of the building complex that had been vacant for a while cheering about something. Whatever it was, I could tell that they were excited about it. They called me over. On the way over to talk with them, I noticed that they were arm wrestling as they cheered the youngest boy on. The oldest brother yelled "I bet you can't beat Homie arm wrestling." I looked at this boy the same age as me, with his shirt off. He sat there smiling with a proud, confident look on his face and a snotty nose. I kind of smiled and wondered why he was sniffing instead of wiping that dried up snot off his lip.

He was scrawny, brown skinned with a dirty brownish afro like mine. Both of us never really picked out our fro neatly but once a day so our afro was always nappy. We made eye contact, but said nothing to each other. I sat at the other end of this raggedy, wooden table they had placed on the porch. The other boys gathered around us. They all had their shirts off. Four of them were brothers of his and one was his cousin Wilbert, so of course I was the underdog. Homie and I locked our palms together and made fist's around each other's hands. The oldest brother Michael was in charge of the action. 'Ready, set, go"! I quickly slammed his hand on the table. "Ohhhhhhhhhh!" they all shouted and laughed.

I was surprised myself because up until that moment I had never arm wrestled before. I had only seen it on T.V. "Awwh naawh, I wasn't ready!" "Let's do it again." Again, Michael gave the countdown, "Ready, set, go!" There was a slight struggle, then before I knew it, my hand was slammed down on the table. Homie jumped up and did the Muhammed Ali shuffle with his hands in the air while his brothers and his cousin Wilbert yelled "Champ. Champ, Champ!" I grabbed my hand and rub it, checking for blood because I felt the splinters from that old worn out wood, scratch my wrist as they hit the table. Suddenly I heard a real cool voice behind me say "Naaawh man, it's a tie, y'all gotta go again." "Best two out of three." It was the voice of Eugene, one of Homie's brothers that was just a little older than us. He was always smooth talking, cool and a peacemaker. Homie sat back down at the table and we locked fists again.

This time, Eugene gave the count down. He placed his hands over our fists to make sure our wrists were straight so that no one had an advantage. "Ready, set, go!" Homie and I struggled as everyone cheered on. This time there would be no winner. The both of us would not give up. We struggled with each other's power until the veins were popping out of our arms, neck and forehead. "Times up!" "Good job my man, what's your name?" I was proud to tell Eugene my name while still holding my wrist. Before I could say anything, the oldest brother Michael said "Awh man that's Snow little brother." I was surprised that he knew my older brother Byron. Later, I realized that my favorite brother Byron and Homie's oldest brother Michael were friends as well.

Byron's nickname was Snow. Eugene said "Ok, ok, we're gonna call you lil Snow" while picking his afro. Eugene was always picking his hair and kept it perfectly round at all times. Eugene was a ladies man. He then said "This is my little brother Homie." I asked Homie, what did they call him? "Muhammed," like Muhammad Ali, he said boastfully. I never heard them call him by that name at all. They called him Homie, so I called him Homie. From that day on, many competitive events between all of us occured. Especially between Homie and I.

Which reminded me of the day Angela, Lisa, Homie and I walked to the corner store that was just outside of the projects, on a warm, sunny, Saturday morning. Lisa and Angela had walked ahead of us to spend the change she had stolen from mom's purse on jungle juice and candy. Homie and I started on our way to the store to catch up with Lisa and Angela.

Once we left the circle, there was a long street called Stonewall, where mostly older people lived in homes that were made of wood and had good structure. I could tell that they had so much more room to sleep in and I often wondered what they looked like inside. There was a long sidewalk that ran down each side of the road. I enjoyed walking on the sidewalk because we didn't have them in the projects. We would get yelled at where I lived if we got caught walking in someone's front yard so we had to walk on the side of the road or walk behind the buildings.

Looking at the beautiful antique looking houses on Stonewall was always a treat. On the way to the store we would play step on a crack, break your momma's, back. It was a game we played and you weren't allowed to step on the cracks that separated each concrete square. It was a long sidewalk leading to the store on each side of Stonewall street in front of the pretty box houses. If you stepped on the cracks of the sidewalk, you lost the game and supposedly broke your momma's back.

At the end of Stonewall was the corner store owned by an old white man and his wife. I never knew their names. They were the only white people we would see in our neighborhood. They seemed to be nice people. I remember that they would allow parents to get milk, bread, and meat products on credit, but all the kids walked to the store only to get goodies. Before Homie and I reached the store we could see Lisa and Angela coming back from the store digging their hands in their bags, tearing off wrappers and feeding their smiling faces.

My sister Angela was skinny and tall like me, brown skinned with pigtails. She was wearing her favorite outfit, little red shorts and red halter top that tied in a bow at the front above her stomach. Lisa was a little shorter than my little sister Angela. Lisa had a caramel complexion and she had on shorts and a t-shirt. For some reason her family called her Porky. I never called her that though. She was always pretty Lisa to me. We could tell they had lots of candy so we quickly forgot about the game and the cracks that broke momma's back. Momma would just have to get over it. We got candy! We ran towards them to get our share of the candy.

Homie and I reached our sisters at the same time. No way would we let the other one be first. Back then we could run for days and not break a sweat. What did y'all get?" I asked, and I was already reaching for the bag. Both Angela and Lisa pulled the bags away and turned their shoulders up away from us. "Uhmmmm-uhmmm," y'all should've came with us!" Angela said as she swiftly walked past us. Standing there in disbelief we both looked at Lisa. Homie asked Lisa for some but she just smiled and kept walking with a smirk on her face as if Angela made her promise not to give us any in return for buying Lisa a bag of goodies. "Some make ya dumb, so ya can't get none," she said, and they both giggled and walked away. "Awwh man, that's messed up," let's go to the store," Homie said, looking at me in disappointment. "You got some money?" I asked

Homie as we continued down the street to the store. Homie never replied, he only complained that Lisa wouldn't give him any candy and that he was going to get her.

"She'll ask me to help her wash the dishes tonight and I ain't gonna do it." By that time we had reached the door of the store. "Let's go in, look and see what they got," Homie said to me and I was willing to do so because it was always exciting to see all the cookies and candy they had. There was a huge window on one side of the door. The other side had a wooden sign that read Corner Store. The cash register counter was located in front of the big window. The old man or his wife would be standing there at all times while the other worked in the back. They could see who was coming in or out from the window while working the cash register. It was a white building that was not very wide, but long enough to have about four long shelves that had pretty much everything you needed for grocery and house items like tissue and paper towels.

The shelves ran long ways and at the end of the shelves in the back was the meat department that was facing the shelves horizontally. You could get rag bologna and cheese sliced up back there. They would always wrap it up in this thick white paper with a toothpick to hold it together. I always knew when mom had been to the corner store when I saw that paper in the fridge. I would get excited because I knew I could make myself a good, thick bologna sandwich with cheese.

There were a few small freezers near the meat counter that had milk, pops and jungle juice in them. Towards the front of the store, on one of the shelves is where all the chips and candy was located. Homie and I walked around the store for a while until the owner of the store asked if we needed help. He was working in the fresh meat department that day. I told him that we were just looking and then the old man asked me how my mother was doing.

I was standing there talking with him at the back of the store and didn't notice that Homie had left my side and continued to browse the store. "She's at home asleep." "She worked the night shift last night." While answering his question, I turned to say something to Homie, but he wasn't there. The old man said "Oh, ok, tell her I said hello and to come see me when she gets a chance." "I know she works hard," he said. I assumed that mom owed some money on her tab, at the store. She loved getting slices of rag bologna, crackers and hot souse, before going to work. This would be her lunch. While I was talking with the owner, Homie walked up to me and asked if I was ready to go. I said ok and we turned to leave the store. "You boys have a good day," the old man said as we left the store. We walked past his wife at the register and out the door. "Bye, bye," she said.

Right after walking out the door, Homie pulled me to the side of the building. There were no windows on the side of the old wooden building. No one inside could see us there. "Look what I got man." He pulled out several candy apple sticks from his pockets. Apple sticks in the early 70's were as long as your finger back then. Not like the little short ones they sell today. My eyes lit up with surprise and anticipation of eating them. I don't think I ever thought at that moment, it was wrong or felt like it was stealing. We were only about seven or eight years old. My thought process was that stealing was a word used for criminals in jail and we were only kids. This was fun, nothing like on T.V. and it felt so good to have candy, especially since our stingy sisters wouldn't give us any.

"Wait till they see what we got, and they better not ask for none," we both said excitedly. It was payback time and a competition between Homie and me. "Hold up man, let's go back in, let me see what I can get", then I told Homie to just wait outside since he had already started slurping on one of the candy apple sticks and sniffing up that snotty nose of his at the same time. I hurried back into the store, not realizing how obvious it was that we kept going in and out of the store without purchasing anything.

I quickly walked to the candy section of the store in order to find something better than the long candy apple sticks that Homie had in his pockets. This would be a hard decision since all of us kids loved apple sticks. The popular choice for the older kids was the Dill Pickle. They would stick the smaller apple sticks like the longer one they sell today, in the top of the pickle and suck on it until it was gone. Then they would eat the pickle. My oldest sister Sheila loved them. I couldn't get the pickles though, because they were kept in a jar on the counter near the cash register. I glanced at the row of Now & Later candy for a moment but I remembered that I could see that my sister Angela already had a bag full of them before she pulled the bag away from me. The Now & Later candy was a good choice but wouldn't impress anyone over the long apple sticks. Eating apple sticks for kids was like steak and shrimp for adults. If you bit off a piece of the candy, folded the wrapper down over the rest of it, you could save little by little for the rest of the day. The only thing to worry about was lint possibly getting on it from your pockets, but that wasn't a problem if you folded the wrapper over it just right. Candy was like gold, precious and priceless to us.

Even if lint got on the top of your candy, the smart thing to do was lick it off, spit out the lint and once again enjoy the taste of clean, strawberry, grape or lemon sensation.

It would be a continuous treat all day long. Sort of like the Now & Later candy. You would eat one now and eat one or two later, but they were small and wouldn't beat Homie's choice. The only thing that came close was Pop Rocks. Pop Rocks packages of candy came in all flavors, they were good, plus they sizzled and popped into your mouth when you ate them.

They made your mouth water with whatever delicious flavor you were eating at the time. Plus, you could eat a little and save some. "Awwwwh yeah, this is it right here," I thought to myself. If I get this, it will definitely make me the winner or at least make me a real close favorite in the bunch. I knew Lisa would be pleased. I looked to my left, to see if the old white man working at the meat section could see me. He had a better view from there because depending on where he was standing, he could see down each row of shelves perfectly.

I knew his wife couldn't see me from where I was standing, but I checked anyway. Quickly I grabbed a bag full of the packages of pop rocks and shoved them in my pocket. My heart rate was pumping quickly and was thumping like a bass drum. I realized that no one saw me and was slightly relieved. The only thing I had to do now was to walk out of the store and be victorious! At that moment I noticed that there was a circular stand at the front of the store. It had various pieces of small plastic toys hanging from it.

I had gotten away with stealing the pop rocks without the nice old man and his wife noticing me, but the toys that I had never noticed before captured my attention. The stand full of toys was in the corner, on the other side of the store, directly across from the cash register counter where the owner's wife was standing. It had water guns in all colors on it. There were little racing cars with shiny rims and wheels, plastic airplanes, and tiny dolls for girls.

While spinning the circular stand around, suddenly it jumped out at me. A bag of green army soldiers! My eyes widened with joy and amazement of seeing realistic looking soldiers. It was the first time I saw toys that actually looked like real soldiers with guns, helmets and military gear. Before then, the only thing I knew of was my older brother Byron who was eleven years older than myself, playing with Cocoa, Cola bottle tops, and imagining them to be soldiers. He would set the tops up like a game of chess across from each other on his bed. He then would attack each side by popping each top with his finger in order for the top he hit to crash into the opposite side. He would make noises with his mouth that sounded like explosions, and gun fire. I remember thinking that I could get this bag of green soldiers for my brother and how happy he would be to have soldiers that looked like the real thing.

I had forgotten all about my competition with Homie and the Pop Rocks, and went into a tunnel vision on how I was going to steal this bag of army men for my brother. I went into action. I pretended my stomach was hurting and began to rub my stomach and moan. I walked around the store a few more times to make sure the old white lady saw me in distress over my stomach pain. This way, I could slip the small bag of green army men into my pants and hold them while I was pretending to have stomach pain and walk out of the store without buying anything, as if I'd changed my mind because I was getting sick. It was a perfect plan and a performance fit for an Oscar, or so I thought.

It was my first time attempting to steal as a child and I was naive to think that I would distract her with brilliant acting skills, not realizing I was only drawing more attention to myself. After I was sure she saw that I was holding my stomach in pain, I walked near the stand with the green soldiers hanging from it, pulled them off and went between the isles and slipped the bag into the front of my jeans and held them in place with my hand under my shirt.

I then walked out of the store, pretending to be in pain. My heart felt like it was going to jump out of my chest in fear and excitement of it all. Once outside, I stopped in front of the store looking for Homie. To my surprise he was gone. "Little snot nose punk!" I said aloud to myself. During those days, calling a kid a punk, as a kid, was the hardest and most insulting thing a kid my age could say, other than something about another kids momma.

After realizing homie had left me at the store, I turned to look behind me at the old lady through the window. She was still looking at me. I turned to walk away. Just as I took my first step, the bag fell out of my pants and hit the ground with a startling noise. I froze in place. My first thought was to pick them up and run, but I couldn't move. I looked back to see if the old lady saw what happened. As soon as I turned to see, she was coming out of the store.

"You ought to be ashamed of yourself!" "As hard as your momma works to take care of you and you out here stealing, wait till she finds out!" In those days, the community looked out for all the kids and if you did something wrong that the elderly saw or knew about, the news of what you did made it home before you got there. All I could do was stand there in the shame and guilt of it all and say "Yes ma'am, yes ma'am, yes ma'am.

To this very day, I never forgot how embarrassed I felt, yet, I attempted a few more criminal acts throughout my lifetime before I truly learned the consequences of my actions. After she was done scolding me, she picked up the bag of stolen goods and told me to go home and think about what I had done. Of course, that was the longest, slowest, saddest walk home ever. I just knew by the time I made it home, momma would be waiting, armed with an accumulation of curse words that made you feel lower than dirt.

Momma had a way of putting words together that would fly out of her mouth with perfection that fucked up your entire self-esteem, for about three months if you had done something wrong or crossed her in anyway. She didn't spank or whoop us, her choice of discipline was to slap the shit out of you. Slob would fly from your mouth and your ears would go numb, in shock from the mighty hand of mom. She didn't take the time to find a belt. Her hands were huge, it would smother the entire side of your head. If she slapped you, it would leave ringing sounds in your ear that reminded you not to do that shit again. Whatever it may have been. She was an in the moment kind of person. She would ask later why did you do whatever it was you had done wrong and then give her opinion. Other than that, she would call one of her brothers over to do the whipping. And she had plenty of options. The dreaded three were Uncle Johnny, Uncle Jean and Uncle Carl. Grand momma Valla had thirteen kids, all boys except for three girls. But mom's three choices were enough to get the job done. She called them her wrecking crew.

Uncle Johnny would talk to you before he spanked you and at least showed concern that what you did was wrong and he hated to do so, but he had to teach us a lesson. After listening to a long drawn out speech, you kind of had the feeling of yeah, yeah, I was wrong, let's just get this whipping over so you can go home Uncle Johnny. Thanks but I'm so tired of sitting here listening to you repeat "This is going to hurt me more than it hurts you." "Can I have a whipping please, thank you, and goodbye?" We respected Johnny after he left though and that would be the end of it.

I hated when Uncle Jean came over because he was just plain ole mean and I felt he just got satisfaction from abusing someone. I say that because, once as a kid, I was spending the night over Grand momma's house with my cousin Brian. Brian was the son of one of my favorite Uncle, James. Brian and I were coloring in a coloring book full of race cars. We both picked out the page we were supposed to color and then we were going to ask Grand momma Valla which picture was the best. I got up from the floor in Grandma's room, where we were playing and went to the bathroom. As I was coming out of the bathroom, Brian was standing there showing me how he had started coloring on the page I had picked out and was planning the perfect colors while using the bathroom. I was furious when I saw it. "Brian, that's my page!" Just as I said that, Uncle Jean was coming through the front door of the projects my grandmother lived in.

He came directly to me. By then I had made it back to Grand momma's room near her bed. I know Grand momma's bed had to have been at least twelve feet tall in my opinion because she had the box spring plus about three to four mattresses on top of it. As small as I was at that time, my uncle asked me no questions at all, he immediately grabbed me by the throat, picked me up and slammed me on top of this giant bed. He was choking me and I was kicking my legs trying to break free. Brian ran when he saw what happened and I couldn't scream from no air.

Once he let go, I ran to tell Grand momma, but she was already on the phone with my momma. She told the both of us to shut up and sit down, in the living room, until our parents arrived. Needless to say, that was the end of us spending the night over. After getting in the car with mom, I tried telling her what Uncle Jean did to me but I don't think she believed me or was too upset that she had to find somewhere else for me to stay overnight since she had plans for the evening. The only other person would be Auntie, which really wasn't my Aunt but my mother's ex- husband's Rev. Snowden's blind mother. I definitely didn't want to go there because the last time I was there she gave me a fish sandwich to eat with bones in it. After I was choking on a small bone, she sent me to the hospital in a cab. I didn't hear anything else about what Uncle Johnny did but I did notice that he didn't come over as much after that.

Uncle Carl was a well- mannered, low speaking calm minister that preached to you and gave you a full Sunday morning sermon that seemed to last forever. He didn't spank or whip you, he just made you listen to the word of the lord for about eight hours, and he never got tired of listening to his own voice because by then, we would be fighting off sleep and haven't heard a word he was saying since seven hours ago.

Our butts would be numb from sitting in one place and sad that we missed outside playing time listening to Pastor C. Pastor C. was the name all the kids in the projects gave him. They would walk up to the screen door where we lived, see him preaching to us, laugh and run before he saw them because he would make them come inside and listen if he caught them at the door. Finally, mom would feel sorry for us, come from her room where she was enjoying herself on the phone and rescue us.

With that being said, my walk home from being caught stealing was like a walk to the death chamber. Dead man walking, so to speak. I was terrified on my way back home. First, I was going to look for Homie. I just knew he couldn't wait for me and was anxious to find Lisa and my sister to try and convince them to give him some of their candy. I didn't care about the candy anymore although it would be nice before I got slapped, cursed out, preached to and had to face the shame and guilt of what I had done. Maybe the sugar rush would increase my speed while trying to avoid the big white belt with holes in it that Uncle Jean wore. It sucked up your skin and left belt marks with the pattern of the holes on my skin perfectly on my legs or wherever he hit you. I'm sure he'd be in jail by now for child abuse in today's society. Since I was light skinned, the red, bruised pattern would show up for all to see. That's all my friends needed to see to give them a reason to laugh and make fun of my ass whipping all day. I would be the joke of the day and the entertainment for all the kids in the hood they told and made fun of me in front of. But I had a plan, I would not be wearing any shorts for a month if that happened.

Finally, I saw Homie, Lisa and Angela in the playhouse we had built out of cardboard boxes, smiling, laughing and enjoying themselves while I felt like a criminal on his way to jail. "What did you get?" Homie said excitedly. He had a proud smirk of confidence on his face. Just then, I remembered the competition and said, "I got pop rocks!" They all got excited and climbed out of our little play house with anticipation of getting some. My frustration of Homie leaving me and the fact that I got caught stealing made me proudly say, "Hell nawh, Y'all aint getting my candy!" As a kid, using a curse word made you feel grown. "You left me and so y'all could eat up all the candy!" I crawled into the playhouse and started eating on one bag of the pop rocks. For the moment I felt good, especially since I had used a curse word I had never used before. It gave me a feeling of power and control. I never told them what happened at the store and enjoyed myself for the moment while making them suffer. I almost felt sorry for Lisa, but she wasn't going to get any either. Her little smile was not going to do the trick this time.

I already slipped her some of my mother's golden, prize winning tea and since I was going to face the end of my Uncle's dreaded belt of death, she would not be getting anymore favors from me today. "Come on Greg, let us have some," they said repeatedly as I sat in the middle of the opening of the cardboard house with my legs stretched out so that they couldn't climb in with me. "Nope, some make you dumb, so you can't have none!" They all started beating on top of the cardboard house like drums to irritate me for not giving them any. I laid back and closed my eyes and smiled while enjoying the burst of flavors in my mouth, pretending not to be bothered by the annoying noise.

Knock, knock, knock, suddenly, Homie forced his arm in and tried to take the candy away from me. I clinched the bag close to my chest, turned to my side and scooted myself frantically past him and out of the box. I ran home so homie couldn't get any. Just as I reached home safely and satisfied that I didn't spill or drop my bag of goodies, I was startled by my mother standing at the screen door. "Boy, what are you running for? Mom asked with a concerned tone.

My heart was already racing from the run home and the thought of her knowing what I had done terrified me so much that I couldn't speak. I stood there, trying to search my brain for an answer, but before I could say a word, she smiled, and said "Where is Angela? I made y'all some peanut butter and jelly sandwiches". At that moment, I knew she had no idea what happened, and it was all good in the hood for the moment. Mom opened the screen door so I could walk in. She held the door and stretched her head out to see if she saw Angela. I heard her calling for my sister, as I went to the back room where I shared with my brother Byron.

I noticed that he had been arranging his bottle caps on the bed, so I sat on the floor. I wished that I had gotten away with getting those green army men to surprise him, but it was probably a good thing that I didn't because I would have had to explain where I had gotten them and big brother Byron was always correcting me on bad behavior. At that moment I felt sad and frustrated that I couldn't provide a simple task of kindness because I had no money to buy them. I quickly jumped to my feet and closed the bedroom door. Before I could sit down again, I heard a knock at the door and my brother's voice. "Greg, open up."

I knew I would never tell him what I had done. I felt shame, although I only wanted to see the smile on his face from not having to pretend that Coca Cola bottle tops were soldiers. Ironically, as my past thoughts of little green army men and the sound of my brother Byron knocking at our bedroom door in the projects. Living in the projects is not all it is portrayed to be on T.V. There was poverty, crime and despair, yes, but there is also a more realistic, lighter version not shown in the news. We had a common bond and strived to escape the false representations that caused police to harass us and others to judge. I can remember it like it was yesterday the good times we had as family and friends. One of those was when my older sister Darlene would stand in the middle of the street and lead all the kids in a game of red light, green light, yellow light and stop until dark. Sheila, my oldest sister, would accompany Byron and Larry, my oldest brother in jumping the fence behind the projects and fill up brown paper sack bags full of pecans, stolen from old man Johnson's tree in his yard. One night, Sheila broke her pinky finger running away when Mr. Johnson caught them. At 7pm every Saturday night, all of us would gather in front of the only, T.V. and watch a movie while cracking open the pecans. By 10:30 pm, all the younger kids would be asleep and mom was headed to work. She had to be there at 11pm.

What the older teens did after that time, we had no clue because Sheila made sure that Angela and I had taken a bath and in the bed by ten. Board games, and made up games like fifty-fifty bee-bee shots, were played regularly and used to bond with others. We played kickball, football, basketball or softball during the day and had to be inside when the street lights came on. Today, you hardly ever see kids playing outside or riding bikes. Advanced technology and social media has taken over and communication with friends and family has taken on a new form.

Janet knocked at the door. It stopped my memories of the good old days in the hood. The frantic knocking at my front door startled me and I was forced to stop enjoying the only peace I found for myself, in a while, since my mother's funeral. I got up from the chair and tried to gather myself and my appearance from a long night of drinking. I rushed to the door and looked out the peephole. It was a co-worker of mine. "Open the door, I got great news!" I opened the door and Janet rushed in and hugged me. She was eager to tell me good news and hugged me tightly with her small, athletic frame, while she jumped up and down with excitement. Janet and I had been on the phone constantly the prior week before, after a protest against mentally disabled people living in their community, trying to reach and obtain a team of attorneys to take the protestors down.

Not just any attorney, we wanted big time, bulldog attorneys that would chop their jaws into discriminators and wouldn't let go until every drop of hateful blood was spilled out and justice would be the choke chain that governed them.

"We got them, we got them Greg!" "We got the attorneys on the phone and they are interested in talking with us about the case. We're sure to get things moving now!" Janet and I were in charge of providing care and protection for assisted living human beings, who were mentally disabled.

We were attempting to rent a four bedroom home in a gated community from a nice old Caucasian lady whose husband was a military war veteran and had recently passed away. She no longer wanted to live in their home without him. We felt that this would be a perfect home for our clients to reside in and we were glad she contacted us to rent her home. She understood the trauma of prejudice and discriminating behaviors and our clients recently obtained a new roommate and needed a larger home to reside in.

Mrs. Barnes' husband was wounded in the Vietnam War that left him paralyzed. She took care of him for many years before he died and she knew too well how the unfair treatment and decisions of ignorant people can destroy lives, she had witnessed and experienced from the treatment of soldiers returning home from the Vietnam War. She wanted to assist us in providing a home for the assisted living care of those in need. It pleased her to know that there were companies that provided opportunities for equal employment, housing, care, protection and the choice to live life as independently as possible and enjoy the world with respect, dignity and as much care, freedom and equal rights, just as any so called "normal" person would expect.

Once the surrounding neighbors found out who were moving into their community, they started protesting under the guidance and leadership of an older, white male. He normally stayed to himself and hardly ever communicated with neighbors unless he and his wife wanted to organize a charity event, fundraiser, or inform neighbors of changes made to rules and regulations of their gated community.

Once a psychiatrist, Mr. Anderson, was now retired from the medical field. He served in the army attached to a Special Forces tactical unit. Tactical training was required in order to handle combat situations when not providing medical assistance to fellow soldiers. Bob Anderson was now older with a distinguished, stern look on his face. He wore his silver and grey hair in a buzz cut and his five o'clock shadow beard was neatly groomed and silver and grey as well. He was very particular in the way he dressed. Fancy suits and polished shoes were a must for him. He was stylish but hard. He had a no nonsense attitude and definitely wasn't going to take any shit off of anyone. Everything he wore had to flow together precisely, and his home was immaculate and sanitary as well.

Mr. Anderson was now a wealthy real-estate investor. He and his wife Dora, were wealthy but lived in a well to do and humble home in a gated community. They could afford to live in a home three times as huge but opted for a beautiful home big enough for the two of them and have room for gatherings. They could stay over comfortably if they wanted to do so. It was disappointing to discover that the man who was investing in re-building lower income communities and had asked the people in those communities to help with the funding events, had disapproval of the mentally disabled living in his neighborhood. His wife Doara was a beautiful fair skinned lady with kinky hair. It was surprising that a white older man married to a younger black woman would have such prejudice, opinions about the mentally disabled.

The protestors walked around the gated community and often stopped in front of the house where our clients lived and held signs that read "no retards allowed". They chanted those ugly insensitive, hateful words as loudly as they could in front of the assisted living home that Mrs. Barnes, kindly and rented to our company. She heard of our reputation for having and providing the utmost care for our staff, involvement with the community and protection, of those, who could not protect themselves. Mr. Barnes passed away of cancer after 50 years of marriage and was paralyzed for 20 of those years after the war. Mrs. Barnes and our company had a great rapport with each other and agreed to provide a larger home for three of our clients.

Inside the home were three kind gentlemen. One was a white handsome autistic young man, 24 years of age that could recite any rap version of an Eminem song with perfection, yet if you asked him a question, he would only repeat exactly what you said to him. Another was burdened with Down syndrome and spoke so quietly, you would have to be at least two feet in front of him to hear his whisper of a voice.

You were not supposed to have favorites in my line of work, but I must admit that I was partial to this soft spoken 50 year old white adult that had child- like characteristics and wore cartoon pajamas to bed. Every evening after dinner, he would watch the same episode of Twilight, Zone. He had it on a VCR and a DVD. The only time he would come anywhere close to a behavior, was if someone had moved it when he was ready to watch it. The last gentleman was a heavy set black male that you really couldn't tell if something was preventing him from enjoying a normal life as described by society. He was diabetic and his misfortune was dealing with hallucinations and voices that would speak to him and he often spoke back as well.

They were all excited about moving into a bigger home and after staying at a hotel for the week-end while Janet and I helped staff move new furniture and their belongings into the new house, they were glad to finally see the house and their new rooms and surroundings. Janet's face was red from smiling as she watched them enjoy everything about their new home. We stayed until the night time staff arrived and we hugged them good-bye. As Janet was walking to her car, she called out to me. "Look, Jasper found his art supplies". She could see him through the window. Jasper always loved to keep his curtains open, so he could see outside and draw. Jasper held an old drawing up to the window and waved good-bye to Janet. The drawing was of a huge, red heart that had the words "JUST LOVE" in all capital letters written inside. Janet smiled more proudly than before and enjoyed the moment as she waved good-bye and stepped into her vehicle to leave.

I could tell that Janet was super pleased with today's events and she always enjoyed her time helping others. That enjoyment wouldn't last long because we both had no clue what the next day had in store for us all. The day staff at the home called Janet and I to the home to assist them with behaviors of the clients that were out of control due to the first day of protesting by the neighbors. The day shift was met with angry neighbors that held signs that called the clients retards. They expressed their displeasure of in their words, violent, retarded people, who may hurt someone in the neighborhood. They felt their kids were in danger and they couldn't be trusted. The day shift staff could not back the company van out of the driveway.

They were attempting to take the clients out in the community to enjoy their day, but the van was blocked by early morning protestors. Staff immediately assisted the clients back into the homes and called the office because the clients were getting agitated and feeling unsafe and fearful of the many people surrounding the van. We were shocked to hear the news and rushed to the home. Janet and I reached the home and found the protestors in front of the house where the clients had just moved into, shouting ugly chants and blocking normal traffic in the area. Janet was furious. She jumped out of the car and immediately demanded that the protestors stop and scolded them about their ignorance and let them know that they should be ashamed of themselves.

I helped Janet through the crowd and up to the front door of the house. The day staff at the home let us in. Janet asked the scared young girl at the door to calm down and immediately headed toward Jasper, the older man who spoke softly and wore cartoon pajamas. Jasper was hiding in the corner of the living room area, shaking and he hugged Janet tightly as soon as she kneeled beside him. "Don't let them take me away," he cried. He sometimes would say that when he felt threatened. I reached for the phone to call the police. One of the female staff reminded me that she had already called them. At that moment I heard a loud smash in the hallway.

As Janet and the young staff lady comforted Jasper, I approached Kelvin, who was pulling pictures off the wall and attempting to bang his head against the wall. I protected his head by putting my hand between his forehead and the wall, while guiding him away from the hallway with my other hand. I asked him to sit down in his favorite recliner and calm down in the living room area. I assured him that everything was ok. I noticed that Kimberly, the young black female staff member, had successfully helped

Janet calm Jasper down. Where is Mike? Mike was the 24 year old artistic client. Kimberly pointed to the kitchen area and Mike was with the other female staff. Todd was mumbling words we could not understand, but he was calm as staff assisted him to his room. Todd felt most safe in his own space. He sat on the bed patting on his chest nervously.

The police knocked at the door and I let him in. I noticed that other officers were outside speaking with the leader of the protest. I asked the officer to do something about the protest and he apologized for their behavior but informed me that they could do nothing about a peaceful protest."Peaceful!" "What's peaceful about assholes scaring the hell out of people who can't defend themselves?" Janet said with tears in her eyes. "I will not allow this to continue!" "If you won't do something about it, then I will!" Janet headed frantically to the door to confront the protestors. "Janet, calm down," I said. "Look, here is my credit card, Take the staff and the clients to a nice hotel, while we get this, straighten out." Janet quickly gathered herself because she knew her outburst would further increase the fear in the clients.

Janet realized that she acted momentarily out of character and her passion for her clients and her job had caused her to speak with anger, although she had good reason to do so. Janet to my card with a look in her eye that said someone will be held accountable for this. The police officer and I assisted everyone out of the home and into the company van. The protesters looked on and smiled as if they had won. "Go back where you belong," one of them said. I turned towards him, and with one stare, he didn't say another word. After getting everyone into the van, I helped Janet into the passenger side of her car. "I'll drive Janet, and follow them to the hotel safely." Janet didn't say anything as she continued to gather herself while shaking her head in disappointment at the actions and behavior of so called normal people. We pulled off behind the van and left the police to deal with the madness.

Janet, was a petite white lady with blonde hair, bright hazel eyes & bushy, well-kept brownish eyebrows. She had a lot of spunk and a fighting spirit in her small little frame. My dreads and my laid back attitude made most people think that maybe I smoked weed and didn't care about much. I never allowed anything to rattle me on the job. In every situation I was confronted with was handled with rational thought and patience. I believed that the calmest person in the room, in any situation had the best chance of survival and problem solving thinking skills. My broad shoulders and the way I wore my casual clothes and suits, standing and walking tall often confused people in the south because a black man with dreads in Memphis Tennessee was associated with crime and drugs. I was often asked about my profession by curious white people and black people who were either proud of me or assumed I thought too highly of myself. It made Janet and me the perfect team. We both had the eye of the tiger when it came to taking care of and protecting those who couldn't protect themselves.

The public's view of me was that I was successful with a meaningful life. It was my private life that was in turmoil. I was haunted by the death of friends and family in my past. I was lonely. I felt handcuffed and trapped because it seemed impossible for me to make a difference in the world. I longed to help troubled teenagers avoid feeling like their very existence sickened people and prevent them from experiencing the feeling of worthlessness or having to witness the unnecessary, up close and personal death of friends and loved ones that I had experienced as a child. My suppressed memories and the local crime scene section of newspapers filled with young black boys photo's often reminded me of the dangers that existed for people of color and my marriage was falling apart.

What could one man do? I thought to myself. What could any of us do without being targeted with bias accusations, criminalized, or like most of our minority leaders, murdered for advocating for peace and justice? It seemed to me, in my career, that so many laws and programs were centered on protecting, educating, and caring for the mentally disabled. I was often elated by just how much minorities in hostile environments or low income communities could benefit from the same kinds of efforts put into the programs to protect the mentally disabled at my place of employment. I loved my ability to help them, but hated that I could do nothing for people of color, still, being victimized in today's society.

I was Program Director, and Janet was State Director of a company that protected the equal rights of the mentally disabled and I often thought, what better career to have than to protect God's angels. We were determined to get justice for our clients. We sought after legal advice from the same attorneys that fought to get justice for the mentally disabled in another state several years before our current situation at a facility setting filled with neglect and abuse by staff and the surrounding community. The mentally disabled were not allowed out in the public and they were often dropped off there by their families and never thought of or visited again. We knew that Mr. Anderson had powerful resources and influences over attorneys in Memphis, although laws were already in place to protect prejudice acts against our clients, we wanted the best non connected attorneys we could find.

Janet was so happy and filled with excitement. I had to gather myself and rescue my troubled soul in order to enjoy this victory with her. It was time to prepare to train, put on the gloves and come out swinging. Janet and I hugged each other as she could hardly contain her joy. She was bouncing up and down while holding me and as small as she was in my arms, I could feel the power in her tiny but athletic frame. She let me go and began to fill me in on all the details. I was anxious to hear because she and I both had been on the phone for months trying to get an appointment with these powerful attorneys that were well known for being bulldogs in the courtroom and in their fight for justice.

I offered Janet some coffee, and she was glad to accept. "Yes Greg, I'd love some and spike that for me please." We both laughed at her statement because we knew we had both gotten pretty juiced the night before at Homie's after hours bar and grill the night before. "Are you sure Miss Janet?" I said with a smile on my face. "Boy, don't you play with me. Nothing like a bit of the hair of the dog that bit you to get the day started." Janet said while adjusting herself on the couch and calming herself since I had pretended that we didn't hang out at the bar Friday night, knocked down a few tequila shots while having fun, intellectual debates with friends. Starting the next day with a bit of a hangover that only spiked coffee would relieve, had become a common routine once or twice a month for Janet and I. Early Saturday mornings, Janet would often come by after or before her workouts for coffee, laughs and discussions about the job, family and friends. We took our profession seriously and never participated in those activities during the week.

I was in the kitchen preparing the coffee and I heard Janet walking around in the living room area. I spiked her coffee with just a shot of liquor and turned around to walk into the living room, when I noticed that Janet was opening the blinds. "Why is it so dark in here?" She asked, "Let some sun in!" "If you haven't noticed Janet, it's raining" I explained with a smile on my face. "There's that crooked smile I love, you should do that more often" Janet said, as she placed her hand on the side of my face. In one motion, she gently slid her hand down my cheek and then pinched my jaw like a grandmother would do, and took her coffee with the other hand.

"Sweetheart, there is always sun if you're willing to see it and allow it into your life," Janet said, as she got comfortable on the couch. She sat with her back against the armrest of the couch, placed one leg on the floor and the other stretched out down the love seat. She took a sip of the coffee, smiled and said "Oh yes, you make an awesome Espresso." Janet took another sip, and looked up at me with those bright blue eyes and said, "We are leaving Monday afternoon." Our flight to D.C. is scheduled to leave at 12:30." "We don't have to meet with the attorneys until later on, so I figured we will use that time to get settled in our rooms and take a quick look at the Martin Luther King monument on the way there." "What do you think?" "Cool, let's make it happen," I said as I sat in the recliner next to the couch near Janet. The sun was coming in behind me from the blinds Janet had opened to the bay windows. My robe opened and exposed my boxers and slight weight gain. Janet reached over, holding her coffee and rubbed my stomach rapidly and said, "You should come run with me," "and turn that four pack into a six pack again"

CHAPTER TWO

SLIPPING INTO DARKNESS

It had stopped raining, and it seemed that Janet's words had indeed, magically, willed the sun to shine. "Cool beans", Janet replied, and she took another sip. "Ahhhhh, great coffee," "We'll meet at the office early Monday morning and drive to the airport". "We'll take my car, there is no way to fit all my fabulousness in yours". "A lady has to slay the city no matter the occasion." Janet smiled flirtatiously and said "look, do you mind if I take this cup with me?" "I have to go take care of a few things and prepare for the trip." I laughed, "Yeah, I bet you do."

Janet turned toward me before she walked out the door. Still smiling, she whispered softly, "Hey babe, I'd be glad to help you, looks like you have a problem with dun-lap." I laughed nervously and asked, "What's dun-lap?" Janet slapped my stomach and said "Your belly dun-lapped over your boxers!" I smiled and gave a fake laugh.

"Ok, I see you got jokes, just make sure while you're running, you don't step in a pot hole and break those skinny legs of yours" Janet gave a loud, short and fake laugh "Ha!, my legs are nothing but tone muscle baby, besides, you know you like them!" "You wish!" I said smiling as I closed the door. I felt rejuvenated by my conversation with Janet, who was a free spirited soul. She was always fun to be around and always seemed to uplift those around her. I watched her get into her Range Rover and drive away. I remember thinking to myself, yeah, you are fine, but I'd never admit it to her.

My smile went away and I wondered, how could she be the daughter of Mayor Hope? Once, honorable and respected by the community, Mr. Hope was now a deceptive man, who used the false representation of minorities, as criminals, for political gain. His re-election campaign also centered on, putting restrictions on same sex marriages and getting votes to overturn judgements designed to protect their rights. Those actions were sponsored by institutions with power and ulterior motives in his re-election that would provide them with more economic power. It would further allow them to influence decisions made by institutions and politicians of the same social status, to control resources, property and the common people. Mayor Nicolas Hope's so called fight against crime, was actually a smoke screen that masked his support for laws put in place by politicians and corporations, to increase the population of minority inmates as a profit. Those who could not afford decent representation in court would be forced to take plea bargains. Innocence until proven guilty would mean nothing for minorities and the war on people of color in the streets, would continue because the color of skin would make them guilty before trial.

  I walked back into my bedroom and opened the curtains. Janet had brightened the beginning of the day with her cheerful and positive attitude. I laughed at myself, as the light came through the window. I noticed the empty liquor bottles. They were all aligned in a row, on the top shelf near the bookcase. I was amused, and thought to myself, only my culture understands empty liquor bottles as decorations. It was like trophies of a stolen, good time, in the mist, of despair. "I gotta get my shit together." I said to myself. I threw them all away and went to my entertainment room. The man cave was a place, I gathered my thoughts and regained focus. On the wall, above my three hundred and fifty gallon, tropical fish tank, was a signed portrait of Muhammed Ali. It always motivated me to watch documentaries about Ali's life, struggles and accomplishments. I felt ready to fight for Janet and our mission although I feared there was no hope for minorities and the decency of humanity.

I thought of her father again, while looking at the portrait of Ali. Here was a man who fought for equality, and justice for all people, all over the world. I shook my head out of disbelief, that people of color were still being victims of injustice, police brutality and political manipulation. Mr. Hope was now a puppet influenced by greed and stood firm on laws designed to protect all communities except minority communities. They were laws that suggested that poverty was a crime and any attempt to stand against injustice was punishable and justified by the ignorance of racist. They were further justified by those not affected by the mental anguish of poverty and criminalized by those who manipulate the judicial system..

It was easy for the mayor to get votes if he played on the belief that crime and drugs only existed in brown communities. His campaign "Down with dope and up with hope" clearly targeted lower income areas, because that was the only image of people of color portrayed in the media. The privileged felt threatened, and votes were obtained. A biased war on drugs and people of color was launched. A hostile environment was created in low-income communities and innocent lives were lost. Politicians like Mr. Hope, used the media to influence a stereotypical image of the behaviors of minorities as a crime. The result was mass incarceration and the ability to get away with aggressive actions towards them. All for political and economic gain. Not for the safety and well-being of all citizens.

His campaign strategies portrayed minorities, as aggressive, drug addicts, dangerous, drug dealers, thugs, uneducated, and violent. Long before any crime was committed, the assumption of who is going to commit those crimes was embedded in the minds of people all over the world. With that being said, being a person of color was the crime before a crime actually existed. Mr. Hope also was throwing the possibility of student loan forgiveness around like cheddar biscuits as well.

Free biscuits sounded good, but taxpayers were asking the question, who's making those tasty biscuits?. Mr. Hope was not telling them that student loan forgiveness came with ingredients that would eventually cause students and prior students to owe the I.R.S. Their forgiveness programs may have promised a ten, fifteen, or twenty year forgiveness. Yet, he didn't tell them that whatever income they made a year, the student loan amount owed would be required to be added to that income at the end of each tax filing period. Even if they added only twenty thousand dollars a year, to a tax payer's income, it would definitely place them in a higher tax bracket. Instead of getting a tax refund, now you owe the I.R.S. The days of paying a little something on it until it was paid off would be over.

It was just another method of profiting or manipulating off the poor working class. Another injustice to the American people. If a teacher made forty thousand a year and was barely staying above the poverty line, then income, she did not make or use to feed his or her family, would be added to his or her income. "How was that a justifiable solution to student loan debt?" Especially when a lot of graduates were not working in their field of expertise. I wondered as I turned on the big screen T.V. in order to catch up on new events going on in the sports world. Watching the mayor manipulate our community was becoming too much to bear.

Mr. Hope was no longer connected to the issues troubling his community. Especially to the precious lives lost of minorities being categorized as criminals and guilty by association, due to the color of skin. Any person of color who stood up against unethical treatment and misrepresentation by the media and politicians, was said to be defending criminals. The attempt to draw attention and awareness to inequality was lost because that person was already thought of to be guilty by association to his or her social group. His plan was working brilliantly. A criminal, defending criminals, to put it lightly. Mr. Hope was now using high profile candidates' methods to obtain votes for his re-election. One that was used to justify slavery and cheap labor years ago, was still affective, and only wearing a new suit. Ironically, he did not realize that his own association with someone in his social group would possibly end his career.

The results of his campaign strategy long ago, was a dominant race forcing minorities by any means necessary to conform to their culture. Laws were enforced mainly, by their way of thinking, without the benefits of enough income, freedom, equality and justice for all mankind. Today, the diversity of citizens in America is phenomenally explosive. One dominant race, continuing to attempt to set the standards, control and distribute resources, was growing increasingly harder to do. The theory in our political system was that institutions and those connected in higher power made the decisions that governed the common people. The problem was that the masses were becoming more aware and diverse in today's society, and politicians like Mr. Hope were fearful of the rapid decrease in numbers of the white majority.

Mr. Hope was once a good man, but now he was imitating the political fear tactics that separated the American people and used the ignorance of those who still held on to prejudice and racist opinions about each other to be re-elected. Those who were disgusted with the election of President Obama, now were an easy target for gaining political votes despite its effects on a diverse society trying to move forward in a positive, more peaceful and functional way. The average day to day working human being had enough problems just dealing with keeping their well-being and mental health intact. The last thing they needed was politicians not addressing the common people issues realistically and shoveling chain locking and dysfunctional theories down their throats. Their so-called true law was only false laws that convicted minorities according to social and economic status.

The great melting pot theory of opportunity and equality was not being distributed evenly. The reality was that status, in all social groups, determined your chances of which spoon full of the pot they may or may not have access to. The diversity of the American people was growing extremely, tired of it. More and more movements by displeased citizens were being formed because of the few higher power decision maker's, denial that the old ways of governing in today's diverse society were increasingly reaching its limitations and having dire consequences to the size of white America. Most people, black and white felt that the salad bowl concept should be the way of Americans, where people don't melt together to conform to one dominant race, instead, the diversity of America complimented each other and worked together like the ingredients in a beautiful, delicious salad bowl.

Candidates Trump and Hilary were supposedly our chosen leaders. It seemed that, leading by a positive presidential example, had taken a back seat to going at each other's throat. In my opinion, Trump, more so, than Hilary. Mr. Hope was jumping on the coattails of Donald Trump's methods of using bia's opinions of the American people to gain political power. Calling all Hispanics rapist and criminals was nothing more than a fear tactic, to make the American people feel threatened by illegal immigration. I honestly didn't feel that Mr. Trump was racist at all. Nor did I feel that Mr. Hope was racist. I felt that they were both using their intelligence to persuade ignorance to place them in office.

Regardless, of the reason or method, the older generations were holding on to, or perhaps, unwillingly trapped into the ways of thinking, learned from America's history of crimes against differences in people. The new, younger generation, who elected President Obama, cared less about racist opinions and were just waiting for the ignorance of the older people, to just die off the face of the earth. Multi-cultured people and advanced technology were growing faster than it could be controlled by one dominant race, or a few institutions and people, with economic and political power.

I respected Janet and wanted to ask her several times about her father but I could tell she wasn't happy with his methods and I just decided to wait for an opportunity to discuss it. It wasn't like I felt she could do anything about it and I was just concerned about how she was handling it, considering how opposite in character, she was compared to her father. I knew how Janet felt about injustice to any individual or group regardless of the color of skin. We both were infuriated by the way the media portrayed young men and women of color, attempting to bring awareness to police brutality. Kolin Kaepernick's situation was one that she and I often discussed, and was dumb founded by the way he was portrayed in the media and stripped of his means of income.

We both wondered why, as decent, human beings, society hasn't learned from past mistakes. Great men and women who could have been powerful, influential people in helping a country with so much diversity, live and grow together in a more prosperous way, were criminalized and treated unjustly because of their efforts. The loss of great people like Martin Luther King Jr. and Malcom X., should've been a shameful reminder to the American people, that injustice and lack of a real connection to the common people, has its negative consequences, on us all. Yet Mr. Hope, the media, corporations, politicians, and institutions continued to be unrealistic, in their efforts to govern the diversity of its citizens. People like Muhammed Ali, and others, were human beings, that would have provided true equal opportunity for us all regardless of color, gender, economic or social status. Janet and I felt disconnected and powerless, like most U.S. citizens in our influence over decisions made that advocate inequality among the common people. Most Americans today could care less about being racist. They needed politicians to realize that the common American citizens were not being allowed to live life as decent human beings, with the amount of wealth inequality and justice in America. The light of hope America briefly had in 2008 was now one that was slipping into darkness.

Janet's father advocated for methods that continued to allow a predetermined assumption, about a person of color or social status determining if they were worthy of health care, justice or the right to live free of the fear of police brutality. I wasn't sure if I would even vote at all for either of the 2016 presidential candidates. Janet and I strongly disagreed with the methods being used in 2016 by local politicians, following the lead of the play on the fear and division of the races to obtain the presidential office. The common people didn't care about e-mails or Trump's association with Russia. In my opinion, as long as his association with Russia meant peace and not war, I was fine with it. Especially considering that Russia had a considerable amount of influence over the use and control of oil. The scary thing about it, was that information was quickly becoming a more valuable commodity than oil itself.

The ability to influence behavior and thinking by way of social media tools was phenomenal. Trump's shady association with Russian leaders concerned me only, because it would not be necessary to be a leader of good character to be elected, when he could obtain the ability to influence millions of people, with the use of informational manipulation. Regardless of my fears, It was clear that minorities needed their own political party. Our dollars were more powerful than our votes. But we were not using our spending power to obtain justice and equality, we were using protest. Protests that were being rebuttaled with violence.

The common tax paying citizen was so wrapped up in making ends meet, that they barely had time to bond with family, outside of the immediate home. Family structure, principles and values took a back seat to the day to day stress of being overworked and underpaid. Therefore, they hardly knew their neighbors, living right next door to them. They were too busy and those who were not affected by poverty lacked empathy for the violence enforced on minorities.. Without order, there would be chaos, yet the price that tax paying minorities paid in exchange for, protection, equality, healthcare, education, justice, and freedom for all, to say the least was a hilarious joke. Janet and I wanted to protect all lives from being discriminated against in any form. We both had the same concerns, just as most Americans were concerned about the future and well-being of their children. Americans of all races were tired of wealthy, political bullshit.

One thing I did agree with Donald Trump with, is that this world was going to hell from being too liberal. You just can't please everyone. Of course, I was liberal in my views, yet even being liberal, should have its limitations. Some things, no matter how many people liked it or disliked it, were just wrong and some things were just right, plain and simple. I wasn't a supporter of Trump at all. I can't say that I didn't know his exact meaning behind that particular statement, but one thing people of color did agree on was that experiencing biased, unethical laws and restrictions in our communities, troubled kids got locked up, brutalized, criminalized or killed in the streets. All while wealthy, privileged, troubled kids, got counsel or support groups. A slap on the wrist, to say the least. They did not die in the streets and have aggressive behavior used as an excuse for deadly treatment. No matter how any political leader tried to sugar coat the problem, it was just wrong.

While watching the 2016 Presidential campaign I felt nothing but despair to witness two candidates rip each other apart instead of focusing on what's important to voters. Concerned citizens care about solutions and wish that candidates could get over the debate, respect differences of opinion and start solving issues despite their differences. Never had I felt so afraid of who would be President in my lifetime. Racial differences of opinions were causing more and more violence each day while Donald Trump's "Make America GREAT again" campaign continued to insult the election of President Obama, people of color, women, homosexuals and anyone who had known the evils of America being not so great, and unethical in so many ways, for centuries.

Donald Trump continued to attack Mrs. Clinton and Mrs. Clinton continued to respond to his accusations and attacked his character and his views as well. All along, while their followers reacted in ways taught to them by the very ones supposedly leading the country. People often learn from observation from those in positions of authority and if they felt that a debate was warranted by ripping each other apart, how could they expect citizens to properly get along with each other despite their differences? Politicians were fighting. Their supporters were fighting. All for selfish gain of power and unrealistic solutions for the common people. While the media highlighted the division of the races, differences in opinion by republican and democratic supporters, carried out those same methods of communication. Their result was, injuries, fighting, jail or death.

It was my opinion that the so-called leaders of this country should've been mindful of their own behaviors, if they expected better behavior from the citizens. I may have not liked Trump's, or Mrs. Clinton's political views, but I respected them both, as human beings. I would've never wished any harm to them or their families. I prayed that Janet's father would see the strain of his decision to follow a high profile politician's example had caused strife with his daughter and his wife.

The ugliness of Trump and Hilary presidential campaign, brought about a familiar looking division of the races that didn't help matters at all. The hope and possibilities of making a difference and "yes we can" seemed to be falling apart with this election campaign.Trump's slogan, make America great again was a slap in the face to those who saw hope for the growing diversity in America. "Make America great again?" As if America went wrong with the election of a black President. I didn't think Trump was racist in his personal and private life, but his play on the angry emotions of republicans, was his brilliant business move. It was also a dangerous threat to the peaceful existence of a diverse nation. Mr. Hope was playing the same game and he was losing his daughter's love and respect.

Janet and I felt that America was at its greatest potential with the election of Obama. Of course, that depends on who you asked about America's greatness throughout its entire history. To people of color and racist white people, he might as well have said "Make America white again'. The 2016 presidential campaign will be documented in history as one of the most controversial election campaigns', ever. Organizations like the KKK were being mentioned, discussed and appearing on the news more and more often, it seemed in retaliation for the Black lives matter movement. Although the Black lives matter movement had absolutely nothing to do with hate, violence or a stand against any other particular race. Misinformed Americans viewed the movement as threatening.

With all the controversy that caused the black, blue, me too and all lives matter movements, the Mayor's re-election campaign was not in alliance with the concerns of the diverse citizens in his community. "It's time to fight for what's right," and "Down with dope" and "Up with hope" and his efforts to overturn gay rights laws were clear evidence, that he had lost a connection with the citizens in his community. I felt bad for Janet and hoped she could get over the negativity caused by his re-election campaign. As for me, I knew I wasn't voting for him and I wasn't going to discuss Janet's personal family business without her consent. I'd be there if she needed someone to talk to and offered my support. I had my own issues as well.

I was haunted by my life as a young man growing up in the projects, witnessing people I knew and my friends losing their lives, being incarcerated, or addicted to drugs, just trying to cope with the unfortunate cards society had dealt them. Now, with the seemingly, increasing brutality of young minorities, and non-realistic actions or solutions by our candidates, I feared for the safety of us all. It was heartbreaking, that only people of color had to talk with innocent kids about not if, but when they experience racial profiling, or being pulled over by the police for reasons not the fault of their own, but only because the color of their skin. It was infuriating for a parent to have had to mix encouragement, with conversations about possible life threatening situations. All due to the color of their skin, not a criminal act. I wanted those issues addressed in the political campaigns but 2016 looked to be in my eyes a highway seventy to hell. This time it was not just affecting minorities in a negative way, it was affecting American society entirely. We seemed to be going two steps backwards in American history during the 2016 presidential campaign.

Another thing about Janet's father's campaign that disturbed me, was health care for those who could not afford it being a problem in America. America spends billions of tax-payer's dollars on medical technology and is considered number one in the nation. Yet, it was only provided for those who could afford the high cost of medical treatment. America didn't come close to being in the top twenty, when it came to the health care for all of its citizens. All citizens of the United States are required to pay taxes. Most citizens barely got by just paying the bills and keeping a roof over their loved ones head.

If they missed one or two weeks of a paycheck, it would most likely mean the difference between a place to live or living on the streets. With the high cost of healthcare and other insurance purposes added on, most U.S. citizens had to take on a part-time job just to be able to afford health care alone. That's if their home was lucky enough to have a two parent household. For a single parent home or senior citizens, the decision to live at risk was far greater than that of two parent homes. Millions chose to put food on the table and provide shelter for themselves and their children over the added high cost of health care, in order to survive.

In my opinion, it made no sense, that as U.S. citizens, they all had to pay taxes, yet those billions of dollars were spent on medical technology that only those who could afford it would benefit from. I was pissed and disgusted that politicians were not taking the issues of the common people seriously. I wondered, if the common, poor working class people paid taxes and they could not depend on their leaders to protect and provide for us all, then surely, those considered not worthy or not socially accepted should be exempt from paying taxes. I was sure that the working poor and minorities could use that extra money to care and provide for their families since the tax dollars they paid wasn't being used equally among all citizens. I loved being an American, but being a minority in America was one that was filled with inequality, injustice and the constant fear of death.

My career with a company that protected the rights of the mentally disabled and Janet's free spirit, kept me grounded, but at home, in the middle of the night, I was always restless. My feelings about Janet were one of a professional manner. I admired her spirit and her caring soul. She was a fighter and a lover of people. I quickly re-directed my focus toward the positive energy of Janet and not her father. I took a long shower, made myself some breakfast and started to gather my luggage for the business trip on Monday. All the while, wondering why minorities rights were not protected in the same way the human rights of the mentally disabled were being protected.

Manufactured poverty produced millions of people in the hood with undiagnosed post traumatic stress disorder and mental health issues yet their behavior due to mental anguish were not treated as a medical condition, it was met with police brutality, plea bargains and discrimination. I wanted so badly to make a difference for minorities, but I felt restrained in how to do so. And according to efforts of those in the past and recently, to do so with too much attention, would result in being criminalized for those efforts. Fucking disturbing, when I thought about it. Most people in America are honest, tax payers and they were tired of being led by men who only had selfish agendas and profited from the disadvantages of the common people and the poor. To them poverty was not only good business but treated as a crime as well. For minorities American society was slipping into the pits of evil from which it came.

I would get depressed nightly after watching the madness arriving from the 2016 election campaigns. I wondered how to end racist views and actions once and for all. I wondered if what I read about Morgan Freeman could be true. He was once asked his opinion about how to end racism and discrimination in America. His answer was one that was so simple and powerful. "Stop talking about it," he stated. Basically, what I think he meant was that people all over the world don't have to give social constructions validity. It is only a biased belief about others that causes people to use opinions and observations as a reason for inequality. I felt that it was long overdue that our leaders were guided by morals and principles and not by greed. Give me a man in a leadership position like Mr. Bernie Sanders, who believes in ending mass incarceration of minorities as a profitable business. Give me a woman like Michelle Obama, who knows what it's like to fight for what's right morally, and lead by example for the sake of all mankind. The diversity of the American people was growing tired of political manipulation that benefited the well-being of the wealthy and the elite. Minorities were tired of their protests being viewed as though they were defending criminals or a stand against the flag or another race. Minorities and the diversity of the American people's voices against inequality and injustice were feared because the elite feared a revolution. They feared minorities wanted dominance. The truth was that the common people cared less about a revolution that provided dominance over another race or country. What they wanted was a political revolution that eradicated social injustice and ended gender, wealth and race inequality.

As diverse and supportive as the mayor's community had been, I was perplexed by Mr. Hope's decision to sell out to what was normally used by high profile political leaders. There once was a time when local candidates were not afraid to roll up their sleeves and get down and dirty for the people in the community. He was once that local candidate that you would often see talking and working with the people. Mr. Hope could relate to the common people and the community once respected his old fashioned, roll your sleeves up and work together attitude. Lately, especially with the 2016 presidential campaign, a lot of local candidates were selling their souls to the devil. It seemed to me that only a few local candidates were honorable in their intentions, for the equality of all in the community. I had to get the mayor's bullshit campaign off of my mind, so I tried to focus on the plans Janet and I had to protect our client's from further abuse.

After getting dressed, I called my friend Homie, who was now Chief of police Bond. I often called him "007" for fun. "Wassup, big homie!" I said jokingly when he answered the phone in his professional voice. I call him big Homie now because during his years in the military, he had used all his spare time as a military police officer to workout. He wasn't the scrawny little snot nose kid anymore.

He was ripped head to toe, although I was still a little taller and had naturally broad shoulders, ripped chest, along with my dun-lap belly that barely showed a four pack, certainly did not compare to the way he had developed every muscle of his shorter frame.

Homie laughed when he realized it was me on the phone. "Wassup, Snow!" "Man, I saw you leave with Janet last night!" "Are you hitting that right or what?" Homie often teased me about my close friendship with Janet. He and I both knew she was single, and she never talked about her private life or jokingly redirected the conversation when someone asked about who she was dating. "You guys looked pretty lit last night," Homie said. "Yeah man, thanks for the ride home."

Homie intended on dropping me off at my home and then taking Janet home further up town but as I was getting out of the car, Janet started feeling a little sick so she asked if she could use my bathroom. After using the bathroom to freshen up, Janet talked with me until the both of us were feeling better. I then gave her a lift home on my motorcycle since I left my old Vintage 1971 Chrysler Newport, locked up at my friend's bar & grill.

His night club was a cozy spot to enjoy live music, food, dancing or just hang out in the VIP sections and enjoy conversations with friends. It was located in the heart of the city, surrounded by other businesses owned by people of all races. You could walk down the street and feel safe at night. Police officers and friends in the community often visited. We knew most of the people there, yet there were more and more people we didn't know attending each week. His cousin Wilbert ran the kitchen and supervised the surveillance room. No one was allowed in the back room of the club without permission from Wilbert.

Live Jazz, Blues and R&B music entertained people, and the food was always amazingly satisfying after drinks and dancing. There was never any of that catchy, say nothing, rap music playing, that's been shoved down the throats of today's generations at his place. Although he and I often listen to the only new rappers we respected during workouts and in the car, you might also hear rap artist playing at the club such as, J. Cole, Bryson Tiller along with the best of old school rappers like Ice Cube, Eminem, Tupac, Biggie, E-40 and A Tribe Called Quest. The night before was a pretty rough night for Janet and I. When we entered the club, the first thing we noticed was Homie standing alone inside the bar area that surrounded him in a u-shaped structure. People were sitting on the stools outside of the bar and we both knew that the always interesting conversations, playful insults, bets on the games and drama was about to start.

When you walk in the club from the front entrance, there are tables and chairs where people eat their chicken & fish plates. The tables and chairs are on each side of a clearance people used to get to the bar area further back. The dining area was small enough for the only waitress "Sasha" to attend. "Sasha didn't take any mess and her small waist and big butt got her lots of tips. Her dark skin, bright eyes, pretty smile and unfiltered vocabulary made her an exciting waitress. She once taught social studies at a nearby high school but quit in order to get away from unruly teenagers. Beyond the dining area, to the far right was a small dance floor with blinking lights and a stage nearby, where live bands would play. This particular night, the D.J. played music, and Homie served the drinks while the big screen TV on the wall at the opening end of the u-shaped bar showed sports highlights and news.

The lights were dim and the music was never too loud where you couldn't hear conversations at the bar. I pulled out a bar stool for Janet to sit in and before I could take my seat, next to her. Wilbert came out from the kitchen with his bald head, glistening from the heat and grease in the kitchen. Sweat was rolling down his forehead and he was still trying to groom his beard by constantly brushing and combing it because he wanted to fill in the two patches in his beard on each side of his face. Since his hair line had receded so badly, he now wore his head bald and wanted to have a Rick Ross look with the only facial hair he had left. Wilbert walked right between Janet and me, and asked "Why do you keep bringing this white girl in here man?" "She ain't down with the brothers." Wilbert often teased Janet when she dropped by the bar and it was sometimes hard to tell if he was playing or not. One thing for sure, he was always starting trouble.

Wilbert was now heavy set, fair skinned with greenish eyes, and he thought of himself as irresistible to the ladies. If his delivery wasn't always up front and raunchy, maybe he'd stand a better chance, but he was always running them away. I smiled and put my arm in front of him and said "bruh, give the lady some space and stop dripping sweat all over the girl's dress." "Wilbert moved back and replied, "My bad, you're right, the girl looks better than a bologna, egg and cheese sandwich." "Baby, ya look delicious!" Janet laughed as she positioned herself comfortably at the bar and said "Thank you Wilbert, and what exactly does down with the brothers mean?" "If it means dating black guys, then maybe it just means that I'm not interested in dating someone whose bald head shines bright like Rihanna's big ass forehead." Janet had a way of connecting with everyone and holding her own regardless of the color of skin.

Everyone laughed and I took my seat next to Janet. We both ordered shots of tequila and Homie poured them up in Pittsburgh Steelers glasses that he kept especially for us. Janet and I shared a common love for the Steelers and although Homie was a Dallas Cowboys fan, he would entertain our preference with our own shot glasses. "Ok, I see you got jokes," Wilbert said to Janet. "I think you got a problem with the brothers because I never see you with a man except for Greg, and I know he ain't doing shit because his wife would kill him."

Homie and all four of the detectives he was talking to all raised their fist, bowed their heads and yelled, "Sista Souljah!" It was a way of joking with me about Lieko, every time someone mentioned my wife at the bar. Lieko could've been a model, but chose a career as an activist and everyone that knew her well knew better than to bring up anything about Donald Trump, or be prepared to do battle. At that moment, the waitress walked into the bar area with two fish plates and gave them to the couple sitting across from us at the bar. She overheard Wilbert's comment and said, "Boy, if you don't take your goat mouth, ass, back to the kitchen and get my orders ready, we're gonna have a problem. "You're always flirting in some woman's face."

Wilbert started to walk away and said, "Shut the fuck up Sasha, don't nobody want her." "She ain't special, I've been with white girls before and some of them got pussy longer than eighty cents in pennies." Janet almost choked on her second shot of tequila as she quickly wanted to respond to Wilbert's accusations about white girls. Janet turned around in her bar stool facing the direction Wilbert was walking backwards in and replied "I don't know what slop jar white girl you were messing with but my va, jay jay stay on right and tight sweet heart." "I got that cream of nature, one taste and you'll live forever." "The old man in the corner holding a glass of Hennessey raised his free hand and did a quick two step and yelled "Got Damn, I need a drink from that fountain of youth baby!" Sasha's loud voice immediately took over again, "Don't pay any attention to Wilbert, he wishes he had been with a white girl." "Don't nobody want his crusty ass." "He needs to take a damn bath and wash them dingle, berries out the crack of his hairy ass."

She then addressed Wilbert before he made it to the kitchen door. "Get your thirsty ass in there and get my orders ready and put a hair net on!" "Stop combing that going bald in the beard, diseased ass hair before it gets in the food." I laughed and said "Awh, that's fucked up!" Sasha laughed and said, "Greg, that boy was washing his beard every night with head and shoulders, trying to fill in those bald spots." "It's a damn shame," Sasha laughed as the old man shouted, "Instead of worrying about using head and shoulders on that busted up beard, he needs to get rid of those dingle berries with some head and ass!" Sasha busted out laughing, threw one hand in the air and the other one across her chest. "Whew lawd!" "You sholl know what to say," Sasha was killing herself laughing. Just then, the couple across from us eating fish looked up and frowned. The woman spit out the food she was chewing into a napkin. "That's it, I can't eat anymore." Her date laughed and said "baby you better eat that fish cause when I get you home, we want to count your pennies." "Shit, ain't nobody trying to hear about Wilbert's nasty ass." "I'm not hungry anymore," she said.

Shaking his head and trying not to laugh, Homie turned away from the group of gentlemen he was talking with and said "Alright that's enough, Y'all making my customers uncomfortable." "Wilbert just had to try and get the last word in again to Sasha. "You need to be at home taking care of those kids instead of worrying about what I'm doing." Sasha put her hand on her hip and said, "Boy, you need to get control over them, menace to society kids of yours and quit worrying about your hair melting off your bald ass head and settling for your face." Everyone laughed while Wilbert stood there with a confused look.

"They're your kids too baby, damn," he replied as he turned and walked through the kitchen door. Sasha didn't care that Wilbert was in the kitchen and couldn't hear her, she replied back, in a loud irritated tone "Yeah, I know, but I don't make it a habit of letting everyone know I have anything to do with your trifling ass!" Sasha and Wilbert had what you would call a love hate relationship but they were dedicated to keeping their boys out of trouble and raising them to be productive citizens. Their teenage boys weren't doing too well in school, but they were decent kids and Sasha didn't want them to fall victim to the streets.

Sasha took two more orders at the bar and asked Janet to take them to the kitchen while she spoke with me in private. "Sure love," Janet said and walked away. Sasha wiped the bar and placed her arms on the counter. She leaned in towards me and said "Hey, baby, how's the kids doing?" "They're great Sasha, Makayla is in New York with her mom. She's going to college to be a Veterinarian and her mother is introducing her to some of her old modeling friends." And of course you know, Kylin is staying with me." "He is away with friends touring different colleges they're interested in attending"

"Child, that is beautiful," Sasha said, "I am so proud of them." When Kylin gets back, tell him to come by and see me, I worry so much about him." "Kylin is fine, I said, "He is still laid back and kind, He will be ok Sasha."

"I know baby but I just think the boy feels like there are no troubles in the world since he's been going to that private school." "Why didn't you send him to the school for advanced learners with more black students?" "And it's free," you can't lose. I explained, "Honestly, Lieko and I didn't even think of it until he had already taken the test and passed, so we didn't change things." "Well, just make sure you keep him aware of the dangers of being black out here in this world, ok?" "I know he's a nice young man, but hanging around all those white kids can be a good thing, but it can also cause him some problems." "You know how some of those fathers are about their precious little daughters dating a black man." "He's handsome too." "You bring him over and let me give him some street, knowledge and a bowl of my famous gumbo." "You know Trump got these racist white folks acting real bold out here like they rule the world and can't take an ass whipping for that shit."

"I took another shot and said "I know Sasha, you sound like his mother, and I got this." "Speaking of his mother," Sasha said, "You two should really work things out." "I like her." "She is militant like me and you could use some TLC on those dreads." "She always kept them looking nice." Give her a call baby," Sasha begged, of me. "I'm gonna speak with her, I promise Sasha." I explained. "Makayla and her friends had a problem with some guy on the college campus protesting against women abortion rights."

"Lawd have mercy, that child got spunk like her momma!" Sasha laughed. "Did she kick his ass?" "You tell my baby if she needs me and my riders to load up and ride up on a mutha fucka, to let me know and we'll go to New York and burn that bitch down if somebody, mess with her!" Sasha laughed again and poured me another shot of tequila. Sasha leaned in again and said "Look baby, you have some great kids and I know you're a great father." "You do whatever you can to work things out with Lieko, ya hear me?"

"Besides, the boys and I love having Kylin over and some of him got to rub off on my boys because I can't get them to take out the damn trash without an excuse why it wasn't done in the first place." "They stay up all night playing these games and sleep all day and don't do shit around the house like I'm their maid or something." "They need to play outside some or get involved in sports or something." "Shit, social media got these kids today lazy as fuck!" Sasha complained. Sasha's oldest son Jermaine, was a few years older than Kylin. A good kid, but he was struggling with his place in the world. He would be out all night and come home with money. Sasha worried about him and what he was doing to have the money she found hidden underneath his bed. Wilbert had two jobs and didn't have much time to be involved in family matters at home. "It's all I can do to keep from choking their ass out and putting my foot up Wilbert's funky ass," Sasha continued to explain. "I must admit that I can honestly see now why Lieko is so militant," I leaned in closer to Sasha. "I teach Kylin to be respectful and cooperative with police if they ever pull him over and question him." "But after what happened in Minnesota, I'm scared to death." " I'm afraid for us all," I added.

Detective Oswald and the new rookie came through the door of the bar and took her attention away from me. Janet came back and stood by my side. Homie saw the two of them approaching the bar. He greeted them with a warm welcome. "Look who decided to drop by!" "Good to see ya, Joe." Joe Oswald was a seasoned detective approaching retirement. He had served the community well and being Afro American, of course he was familiar with the high expectations of him from people of color. He knew well, the hardships of seeing the negative side of people according to the negative images of police officers portrayed in the news, and social media. Officers got a bad wrap as well and sometimes a clip of law enforcement was not shown entirely. He was a firm believer that there were always two sides of a story and oftentimes, three or four. So, to him it was best to gather as much information he could to avoid irrational acts.

Oswald fully supported Blue Lives Matter and wanted to bring the communities he served and protected closer together in their understanding and cooperation with each other. Detective Oswald wanted the rookie to get familiar with the bar and relax a little because he was so uptight. All the older detectives called him "Bruce Jenner" because he was the only young white rookie that could out run all of the black recruits. Plus he had a pretty face. Of course, Bryson, which was his real name, didn't like being called Bruce Jenner since he only knew of him as the guy who changed his sexual identity.

We all meant as a compliment because the Bruce we knew was an Olympic Gold Medalist. We all greeted Bryson jokingly and tried to make him feel comfortable. "Bruuuuuce!" all the detectives and some of the others who knew the nickname in the bar yelled together. Bryson gave a halfhearted smile, put his hand up and said "That's Bryson please." Oswald put his hand on Bryson's shoulder and shook him around some happily. "Come on Bruce, lighten up, enjoy yourself and unwind."

All at once, a mixture of emotions rang out from the people around the bar. One guy jumped to his feet facing the big screen above the bar. "That's fucked up man, why the hell are they handcuffing him!" he said. "They should be arresting the mother fucker that hit him!" Homie and his detective friends stood there watching the fight that broke out at a Donald Trump rally on the news. Homie wanted to see exactly what happened but he had to take control. "Turn the music off!" he shouted. "Everybody just calm down!"

The other detectives all seemed to be in disbelief and analyzing the facts. The man shouted again. "You see that shit, the old white dude jumped up and hit that black boy with the dreads in the face and they are fucking with the black dude!" "Hell he's the one that got hit!" One of his friends said "It's a damn shame the police treat black people with patrol and control and treat white people with a protect and serve mentality." "White people getting too bold with this Donald Trump shit and before you know it, they are gonna think they can just go out and start hanging niggas again and get away with it." Another black gentlemen at the bar said "Shit, I wish they would, I'm ready to fuck up anybody think they gonna get away with that bullshit."

One officer in plain clothes said "we don't go out there looking to harm anyone." "Our job is not to settle domestic disputes. 'We are not there to listen and determine who's wrong or right, that's for the judge." "Our job is to contain the situation and prevent people from hurting themselves or others." The upset guy at the bar asked "Well why the hell it's always us that are being contained or being shot because we look a certain way?" "Hell, aren't we free to ask why we're being detained or is that just for white boys?" Before the officer could respond he said "Hell nawh, we ain't free, even the Statue of Liberty, has shackles at her feet!" "I know it's supposed to represent the breaking of the chains but why have them at all," the man added.

"Sir, we have families too,' the officer said, and we want to get home safely as well." "So if we run into any situation where the person being questioned is being uncooperative or threatening then we have to diffuse the situation for everyone's safety. 'So, are you saying that shooting an unarmed man is right?" "No, I'm saying that people should be mindful of their own behavior that causes an unfortunate event." The officer replied.'Unfortunate event!" "What the hell are you talking about?" "Oh because in your eyes, all black people are angry and aggressive huh?" "Why can't it be that we are tired of the bullshit and injustice?" "Shit, don't we have the same rights as anybody else?" "The Statue Of Liberty supposed to stand for America becoming this huge melting pot of all races with equal opportunities, but if you ask me, the broken chains at her feet are letting our ass know that you're only equal and free as white America allows you to be!" "Minorities got fucked out of the equal opportunity pot!" He added.

"We don't have to put on a smiley face and skim and grind just because you have a badge." "That's just a kill a nigga free card, to say they were angry or aggressive and you feared for your life." The man replied. "Calm the fuck down before I put yo ass out!" Homie instructed the angry man. One of the angry man's buddies told him to just chill. "We can't hear what happened." The man took his seat and apologized and spoke in a softer, but still heated tone. "See, that's the shit we gotta deal with." It's always the black man's fault whatever the situation is."

The young lady next to him put her hand on his shoulder as if to soothe him and asked everyone around the bar "Why is it that we love the diversity in animals, flowers and any other species except for our own? "Isn't the human race supposed to be smarter than that?" "Aren't we supposed to be smarter than them?" She asked. Animals stay among their own kind, yet they live together in peace." They see and sense danger, so of course they recognize differences in many situations and use that to survive and protect themselves." "Shit, I'd say that they have more wisdom than we do." "We're the fucking problem." She said, almost ashamed of her realization. The angry man replied. "What the fuck!" See, there you go blaming black people!" "No." She stopped him immediately. "Human beings are the problem."

The older gentleman took another sip of his Hennessey and said "young lady, you are right, we are supposed to be smarter, but we haven't learned to treat each other with respect." "Unarmed black people have been getting their ass whooped by police since the beginning of time and these young folk don't help the situation by acting like thugs and killing each other over shoes, drugs, money, cars, women and territory that don't even belong to them. The man sitting beside the young lady said "Well what are we supposed to do, pop, not have shit and bow our heads?"

The old man replied, "I'm just saying in addition to peacefully looking and fighting for justice, we can stop killing each other over bullshit. I agreed with the older gentleman and added that we needed to find ways to ensure that our kids keep their self-worth, pride and respect for others, in and out of the educational system that teaches them that the only way to be successful is making all A's, or going to college. "There are other ways to provide for your family like good honest work ethics and keeping a good credit score." I said "Fuck an A, if trying to get it destroys you as a decent human being." "Are you saying that education is not important?" a young lady asked. "No, not at all," I responded. I'm only saying that realistically not everyone will make all A's or have a chance to go to college, but that doesn't mean that a child cannot be successful or happy."

'There is nothing wrong with learning a trade and loving yourself regardless of what you may or may not have." "True Happiness means different things to different people, and everyone could use some education on self-worth without expensive material things" I added.

"Nigga, if I want to buy an expensive car, that's my business and I shouldn't have to be pulled over because I'm a black man driving a nice car!" the upset gentleman said. I smiled, holding in my frustration that he was missing the point. "I agreed and said, "You're absolutely right." "I'm just saying that we lose a lot of kids that first start feeling worthless in school because they are not making straight A's." I asked everyone a question. "What is the first thing they do to a child acting out, because they are not making good grades and being picked on?"

Before anyone could answer I said, "They end up in alternative class, or pushed through the system without learning anything of value about themselves." Sasha quickly added, "Child you're right and they'll end up in these streets if they're not careful, they'll end up like Wilbert's goat mouth, dumb ass." "Wilbert replied "The fuck you mean Sasha, I may have not been the smartest in school, but I got yo ass sprung on this donkey kong!" "Sasha responded, "If it wasn't for those pretty eyes, I wouldn't have given you the time in the day, because you was a dumb mutha fucka." I could tell that the hamster was there, but your wheels were not spinning. The hamster was dead as yo donkey- kong is." "Fuck you bitch," Wilbert said smiling, going back into the kitchen. Sasha shook her head. "These kids today get caught up in this bullshit America's shoveling them and feel worthless, next thing you know, they are trying to look the part and buy the expensive clothes and cars they can't afford to add worth to themselves," Sasha added.

"Yeah, that's all these young kids music talk about is how much money and bitches they got or killing some damn body!" the older gentleman said while holding his crotch and pretending to shoot in the air forgetting he had a drink in his hand. "Stop wasting my good liquor," Sasha said "and sit your old ass down." I interrupted and said, "I think what he is trying to say is that we have to continue to teach our kids to have some pride, respect and self-worth about themselves in addition to taking on injustice in a positive and peaceful way." "The upset man replied, "Bruh, what do you know about the hood?" "You haven't been hood, since you left the hood." "What does that mean?" I replied, confused by his comment. "Just because I'm trying to provide a healthier environment for my kids than what we had to go through means I don't know what's going on anymore?" "Maybe you need to quit glorifying what news, and the movies portray the hood to be". "I don't have to go around with my pants hanging off my ass or talking a certain way trying to prove where I'm from or act like I'm hard."

"I know who I am and I'm proud of what I've learned from the hood" I explained further, " It's that acting hard shit people see on T.V that helps feed that same shit you're mad about, so do you want a war or do you want peace with the police." "The upset gentleman said, "shit if the police ain't, being peaceful with me or treating me with respect, then I'm not gonna act like that shit is ok." "I don't care if there are police in here, don't come to me or my kids with that police brutality shit or suffer the consequences." "This Trump shit got people acting all bold out here, hell, his ass talking about building a fucking wall and making Hispanics pay for it." "What the fuck kinda shit is that?" "If you ask me, all Trump ass trying to do is control the product!" "He knows weed will be legal soon and he wants to be the drug king," the man added. His friend beside him said "This shit ain't no different than back in the day separating black families in slavery times, hell he keep fucking with them Hispanics families, trying to be the drug lord of America gonna get his ass fucked up by the Cartel." "I know I'm tired of these black boys being killed in these streets," he added. "They need to focus on getting this murdering and poverty shit straightened out over here and leave other countries alone, is all I have to say," one lady added.

Another officer tried to speak to him and said "look, I understand what you mean." "We feel the same way about our life and kids as well and there are some bad cops out there." "We try to identify and get rid of the bad ones." The upset gentleman said, yeah but in the meantime, it's our black ass dying out here in these streets." "I mean, damn, how long is it gonna take, the old dude already said this shit been happening since before Moses!" "When we patrol a neighborhood, we are only trying to do our job and protect the community, but we also make no hesitation in protecting ourselves in a potentially dangerous situation." "What the fuck is this blue lives matter shit?" The angry man said. "You just gotta downplay black lives matter, like it's a joke." He added. Euhommie told him to lower his tone. The angry man gathered himself and said "Look, I'm just trying to understand what the man said." They act just like the gangs around here and don't tell on a mutha fucking cop they know out here doing wrong." "They protect their own, wrong, right or indifferent." "They expect nigga's in the hood to snitch and then leave em' in the streets to die, but they won't snitch on the crooked ass cop out here abusing the badge. The man further expressed himself. "Hell, sounds like to me, ya'll the biggest gang out here and blue lives matter only means we protect our own and not the community."

The old man said, "It seems to me that if you're so afraid in particular communities, then you guys would take that opportunity to hire people in those communities that know the people well and let them patrol and protect their own neighborhoods." "Or actually train officers to contain without killing unarmed people even if they are being aggressive." "You're the ones with the guns in the situation, what is it to be afraid of?" "You have the upper hand." The old man, now sitting in a chair at a nearby table said "I think we can all agree that there is more than one issue to be addressed here." "It's more than a black and white thang." "It's more than blue lives matter, black or all lives matter." "It's a sign of the times, like Prince said." "If we don't learn from past mistakes we are destined to repeat the same mistakes." "Anybody, in here, ever read Huckleberry Finn?" the old man asked. "What the fuck? "This old negro, spiritual dude, talking about Prince Sugar britches ass and slave time Huckleberry Finn." The upset man protested and I was annoyed, especially since I was a huge fan of Prince.

The old man continued, "I'm just saying that even the little white boy in the book felt something in his heart and knew it was wrong to enslave people." "He had a guilty feeling inside about his friend who was a slave and struggled with helping him escape because he knew in that day and time in history, society would kill the slave and possibly him too for helping him escape." "So what's your point?" Janet asked the older gentleman while drying the wasted liquor on his shirt with a napkin. "The consciousness and compassion of America for its people should be on trial here, not whose lives matter the most." "Any rational mind can agree that all lives matter, but what was tolerated in those days by force cannot be tolerated by choice today." "Human lives should not be penalized because of color, age or not having health insurance," Insurance is high as hell, shit, I can't afford it." "Why do I have to die because I'm broke?" he added. "Amen, baby," Janet replied and kissed him on the cheek.

By that time a commercial was on and everyone seemed uncomfortable so Homie decided to call it a night and ended the business hours for the night. Everyone was calm but a few of them were asking the detectives if they thought it was right that the police officers at the rally did nothing to the man who struck the boy but arrested him. Although the bar was a mixture of white and black people, Bryson seemed uncomfortable around too many black people addressing him at one time. Officer Oswald accompanied Byson with one last shot and Officer Oswald asked the rookie, "Why are you here?" Bryson responded, "Because you asked me to come." Officer Oswald said "No, why are you here?" "Why do you want to be a police officer?" Oswald placed his hand on his shoulder and said, "If this environment where people freely express themselves makes you uncomfortable, what makes you think you can handle yourself professionally in the streets?" "Or is it that you just want to bust a nigger's head open?" Before Bryson could answer, Oswald said, "Look, I read your file and I know what happened to you." "Make sure the past is the past, keep a level head and if you have any problems keeping your code of ethics together, you make damn sure you come talk to me immediately, ok?" Bryson looked somewhat shocked and confused and said "Sure man, no problem." Officer Oswald continued, "Look man, we come here so that the community can see us in a different perspective." "We could have our own place just for us but we'd rather get to know the community even if there are differences of opinion." "Don't let those differences cause you to judge, unless you're willing to be judged."

Bryson used to live in a low income neighborhood as a teenager and being a white boy in the hood was difficult for him and his mother. He often told the story of being jumped by some black teens he originally thought were his friends and no one helped him. After that he knew he wanted to become an officer of the law. Bryson's discomfort was nothing new to the detectives at the club because he was a bit standoffish during training as well. Officer Oswald and Byson gave their opinions and quickly exited the bar. Janet and I were both feeling a little juiced and didn't get a chance to eat before the commotion started. Straight tequila shots on an empty stomach didn't go well for the both of us, so Homie offered to take us home and secure my car for the night.

We said our goodbyes and Homie asked Sasha & Wilbert to hold the fort down until he returned. He whispered in my ear before getting in the car and said "Thanks for coming by bruh, don't forget to be at the gym tomorrow." I smiled as he helped me in the back seat and opened the door for Janet on the passenger side. I had secretly been working out with Homie to try and get my six pack back since Homie had informed me a month ago that his sister Lisa was coming home on leave. He joked with me about Janet because he knew that Lisa and I wanted to be together long ago, but life would take us in different directions.

She also joined the military and became an officer in the Air Force and I went away to college. Before heading to the gym the next day, Homie joked about Janet again while we spoke on the phone. "Did you tell Janet you were hitting the weights?" He giggled because he felt that we had a thing for each other but were too afraid to admit or commit to each other.

CHAPTER THREE

DIFFERENCES

"You know Lisa ain't gonna be too happy to see you with a snow bunny after traveling across the country to see ya bruh" I laughed, and redirected the conversation. "Look man, are you gonna be ready to meet me at the gym today or are you expected at the nightclub early?" Homie laughed, "Ok, man, I'll leave you alone for now bruh, meet me there around two thirty or three o'clock." "Dig that big Homie, see you then." I hung up the cell phone and placed it on the bar in the kitchen. Normally my kitchen was spotless with the help of my son, but he was away on college tours with friends.

The wooden white cabinets had glass doors in front. They looked great as long as the drinking glasses and plates were organized inside. My son was an artist and he always kept my cabinets looking like an art gallery. He'd be disappointed that I had dirty dishes in the sink and the ones that were clean were scattered in the cabinets and ruined his hard work. I turned the cabinet lights out so I couldn't see my mess, wiped the sugar off the marbled, counter tops and attempted to wash dishes before preparing for my work out later on. I was interrupted by the buzzing of my cell phone on the bar. I hurried to reach it because the buzzing was making my phone vibrate and move towards the edge. Just as it was falling over the counter, I caught it. Without looking, I answered. "Hello!" I said with a frustrated tone.

"Well damn, don't you sound excited to hear from me"? Lieko said with a sarcastic tone. I caught my breath and gathered myself. "Babe, I was running to get the phone before it fell off the counter," I said, hoping my wife wasn't going to start some shit with me today. We had been separated for about six months due to her militant nature and our differences of opinions about raising kids. "What the fuck you running for"? "You got some bitch over there holding you up"? Lieko was always ready for a fight and I just didn't have it in me to entertain her shenanigans today. "Look babe, no one is here but me, Kylin is away with friends," "Wassup"? I asked with an irritated but calm tone. Lieko seemed to calm down and asked "Well, I was just calling to check on you and speak with my son."

"Where is he and what damn friends, you letting him hang around with"? I sat down at the bar stool behind the counter in the kitchen and placed my head in my hand and rubbed my eyebrows while looking downward, shaking my head before answering. "First of all, he's our son, and he is touring colleges with his usual friends from high school," I explained. My son was attending private school, and he had become friends with some pretty cool young gentlemen. Most of them were white and because of Kylin's laid back nature, his mom was afraid that he was not aware of the real world that didn't see him as the kind, person, he is, but outside of our home, he would be viewed as the angry black teenager, especially with everything going on with the police shootings of young black men and the racist nature of people and social media during Donald Trump and Hillary Clinton's Presidential campaign.

She was diligent in always talking to him about not being fooled into thinking just because he has white friends and went to a private school that life wouldn't be as easy for him as he may think due to the color of his skin. She was afraid for him if he or anyone she loved, was pulled over by the police. So many young black men and women were victims of the false image of angry black criminals that have nothing better to do but do drugs and commit crimes. She had valid reasons for fearing for Kylin's life.

But I did not agree with her militant way of trying to make him aware. I felt that as long as he carried himself in the way he always did, which was laid back, rational, and he treated people with respect, he wouldn't have a problem with police officers if he cooperated and treated them with respect. Kylin had a calm nature about himself like his father, and I was proud of him for that. My way of making him aware was to continue to tell him the same things as his mother but I would also talk calmly and asked him to continue to not be confrontational. Sadly, while white teens are being talked to about college, careers, opportunities and the hopeful things in life like love, relationships, great friends and supportive family, black parents have to ruin a precious moment like that with conversations about how not to be killed by police due to the assumptions of who you are by the color of your skin or the way you dress. Lieko had her valid points but our differences of parenting styles tore us apart.

Lieko was pumped, and the Presidential campaign, police shootings, Ferguson and the Trayvon Martin case had her ready for battle. She deleted any of her long time white friends from Facebook that supported Donald Trump or made any remarks about how people of color was owed nothing from the injustice of slavery and denied the inequality in America. I didn't support Donald Trump myself, but I felt that an opinion was like assholes, everybody has one, and the ability to get over the debate of who's right or wrong was crucial for starting a plan of action for realistic solutions. In 2016 the word compromise was becoming a traumatic disappearing act.

The so called leaders of America and the running candidates for the presidents seat in the white house, continue to tear each other down with accusations and deliberate tactics to discredit one another were prime examples of why the citizens that the American leaders govern couldn't agree to disagree and find peaceful solutions. If the leaders of our nation couldn't focus on solutions without fighting each other because of differences of opinions then how can they influence the people to strive for peace, love, humanity and treat each other with respect no matter their differences? My wife and I were being torn apart by our differences in opinions on raising black kids in a society that was led by the elite. The elite seemed to have had no clue of the consequences of injustice, or they felt that minorities of a particular status, are expendable with no effect on society. Truthfully, it affected us all. It tore apart families, the economy, the educational system, religion and the common people's connection with the rest of the world. Lieko continued to scold me.

"Will you please stop blaming me for his choice on who he wanted to live with"? "Kylin loves you and he doesn't want to see any of us unhappy," I explained to Lieko. "Well, if you weren't so lenient on him, he wouldn't be so naïve to what's going on in the world and think he's going to have it easy all his life". "He chose to live with you because you baby him," Lieko complained. I was annoyed because this was a repeated conversation and I knew that our son wasn't naïve to his surroundings and the world he lived in at all. Kylin was very observant and optimistic. He was fully aware from the conversations we had, plus he listened to some crafty rap artist that threw some political lyrics in from time to time.

"Look, he's ok babe, and he is with his friends," which is another reason he chose to stay home with me," I pleaded. "How is Makayla? I tried calling her last night but couldn't reach her?" Makayla lived with her mother during the separation and has a heart of gold. She's beautiful like her mother. She too, was outspoken but with more of a kind nature than her mother. Makayla's love for all races made me proud and I often warned her about putting too much effort in trying to change those who were not ready to change or didn't treat her with the same respect and care as she invested in them.

The funerals were extremely hard for my baby girl. She worried about us and tried to be strong for us but she was overcome by her own emotions for her grandmother and was sad for me because she knew how much my brother Byron, my mom and my grandmother meant to me. It was a lot for an eighteen year old to deal with. Makayla was only one year older than her brother Kylin, yet she cared for him and kept a watchful eye over him as if she was his mother. They spoke on the phone more than they did at home when we all lived together and since the funerals, they became even closer.

Lieko explained that Makayla was doing well in college and was enjoying her summer break, before going back to classes. "Tell Makayla to call me, I want to speak with her before I leave Monday morning," "You can speak with her now." "She just walked in." Lieko said and handed our daughter the phone. "Hey sunshine." I said, smiling and happy to hear her voice. "How's everything going baby girl." Makayla was excited to hear from her dad as well. "Hey, dad." She said. I replied. "Hey, Makayla." Are you ok?" "What happened at the college campus?" "Some asshole man was there trying to tell women what they can and cannot do with their bodies." Makala was a fast talker, so I wasn't able to get a word in before she went into a rant about that day.

Makayla continued. "It's not fair for men to get to decide about things that they know nothing about." "He got smart with one of my friends, so I told his ass that I hope that they stop using taxpayer's money to pay for his old, wrinkled, ass to get an erection!" She added. "If women are not allowed insurance to assist with abortions and fools like him make it illegal, than the days of women taking drastic matters into their own hands will come back." "Too many women have lost their lives or put their lives in danger, just because men think they have the right to tell them what they can do with their bodies." "But it's ok to use insurance to bring their dead ass dicks back to life." Makayla said with fire and passion in her voice.

I knew she was just like her mom, and once they were in that zone, there was no easy way of calming them down. "I hear you sunshine." I sighed. "It's not fair at all, if you look at it that way." "What do you mean, if I look at it that way?" Makala asked. "Nothing, baby girl." "You're absolutely right." "I just want you to be careful and choose your battles wisely." I said with a calm voice. "We'll talk more about it when I get back." "Just understand that although I don't look highly upon abortion, I do understand that women should have the right to that choice." "Especially in situations like pregnancy due to sex without consent." I added. Apparently, Lieko had the phone on speaker and interrupted immediately.

"Where are you going?" "Janet and I are going to D.C. to…..before I could finish my sentence, Lieko quickly and rudely interrupted. "What the fuck!" "Why are you still spending so much time with her and why the hell are you taking a trip with her?" 'I knew it was something going on with you and that bitch!" Regretting I had mentioned Janet and the business trip to D.C., I shook my head and ended the conversation. I had forgotten that my wife didn't like the bond between Janet and myself. It was another reason for the separation. Her jealous nature allowed her assumptions about Janet and I to cause unnecessary arguments in the home and it had become unhealthy for the kids to hear.

I felt it was necessary to separate for a little while because I didn't want the kids to think I was having an affair and I didn't want them to think that a healthy relationship consisted of continuous arguments and sleeping in different rooms. It had become a regular routine that I was on the couch. It was easier said than done. I was miserable without the entire family at home. It helped that Kylin chose to stay with me and I was thankful for that, yet it was quieter at home than usual. Never thought I'd miss the noise of the T.V, at night in every room, and the constant interruptions of teens asking for things when we were trying to have one on one conversations or private time together.

A good old home cooked meal had become a distant memory. I could cook, but not like her. Lieko made melt in your mouth meals, and was always exciting and fun to be around. Although she didn't always have enough time to cook breakfast, or prepare a meal for us all to eat together, when she did, it was delicious. I complained so much about her not having time for us to eat together. To me, it was a chance to talk and communicate about anything in each of our busy lives. Lieko and I, with work, and the kids with school. She grew tired of my complaining. Just one of the reasons, we fell apart. Now, I missed her efforts and a good home cooked meal. I responded to Lieko's accusations, of me and Janet, having something going on, other than a platonic, relationship. "Look, it's not like that," I explained, "Just tell her to call me please or I'll catch her myself before leaving Monday." "I'll be back before Kylin gets back home

Friday," I said, trying to be as comforting as possible. I hung up the phone and prepared to go to the gym.

On the other end of the phone, Lieko was extremely annoyed that I ended the conversation so abruptly. Makayla noticed that her mother seemed upset. "Is everything ok?" she asked. "How is dad?" Lieko responded with "That yellow, pie face mutha fucka hung up on me!" "That's ok, I'm gonna put my foot so far up his ass when I see him, he'll be tasting my toes for breakfast for the rest of his damn life." "Mom, don't say that," Makayla said. "Girl I'm just blowing off steam, ain't nobody gonna do nothing to his stubborn ass." Lieko said as she made herself some coffee and pulled from the long cigarette in the corner of her mouth. Makayla laughed and said "You need to stop smoking or you won't be able to whip anybody ass." "Is Kylin home yet?" She quickly added. "No, not until Friday, miss smart ass," Lieko replied with a motherly, ``don't be cussing in my house," look on her face. Makayla excused herself from the kitchen with a smirk on her face before she pushed her boundaries too far. They both were charismatic, beautiful, smart and funny, but they both also had the fight of a tiger inside of them. You definitely didn't want to push their buttons or challenge their opinion unless you were prepared to go fifteen rounds, blood, sweat and tears. Makayla knew this of herself and her mother so today she decided to give her mother some space.

Makayla went back to her room where her new Korean friend was studying. Mee-Yon was very intelligent but not used to the leisure time that Americans took for granted in college life. Makayla, oftentimes tried to loosen her up to experience more fun but Mee-yon was always reluctant to participate. She wanted to prove to her family that she could live up to their expectations and if it meant not having any free time to do so, she was unhappily willing to do so. Mee-Yon noticed Makayla standing up against a man being rude to students on campus because they did not like his statements made against women having abortions rights. Mee-Yon admired Makayla's courage and introduced herself. They have been cool since that awful day of people protesting on campus.

Makayla laid across her bed and entertained herself on the internet while Mee-yon was assumed by her studies. After a few moments of silence, Makayla cried out with laughter. Again there were a few moments of silence and Makayla's laughter burst out even louder. Mee-Yon looked up at her each time and smiled but she did not ask what was so funny. Loud laughter again from Makayla and this time she said with joy in her voice, "Mee mee, come look at this old lady whip this teenager's ass." "That's what she gets for disrespecting her elders." Makayla called Mee-Yon Mee mee because it just sounded better to her and giving her a nickname meant that Makayla liked her as a close friend.

Mee-Yon was curious and finally was willing to see what was so hilarious. They both laughed while watching it but Mee-Yon quickly gathered herself and returned to her seat. Makayla noticed the sudden change and asked what was wrong. Mee-Yon just shook her head as if to say nothing is wrong or that she didn't want to talk about it. Makayla in her loving persuasive way, persisted. "Come on Mee mee, what's bothering my little Mee mee, " Makayla said, pretending to pout and poking Mee-Yon with her finger on each side of her stomach.

Mee-Yon laughed, stood up and said "Look, don't take this the wrong way but you Americans have access to so much technology and have the freedom to do as you will with it." "You can even start a worldwide conversation with the touch of a button to do something meaningful for humanity, yet you waste it watching and recording foolishness that doesn't do anyone any good." "Violence or someone acting a fool, fighting or smoking a blunt on social media is entertainment for others instead of someone doing something about it. "You guys take the technology you have for granted." Mee-Yon added. Makayla then stood up with no expression on her face and stared at Mee-Yon, for a few seconds.

Mee-Yon, feeling like she may have offended her new friend, took her seat again and uncomfortably opened her book again to read it. Makayla walked closer and said "Mee mee, you're right." "I can respect that," Makayla added. We definitely could spend more time using technology to make a difference." Makayla smiled and said "but Mee mee, you gotta admit, she beat that bitch ass, didn't she?" Mee-Yon laughed and said "On God," using western ghetto slang she had heard Makayla use. They both laughed at her attempt to talk slang. Makayla said "Yeah, we're some dumb lazy ass Americans but step to us wrong and we'll treat that ass!" she said while popping her palms together three times. Lieko yelled from the other room, "Stop cussing in my damn house!" Makayla and Mee-Yon giggled silently with their hands over their mouths.

Makayla hugged her friend and said, "Look, I understand where you're coming from" People are just not present anymore." "We miss out on moments like this, between you and I." "A simple hug or touch can do so much more than a text on the phone." 'The news, social media and this political, racist shit, have us prisoners of our own mind." Makayla stopped hugging Mee-Yon. "I got an idea!" Makayla said, excitedly. "Let's practice using social media, only one hour a week." Mee-Yon looked at her with a smirk on her face and lips twisted to the side. "One hour a week?" "How about one hour a day?" "I think you need to slow your roll a little bit." I'd hate to see you acting like a crack head over that phone." Mee-Yon added as she imitated Pookie, from the movie New Jack City. "It just keeps on calling me," "Mee-Yon said, laughing at Makayla standing there, giving her the eye. Makayla shrugged her shoulders and said, "Look they say social media makes people feel miserable but I have a ball on there." "The shit is hilarious to me." "Maybe they're just miserable themselves, but who am I to judge?" Makayla added as she noticed that Mee-Yon was serious.

Makayla shoved Mee-Yon's shoulder and acknowledged Mee-Yon's suggestion. "Yeah, you're right." "We'll do one hour a day." Mee-Yon was pleased. "It's a good thing Makayla." "I've done the research." "Too much social media can cause anxiety and depression." "Besides, you could use the extra time to help your mother educate these fools around here." Makayla nodded. "Yeah, and we also can use our time on the internet to find your uncle." Mee-Yon smiled and they hugged each other again.

CHAPTER FOUR

WHERE IS THIS PLACE

Before going to D.C. I wanted to hit the gym. That early morning, I went outside to pick up the newspaper. Jermaine, Sasha and Wilbert's oldest son was standing there beside his motorcycle. He didn't smile at all when he saw me and had no expression on his face. He seemed troubled by something. "Wassup Jermaine." I said smiling at him. "Did you get that job working for the state you wanted?" Jermaine was a good kid and had a good chance at getting a great job with benefits. "Nawh, man, that job was on some bullshit." Jermaine said. I could tell he was disappointed. I asked him what he meant by that statement. "Man, I come from the hood, where the chances of getting into trouble is off the chain out here." "I don't do drugs and I haven't gotten into any trouble." "Do you realize how hard that is?" "Yeah, son, I do." "I was raised in the projects too." "Believe me, I understand." I quickly added. "So, what happened?" I asked Jermaine to explain.

'I took the background check and the guy that interviewed me, said that it showed that I had a criminal history." "I knew that couldn't be right, so I asked him what was on it." "It just had to be a mistake." Jermaine explained, further. "He told me that I had a failure to appear on my record." "When he said that, I remembered, a few years back, I got a traffic ticket, and the officer told me that all I had to do was pay the ticket and I didn't have to go to court." I could tell that Jermaine was getting upset as he explained. He was a good kid, trying hard to stay away from trouble in a community, where trouble is lurking in each and every corner. Jermaine continued. "I paid the ticket and a few years later, I was stopped again by the police, asking me about my bike." "I didn't do anything wrong, he said." "But he ran my license." "Then he tells me that I had a failure to appear." "I explained to him that I paid that ticket years ago and told him what the officer, that stopped me, instructed me to do." "He said that it didn't matter and that I had to go to court and explain."

Jermaine continued explaining and became even more irritated by it all. "They didn't give a damn about me in court and said even though I paid the ticket, I still should have been in court, and gave me probation." "I had forgotten about it and had no clue, I was listed as a criminal!" I shook my head in disbelief and thought to myself, in a community, where the opportunities to get in trouble are so enormous, why a boy, who has managed to stay away from it all, should be punished for something as simple as a failure to appear. Especially under the circumstances, he explained. I knew him well and I knew he was telling the truth. If anything, kids who make it through those high risks, situations, should be awarded and given a break, with such minor things in their background. My mind was racing for answers as Jermaine explained. No other culture has those high risks, so they shouldn't be judged so harshly, when they are trying to become a part of mainstream society. I thought to myself. I had no answer for him. All I could do was try to lift him up, although I felt horrible for him and knew how disappointed he was feeling. "It will work itself out, son." I said, knowing his chances were slim to none. "Man, fuck that." Jermaine said, as his mood changed with the more infuriated, scowl on his face.

I asked Jermaine how he was doing and what was wrong. Shaking his head, Jermaine reluctantly delivered a message from people he claimed he worked for. "You and your boy Homie need to be careful who you piss off," Jermaine said. Confused by his demanding comment, I was concerned, especially since Sasha had confided in me about her concerns over Jermaine's strange behavior. I knew him well and noticed a troubling change in his demeanor as well. "What are you talking about son?" Come inside, let's talk for a moment.

"Nawh, bruh, you know I respect you but if you don't take this warning seriously, the consequences that come down on you, is out of my control." "My people ain't the kind of people you want to mess with. "What damn people are you talking about son?" "Do you know that your mom is worried, to death about you?" "What the hell are you doing coming here making threats and demands for some mutha fucka who could care less about what happens to you," I said angrily. "What the hell is going on with you?" "You're a good kid with a good head on your shoulders." "Don't fuck up your life out here trying to be somebody you're not." Completely forgetting about his reason for coming by, my love for him made me ask the hard straight forward questions as if I was his father. "What the fuck do you know about me, huh?" Jermaine said, raising his voice. "I got good grades, hell, I don't do drugs as bad as I need to smoke a blunt dealing with this bullshit out here in these streets, and I didn't!" "Shit, I might as well do what all these other nigga's doing out here in these streets." "If you don't hustle, you don't eat and I'm tired of seeing my momma slave at that damn club." Jermaine had a look on his face of anger and disappointment. He continued to yell, "I got a clean background, good grades, and I don't do drugs despite what my momma thinks and I still can't get a decent paying job!" Feeling his pain, I knew of many college graduates who were not able to find jobs and had the same frustrations about it. I knew I had to choose my words carefully and try to encourage him to be patient although there was a disturbing truth to his frustrations. People of color know this painful truth too well. "Son, take it easy, I understand." "Come inside," I asked. "Fuck that, you and Homie just keep Miss Snow-white out of shit that don't concern her and you won't have to worry about the consequences," Jermaine said, getting on his bike and rushing away. I yelled for Jermaine to come back but he was not trying to hear anything I had to say to him. I took the paper inside and headed towards the gym. I wondered if I should tell Homie about what happened before going to Washington. Instead, I called his mother Sasha.

Sasha was sitting in the living room of their home. Jermaine opened the front door. Immediately, Sasha got in his ass. "Boy, where the fuck you been, and why the hell you over there bothering Greg with that bullshit?" "Ma." He said and before he could say anything else, Sasha continued questioning Jermaine. "I don't know what the hell that white man got you doing, but whatever it is, it can't be good." "You stay the fuck away from him and get your shit together and be a good influence in your brother's life, before I send your ass off to the military!" "I'm not going in nobody's military mom." Jermaine said with conviction. Jermaine was holding on tight to the straps on the book bag he was wearing on his back. "Oh, yes the hell you are." Sasha said. "Who the fuck you think you are telling a grown man who to stay away from?" That man has been good to you." "That white man don't give a damn about you!" "I work my ass off taking care of y'all, so you can stay away from dumb ass shit!" Jermaine interrupted.

"And what the hell did it do for us mom?" The younger brother came out of his room and was confused by the altercation and shocked that his older brother used a curse word and raised his voice at their mother. "You got scammed on this house mom." "The fucking interest rates blew up on you, now we're gonna lose this house!" "At least I'm making money." I'm trying to fucking help!" Sasha looked at him with a stern face. Her voice lowered and said, "You know what, you're right." So what if we lose this house." "There are other houses and next time, I won't be fooled." She continued. "You let me and your dad worry about this house." She concluded. "And the next time you raise your voice at me, I'm gonna snatch your soul out." Sasha said through her teeth and shaking her head. "Take that book bag off and get the fuck out of my face."

She watched him take it off as he was walking away. "Wait." Sasha said. "What's in that bag anyway? "You ain't been to school, and even when you were, I hardly ever saw you with a book." Jermaine knew he had pushed his boundaries to the limit and hesitated giving Sasha the book bag. "Ma." He said,"Don't ma, me." "Give me that damn bag." She said, as she snatched it away from him and started searching the book bag. "Oh, hell nah!" Sasha said, after seeing the contents of the bag. She told her younger son to go to his room. "What the fuck is this!" "I know this isn't ice!" Jermaine said nothing and took a step back. Jermaine was stunned that his mother knew what it was. "I know what the fuck this is Jermaine!." Sasha yelled. "This shit been in your bookbag and it's not melting, so I know what it is." "It's meth and crack mixed together." "So this is what he has you doing?" "Putting this shit in the streets for him?" "Your father is going to be pissed, when he finds out." "What father?" Jermaine said. "He's never here." "Boy, get the fuck out of my face, before I slap your ass, into next week!"

Jermaine went to his room where his younger brother was. His brother looked at him and asked him, "Why are you doing this?" "You don't understand lil brother, we are about to lose this house." "I gotta do what I gotta do." His younger brother tried to convince Jermaine to stop. "You could go to jail for this, it's not worth it." "Mom and dad can handle it." His younger brother pleaded. That seemed to anger Jermaine even more. "Dad!" "Where the fuck is he?" "He is never home and I heard mom arguing with him about not having all of his money for the bills." "I don't know Jermaine." The younger brother pleaded again. "Just stop, please." "I can't make it out here without you man." "If you go to jail, I gotta deal with this shit out here in these streets by myself."

Jermaine paced back and forth for a minute and then said, "Look, I gotta go handle something. "Where are you going?" His younger brother asked. Jermaine didn't answer and silently slipped down the hallway to see where his mother was located. Sasha was on the phone, in the kitchen, trying to reach his father Wilbert. Jermaine saw the book bag on the couch and picked it up carefully, not to make a sound and slipped back to his room. "What are you doing?" "Mom is gonna kick your ass." The little brother asked. "Shut up." Jermaine said as he was climbing out of their bedroom window. "Don't worry, I will be back." His little brother looked worried. Before closing the window, Jermaine asked his younger brother to trust him. Jermaine pounded on his chest twice and reassured his little brother. "I got this." "I'm gonna make things right." Jermaine hopped on his motorcycle and quickly roared away.

Wilbert was not answering Sasha's calls. She heard the roar of Jermaine's motorcycle, speeding away. Sasha ran to the front door and flung the door open. She ran outside and yelled. "Jermaine!" Jermaine did not stop. Sasha went back inside. "That boy is going to be the death of me!" She complained to herself. She then noticed that the book bag full of drugs was now gone. "Lord, Jesus, help me please!" Sasha yelled. She tried desperately to reach Wilbert. She called her youngest son out of his room. "Come on," she said. "Get in the car. Sasha knew Wilbert volunteered at the office downtown, helping people get registered to vote for Mr. Hope. It was getting late and she figured he'd be leaving soon.

Sasha drove past the office and saw Wilbert through the window holding papers in his hand. She dialed his number again. Wilbert did not answer. She didn't want to go inside, but because he wasn't answering and it looked as though everyone else had already gone home, she parked the car and walked towards the building. To her disappointment, she now could see that her husband Wilbert, was embracing and cuffing the ass of a woman she recognized. She burst through the door. "What the fuck is this!" The woman stepped back from Wilbert. Sasha rushed Wilbert, hitting him several times. Wilbert tried to contain her.

"Baby, it's not what you think!" "Calm down," he pleaded. "Calm the fuck down?" Sasha said. "This is the insta-gram bitch, you spending our money on?" "Wait, hold up, I ain't no bitch." The woman said. "Stay the hell out of this before I snatch them fake ass, eye lashes off your face, bitch!" Wilbert stood between the both of them. "Baby calm down please!" The woman left in a hurry. "This is what you've been doing?" Sasha asked. "You claim that you're so damn tired from cooking at the club all night and not sleeping with me." "But you can get your ass up, every day and volunteer to come down here?" "Now I see what it is, you lying mutha fucka!" "It's not like that." Wilbert tried to explain. "Nigga, you think I don't know." "Don't try to play me." "I saw the bank statements." Sasha continued. "I saw where the money was going and I looked the bitch up." "Lacey Love, Lacey Love!" A whole page full of withdrawals going to Lacey Love!" Baby." Wilbert interrupted. Sasha, cut him off immediately. "Don't baby me!" Sasha said. "We're about to lose our home and you spending money on your insta-whore?"

"Do you know where your son is?" Sasha said, hitting Wilbert in the chest again. "Who?" Wilbert asked, confused by the transitioning. "Your son, Jermaine!" "You remember him, don't you? Sasha said sarcastically. "He is out there selling drugs because your sorry ass can't be a man and handle your damn business at home!" Sasha tried to walk away. Wilbert reached out to her. "Don't touch me!" Sasha said, crying and walking to the car. "Where is he?" Wilbert asked. "I don't fucking know!" "I've been trying to call you." "I can't find him." Sasha continued to her car. Wilbert took a few more steps after her, but then saw his youngest son looking at him in disappointment. He stood there, embarrassed and worried about Jermaine. "I'll find Jermaine." Wilbert assured Sasha, as she was starting up the car. "Fuck you!" Sasha said. "Go find your insta-bitch. Sasha drove away.

Janet was infuriated with Mr. Anderson, the leader of the protest against the special needs people living in his community. She had no tolerance for mistreatment of the mentally disabled and couldn't understand why anyone would feel so superior of themselves to judge them simply because they were different or in their words, retarded and a threat to others. Just as I couldn't understand why the division of the races was once again, raising its head, during 2016's Presidential campaign. The both of us were a little annoyed by the debates at the club and I think we both wanted desperately to make a difference.

It was a quiet ride home from the club as Homie, myself and Janet gathered our thoughts. I myself felt that the common people of all ethnicities were feeling that their voices were not being heard more than ever before, when it came to their wishes for justice and a peaceful nation. Once again, a civil war seemed to be inevitable, and they were not happy about it. The days where police brutality were the norm seemed to be dangerously reincarnating itself in 2016. Like the over looming cloth of death and despair over the hood, the common people all over America were beginning to feel the ghostly pressures of barely staying above water. They felt like they were nothing more than consumers working hard to pay taxes only to fulfill the needs of the wealthy and the elite.

Janet and I invested our lives in order to protect and serve the mentally disabled, but there were still those who treated them indifferently, even though our company and others like it, put programs together in order to prevent the mentally disabled from hurting themselves or others. One thing for sure though was if caught or suspected of denying them a life of social justice and well-being would come with dire consequences.

We utilized corporations and professional programs to create equal employment opportunities and provide opportunities for them to live a more independent, healthy and meaningful life. They were victims of ignorance and cruelty much like people of color, same sex couples, women, and the poor. Crimes committed against them existed when Trump and his followers claimed America to be so great. Companies like the one I work for strived to make sure that the mentally disabled are treated with dignity and respect. It haunted my spirit that somehow society was so focused on powerful men in the news fighting over more power, all the while the common needs of decent humanity went astray and minorities were still struggling with inequality and injustice.

"Where were minorities established companies and programs designed to protect them?" I thought to myself as a slight bump in the road caused us all to bounce around simultaneously in the car. I knew that watching the news had taken its toll on me and I couldn't stand to see young men of color during the crime scene on the news. I had even stopped watching all black movies for fear of the same portrayal of us. It then occurred to me that if I was able to stop watching what was happening to people of color on the news in an attempt to ease my pain, how easy it must have been for white America to ignore or deny that racism and injustice to minorities actually existed. No one cared enough to stand for justice on our behalf because it wasn't real to them. To them our protest was all like a television show that could be turned off with the push of a button. In my realization of discovering that although trying to escape my pain, by clicking the off button on the remote, I somehow contributed to the denial of its existence.

Ironically, it was why Leiko felt that I had become too comfortable in believing that justice would prevail for black people who were careful of their behavior and choices, versus what some would call criminals, those that were irrational in their thinking and actions. On the way home from the bar I thought about heated discussions and came to the realization that decent black folks and criminals were all viewed as not worthy of justice and equality. My careful choices may have got me somewhat ahead of the game but my choices made me no different in how I'd be treated in the courtroom or by a racist police officer. I was horrified and knew if we ever had a chance to make a difference, we all had to make that change standing together as one, despite our similarities or differences.

I wondered if the mentality of labeling others had crippled the thinking of all human beings of any race. Differences in skin color, social or economic status, had been America's way of separating the privileged from those whom they felt were not worthy simply by the color of skin for centuries. The fallout of it was still effectively justifying injustice and providing white Americans with a silver spoon. Although most Americans were not racist, the psychological effect of categorizing people by the difference in skin color, culture or religion was still causing crimes against humanity. I had unconsciously did the same thing and divided people of color by their choices or behavior. My thinking was that I loved god, but some of his children got on my last fucking nerves killing and committing crimes against each other as if we didn't have enough crimes against humanity being committed against us. Some people described it as the difference between decent hard working black people and niggas. I realized, that anyone ignoring the real issues that created those so called, crime committing niggas, was just as damaging to minorities as committing the crimes themselves.

    The conversations at the club and black man on the news getting killed while fully cooperating with the police,brought me to the real truth of it all, as I rode in the back seat quietly thinking to myself.. Being black in America came with a heavy price over your head, period. It didn't matter your social, political or economic status. There were no nigga's. We all had the same price to pay and that's why Lieko was so afraid for Kylin.The common ordinary day to day people themselves pay a heavy price in America, not as traumatizing as minorities, but a heavy burden the same. Most of us live paycheck to paycheck, underpaid while the cost of living rapidly increases higher and higher.

    For us it was a money thing, not a black and white thing although the media portrayed it to be about race. It was just us in danger of the decisions made by those who lacked empathy and understanding of what it is to live struggling to keep your head above flooding waters. I realized that all god's children, black, white, red or brown, had different circumstances that caused particular thinking and behavior. Most of them, caused by the American culture, not addressing issues of poverty, inequality and injustice realistically. I had inadvertently adapted the biased thinking of American culture. In 2016, political candidates and the media highlighted racism as a fear tactic in obtaining votes. It was us against them according to what was shown on the news. In some states that political game was just waiting to blow up. Racial tension was boiling over, although the truth was that most people didn't care about racism at all anymore. The damage that all of us were doing to ourselves and each other was just as awful as allowing ourselves to be so easily manipulated. We were being micro-targeted and our personal information was being used against us. It was political manipulation at its best in destroying a nation for political and economic gain.

Many of us had lost our way and I was beginning to understand why I couldn't see eye to eye with my wife. It was like the guy said at the bar, I had lost my hood card. I had forgotten what all good in the hood meant. It meant despite our hardships and differences, we shared a common bond and made the best of what we had or didn't have. Somehow, we were still able to still smile and love each other. My mother, and millions of people like her were good, decent and honest working human beings, despite living in low-income areas. Most of us were just hanging out and passing the time away, the best way we knew how. No real crimes were being committed, except by a few. We were, Just having fun, despite our circumstances. The police helicopters and political leaders, made our community a war zone. The crimes and massive arrests of minorities, in the news, portrayed us all as criminals. "Are you ok?" Homie asked while driving Janet and I home. I hesitated before answering, noticing a billboard advertising Micheal Jordan sneakers. Homie asked again. "My man!" He chuckled. "Are you cool bruh?" "You're a little quiet over there."

I was deep into my thoughts but I let him know I was cool. "Yeah man, I'm good." I noticed that Janet had dozed off to sleep."Do you realize how many billions and trillions of dollars black people spend on products not owned by us? Homie chuckled again, "Nigga, what do you know about billions and trillions of dollars with your tight ass?" I laughed and replied. "Yeah, but I aint broke, ya feel me." "Shit the only way to keep money is not spend it on shit you don't really need." "Yeah, you're right," Homie said, turning the corner near our old neighborhood. "Man, if I wanted only to spend my money with black businesses around here, I wouldn't have many choices." I was thinking to myself but inadvertently said out loud. "We gotta do something about this shit bruh." Homie said as we both looked around at how much the hood had become more worn out and run down than before when we grew up there. I sank more into my thoughts again.

Celebrities and minority leaders didn't live in the hood and success, to the common kids, of common people, looked as if it was so far away. Little did they know, success was right there in front of them. Celebrities and the wealthy, did not live in the hood, because they were afraid, and it was possibly warranted. Especially if their only connection to the common people was through the media. I couldn't blame them because I myself was haunted by the pain of what could one man do and how?. I wanted so badly to change the circumstances for the poor and yet at the same time, deal with the heartache of not knowing how or having enough power to do so. As a black man with a promising career, I was being judged because I was a step or two ahead of the game. I was being accused of somehow turning my back on who I once were. Little did they know how isolated and alone I felt and the hardening of the heart it took to remain focused for the sake of my family.

They didn't realize that I carried the heavy burden of how the fuck could I change this world for the sake of all of us? For the most part I was still the same person and wanted so badly just to be myself again and feel free of the responsibility. But for us all, there was more stress and pain than joy. Feeling free was a luxury we could not truthfully be without unity or at least our own political party. I was once again saddened to feel that maybe it was just me to think it was a possibility. We were all shackled to the restrictions of giving a piece of paper validity that allowed crimes against humanity. Social constructions were enabling society's ability to agree. Or at least agree to disagree in peace. I would pray daily for the courage to stand alone, knowing my political convictions would cause ignorance to criminalize me.

I reminded myself. that it was up to us common, everyday people, to take back the position of role model, instead of allowing T.V., celebrities, athletes and social media to tell us what success should look like. The zombie effect of advanced technology and misinformation were toxic to human relationships. The negative energy poisoned the brain. Of course, I felt that anyone should outgrow their surroundings, physically and mentally. Moving away from the hood, in my opinion, should be a moral developing process, in order to expand the mind, body and soul, into a much bigger and healthier environment, connected to a non biased society. Looking around at the old broken down buildings that once used to be homes for struggling minority families, I felt joy and pain remembering those days as a kid. I rolled down the window to smell the air of long ago and was elated to discover that holding on to my connection with the hood was not one meaning that I should stay down, but one of being proud of the lessons learned in the hood that allowed me to grow.

Almost approaching my home I now strongly felt that people of color had to start buying, owning and building the hood up. That way, our children and their children would see that success was right there in front of them. It is not impossible. Someone once said to me that excellence was as difficult as it is rare. Basically, if we put in the work, the impossible is doable and the rewards of the sacrifice and efforts are great. It is not far away. If we show them that they can own that home in the hood and rent it out. Leaving the hood for a bigger better home is a good thing, yet they would've left their mark in the hood by beautifying it and making it possible for the younger generation to buy, own, rent and raise the property value. If we had no corporations or policies that truly protected the well-being of our society then it would definitely be up to us to teach our kids that Good credit, good work ethic, good character and money management are just as powerful or possibly more powerful than good grades to those in the hood who were not being properly educated and misunderstood in school. Controlling and managing our spending power wisely in America along with advocating for our own political party and abolishing the electoral college voting system were discussions Lieko and I debated over. I was now more clear on her stance as well as enlightened by my newly found motivation as to how I could make a difference for the younger generation in my community.

Protesting and asking those that deny the devastation of a people to stand for us all, looked as though it would never happen. I remembered when I was a teenager, wanting to open a community center in order to provide a safe environment to entertain the kids in the hood and provide them with fun activities during summer breaks. It sparked an idea that now I could take that idea and expand it further to educate and provide support programs as well. Janet and I shared the same ideas about equal justice and opportunities for all, no matter what race, sex or misfortune. If only Lieko would get to know Janet, she'd respect her and we could get past her accusations. They would make a great team just as Janet and I had become. "I'll see ya later bruh." "Thanks for the ride my guy." I said, helping Janet out of Homie's car.

Before Janet and I would be leaving for D.C. she stopped by the hotel Sunday morning to see her clients before attending church with her family. Her father planned a dinner at his home after church that included staff members and sponsors for his re-election campaign for Mayor. Janet had confided in me that she really didn't want to attend the dinner because she didn't agree with her father's views in this re-election. I knew about his re-election announcement next week and wondered how she felt about it, but I didn't ask. She expressed her disapproval voluntarily and stated that she and her mother both were not pleased. "Why?" I asked. "This time, it just feels all wrong, there's something different about him and the entire election." Janet added, "I don't know, but I fear that there is nothing we can do to change his mind." Janet was always willing to stand for others and what she believed in even if it made people she loved uncomfortable.

Mayor Hope was planning a huge campaign event where he would pitch his views and intentions for the next four years. One of those topics was getting some gay rights rulings overturned. Janet was extremely disappointed in his decision and publicly expressed her views when asked by reporters. A Gay activist caught wind of her statements and asked her to speak against those views directly across the street from her father's campaign event. Janet, in her heroic, feisty and spirited manner, agreed immediately without giving it a second thought. I was with her that day and was asked my opinion as well. My statement was short and sweet, "To be human is to have equal rights, no matter your preferences," I said as I assisted Janet into the car and we drove away. Of course, her father was furious when he heard about her comments on the news.

Janet spent as much time as she could at the hotel before leaving for church because she knew she wouldn't see her client's again until Friday and she was worried about them. The protest had caused some setbacks in their behavior and her concern was certainly warranted. Staff had worked well with them and the programs put in place to encourage a positive and healthy lifestyle were working perfectly until the ugly actions of the protestors.

Janet walked up the hallway of the Hilton hotel. She was smiling as she could hear Kelvin listening to and singing one of his favorite country music songs as she approached room 132. She paused for a minute at the door to hear Kelvin sing. "It can buy me a boat"…."It can buy me a truck to pull it"…."It can buy me a Yeti 110, iced down with some silver bullets." "Yeah I know what they say, money can't buy everything." "Well maybe so, but it can buy me a boat." Kelvin was singing his heart out and it always amused Janet to hear and see these large black gentlemen singing country music with such passion. Janet giggled softly and put her hand over her mouth so they wouldn't hear her outside the door. She took a sip of her freshly made smoothie and privately entertained herself. As much as Janet was enjoying her little moment she gathered herself and knocked at the door.

The week-end day staff opened the door. Janet walked in excitedly and said "Hello, everyone." Kelvin stopped singing and Kelvin and the other two clients were happy to see and greet her. Jasper, surprisingly, was the first one to reach her. Normally, he moved slowly, but today he was at top speed. He walked swiftly towards Janet with his arms spread wide in anticipation for a hug and said "Hey, sugar shorts." Jasper called Janet that when he was really happy. Janet said "I just love your hugs Jasper." "Did you bring your DVD player?" "Yes," he said softly and asked Janet to watch his favorite episode of the Twilight Zone with him. She hugged him tightly. "Maybe next time, ok?" Jasper looked disappointed. "Ok, just for a little while." "Put it in." Janet said. Jasper did so happily. Japer hadn't watched the episode all the way through and Janet saw that it was a Twilight Zone episode she remembered.

"Oh, yes, I remember this." "It's a good one." Jasper smiled. This is the one where a lady hates her face and wants to look like everyone else and at the end, everyone else, including the doctors look like pigs!" Janet was excited and started quoting the narrator's part at the end. "Where is this place, and when is it?" Jasper joined in with Janet and they both quoted more. "What kind of world where ugliness is the norm and beauty the deviation from that norm?" They both continued quoting. "You want an answer?" "The answer is, it doesn't make any difference." "Because the old saying happens to be true." "Beauty is in the eye of the beholder, in this year or a hundred years hence." "On this planet or wherever there is human life, perhaps out amongst the stars." Janet teared up, and hugged Jasper as they quoted the last lines together. "Beauty is in the eye of the beholder." "Lesson to be learned, in the Twilight Zone." She looked up for the other two. Both Kelvin and Mike, joined in on the group hug. It was out of character for Mike, who was autistic to hug for a long period of time because he rarely liked to be touched. Today was a unique day. Mike smiled and gave a few more seconds of affection.

"How are you Kelvin?" Janet asked and Kelvin responded "I'm good Miss Hope." "Heyyyy Mike," Janet said, still smiling and amused by the few couple of seconds she received from him. 'How are you guys holding up?" Janet asked. "I brought you guys some home- made cookies." Janet smiled and handed the cookies to the day shift staff. "Please don't give them too much at a time." Janet, instructed staff. Staff replied "Ok, they are holding up well, they're just wondering when they will be able to return home." Janet told the staff that she could tell that they were home sick. "Don't worry." Janet explained. "We are leaving tomorrow morning to get this all straightened out." "When will you be back Miss Janet?" Staff asked. "Hopefully by the end of the week." "You guys call me if there are any problems ok?" Janet explained that she has left her personal number in the documentation book for staff to reach her.

"We want all of you to be as comfortable as possible during your stay here." Janet explained to the staff that breakfast, lunch and dinner will be served downstairs each day for clients and staff. "Please make sure to continue their scheduled outings each day until we can get you guys back home ok?" Staff replied "Yes, ma'am Miss Janet." "We love you, be careful and have a safe trip." Janet smiled and said "Thanks, we will."

Janet hugged all the clients and said good-bye to the staff on duty. Janet reluctantly left and sighed because she did not want to attend her father's and definitely did not want to have anything to do with his meeting afterwards at his home. Janet enjoyed her time with clients most of all and didn't want to be mentally drained listening to her father's campaign sponsors with their biased, cognitive distant views and opinions on how to influence voters that they care about the community. Because Janet has such a caring soul, she decided to visit the Anderson's and give them a chance to reconcile the situation before going to her father's church.

Meanwhile at Anderson's home, Mr. Anderson was standing in the mirror adjusting his tie. He heard his wife talking in her sleep. She mumbled words together that didn't make any sense. Mr. Anderson walked toward her bedroom across the hall from his master bedroom. He was startled as he approached her because she woke up screaming again, like she had done, several times before. She was drenched in sweat and her hair was sticking to her face and neck.

"Calm down, it's just a dream" he said. She looked at him with fear in her eyes. She yelled, "Why are you trying to kill me Bobby?" "Get away from me!" She frantically pulled away from him and jumped out of her bed on the other side of the bed so he couldn't touch her. Mr. Anderson attempted to slowly walk to the other side to comfort her because she could be incredibly strong when she wasn't on her medication. She screamed "No, get away from me!' Mr. Anderson pleaded with his wife to calm down. "You just need your medicine dear, please just settle down and wait right here while I get them" Mrs. Anderson started pulling and scratching at her arms trying to control herself.

Mr. Anderson gathered her meds from his locked drawer in his bedroom and hurried back across the hall. Before he could reach her room, Mrs. Anderson darted away from him screaming. "Stop fucking with my head!" Mr. Anderson reached out quickly to grab her arm as she was fleeing by. They both fell to the floor. Mrs. Anderson, barefooted and in her nightgown, swiftly got to her feet and ran. Mr. Anderson tried to catch her, but his church shoes prevented him from having good balance as he slipped down again. Mrs. Anderson reached the stairs. She grabbed the wood rails and rushed down the stairs as quickly as she could. She was fast and strong. She was younger and still in great shape. She was hard to say the least.

By then Mr. Anderson had gathered himself and was catching up to her fast. As Mrs. Anderson reached the bottom of the stairs, she crashed into a table by the window. Mr. Anderson caught her by her arm once again. "No, no, no!" she cried, "I don't want them!" Mr. Anderson held her from behind and pleaded with his wife to just take her pills while holding the tablets in his hand in front of her mouth with his free hand as he held her tightly against his chest. She sobbed on his shoulders. When she opened her eyes standing behind Mr. Anderson was a ghostly figure of herself with kninky hair and eyes burning in flames. Dora screamed again and tried frantically to get away. As suddenly as the woman with burning eyes appeared, she was gone as Dora feared for her sanity.

"Take them!" he yelled. "Please just calm down and everything will be alright!" Breathing heavily, Mrs. Anderson started pulling at the skin of her arms again. She reluctantly swallowed the pills. "That's it, just breathe." Mr. Anderson said as he released her. He walked to the recliner nearby and took a seat to catch his breath. Mrs. Anderson calmed herself as the medicine took effect. Tears rolling down her face, she turned her back to her husband towards the window and said softly to him, "You don't love me." "Of course I do dear, I'm trying my best to help you."

Mrs. Anderson noticed Janet coming towards the steps in front of the house to knock on the front door. She didn't say anything to her husband and opened the door. "May I help you," Mrs. Anderson said rudely to Janet. Janet was taken a bit back by the appearance of Mrs. Anderson. Janet noticed that she had been in some kind of struggle and immediately became concerned. Before Janet could speak, Mr. Anderson placed himself in front of his wife and asked Janet ``What is your business here?"

Janet, still puzzled by what she saw, asked what was going on and asked if Mrs. Anderson was ok. "That's none of your concern Miss Lady, but yes, Dora is just under the weather this morning." Janet, still looking confused, said "well, I was just wanting to ask you to stop your protest before I seek legal action." Mr. Anderson replied, "Legal action? "Why, there is nothing illegal about a peaceful protest." "Is that what you call a peaceful protest, by scaring and intimidating people who are incapable of defending themselves?" Mr. Anderson said calmly, "Look I'm aware that things got a little out of control but I assure you that it won't happen again." "How about you assure me that you'll stop completely and we won't have any issues with each other?"

Mr. Anderson looked back at his wife and turned back toward Janet and said, trust me, I can't do that." Janet gave him a look of disgust and asked, "What do you have against them?" Before he could answer she said "How do you think my father will react when I tell him that one of his campaigners is a racist bastard!" Mr. Anderson replied, "Dear, I assure you, I've already spoken with your father about this matter and gave him my sincerest apology, especially since the protest offended his lovely daughter". "Well, we'll see about that," Janet said as she noticed Mrs. Anderson mumbling to herself behind Mr. Anderson. Mr. Anderson told Janet that her father was a dear friend and asked if they could be friends as well. Janet leaned her head to the right of him to check on Mrs. Anderson. Mr. Anderson put his hand forward for a hand shake. Janet looked at his hand and looked him in the eye without shaking his hand and replied "No, we can't." and walked away. Mr. Anderson closed the door and turned toward his wife who was now calm and said "Look what you did!" and slapped her to the floor.

Janet called Homie and explained to him what she had witnessed at Anderson's home. Homie told Janet that he couldn't just accuse Mr. Anderson of beating his wife but he would definitely look into it and keep an eye on the situation. Janet got off the phone and attended church, but seated herself towards the back away from her father. She listened to the sermon and cited a silent prayer for her clients and a safe trip. Once service was over, she noticed her father arrogantly communicating with members of the church. In his million dollar suit and cufflinks, he spoke without really listening and rarely gave eye contact long enough to establish that he wanted to be in the presence of any one particular person at a time. Janet noticed that he was turning to look in her direction. Before he could motion for her to come near his side, she gave a half smile, waved and turned to exit the church doors. She was near the back and her escape plan worked well.

Janet arrived at her father's home shortly after leaving church. She drove up the long driveway that was beautifully aligned with purple crape myrtles. Janet loved the color purple and she always admired how beautiful they looked dancing in front of a blue sky. She drove up to the front entrance of the house and enjoyed the different colors of flowers that were perfectly placed and greeted anyone entering the huge mansion with warmth and kindness. Just as Janet was reaching the steps, her mother opened the door excitedly and said "I'm so glad to see you honey bun!" "I was hoping you would come, you know your father really needs you to be here." Janet smiled and hugged her mother.

"Your hair is nice." "I like that short hair style on you, mom." Janet said while gently playing with her mother's hair. Janet's mother was just as kind as her daughter and they both had energetic, free spirited souls. Mrs. Hope rubbed Janet's back and guided her inside the house. "Get your tiny butt in here so I can feed you girl!" "Doesn't look like you're eating enough" Mrs. Hope said smiling and eager to spend time with Janet before the guests arrived. "I'm eating just fine mom, I'm just trying to stay fit so I can be as gorgeous as you when I get older."

Mrs. Hope posed and put her hands on her hips, and said, "Well, I do look fabulous for my age baby girl." She said jokingly as she hugged Janet again and kissed her on the forehead. "I'm just kidding honey bun, you look amazing." Mrs. Hope smiled and gave Janet a slap on the butt. "Look at you all perky and firm" I wish gravity would give me a little break, how I miss going without a bra and letting these bad girls breathe." They both laughed as Mrs. Hope used her hands to make her breasts bounce. "Really mom?" "How much money have you made dad spend to keep them looking like that?" Janet said jokingly, knowing her mother flaunted her new boobs, every chance she had.

"Mom, I can't stay long," Janet said to her mother. "I just wanted to stop by before my father and his guest arrived from church." "Awwwh, honey bun, your father will be disappointed, besides I'd like to have more time together with you and catch up on that handsome devil of a man you're going to D.C with." "Janet laughed, "It's just a business trip mom and I just don't want to hear about his plans to support laws to overturn the Supreme Court decision in making gay marriages legal."

Janet's smile disappeared as she was speaking of her father. "I wouldn't worry about that Janet," there is probably nothing he can do about it anyway." Janet replied, "Yes, I'm hoping so, but his methods of getting votes by kissing up to people who have no right judging others are just shameful mom." "They're all hypocrites." Always the caregiver and fighter", Mrs. Hope said to Janet while holding her hand. "I love you honey bun." "It's ok, I'll cover for you." Besides, if he wants some of my goodies tonight, he won't put up much of a fuss," Mrs. Hope said smiling and posing again. Janet pretended to throw up and frowned. "Too much information mom!" Janet smiled again and reached out to hug her mother again. "Look, we are leaving in the morning, I'll call you as soon as we reach D.C." "There's that pretty smile I love," Mrs. Hope said, "you go ahead and enjoy yourself and call me soon as you can." She assisted Janet to the door and before she closed the door she placed her hand on Janet's shoulder.

As Janet turned to face her, Mrs. Hope smiled and winked her eye. "Tell Greg I said hi," Mrs. Hope puckered her lips and made kisses, kiss sounds and closed the door. Janet shook her head in surprise of her mother's curiosity and assumptions Janet hurried to her Range Rover and drove away. It was a Beautiful, sunny day and Janet wanted to stay, have dinner and enjoy her mother's silly stories about her rich friends and secrets they shared about their husbands, but she did not want her father to arrive and see her pulling away. Just as she reached the end of the driveway, she could see her father's limo pulling around the corner.

Mayor Nicolas Hope recognized his daughter's vehicle as she passed by him. He leaned toward the window in anticipation of speaking to her, but Janet didn't acknowledge she saw him and looked straight ahead as she moved forward past the barricade of black limos that carried her father and his sponsors. Janet looked in her rear view mirror and felt bad about not speaking because she loved her father but she did not care for his tactics in his re-election campaign.

Her father used the anger of people who were upset about President Obama's term in office to gain supporters. They viewed same sex marriages as abomination and denied that injustice to people of color existed. In their opinion, Affordable Health Care, and employment opportunities were failed attempts by the President. Angry republicans were targeted, supporters sought out by her father. He had used the same method as Mr. Donald Trump's presidential campaign. Janet continued her drive home to finish packing so that she could be rested for the drive to the airport the next day.

The flight to D.C. would be leaving early the following Monday afternoon and Janet always enjoyed arriving anywhere a little early in order to enjoy conversation and prepare her mind for old and new adventures. Fortunately, Janet did not stay at her father's home long enough to see that Mr. Anderson, the retired physician and the leader of the protest against Janet's clients living in their community, was in the limo with her father. Homie was in the area and saw that Mr. Anderson was away from home so he took the opportunity to visit Mrs. Anderson and investigate.

Janet would have been furious and even more disappointed in her father for his inability to decipher between blood money that would keep her father in the grips of evil intentions and supporters that would actually stand together with him and the great values he once stood for. Janet wanted her father to have supporters who wanted a community with realistic solutions for violence, crime, poverty, health care, education and funding for programs that served the needs and advancements of all races, no matter their economic status. One of the most common complaints from inner city teens, was that they did not feel a part of the community, because other than small adjustments at school or work, the community events did not cater to the diversity of its citizens. Freedom to participate in community events without being watched or judged are a privilege not enjoyed by minorities.

Inside the Limo, Mr. Anderson explained to the Mayor that he had a visit from his daughter and that she was not happy with the protest. "Don't worry about it, your protest won't last long and you just make sure it is a peaceful one and end it, before the police get involved again," the Mayor said. "I want her to like me," Mr. Anderson said, "She doesn't understand why I'm doing it nor is it helping our situation." "Our situation?" the Mayor re-directed, avoiding the conversation. "It's your situation, and whether or not my daughter likes you is her choice not yours so you just handle the protests and let me handle my daughter." You understand?" the Mayor said with a stern face.

Mr. Anderson leaned toward him and replied, "Do you understand what would happen if she knew?" They both grind their teeth together and stare at each other as if to be challenging each other to an old fashion shoot out in the middle of an old dirt road. "Look, my daughter is not your concern, you just make sure you handle that thug coworker of hers." "Make sure he understands that the information I have will do to his career." "Mr. Anderson leaned back again and relaxed. "No problem, Mr. Mayor" Bob said with a sarcastic, evil smirk on his face. "Well since we have an understanding Bob," The Mayor said, putting an extra loud emphasis on the name Bob. "Maybe you shouldn't attend this dinner and take care of business." The mayor got out of the limo and proceeded up the stairs into his home.

Meanwhile, back at Anderson's home, Homie knocked at the door until Mrs. Anderson answered. Dora would not completely open the door but Homie could see that she was in distress. "Ma'am, it's been brought to my attention that your safety may be in need of some protection," he explained. Mrs. Anderson rudely replied. "Look, you tell that nosey meddling, girl, to stay out of my business." 'There is no need for concern here." "I understand ma'am, I just want to make sure that everything is ok." Homie explained. "Just say the word and I'll have anyone who harms you picked up."

"You will do no such thing, and if you are implying that my husband has hurt me, then don't you go near him or I will see your ass in court and your little loud mouth friend too." "There is no need for that ma'am, I'm leaving but you call if you need to talk, ok ma'am?" Homie excused himself and got back into his vehicle. He knew something wasn't right so he decided to look further into the situation first thing Monday morning.

Dora called her mother who was a white woman barely holding on to her sanity as well. There was no answer. Alone in the big house near the old covered up water well, Dora's mother stood in the window upstairs, staring over the water well into the field where beautiful wild flowers used to grow. She thought about Dora as a little girl running and playing in the wild flower field. No flowers grew there anymore and the field looked like a deadly reminder of what happened long ago. Dora called again. Her mother heard the phone ringing but again, she did not answer. She didn't even move and she was trembling with fear. Tears ran down her pale cheeks as she could see a blood trail coming from the field towards the water well. She closed her eyes tightly to get rid of the horrifying vision. She opened her eyes and to her disappointment the blood trail was gone but kneeling there by the well stood a naked figure of a black woman crying. The crying turned into a snarling wind of dust that prompted Dora's mother to move away from the window but her body would not listen to her mind. She was frozen in time as tears of guilt streamed red unto the floor.

She wiped her eyes and noticed the blood on her hands and the puddle of blood beneath her bare feet. She struggled for air as she gasped in horror. As soon as she broke free of the snarling grasp of the naked woman's cries she was able to take a step back away from the blood on the floor. She turned to get away from what just couldn't be real, and ran into the naked woman, suddenly in front of her. The woman had fire holes all over her body and small flames flickered out of them like burning wood. "No, no, no!" Dora's mother pleaded as the burning lady with kinky hair released a loud terrifying scream. The force of it threw Dora's mother across the bedroom and she landed at the base of the window. She struggled to breathe as she landed with the sounds of the snarling winds. And then there was a deadly silence and the burning lady with fire in her eyes was gone.

Dora's mother heard the phone ring again as she laid there unable to answer. Dora sighed and gave up trying to reach her mother. Dora then tried to call her husband who was too busy with his dealings with the mayor or didn't care at all about answering her call. Mr. Anderson grunted after noticing her call. He rejected it and continued speaking with the mayor and his wife. After a few hours of dinner and campaign strategies, the Mayor and his wife adjourned the meeting and welcomed some time alone. Mr. Anderson and others got into their limos and drove away. The mayor smiled at them as they departed. He sighed as his facial expression turned into one of dismay. Mrs. Hope asked the Mayor what was wrong. "What's troubling you," she asked. "Why is the baby girl avoiding me?" "I guess she's too busy to support her father these days and spending all of her time hanging around those people." "Those people?" "Who are you referring to when you say "those people Nickolas? Mrs. Hope asked. "She loves her work and "those people" deserve respect like anyone else." "Janet is a fighter just like you used to be and she fights to protect the rights of the mentally disabled so they don't have to put up with being called "those people." "I'm surprised to hear you say that, don't take your campaign frustrations out on them or us," she pleaded.

The Mayor responded, "It seems to me that her only stand lately is against her own father". "Do you know how awful that looks to my supporters?" "Can you imagine how that must feel to me?" He took another shot. With each drink, his voice became louder than before. "Besides," the Mayor added, "I meant her Afro-American friend and that club she hangs out at every weekend." "Why doesn't she settle down and spend some time with her parents or take the time with that kid, Brandon, instead of that fucking thug ass criminal?" "Carol looked confused and chose her battle, carefully.

"Look, Brandon is a nice boy, but Janet makes her own decisions and dating may not be on her mind right now." "And his name is Greg by the way," she explained. "Who?" The Mayor asked. "The Black American you described as Afro-American." "He doesn't have an afro," Mrs. Hope said sarcastically. The Mayor turned away from his wife and poured himself a shot of bourbon. "I have no idea what to call them, if you try to be politically correct, it's Afro-American, since they weren't satisfied with being colored." The Mayor took a huge shot of his bourbon and asked his wife to cut him some slack. "Why don't you just support me and give me a little peace of mind, I'm already dealing with enough pressure from the community," he said with a frustrated tone. Mrs. Hope shook her head and said "Look honey, I'm just saying that if you're going to speak about someone, why not use their name." "Well, how would you describe him?" he asked, since Afro-American is not the correct way?"

Mrs. Hope immediately responded, "If you asked me, I would describe him as a gorgeous black man." "He is so kind to our daughter and if I'm speaking to him or about him, I call him by his name." "Not all black people have afros and no one ever colored them." "If you listen to Janet the way he does you'd understand her." Mr. Hope put his empty glass down on the counter, put his hands up and said, "Look Carol, I'm tired, and I don't have the energy or the time for this conversation." Mrs. Hope said that's fine love, but we really need to talk."

"About what?" He asked. "I love you and so does Janet, but you've lost touch with us and the community." He looked at her with confusion. Carol continued, "Nickolas, You listen to everyone around you who has no other interest in you other than what they have to gain by your re-election." "We don't need this honey." "You don't need this, not this way." She begged. Mr. Anderson sighed, and his shoulders seemed to drop in a brief moment of acceptance. "What do you mean, not this way?" "Baby it's already too much tension in the world with this Presidential campaign and people are afraid of some kind of race war." "I'm tired of the racist's nature of this election and I don't want to be caught up in the middle of some war between men with power, fighting over more power, while the racism rages out of control." "The community loved who you were, not who you're becoming," she added. "Let the United States get past its own differences before you even think about another run for the Mayor's office, "she begged.

"I voted for President Obama because of what he stood for and I'm definitely not voting for Donald Trump for what is portrayed in the news that he stands against."

"You're caught up in this us against them foolishness, trying to straddle both sides of the fence and it's going to destroy you." "It will destroy us baby." She sighed. "Give it up," she pleaded with him. This re-election is not good for our family." "It's not good for anyone, if you continue using Trump's politics." "Let's just focus on our family and sit this one out?" Mrs. Hope placed her hand on his face and waited for his response. "I can't, I've invested too much," he said and walked away with a concerned look on his face. She watched him walk up the stairs and poured a shot of bourbon herself and wondered why she couldn't get through to him. Carol sat on the couch and hoped she wasn't too hard on him, but she knew she desperately needed to save her marriage and restore the love and respect Janet had for her father. She later joined her husband upstairs and fell asleep.

Before leaving for D.C., I decided to pick up a few things at the corner store. At the checkout I noticed the young teenager, I often spoke with him about his plans for the future. He was always willing to listen, well-mannered and seemed concerned about furthering his education. I hadn't seen him in a while and waited anxiously to ask him how he was doing and where he had been in the last couple of weeks. It was a slow day and no one was behind me in line. There was only one woman in front of me, So, I hoped I'd get a chance to chat with him for a moment. The beautiful, dark skinned lady, in front of me, proudly wore her hair in a natural, kinky twist. She had a little girl with her. The little lady was well mannered. "Hello, precious." I said when she smiled at me. She smiled and said "Hello." "That's her name by the way." The mother said. I was confused. The beautiful dark skinned lady smiled. "Precious." That's her name." She explained. "Oh, ok." I smiled. "It fits her well." "She is adorable." "My name is Greg, Precious."

"Nice to meet you." "Nice to meet you too." The little girl said politely. "My momma's name is Elaine." The little girl said smiling at her mother. Her mother looked at her as if to say don't start. Her mother smiled at me and said "nice to meet you," as she was reaching in her purse to pay for her groceries.

Suddenly, the little girl said, "momma, I can't stand that man. The mother looked at me and then looked down and noticed that she was pointing at a magazine. On the front was a picture of Donald Trump. Elaine Laughed and was a little surprised. "That's not nice, precious." "I see you've been watching too much news with your grandmother. Elaine said, "I swear this one has been here before." "She has too much grown, folk's sense." I chuckled. "It's ok." "Damn, even the little ones know that Trump ain't right." When Elaine finished paying for her groceries, I smiled and said hello to the teenager, I knew, bagging her groceries. "What's going on Mr. Snowden?" He asked. "Not much, I'm getting a few snacks for the trip to D.C." I replied by gathering my things. "Oh, yeah?" "What for?" He asked. "Just a little business trip." I replied. "I wish it was for pleasure, Lord knows I could use a break." He smiled a little and said, "I know what you mean Mr. Snowden." "It's hard out here."

I noticed that he wasn't as enthusiastic as he normally is, so I was a little concerned. "Where have you been man?" It's good to see you." "The service in here sucks without you." "You know they can't function without you bruh." I added. He laughed and said, "I know, but I been locked up." I was stunned. "Locked up?" "You mean like in jail, locked up?" He replied. "Yeah man, I got caught with some weed." "This shit crazy out here man, this is my third time." "Third time?" I asked in confusion. "You know how it is for us man." "That's life." He said acceptingly. "Nawh son, that's not life." "It doesn't have to be your life." "You're too smart for that young blood." "What's the problem?" "Man, they keep stopping me and my boys." He said. "I swear, we be minding our own business and here they come with the shit." "That's just how it is." He explained.

I noticed someone else coming close by so I got right to the point. "Look, you and your boys need to make better choices." If you just gotta smoke, why not smoke at home instead of riding around." "I understand what you mean about constantly being stopped by the police, but don't make it easy for them." "Don't waste your life smoking weed all day young blood, ok? He nodded, "Fa-sho, Mr. Snowden." I paid for my snacks and shook his hand. "Stay up, young blood." "You're a smart young man." Change your surroundings some, and be careful of your choices, ok? "No problem man, I can't keep getting locked up over some B.S. Mr. Snowden." "Have a safe trip man." He said, looking concerned about what to do and thankful that someone took the time to speak with him about it. "Alright young blood." "I'll see you when I get back." "We'll talk some more." I said making my exit.

Meanwhile, Mr. Anderson and two of his associates waited outside the grocery store as I was talking to the young man. As I was walking out the door they stopped me and warned me that the Mayor was not happy with my association with his daughter and threaten to ruin my career if I didn't take drastic measures to ensure that Janet did not participate in the gay rights rally across the street from her father's fifteen hundred dollars a plate event announcing his re-election campaign. I laughed at the boldness of them insulting my intelligence and assured them that Janet was definitely not under my influence and that no one was going to tell me who I can or cannot associate myself with.

Mr. Anderson stood there with an arrogant stern look on his face while the other two men stood behind me as if to say that I wasn't going anywhere until I agreed to do as they requested. I started to walk away with a sarcastic remark. "You gentlemen have a nice day," I said. I look over my shoulder at the two gangsters standing too damn close for comfort and said "You wanna tell your boys to back the fuck off me?"

At that moment, Mr. Anderson said, "You should think about how your family will feel if they knew about a 45 automatic with your finger prints on it." "That took a man's life." Mr. Anderson nodded his head for his well-dressed gangsters to allow me to move. He smiled and they all walked away as I stood there stunned. I often had nightmares about that night. I was only a teenage boy. Only one person knew what happened that night, and she would never speak about it or betray our friendship. I walked to my car wondering how Mr. Anderson knew anything about that night. I heard a familiar roar of a motorcycle and turned to see. It was Jermaine, Sasha's son. He was talking to Mr. Anderson and his gangsters in suits. I couldn't hear what they were talking about, but it didn't look good.

Jermaine handed Mr. Anderson the book bag. "What is this?" Mr. Anderson asked. "I'm done." Jermaine said, still sitting on his motorcycle. "Done with what? Mr. Anderson asked, looking inside the bag. "You people never fail to amaze me." "Didn't I tell your sorry ass, to never approach me in public?" Mr. Anderson said in a muffled tone, grinding his teeth. "We do business at my office only." "Do you understand me?" Mr. Anderson insisted that Jermaine look at him and answer. Before Jermaine could respond, Mr. Anderson asked his last question. "Where is my money, son? Jermaine took off his helmet.

"First of all, I'm not your son." Jermaine explained. "Secondly, you can miss me with that you people bullshit." "You of all people, shouldn't judge." "I never would've imagined a gay man being racist." "And as far as your money, there's your drugs." "Sell that shit yourself." "I'm done!" Mr. Anderson laughed. Jermaine gave Mr. Anderson pictures he had of him and the Mayor embracing each other intimately. "You can have those, I have copies," Jermaine said. Mr. Anderson laughed again. "Ok, let's see how that works out for you." "It's a shame your mother will lose that piece of shit house." Mr. Anderson said calmly. "On second thought, shit smells good to me." "I'll just take it myself and sell it to make up for my loss today." 'As for the piece of shit in front of me." Mr. Anderson suddenly back handed slapped Jermaine. Jermaine fell off of his motor cycle as I was walking in closer. "Hey!" I said, rushing towards them. The two men grabbed me and put a gun to my side. Jermaine waved his hands for me to get back. Jermaine got up and Mr. Anderson continued laughing.

The two men let me go and backed away. They drove away. Jermaine put his helmet back on and got on his motorcycle. "What the fuck was that about!" I asked Jermaine. "Just stay out of this!" Jermaine said. "Nawh, nawh, son, I can't let them get away with this. "I'm not your fucking son!" Jermaine pushed my hand off of his shoulder. "Just stay out of this." "I got this." 'I got on my cell phone, to call the police." "Hey, what are you doing?" Jermaine yelled. "Trust me." "Say nothing to anyone about this if you care about my safety." "Not even to my mom." I saw the seriousness and fear in his eyes. I hung the phone up before anyone answered. "I got this!" "Trust me," Jermaine said again, "They're not the kind of people you want to mess with." Jermaine drove off quickly and left me standing there in the smoke, confused as the sound of his roaring motorcycle faded in the distance.

CHAPTER FIVE

FAT PIMPING

The next day, Janet and I boarded the plane and settled comfortably into our seats. I took the opportunity to call my son Kylin informing him that we were about to ride the clouds, Kylin seemed upset about something and I asked what was wrong before we had to turn our phones off. "Have a safe flight," Kylin said. "Let me know when you guys land." "Of course I will, but what's bothering you?" "Did you not have a good time touring colleges with your friends?" I pressured him for answers. Kylin normally doesn't get upset easily, so I was concerned. "Nothing dad, I'm just confused about why Nate got kicked off the football team and got nine years' probation for simple possession."

Nate was a friend of Kylin's and he had another friend's joint in his hand while his friend went to use the bathroom at a party. Someone called the police about the noise and they came by and searched everyone. They found the joint Nate attempted to hide in his pocket. Kylin told me that while touring colleges, Patrick knew some wealthy friends in Portland Oregon and they decided to drop by and attend a party at the enormous home with a pool in the back. Kylin informed me that he had never seen so many drugs in his life. He even described drugs that he had no clue what they were. What troubled Kylin was that the wealthy family had officers as security where those drugs were being used as recreational activities. I tried to reassure Kylin that justice did indeed exist despite its often tilted scales. He was not convinced and in his kind nature, he re-directed the conversation and suggested that I have a good time and that we should talk about it when he arrives home.

Janet was excited about the trip and was overly talkative to everyone she came in contact with. Not in an annoying way, but her natural free spirited kindness was on a higher level that day. Everyone smiled and didn't want to stop communicating with her because her joyous laughter spilled over into everyone's life around her and filled the crowded airport with peace and sunshine. Janet rushed to drink up the rest of her fresh vegetable and fruit juice she had made earlier before boarding the plane. She was trying to watch what she ate because she knew she wanted to treat herself by indulging in some good binge eating while in D.C. People around her were amused by her kind nature and continued to converse with her about numerous things. To be able to watch her interact with people was intoxicating.

I managed to capture her attention before the plane took off and she held my hand. Janet loved flying, but the take- off was always uncomfortable for her. I was tired from being up most of the night, speaking with Lisa on the phone. I welcomed the late night conversation because I normally didn't sleep well and she and I had a lot of catching up to do. Lisa would be home on leave in a few days and we both were excited to see each other again. The flight from Memphis to Washington D.C. was only a couple of hours so as soon as Janet was comfortably over the climb in altitude, I immediately took the opportunity to catch a quick nap. Before I knew it, my subconscious took over and I was in dream land.

There I was, a young boy about 11 or 12 yrs. old with a reddish afro. I was walking up the street to visit my friend Euhommie, but half way there, his brother Hercules met me in the middle of the street complaining that I had promised him that I would let him use the rest of my Sta-soft fro, moisturizer but had instead given it to Homie. I had forgotten that I had told Herk that he could use it when homie asked to have it earlier. I tried to explain, but Herk, a few years older than I, pushed me. I stumbled backwards and took a swing at him. Hercules ducked and caught me in the stomach with a right hook. I bent over from the blow and simultaneously caught him in a headlock. Hercules wrestled to get out, but my upper body strength was incredibly surprising because of my lanky build and tall frame.

"Let me go Snow!" Hercules yelled, "When I get out, I'm gonna bust you up!" He said angrily because he was being handled by someone a year younger in front of his friends and couldn't get free. In the 70's, most fights were handled with your bare knuckles and guns and knives were something boys our age had only heard or witnessed from a few older kids in the projects and what we saw on T.V.

Suddenly, Eugene rushed through the cheering boys and stopped us from fighting. To me, Eugene was the coolest of all the brothers. He was a few years older than Hercules, so he was about 16 or 17 years old. "What's going on, why are y'all fighting?" Eugene asked in his cool, calm and collective voice. Hercules began to explain while I was checking my face for blood. The afro pick in herk's hair had somehow struck me in the face while I wrestled him to the ground. Before Eugene's younger brother could finish speaking, Eugene quickly realized how stupid the reason for fighting was among friends.

Eugene braced himself between the two of us and grabbed us together by our t-shirts in the front neck area with his fists and made us apologize to each other. Being that we admired him as a ladies man,. Eugene captured our attention and suggested that we needed to be enjoying the company of the pretty girls instead of fondling with each other in the dirt. Everyone laughed and agreed with him. Eugene then told us that he was getting ready to go and get the rest of his hair done by a pretty girl he knew before in Lincoln Courts, another project housing complex nearby.

Eugene and his family had lived in the Courts before moving to the projects where I lived. The LBC, they called it, for Lincoln Black Courts. "Dreamy," the girl he met in the LBC, used to be a child crush. She had now learned to braid hair well in her young adult life. They both fancied each other before Eugene and his family moved away. Dreamy now had a baby girl and an older boyfriend. Eugene let us go, smiled and asked us to get along. He told his younger brother and I that he didn't want to hear of us fighting again when he came back home. Eugene asked, "Are y'all cool?" We both said yes. "Yeah man, we're good," we assured him. "Alright then," Eugene said while nodding his head.

Standing between us, he put his arms around our necks and gave us a little quick hug. He was a little taller than us, so when he pulled us closer to the sides of him, our heads fell in towards each side of his chest. We were both in a brotherly headlock for a second as Herk and I made eye contact with each other and smiled. At that moment, we knew for sure we wouldn't be fighting again. Eugene let us go and said "Alright now, y'all be cool and go find something to do." He walked away swaying from one side across the playground field in the center of the projects. In those days the cool walk was known as the pimp walk. At the end of the field was the street that led to the LBC. His friend, fat pimping, was waiting for him at the end of the field.

I watched them walking further away and suddenly recognized this familiar scene. "No! Stop! I thought to myself. Eugene's hair was braided only on one side and the other half was still in an afro. I've lived this dreadful day before! The devastating experience of that dreadful day was carved into my brain forever. Realizing I was dreaming of that awful day, I wanted to wake myself. I tried to shake myself free of this disaster but I couldn't move. I tried to reach for Janet to wake me, but my hands only gripped the armrest of the plane seats. I knew what would happen next and I didn't want to see my friend lose his life. It would be the last time I would ever see Eugene again.

Death had a way of constantly visiting the hood and it didn't matter if you were kids, death made his familiar visits a repeated gruesome event. In the hood, death made its acquaintance early in a child's life and left behind realistic evidence of a promise to return. Psychological effects of not having enough essential survival methods started long before any beneficial moral development could influence mental stability in the life of a growing child in the hood. Poverty was your teacher and your outlook on life was scorned. A man in a red suit or a rabbit with painted eggs, were comical tales to relieve the constant fear of poverty's wicked, Uncle Death.

Eugene walked away, afro half braided and he moved in a cool slow-motion fashion. Eugene could not hear me screaming his name to stop him from going to a place he would not return. I quickly ran across the field but the grass turned into quick sand beneath my feet and no matter how hard I tried to keep myself from sinking into the ground, I slipped and fell over and over again. Struggling to stay above ground, I could barely see him anymore. I yelled his name as loud as I could and before I could catch my breath to yell again, he was gone.

In my dream, I was trying to stop a horrible thing from happening again. I recognized that I was reliving something that had happened to Eugene years ago when I was a young boy. Eugene never came back home that day. He was shot in the head, by Dreamy's jealous boyfriend. Dreamy and her boyfriend had an argument about inviting her little girl crush over and Dreamy tried to explain that it was an innocent gesture between friends. She pleaded that there was nothing more than that going on.

She had braided another guy's hair at her home before and had no problem other than his anti-social behavior towards them until she invited someone her older boyfriend knew she liked before she met him. The argument got way out of control and her boyfriend struck her in the face and pulled her by her hair into the bedroom. She had heard about his reputation of getting drunk and beating on his prior girlfriends but he had never shown any signs of violence toward her at all. She was caught by surprise and struggled to get away from him. He struck her again and then tried to pull her pants off and rape her. Dreamy couldn't call Eugene and warn him because in those days there were no cell phones and Eugene and his friend were already on the way. Besides she had found herself in a fight for her life.

Eugene never stood a chance. He knocked at the door, not aware of the brutal horror unfolding inside. The angry man knocked Dreamy unconscious and answered the door. He came to the door waving a gun and before Eugene could speak, the man said, "You're the mutha fucka been calling my girl?" "Get the fuck off of my porch!" "Eugene apologized and tried to explain that Dreamy was supposed to be braiding his hair and that's the only reason he was there. That only enraged the man even more. "Her name is Shae!" "Get the fuck off of my porch with that Dreamy shit!" Fat pimping shoved Eugene out of the way and said "Look man, we don't want any problems, you need to check your attitude!" Fat pimping and Eugene turned to walk away. At that moment for no reason at all, the man pulled the trigger. Fat pimping panicked and reacted with violence. Fat pimping, yelled and knocked the gun away from the man and started beating him relentlessly. He threw the man off of the porch and jumped on top of him.

Crying and yelling, fat pimping couldn't control his rage and continued pounding his face with his fist until the man was bloody and unresponsive. Fat pimping had to be pulled off the older man by neighbors who heard the gun fire. Fat pimping sat on the ground shaking from shock and disbelief of what had just happened. The police and the ambulance arrived shortly afterwards. By that time some of Shae's friends arrived and were terrified by what they saw outside. They immediately rushed inside and found Dreamy laying on the bedroom floor bruised, battered and unconscious. They all screamed for someone to help her. Dreamy was taken to the hospital while officers secured the crime scene.

Fat pimping was never the same after what happened to Eugene and as small boys, we didn't know how to approach or comfort him. All of us changed a little after that day. We hardly ever saw him after that and whenever we did see him, he stayed to himself and he barely spoke a few words to anyone. My heart always felt heavy when I would see him in the neighborhood. He never really smiled again and he seemed distant and didn't participate in any activities anymore. He was one of the older guys we looked up to in the hood and on the football field. After the shooting, fat pimping, appeared to us as a person who had lost his joy for life.

I suddenly woke up, as the plane had landed and came to a halt at the Ronald Reagan Airport. Janet was holding my hand. She asked if I was ok. "You didn't sleep well," Janet explained. At that moment a gorgeous flight attendant put her hand on Janet's shoulders and asked if everything was alright. She assisted us both out of our seats looking curiously at Janet and said "He's hot, you take care of that cutie pie." Janet didn't respond and I thanked the smiling attendant as we exited the plane. Janet suggested that I go ahead to the hotel, check in and go see the Martin Luther King Jr., statue alone while she spoke with the attorney. She knew I often felt despair living in a city where Mr. King was assassinated, so she felt that I would be inspired by the monument. "I'll meet up with you later." Janet said with a cheerful excitement.

That same Monday evening in Memphis, Janet's mother was attempting to seduce her husband. She had grown tired of entertaining the wives of wealthy men who all had stories of being left alone and poor performances by their husbands in the bedroom when they did try to show some affection. Mrs. Hope was always in good spirits and her joyful nature, like her daughter, would always cheer her friends and family up. Sadly, her smile was a mask that prevented anyone from knowing of her own unsatisfactory relationship with her husband. She loved him and admired his determination, yet she did not understand why he let go of the morals and values he once stood for that got him elected as Mayor. Mrs. Hope was a woman with a caring nature who enjoyed solving problems for family and friends, yet she herself often wished she had someone to lean on from time to time, especially now that her husband had become distant.

She would never tell her wives group such personal things like bedroom issues the way they so openly did. Her daughter was her only lasting relationship, but she had not yet figured out what was wrong with her marriage and she didn't want to burden Janet, especially since Janet was recognizing changes in her father herself. There would be no holding their family together if Janet also knew her father was being distant and avoiding intimacy emotionally and physically. Mrs. Hope was in the kitchen while her husband was watching television in the entertainment room that was connected to the master bedroom up-stairs. She poured two glasses of red wine and cut one piece of vanilla bean pie for her husband. She strategically placed strawberries beside the pie and drizzled some chocolate over them. She hoped to use the leftover chocolate in the small white porcelain container, so she placed it on the carrying tray as well.

She walked up-stairs and entered the bedroom seductively in her white robe. Carol was in amazing shape for her age and was confident about allowing her robe to sway open as she walked behind the sofa her husband was sitting in. "I brought you a light snack love." Carol said in a soft voice. She walked around in front of him holding the prepared tray with wine, pie and strawberries. Mayor Hope looked up at the tray and noticed that her robe was opened, exposing her brand new breasts, and silk, laced panties. "Sweets for my sweetie," she said.

The Mayor, Nickolas Hope did not respond, and took the glass of wine in one hand while placing the tray she handed him on the table in front of the sofa. He calmly picked up the newspaper beside the tray, opened it and said "Carolyn, you're being a naughty girl." "Yes, I am, why don't you come over here and punish me," she said, placing herself on the sofa next to him. Carol leaned back on the armrest with one leg up on the sofa and the other on the floor.

Noticing that he was still pretending not to be bothered by her advances, she crawled close to him and pushed the newspaper down in his lap and started kissing and nibbling on his ear. She turned his face towards hers and kissed him passionately on the lips. He responded and kissed her back.

Breaking news on the television interrupted Carol's advances. The reporter explained that people were in the streets in front of Mr. Anderson's building site protesting its completion because they had discovered his intentions of raising the rent and purchase prices of homes, in order to force those with low-income out of their communities. They were also furious about his insensitivity towards people with special needs. Mayor Hope stopped kissing his wife and reached for his cell phone to inform Mr. Anderson. "This is not good," he said to himself.

Disappointed, Carol tried to convince her husband to stay home. "Why don't you let him worry about his own problems?" she asked. He explained that he had to go and that the people knew that Mr. Anderson was a major player in his re-election and he had to do something to rectify the situation. Homie had been trailing Mr. Anderson and discovered that he was going in and out of a penthouse downtown. It looked as though he was living a double life and spent a lot of time there away from his wife. Homie could see that a female and a young man also resided in the same penthouse.

While waiting in the parking lot downstairs, Homie received a phone call from detective Oswald, who informed him that Mr. Anderson and his wife had a son while living in another state that mysteriously died and moved to Memphis afterwards. After the accident, Mrs. Anderson was mentally unstable for a while and was under private care of her husband who has extensive experience in treating depression. "Homie was confused by the news and asked "Why would he form a protest against the mentally disabled if his own wife suffered from mental issues?" 'I'm not sure, but police records state that Mrs. Anderson didn't believe that her baby boy died at all because she never saw his body and caused her severe grief and depression"

"So what happened to the child?" Homie asked. "Mr. Anderson was driving from an amusement park when he claimed to have swerved the car to prevent hitting a deer in the road." "The vehicle hit a tree and knocked him unconscious." Detective Oswald further explained that Mr. Anderson claimed that when he woke up, the car was in flames and he desperately tried to get the child out of the back seat that was already in smoke and flames." "Mr. Anderson suffered burns on his hands and arms and police found evidence of an unidentifiable, small body in the back seat." Oswald explained.

"It doesn't add up," Homie explained. "Why the protest if he loved and took care of his wife?" "Why would he be abusing her if he's having an affair? "Why not just divorce her?" "Is that why you asked me to look into their marriage?" "Is he abusing her?" Oswald asked. "I'm not sure yet, but I have a witness who noticed bruises and strange behavior from Mrs. Anderson," Homie replied. "In the meantime, I'm faxing over a picture of the female in the penthouse, see if you can find out who she is and get back to me as soon as you can." Homie instructed Oswald.

Mr. Anderson arrived home Monday evening. He walked inside and found his wife combing her hair gazing into the mirror as if not to recognize herself. She slowly turned and acknowledged his presence and asked "Back so soon?" "Must there be trouble in paradise?" she said sarcastically. "For once you're home while dinner is still warm." "We didn't discuss much today, besides I have to prepare to be at the building site in an hour." He looked at her swollen eye and said, "I'm sorry you made me hit you." "You have to take your meds dear." "You're not yourself without them." "You want me to be myself?" "Then let me live a normal life." "You're never home, our son is dead and we sleep in different bedrooms." Mrs. Anderson explained. "Our son is in a better place now and I'm trying to provide for you and take care of you Dora." Mr. Anderson kissed Dora's forehead and walked to the kitchen. She followed him with her eyes with an evil smirk on her face. Mr. Anderson assisted himself to a warm plate of chicken casserole at the dinner table and a glass of wine.

Homie had followed Mr. Anderson from the penthouse of the building he owned. He had discovered that his wife knew nothing about that particular building and Homie wanted to know why. Mr. Anderson went inside his home with his wife Monday evening after leaving the penthouse. Homie drove slowly, past Anderson's home after he went in and received another phone call from detective Oswald. "I got information on the woman at the penthouse," Oswald said. "What's up," Homie eagerly, pleaded for more information.

"The female you identified is Mrs. Melanie Bautista." "And get this, she is a hired nurse to take care of the young man while Mr. Anderson is away." "Apparently, the young gentleman is autistic and she is married, so Mr. Anderson may not be having an affair." Homie shook his head and replied, "Why would Mr. Anderson hire someone to take care of his autistic son, if he doesn't want special needs people living near his home." "He didn't hire her, Mayor Bobby Hope did," Oswald explained. "You have got to be kidding me." Homie said, even more perplexed by the information. Homie wondered if the Mayor was having an affair with the young lady and using Mr. Anderson to hide a son, Janet's mother knew nothing about. Detective Oswald, mentioned that he would be going by the penthouse to investigate soon.

At that moment, Oswald received a call from the police dispatcher that officers were needed at the building site of Mr. Anderson. Someone had called in concerned that protestors were blocking traffic and things may get out of control. Oswald informed Police Chief Bond and they both dismissed their conversation and headed towards the area. On the way there, two streets over from where mostly black communities were expressing their concerns about a new building project in their community with rental rates they could not afford, a white supremacies group were marching with signs supporting Mr. Trump.

"Dear God, help us!" Chief Bond said to himself. Before he could gather himself, a reporter came to the window of his car. "What do you think of the march Mr. Bond?" The reporter asked. "As long as they behave within the law, it should be no problem." Chief Bond replied. "Are you not concerned that a racist group supports Mr. Trump?" The reporter asked. Chief Bond replied quickly and disguised his fear that they would be seen by the large group of black people nearby. "I am certain that not all white people who support Mr. Trump is racist but clearly it seems that all racist groups support his election." Chief Bond rolled the window up and drove away. He immediately got on the phone. Chief Bond called the station. "Get some guys over here immediately at the corner of West end Street and 5th Avenue." "Why the fuck don't I have any information about a supremacies' rally for Trump today!" He said. "Get here now and make sure nothing pops off." Chief Bond waited until officers arrived.

A few officers were black officers. One asked "why do we have to protect these fools." "If they ass is bold enough to come down here, they're bold enough to take an ass whipping." "Shut the fuck up and do your job." Chief Bond said. "It's time to earn your pay." "It aint always pretty but its' necessary. "They pay taxes too." Chief Bond added. "Yeah, but entertaining this kind of ignorance always has its consequences." The black officer said, shaking his head. "Damn right." Officer Bond said. "So get your ass over there and protect and serve." Chief Bond gave a reluctant half smile while shaking his head in agreement with the officer. Chief Bond returned to his vehicle and proceeded to go to the construction site to maintain order. "Lord, help us." He said to himself.

CHAPTER SIX

BALL OF CONFUSION

Mr. Anderson received a call from the Mayor while eating his dinner and immediately rushed towards the door. "Leaving again", Dora said grimly. Suddenly, Mr. Anderson realized that it was time for Mrs. Anderson's medication so he quickly went upstairs to get them from his locked drawer. He came back down with a glass of water. "Here love, take these, I have to take care of business." She put the pills in her mouth and took a drink of water. "I promise, I'll be right back," Mr. Anderson said and hurried out the door. Mrs. Anderson watched him leave with that same evil smirk and spit the pills into her hand. "Business huh?" She mumbled to herself.

By that time Kylin and his friends were arriving back home from touring college campuses. They arrived back home early before Friday because Kylin was bothered by the party they attended with all the drugs he had never seen before in his life. Kylin wasn't one to judge others for what they did in their life and he was comfortable having the courage to say no despite what others did around him. The drugs were not the problem. What disturbed him was seeing officers participating and protecting rich kid's indulging in criminal activity. His basketball teammate had been kicked off the team and criminalized for having a small joint in his possession, yet these privileged kids had coke all over the place and other drugs he'd never heard of. Kylin was glad he had good friends and they all agreed to leave. For the first time in his life, Kylin was now realizing the world he lived in was not as equal and justice for all as he had originally anticipated. His mother's words sounded off over and over again in his head. "Boy you better work twice as hard as these white boys out here to prove yourself" "They're gonna have it easier than you because they're white." His mother would say. 'Don't think because you go to that private school your chances for success will be the same as theirs," she would say. At the time Kylin didn't want to believe that, but his innocent, kind, laid back nature was being awakened and tested. Confused and saddened, Kylin missed his mother and looked forward to calling her when they arrived home. Still holding on to his faith and the exciting universities they had visited, they all had ambitious goals to pursue.

They were excited to be starting new adventures and were eager to tell their parents about their time away and all the possibilities they had discovered. I was glad I had a chance to meet young white teenagers who did not see the color of skin as separation, they saw it as only an observation of diversity in greatness and character. Ignorance, racism, and negative organizations along with the media's biased coverage of it, had a way of deteriorating young hopeful minds into weary, and frustrated adults. It was refreshing to meet them and I felt blessed to have gotten to know such humble and well-cultured young men. All five of them attended private school and were very intelligent, handsome young men. Kylin was interested in designing his own game and going to an art & design school. All four teenagers in the car with him had plans for a bright future.

Evan, Nick and Patrick visited my son kylin often. They were cool white teenagers who had wealthy families, yet they were humble and kind. My son respected them and they respected Kylin. Patrick had what I would call a beach boy look. His hair was long and layered down to just above his shoulders. He dressed well and was well mannered. He would always address adults with yes sir or yes ma'am. He was always helpful and would always offer to buy pizza or McDonald's for everyone when the teens were all together.

Patrick spoke and carried himself with confidence and was interested in becoming a doctor. He also studied music and played the guitar well. I think he secretly had a crush on my daughter Makayla who was a year older than him and I can't say I blame him. Makala's social skills were off the charts like her mother and beautiful as well. Patrick noticed that Makayla had a guitar and I hoped he would teach her a few tricks of the trade. His parents were in the medical field and admired their son's musical talents.

Nick was tall, clean cut and lean. I had fun teaching Nick how to do the universal head acknowledgement known to all black people as "wassup." The smile on his face the first time I taught him to slightly throw his head back as a sign of respect, told me that he was either amused by it or just being nice, because he already knew the cool move. Regardless if he already knew or not, Nick took the time to humor me, and I respected him for that. After that each time he came over the first thing we would do was the universal "wassup," move. Nick also drove us crazy with his favorite lyrics of Drake's summer sixteen.

Nick was constantly trying to dance and throwing his hands in the air, bouncing his slender shoulders and singing, "Looking for revenge, all summer sixteen, all summer sixteen, playing dirty not clean." "Shut up!" We all would say. "Say it one more time and we're just gonna dive on you." Nick would laugh, smile and go to another room by himself and then you would hear him again. "Looking for revenge!" We would just shake our heads.

Nick was interested in becoming a Chemical engineer. His parents were Jewish and I would always inquire about their beliefs and traditions. Nick would gladly educate me. He was so tall and slender like my son and I just wanted to feed the child a sandwich every time I saw him but he wouldn't eat anything after about seven o'clock.

Evan was the first white friend of my son I met when Kylin first started attending private school when they both played basketball. My son was shorter back then and on the chubby side, but his personality was always strong, full of vigor and caring. After the game I walked down the bleachers and talked to Kylin and to meet his new friend on the sidelines.

Evan at the time was so tiny compared to my son. Without realizing it, my voice would change when I was talking to him. He just smiled and said hello. Later that day my son said "Dad, did you know your voice changed when you were talking to Evan?" "No, what do you mean," I asked. He laughed and said "you were talking to him like he was a little kid." "We're the same age dad," Kylin chuckled. I laughed and was kind of embarrassed that I hadn't noticed it, but I knew exactly what my son meant. I love kids and I do have a tendency to soften my voice when I'm speaking with them. Kind of like a kindergarten teacher.

I apologized and asked my son to tell his friend Evan that I didn't mean any harm. They remained friends throughout each school year and they both decided not to play basketball after the second year to focus more on their homework. Evan was kind and the smallest of the bunch, but like Kylin, he radiated with vitality and was enthusiastic about life and adventures. At that time my family was all together and Evan's mom, who was a sweetheart, got along great with Lieko. Evan was interested in computer science and I personally liked that he loved "The Walking Dead" because it was one of my favorites as well. Of course, I invited him to all my start of the season "Walking Dead" parties.

Drake, known as "Shake & Bake" Drake was the only other black friend in my son's crew. Drake didn't visit as much because he was always in basketball practice or doing homework, yet at school he was part of the fabulous five. Drake was tall, handsome, stocky and physically fit. He played the power forward position and I'm not sure what major college wasn't trying to recruit him to play college basketball. That Monday evening Drake was sitting in the front seat with Kylin. The rest of the crew was sitting in the back seat of Kylin's old 2008 Lincoln Navigator. It was black with tinted windows.

They were looking for Homie since Kylin knew I was away and I instructed him to let Homie know as soon as he got back in town and stay with him until I returned. They all were excited and Nick begged them to play Drake's "Summer Sixteen" as they were heading towards the inner city. "Bruh! "Not again they sighed. "Alright, alright, just one more time," Nick said. Kylin shook his head and said "I'm gonna play this shit one more time for you then I'm throwing it out the window."

Kylin called Homie and asked where he was. Homie explained that he was at the new building site and protesters had the streets blocked. Kylin explained to his friends what was going on so they decided to go to a near-by Starbucks to wait it out. They all agreed and started blasting Drake on the way over. Nick of course, Nick bounced around in the SUV the entire ride on the way there. They parked the car and were walking in the direction of the Starbucks. They passed a news reporter in the parking lot. She was not filming the protestors close by. The lady reporter was talking to the head of the news editing room who was instructing all the camera crew on which angles to shoot and record.

"We can't get a good story from that location," the head of editing explained to the reporter out in the field. "Try to get closer and make something happen." "What do you mean?" The lady reporter inquired. "If I have to tell you your job, maybe I should do it myself," the man said. "Ask questions, get involved, and get a reaction worth covering!" "I don't care, just get it done!"

By that time Mr. Anderson and Mayor Hope were attempting to answer questions from other reporters and a few protestors. "You claimed you were re-building our community in order to provide better living environments and provide businesses that would create better jobs for the community." One protestor shouted. "Why is the rent on the apartment complexes so high?" No one here can afford those prices!" He yelled.

"It seems to me that you're only interested in running the poor out and fattening your own pockets, "a woman nearby accused Mr. Anderson. Another lady added with frustration, "He doesn't care about us, if he doesn't care about the mentally disabled, how the hell is he gonna pretend to care about the poor!" "I assure you that it will all work out for the best if you will just be patient and give it a chance," Mr. Anderson pleaded. Mayor Hope stepped in and said "I think what he means is that the employment the businesses will provide will help the community afford living cost and purchases of homes in the area." "We must keep up the Hope, and drive out crime and dope."

"How are you gonna back up this greedy, evil, selfish man," an old man asked. "You want our votes but you don't want to listen to the needs of the people." "We need affordable housing, good paying jobs, and affordable health care!" The old man explained. "Not everyone here is a criminal and uses drugs." 'Most of us are hardworking taxpayers and educators of our children." These kids are afraid to go outside lately, not because of drugs but because more crime is being committed against them from the police, not criminals," the old man explained.

"Do you hear yourself?" The Mayor asked. "You defend the criminals and crime we're trying to control and expect a better community from it." The Mayor said in confusion. "A lady with her two kids said "No, we don't defend crime, we defend the right not to be assumed as though we are all criminals because we are black and lose innocent lives at the hands of the same people who say they are protecting the people."

"It seems to me that the community they protect are their own and come to our community to rage war on anyone black who looks threatening rather they are armed or not." She added while placing her hands on the chest of her little boys standing in front of her. "It has to stop now, so keep your new buildings if your solution is to drive us all out into the streets with no place to live while Mr. Anderson gets rich.

The reporter from the Starbucks parking lot had obtained a better position to please her boss and was starting to ask questions among the protestors. It was night time now and around 10 pm. Starbucks was closing and the crowds were getting larger and irritated by questions by reporters who asked questions like "What will you do if you can't afford to live here, where will you go?. The tension grew and angry people shouted and waved their fist in the air. Kylin and his friends noticed that the Starbucks they were at was now surrounded by more people closer to the nightclub Homie owned.

"Are you afraid you and your kids will end up homeless because of Mr. Anderson?" The lady reporter in front of Starbucks asked?" "You're got, damn, right I'm afraid, "the concerned lady said. "Wouldn't you if you couldn't afford to live anywhere else? More people gathered and more signs went up in protest. People started moving swiftly towards where the mayor and Mr. Anderson stood speaking to the citizens.

The police noticed that things were starting to be a little uncomfortable, and was attempting to dismiss the protestors and maintain order. Kylin and his friend were walking out of Starbucks and Kylin could see Homie from a distance approaching the

Mayor and Mr. Anderson. The Mayor recognized Homie and knew He owned the club his daughter attended regularly, so he wasn't too quick to cooperate with Homie's suggestion that they should live in fear for their safety. "We're not going anywhere son!" the mayor boastfully replied.

"Sir, we need you to move and move now," Homie explained that the tactical unit was moving in and he was not sure how the crowd would react so he pleaded as nicely as he could for them to get to safety and then turn toward the crowd and advised them to leave as well. Officers in police riot gear had placed themselves in position but had not yet made any moves. Chief Bond spoke into his walkie-talkie and asked officers to disperse the rally for Mr. Trump as well. Detective Oswald and the rookie were on the back end of the crowd near the club and Starbucks.

They were also advising protestors to leave the area. Now that the tension was greater than before. Live broadcasting started in anticipation of a huge story. The Mayor and Mr. Anderson finally took Homie's advice and hurried themselves to the waiting limo. While in the limo, the mayor expressed his frustrations to Mr. Anderson. "This has to end," he said angrily. "Don't let it get you down," Mr. Anderson said while placing his hand on the Mayor's knee. The mayor pushed his hand away and said "No, this all has to stop now!" I don't need this election and I don't need you." "You can't be serious?" "Bob asked the mayor in an angry tone." "Life ain't worth living if you can't be true to who you are." Bob added. "I am being true." "True to my family, and that's all that matters." The mayor said. Bob became enraged. "Your family? "What family? Bob asked. "Your daughter doesn't support you, and your alcoholic wife doesn't love you like I do." "You think you have a chance of reelection without me?" Mr. Anderson scolded. "I took care of the competition!" " "He's dead and you still have a chance." "This loud mouth woman doesn't stand a chance of being elected." Mr. Anderson added. The mayor looked at him with disgust and fear in his eyes. The mayor respected Mrs. Watkins although she was fairly new in the political field, the Mayor felt that she was intelligent and highly qualified. Although the favored state representative was his biggest opponent, he knew that Mrs. Watkins would put up a good fight. The mayor now knew that Mr. Anderson had done a horrific thing to an innocent man and his wife.

For the first time, the mayor realized how dangerous and disturbed, Bob was. He knew now that the state representative and his wife were murdered. It wasn't just a hit and run, by just anyone, Bob had ordered the hit. The mayor tried to conceal his realization and redirected the argument. "Look Bob, it just doesn't feel right this time around." The mayor continued explaining. "How can I advocte for L.G.B.T.Q rights to be overturned, if I identify with one of them?" "How can I ignore minorities being judged by the color of their skin when I myself, know too well my fear of being judged if I tell my family and the community who I really am?"

"Besides, I am not the one hiding my son away from the world, you are." "So just keep your judgements to yourself." The mayor said while getting out of the limo. Mr. Anderson tried to grab his arm before he got out, but the mayor pulled away. The mayor knew now what Bob was capable of. He was frightened by the thought of his decision to break ties with him, meant for his family's safety. A cufflink Mr. Anderson had given him fell off from violently snatching his arm away. Mr. Anderson picked the cufflink and held on to it as if to cherish the memory of the night he gave it to the mayor as a gift. He said nothing but only turned on the radio loudly. A song came on that reminded him of that night. As "Take me to church" by Hozier played, Mr. Anderson bald up his fist and slowly tapped his forehead with the cufflink inside. He grew more disappointed, sad and angry as the lyrics to the song pounded in his heart and exploded in his mind. He felt that all was lost. He picked up his cell phone and dialed a number. When the person he dialed answered. Mr. Anderson said sternly, "You know what to do."

Mr. Anderson was furious, not because of the protestors but what it meant to his financial plans and his disappointment in the Mayor's decision to distance himself from Mr. Anderson's advances. They were secretly lovers and the Mayor wanted nothing more to do with Mr. Anderson. Mr. Anderson had faked his son's death to protect his son from Mrs. Anderson, who thought that a child born with disabilities were the devil's children. Mr. Anderson was afraid that Dora would try to harm their son. Mr. Anderson knew about her past. She was suffering from mental issues due to a traumatic childhood event. Dora, later met Mr. Anderson, who at that time was a young psychiatrist. She was seeking treatment. They married later. After they had a baby boy, Dora's condition worsened. Mr. Anderson retired as a psychiatrist, made some investments and they moved to Memphis after the suspicious death of their son.

Suddenly, the building Homie owned exploded into flames. A dark hooded figure ran away from the back of the building into the wooded area nearby, people were running away from the burning building. This angered some protestors and a few reacted with violence against officers who had started to arrest innocent bystanders. No one knew who started the fire but officers and protesters erupted in fights with each other. Protestors were frantic and afraid. Everyone was running to safety and others were still protesting or arguing with officers arresting those who refused to move.

Kylin, noticing that the building that exploded was his dad's friend Homie's place of business, made him desperately look for Homie again and tried to help get his friends and himself to safety. They saw the hooded figure again watching the flames from a safe distance near the wooded area. It looked like a female but her face could not be seen completely.

As they were working their way through the scared, angry crowd, a few of them started destroying property and others were arguing with officers in riot gear. They decided to give up the search for Homie and get away from the scene. Struggling through the protestors, an officer grabbed Drake and Drake, with fear in his voice, pleaded that he had done nothing wrong and tried to get away from him. The rest of Kylin's friends including Kylin turned to help Drake explain. Drake freed himself and the officer's attention was taken by another explosion nearby.

They ran towards safety and Drake mistakenly knocked down a Caucasian woman coming out of one of the businesses where the windows were being smashed in. She was screaming and Drake tried to help her up. Once again, Kylin and his friends tried to help Drake. As they were attempting to calm the older white lady, her frantic behavior made the situation worse and at that moment a voice rang out to freeze, they all turned towards the voice. Drake released the woman and turned towards the officer, walking towards him with his hands up trying to explain that he was only trying to help. Suddenly a single gun fire went off like thunder. Drake fell to the ground fighting for his life. Kylin and the rest of the guys were shocked to see Bryson, the rookie cop standing there with the smoking gun. Detective Oswald recognized the high profile high school football star, shake and bake Drake, as the victim and yelled at the rookie cop to stop what he was doing. The wind snarled with a crying sound and smoke violently, swirled around the buildings where drake laid on the ground. "What the fuck!" Oswald said, fighting the debri in the air, as he forced the stunned officer's gun downward. At that moment, the young teen who worked at the grocery store saw Kylin in distress and pleaded with them to get in his car and left the scene while detective Oswald assisted their wounded friend. "We'll meet them at the hospital!" The young teen yelled." Kylin and the rest of his friends were frantically trying to see if Drake was ok but couldn't see much as the car was speeding away and people were running around everywhere. They were confused and sobbing. "Go, go, go!" "Go to the hospital," they yelled!"

Officers on 5th Avenue noticed a group of black protestors leaving the area had made their way where officers were attempting to get the supremacies group and reporters to safety. "Awe, hell nah!" A black man noticed the signs that read make America white again, and started arguing with the white men holding the signs. Confusion erupted and before you knew it, people were fighting. The smoke from the flames and sounds of sirens just a few blocks over were now swirling around the supremacist group and the men they were fighting.

Chief of police, Bond quickly got to the scene and ordered his officers to block off the streets to prevent more people from the construction protest accidentally coming across the fight with the Trump supporters. Reporters were on the scene quickly as well. Miraculously, the road block worked and people who could not get through were furious that it seemed to them that the chief of police was protecting a supremacist group. As soon as Chief Bond, arrived at the scene, a reporter asked, "Why are you protecting a white supremacies group?" "We protect human beings," Chief Bond replied. "Now please get those cameras out of here!" Chief Bond was clearly annoyed by the ignorance of the questions being asked, and was concerned for everyone's safety. I'll be glad when this election is over, he thought to himself, pushing through the furious crowd and trying to establish order.

More fights broke out between the black and white protestors, as reporters, remained relentless in their attempts to cover the unfolding events. Again, they interrupted Chief Bond's duty to protect and serve. "Get those cameras out of here!" He said again, as the winds howled in despair. "Who are you protecting here?" The reporter asked?" Extremely annoyed, Chief Bond replied, "Look, a crime is a crime, no matter who commits them." Chief Bond hurriedly replied. "Some people just belong in jail." "Now, get out of here and let us do our job." He demanded of the reporters. Tear gas erupted in the skies and order was re-established with several arrests made. Luckily, besides a few bloody noses, broken bones and bruises, the fight ended quickly and officers arrested those involved. What was our community becoming. Minorities in Memphis felt that Martin Luther King's death and the suffering of his family and people all over the world who fought for justice had made a difference. It had now become clear that people's true colors were showing and the racist actions and thinking of long ago had only changed its appearance and was now taking off it's disguise.

CHAPTER SEVEN

DORA

Watching the flames and the crowd from the wooded area, the hooded female enjoyed the chaos she had created. Her intention was to burn Chief of Police Euhommie Bond's place of business down as a warning to stay away from her husband. Dora, with a disturbing look on her face stepped back further into the trees chanting to herself. "Mary, Mary," she said softly over and over again. "Mary, Mary," she said, pulling her hood off of her head. She crouched down in the darkness and continued to chant. "Mary, Mary, lost her faith, burned her cross and cursed her father's name," she mumbled as black tears from mascara rolled down her face.

Looking down upon the screaming people in the streets, Dora heard the growling wind and saw the smoke filled debri gathering and coming up towards the trees she was hiding in on the hill. It terrified her and she stood to get away to the other side. As she turned to go down the other side, the smoke and the horrific sound vanished into silence. Dora was stunned at the silence and thought she'd suddenly lost her hearing. She looked over her shoulder and screamed at the sight of the image of the burning woman reaching for her shoulder. Dora fell backwards screaming as she tumbled down the other side of the hill. She stopped at the next street over and ran away, as fast as she could. When she felt safe and nothing or no one was chasing her she slowed her pace. Just ahead of her was a police car with flashing lights.

As she walked closer, she saw one officer hitting and slaming a young black man around as the other officer was standing there watching. Dora walked to the other side when the officer saw her approaching. "Get out of here," The officer instructed Dora. Dora heard the young man trying to explain that his identification was in his wallet and that he had done nothing wrong. "Shut up!" The officer told the young man as he slammed his head into the hood of the police car. Dora kept walking past the scene on the other side and placed her hood over her head.

Dora knew she had just committed a crime and didn't want to draw any attention to herself. While she was swiftly trying to escape the horrible scene and conceal her face, She saw the kinky haired lady again, who resembled Dora, standing near the officer hitting the young man. This time she did not look as though she had been burned and there was no fire in her eyes. This time she looked sad and sobbed as she watched over the young man pleading his innocence. The lady slowly looked over at Dora as the sobbing image of herself vanished into thin air. Dora reached the corner on the other side and trotted away fearing that she was insane.

As a child in her hometown, Dora was a sweet innocent little girl with beautiful caramel skin. She was an only child. She had a close loving bond with her mother, who loved to bake apple pies and sew handmade quilts. Her mother sold them to neighbors and friends for extra money. They both lived in a beautiful humble home on a farm left to them by Dora's father who disappeared when she was only four years old.

Dora didn't remember much about her father except that he was always working in the fields. He was a strong dark skin man and he was proud. Dora would watch him tend to the animals while she played by herself on the porch. The smell of apple pies being baked by her mother always made her anticipate eating dinner just so she could eat desert afterwards. Just before sun down, her father would walk up the steps and Dora would have a cool glass of water given to her by her mother to greet her father Stanley after a long hot day of work. At night, Dora could hear her parents screaming at each other and often cried herself to sleep. One day he was gone and never returned.

Her mother didn't seem upset about it and didn't give Dora any details of his disappearance other than that they were better off without him and that she would do her best to maintain the property and provide for the both of them. Dora's mom would later have random strange men in and out of the house late nights attempting to hide her visits from Dora. Dora would hear them because she stayed up late looking out her window, over the water well, where the Black Eyed Susan's grew wildly wondering if her father would return. The brilliant gold colors of the Black Eyed Susan's made Dora particularly partial to them, although other wild flowers grew just beyond the well in the field just before the tree line.

Dora had a close bond with her mother but after the random men were visiting late nights and her mother became more and more angry and stressed out because she was having a hard time paying the bills and keeping the property and animals tended to, Dora felt alone and depressed. Her mother often allowed her to stay the weekend at a friend's house where there was a little girl the same age as Dora who had grown to be fourteen years old. It was her time there that changed her life forever.

Fourteen year old Dora and her friend Jessica wanted to play with Jessica's older sister and her friends but they were not allowed to participate in their adventures in the woods at night. Kelly was a redhead with freckles. Her fair skin, beautiful smile and dazzling eyes made her a favorite with the teenaged boys and older men. Jessica enjoyed the attention and often teased them by wearing revealing tops and tight blue jean shorts that revealed the cuffs of her behind. Kelly and her friends liked to play softball every day, in the fields and she had developed great muscle tone and her breast was fuller than most teens her age. At night they spent time in the old barn in the woods which they called the lovers lounge. There, they would build barn fires, tell stories and participate in activities that Kelly's little sister Jessica and Dora could not attend no matter how much they begged.

It was always a treat for Dora and Jessica to sneak out to the lounge at night, peep through the holes and laugh at the older teens and the funny sounds they made. Dora and Jessica would giggle and imitate the noises and run back to the house to play their own games while talking about what they had seen the older teens do in the night. One night one of the older teenage boys who would always tend to the fire while the couples would go inside the lounge, noticed Jessica and Dora sneaking up to the barn. Todd was a strange teen and kept to himself most of the time. He was not popular with the girls and he was always being teased and pushed around by the other teenage boys who enjoyed making out with the girls late at night. Todd, although offended by being pushed around and being the butt of the jokes, wanted to be accepted and endured cruel treatment as long as he would not be alone. He would keep the fires going and anticipate anything they would involve him in even if it was demeaning to him.

Todd didn't say anything to girls to let them know he saw them. Instead, he hid himself and watched them. It was his first time seeing Dora and he was curious about who she was. He admired her kinky, curly hair and caramel skin. He stood there watching her in a way that no eighteen year old should look at a girl fourteen years of age. After about twenty minutes or so, little Dora and Jessica had enough laughs at the older teens making out in the barn and started walking back home. Dora's mother would be picking her up early Sunday morning, so they went back to pack her things for the night and get some sleep after some girl talk.

Todd silently followed them as far as he could without being noticed. Todd hid himself behind a tree as the girls exited the woods headed towards Jessica's mother's home. Todd hurried back to Lover's lounge to attend to the fire. Just as he was getting there, one of the boys he admired rudely asked him, where he was and scolded him for not being there to be the lookout. Jessica's older sister Kelly tried to stop the young muscular teen from bothering Todd. Todd, with fear and frustration in his eyes, said "Why do I always have to be the look out anyway?" Because no one wants to make out with your big head ass," the teen said and pushed Todd down. "Stop it," Kelly yelled. Todd got up and spit at the teen and quickly ran away. The teen attempted to run after him but Kelly grabbed his arm and said no. The other teens came out of the lounge adjusting their clothes and asked "What was going on." The angry teen bit his lip, frowned and said "Nothing, Todd-doe the creep-poe ran home to beat his meat. All the other teens giggled but Kelly looked at him with disappointment and announced her decision to go home and call it a night.

When Todd made it to his home, he went upstairs to his room and punched a hole in the wall. Todd felt humiliated being pushed down in front of Kelly. His anger consumed him and after punching a hole in the wall, the thought of little Dora brought him comfort so he calmed himself and fell asleep thinking of her. Dora was picked up by her mother the next morning. Dora and Jessica said their goodbyes, hugged each other and pinky promised to see each other the following weekend. Dora got in the car and anticipated her return.

The following weekend, as pinky promised, little Dora arrived at her friend Jessica's home again. They were excited about keeping secrets and spying on the older teens at Lover's Lounge again. Just before dark Saturday evening, Dora and Jessica started their way through the woods. Halfway through, Jessica had a bright idea. "I should've brought some sandwiches," Jessica said. "Wait here until I get back and we'll have something to snack on our way back." Dora waited patiently when she was surprised by Kelly, who quietly slipped up behind her in the woods. "Boo," Kelly yelled as she grabbed Dora by her shoulders.

Dora screamed in fear and started laughing with Kelly after recognizing her. "You scared me," little Dora said. Kelly apologized and asked why she was there in the woods alone. "Where is Jessica," Kelly asked. Dora told Kelly that Jessica went to get sandwiches so that they could have a pic-nic in the woods. 'Cool," Kelly said. "You guys shouldn't be out here alone." "I was going to the house to get more blankets," Kelly explained. "Come with me and you and Jessica can sit by the barn fire with us tonight." Dora didn't expect the invitation and knew Jessica would be just as excited as she felt knowing that tonight, they would finally get a chance to hang with the older teens.

After Jessica made the snacks, and was walking out the door with the sandwiches, she was surprised to see her older sister Kelly with Dora. Kelly greeted her little sister and insisted that the both of them join her at Lover's Lounge. Kelly ran inside and got more blankets. Jessica and Dora had smiles on their faces and joy in their hearts. After Kelly got her things, Dora and Jessica eagerly followed her to join the gang. They reached their destination just as it was getting dark. The barn fire was flickering and all the teens were nice to them as they all gathered and sat around the fire. Jessica and Dora held hands in excitement next to Kelly. The older boys were putting hotdogs and marshmallows over the fire.

Kelly asked her little sister to tell everyone the joke she shared with her the night before at their home. Jessica jumped to her feet in anticipation. "Ok", she said. Dora looked up at her smiling and paying close attention to her friend. They often shared jokes with each other and she wondered if this was a new one or one she had heard before. Jessica wanted to impress the older teens, so she did not tell the joke she had shared with her sister Kelly. Instead, she told the most mature joke she had heard recently. "An elephant and a mouse were walking through the jungle." "The elephant suddenly fell down a deep hole." "The elephant cried out for the mouse to help him." Jessica, smiled and continued. "The mouse, feeling helpless, ran away from the jungle and got in his Mercedes Benz." "Mercedes Benz," one of the older boys mockingly asked. "Un huh, Mercedes Benz," Jessica assured him.

Jessica continued. "The mouse jumped into his Mercedes Benz and hurried to the sore and bought a long rope, threw it in the trunk and rushed back to the jungle to help his elephant friend out of the deep hole." "The mouse tied the rope to the back of the Mercedes Benz and dropped the other end of the rope down the hole." "Hold on to the rope, the mouse shouted and pulled the elephant out of the hole." "They became even closer friends after that and would do anything for each other." The older teens were now listening to Jessica closely and she felt important. Smiling, Jessica continued telling the rest of the joke while the warm fire flickered in the calm night.

"The next week, the elephant and the mouse walked through the jungle again enjoying their day, when suddenly, the mouse fell down a deep, deep hole. "Help, help, the mouse cried out to the elephant." "The elephant threw down his thang down the deep hole." His thang?" Kelly asked, amusingly surprised by the joke her younger sister was telling. "Jessica smiled more intensely again and continued the joke. "Yep, that's right, his thang, Jessica assured her sister. "The elephant threw down his thang and told the mouse to climb on and pulled the mouse out of the deep, deep hole." Jessica ended her joke with, "The moral of the story is, if you have a big thang, you don't need no damn Mercedes Benz." They all laughed and Kelly playfully slapped Jessica on her leg to sit down. "Where'd you hear that joke?" Kelly asked her while still laughing and once again impressed by her sister's joke for tonight. Jessica told her that she heard a comedian tell that joke. Jessica and Dora smiled and hugged each other.

Enjoying the warmth from the flames in the night, the handsome muscular teen asked everyone if they knew about the curse of Mary. Whose Mary, they asked. With no emotion, the young man explained that Mary was raped by her father, who was a priest, long ago. Mary once lived somewhere in these woods to get away from her father." "Mary gave birth to a baby boy and buried him out of shame." The young man continued to tell Mary's story. He could tell that the girls were getting uncomfortable but paying close attention. He continued. "It was told that Mary's father found out where she lived and where she buried the child." "Her father was angry and told Mary that she had murdered a child of God and that she would be punished.

"It is said that Mary fought with her father after being attacked and killed him as well. She burned his cross and threw it in his grave." The young man added and told them what happened to Mary. He could see that the girls were even more uncomfortable and frightened. "They say that Mary was haunted by the priest and one night in the woods where she lived and buried the bodies, the child came back deformed and took revenge on Mary for murdering his father and burning the cross." "Stop it, another teenage girl said sitting next to Kelly." "That isn't true, asshole, don't you see that you're scaring the girls," she said, referring to Jessica and Dora. Dora didn't say anything although she wanted to go home. Dora was afraid that the story was true and she didn't want to be in the woods anymore. "I'm not trying to scare anyone," the young man said. "I'm just telling you what I heard." "They say it's true and that each year, when he is summoned, Mary's son comes back to claim those who have lost their faith and sin against the righteous." Dora became even more afraid because she knew she had lost her faith when her father abandoned her and her mother. Her family was never the same after that and Dora wondered why God would allow that to happen. Dora and her mother stopped attending church each Sunday morning and kept to themselves.

"Are you guys ok," Kelly asked her sister and Dora. "Yes, were ok," they both said, to save face, knowing that they didn't expect to hear about curses, murder and revenge tonight. The young man told the rest of the story while they sat around the flickering flames. The shadows from the flames gave Dora an even worse feeling about being in the woods. "They say that if you recite the tale on any given night, he will come to claim his revenge," the handsome teenager said with a stern look on his face. The dark shadows from the flames danced across his face as he began to recite. "Mary, Mary, dark and scary, was frightened and deranged." "She lost her faith, burned the cross and cursed her father's name." "She fell asleep, as she wept and darkness came to claim." "Without a doubt, she pushed it out and threw her child away." The young man paused and stood up. All of the other teenage boys stood up as well and set wooden crosses on fire as if they had rehearsed this routine before. They continued as Dora watched, feeling uncomfortable and afraid. "Burn a cross, hold it high and call Mary's name." "Her son will come and you can run, but you will surely die the same!" The boys all yelled.

Suddenly, Todd jumped out from the dark woods, disguised as the devil and all the girls screamed. The girls all ran in different directions as Todd ran after them. The older teenage girls eventually laughed in relief, after recognizing Todd's voice and cursed at him. Todd continued to chase after those who didn't run into the dark wooded area. Kelly screamed out. "You asshole!" Kelly looked for her little sister and Dora. "Jessica!" Kelly yelled. "Dora!" She yelled. Kelly then heard a familiar scream. "Jessica!" Kelly ran towards the distant sound of her little sister screaming in the woods. Everyone near the fire ran with Kelly to help find the little ones.

They searched for the girls for what seemed like hours, yet, it had only been about 20 minutes. Kelly was growing more and more frantic and extremely upset with her friends for scaring the girls. Kelly tripped over a branch and fell. Her boyfriend tried to help her up and held out his hand to assist Kelly in getting up. "Get the fuck away from me!" Kelly smacked his hand away from her. "Why the fuck did y'all do that!" Kelly yelled, as tears began to form in the corners of her eyes. "We didn't know they were gonna be here." "I'm sorry." The young man pleaded with Kelly. "Maybe they ran home." He added. He tried to help Kelly knock off the dirt and dried leaves from her body as she got up from the ground. "You better hope and pray they're at home, you stupid mother fucker!" Kelly said, gathering her composure and hoping that he was right. They all started making their way towards Kelly and Jessica's home with flash lights.

They hadn't walked but about 50 feet before they noticed Jessica lying next to a pile of broken tree trunks. "Jessica!" Kelly yelled, as they all ran to see if she was ok.

Kelly reached her sister first and picked her up. "Jessy, are you ok?" Jessica woke up holding her head in pain. They noticed blood coming from the back of her head. Jessica had tripped and fallen on a near-by rock that injured her head. Apparently, she was knocked out from the blow and didn't remember what happened to Dora. "I'm ok, where is Dora?" Jessica asked.

"We were hoping she was with you." What happened?" We were running." "I fell." "I don't know where she is." Jessica said in a soft and confused voice as her sister was checking the back of her head. The young men suggested that the girls get Jessica home and that they would continue looking for Dora. Kelly's boyfriend asked her to let him know if Dora was at the house and she agreed as the girls helped Jessica to her feet. "Maybe Todd has seen her." He and the rest of the boys rushed anxiously in the other direction, towards Lover's Lane.

Helping Jessica home, the girls began to see police lights as they were reaching the edge of the woods. Several flash lights were coming towards them and they could hear Kelly and Jessica's mother screaming out to them. Several officers surrounded them before Jessica's mom could get there. One of the officers noticed Jessica was in need of assistance and carried her to the home. The others walked with the girls and asked questions about what had happened in the woods. Jessica and Kelly's mom was terrified and worried that Jessica had been sexually assaulted because Dora had made it to the home but was in shock and fearful that someone was going to get her again. "What's going on?" Kelly cried.

Officers informed the girls that Dora said that the devil raped her in the woods. They were not able to get much more than that from her because she was so afraid that she could hardly speak. Jessica's mom hugged her and Kelly with tears in her eyes. "What happened to Dora?" She asked. "Are you ok?" "Kelly, what happened?" Officers assisted all of them to the house and informed Dora's mother that the ambulance had taken Dora to the hospital. The other officers went to the home of the teenage boys after finding out their names from Kelly and the other girls. Unaware that the police were on their way to their homes. The boys found Todd sitting in the corner of his room. Still half dressed in the devil costume he had made himself, Todd was covered in dirt and sweat.

"Todd, have you seen Dora?" They asked. "She wouldn't stop screaming." He said in a frightened voice. "She just kept on screaming and screaming!" Todd said while banging both sides of his own head. "Todd, where the fuck is Dora!" One of the boys asked. At that moment, they heard the police coming up the stairs. The police rushed in the room and knew immediately which one of the boys Dora was referring to. Dressed in a dingy looking self-made likeness of some sort of devil, they knew Todd was a key player in whatever happened to Dora. They arrested all of the boys and took them down to the station for questioning.

As they were loading Todd in the back of a squad car, a strange teenage boy was hiding near-by watching. He was not one of the boys in the woods but He and Todd knew each other. The strange young teen looked worried about Todd. No one saw him but Todd as the squad car drove away with him hand-cuffed in the back seat. Todd and the strange teen locked eyes at each other until Todd couldn't turn his neck any further. "Bobby." Todd mumbled to himself when he couldn't see the strange boy anymore.

It was never clear exactly what happened that night between Todd and Dora. Todd hung himself later that night while in custody and friends and family of Kelly's' never saw or heard from Dora anymore. Dora's life forever changed and she was never the same again. She became mentally unstable and moved away as an adult to start a new life. Remembering the events of the devil raped her, Dora chanted to herself. "Mary, Mary, as she ran away from the protestors and the explosion of Chief Bond's bar and grill. It was a disturbing sight to see. There was tension in the air and the night exploded into pandemonium.

CHAPTER EIGHT

AWAKENING

Arriving in D.C, Janet and I were not aware of the events unfolding in Memphis. Janet quickly unpacked her juicer and made another fresh vegetable and fruit juice drink and immediately prepared to meet up with the attorney at an old asylum that the mentally disabled once resided in. The attorney wanted to meet at the now worn down site that was barely standing but still had evidence of the filth and negligence by the staff and the providers there. The attorney wanted Janet to see it because he himself had personally witnessed as a child, his uncle being kept in such an inhuman place. After his family took their relative, out of the facility, it was then he decided that he wanted to become an attorney in order to prosecute anyone who harmed or mistreated others.

They both entered the old abandoned building as they discussed Janet's concerns about the safety and cruel treatment of her clients. It was light outside yet inside of the building felt dark, gloomy and gray. Dead leaves and tree branches covered the floor. As they walked, the leaves crackled and blew around at their feet with a ghostly breeze. Mold was on the walls and windows were broken out. The ceilings were water stained and the hallways were long and dark. There were old pictures of ghostly looking nurses, doctors and staff still hanging on the walls. There were no smiles on the faces of the client's, just faces of pain, suffering and despair as the people supposedly taking care of them looked upon them as if they had no compassion for their misery.

The grass was growing up through the cracks of tiles and dead birds and rats didn't bother Janet as much as seeing the bathrooms with feces on the walls. Dried blood and dirty stained sheets were in the bedrooms. Iron doors to each room had scratches and dents, clearly from a tortured soul inside trying to get out from behind the locked doors. There was only a small, wire caged window in the door and no way to see the sun in each room.

They came across a room in the basement where there was still evidence of electric shock equipment that was used on the mentally disabled. It was a brutal way of trying to manipulate the brain. Janet thought to herself. Electric shock therapy was more like torture and cruel punishment instead of treatment. The smell was unbearable, yet Janet and the attorney endured it in order to respect those who had no choice but to be confined to this haunted, miserable dark place. If they felt this miserable and disgusted in the short of their visit, it must have been a horrible nightmare for human beings to be left behind, mistreated and imprisoned in such a cruel place.

The attorney told Janet what we already knew. It was inhumane and unlawful for Mr. Anderson to try to stop her clients from living in any community of their choice or their caregiver's choice. Janet also knew there wasn't much she could do about a peaceful protest but she could definitely stop the endangerment of her clients due to unruly protestors. He further confirmed that he has no right to stop the mentally disabled from living in any community. Either way, Janet was excited about returning and putting a halt to it once and for all but for the moment, she and the attorney stood there awhile silently gathering their emotions. It was time to leave and fight for rights, an option the client's abused and beaten there never had. Janet knew how I felt when I spoke about how awful I felt seeing people of color affected by crime and drugs and how unfair the media and the news betrayed them. As she was leaving the building, she wondered to herself how she could help people of color create opportunities for themselves and be protected from unethical treatment the way the mentally disabled and homosexuals are now being protected and given the rights that they have been denied for so long.

    Janet returned to the hotel before I arrived, made another vegetable and fruit juice, and started to make plans for celebration at a nearby nightclub she knew well. Janet knew D.C. well because she visited a few of her relatives there regularly. I was standing in front of the Martin Luther King Jr. Monument until just before dark. I decided to walk to the site after getting off the trolley. With each step closer my visions of all the media clips I had seen of Martin Luther King Jr. being assassinated made me feel more and more ashamed to reside in Memphis. I thought of all the marches, speeches, sacrifices he made for justice. I thought about all the pain and suffering they went through and what his family must have had to endure. I saw each clip I'd ever seen on T.V of the violence & resistance he and his followers suffered at the hands of police, politicians, dogs and racists people during that time.

With each step closer my feet felt heavier and heavier. My shoulders hung low and my heart could not take the fact that he would possibly be ashamed of our complacent attitude and inability to continue to stand together and further grow, fight for and accomplish his dream.

I considered not going to see it and turn around but just as I was feeling unworthy, I could see it from a distance. I could tell it was huge. People were everywhere of all different races and nationality, just like on the trolley. People from New York, Virginia, Pittsburgh, and tourists from all over the world. Just as I reached the entrance there was a huge granite wall leading up to the statue. The wall had different powerful quotes taken from various speeches throughout his time in his fight for justice.

I could see the statue and could tell it was about thirty feet tall. I was amazed and I anticipated standing in front of it, but I could not ignore this beautiful wall and I just had to read each and every one of them on my way to the statue. With each scripture, I became more and more proud. My feet were not heavy anymore and they moved swiftly in anticipation of the next quote. My shoulders began to stand up straight and not slouch. My vision became ones that were not of shame but of a glorious reminder of those before me and the work to be done. With each different race I saw admiring the same sacrifices and accomplishments of Martin Luther King Jr. I was once again refreshed and aware that humanity was not lost.

Just as refreshed I was to meet my son's white friends and their non-judgmental, young inspiring and hopeful minds, here at the monument I was reminded that adults too, were still just as hopeful and justice for all was not just a dream, it can still be a reality. The President was black and I was once again proud. Whatever happens with this

Presidential election, I was reassured that those same rational, non-judgmental minds of all races that voted for President Obama did not hide under a rock and were still ready to preserve and speak out against injustice.

The negative media coverage of the KKK, fights between blacks and whites at campaign rallies, police brutality acquittals, talks of building a wall, groping crotches, email security risks, black, blue and all lives matter, all seemed to become small hurdles to jump in the mind of a refreshed giant. I understood that it didn't matter if you voted republican or democratic. Whatever the choice may be, it didn't mean you were racists like the popular talk suggested or the craftiest headline story implied. I didn't feel alone anymore.

I felt empowered. I wasn't worried about the negative images that portrayed young black men and women as criminals and thugs anymore. I was ready to lead with my blackness not my fear of what false image some people may have about it. I understood that it was my identity first, and my own unique representation of intelligence, creativity, power, and dedication to myself, my family and non-bias service treatment of others who may or may not look like me or share my opinions.

Walking tall and proud, I wanted others to see my blackness first and respect the character that came along with it. People look for evidence to confirm their negative images or suspicions about a person's character and now I understood, that we all are guilty of some form of biased behavior and I would no longer allow it to restrain my mind in the tiny dark boxes of judgmental society.

Finally I reached the statue and was in absolute awe of its likeness of the King and was stunned by the brilliant detail and realness in the statues eyes that seemed to look over and conquer any frivolous or serious issue in the world. I thought to myself, that if this man could go through all of the madness in his time and era, and still push through, then surely I could stop being haunted by my past and struggles of people of color today. Giving up is not an option and I most definitely must seek, find and execute a plan of action in order to do my part in making the world we live in today a better place for us all.

I noticed that it was starting to get dark. I didn't want to leave but I was rejuvenated and practically skipped back to the trolley, never stepping on the crack that breaks momma back with ease. I had a new unselfish attitude and thirst for life. I got back to the hotel and stopped by Janet's room to hear about her visit with the attorney and tell her how much the time alone at the monument helped me. I knocked at the door but there was no answer.

I could hear music and Billie Holiday was playing softly. I checked the handle on the door and it was unlocked so I knew Janet was in her room. I walked slowly in announcing myself. "Hello, Janet, it's me," The light in the room was dim and I could see that Janet had glowing diffusers giving off relaxing aroma's. Janet often relaxed with essential oils burning and listening to Billie Holiday was one of her favorite ways of centering her emotions. "Hello, Janet," I said once more while walking through the dim living room area of her suite.

Maybe she's in the shower, I thought to myself, because I could see that the bedroom door was slightly open, although the room was dim. "Janet," I called out again while approaching the bedroom door. I pushed the door open a little wider. I walked in cautiously and to my surprise, I saw Janet making out with another woman. Shocked by Janet's sounds of enjoyment, I was even more shocked when I recognized the other woman to be the beautiful airline stewardess from the flight. I tried to back out slowly but knocked over the other glowing diffuser in the bedroom.

They both jumped up and grabbed the sheets to cover their breast. They still had their panties on both I could tell that Janet was more bothered by the interruption than the airline stewardess. "Hi, gorgeous," the stewardess said after recognizing my face. "I apologized and exited the room after fumbling with trying to pick up the diffuser and getting out of the room as fast as I could. I managed to get out of Janet's suite completely before she caught up with me in the hallway. She didn't seem ashamed that I had discovered her naked and now knew her secret. Instead, she had a kind of proud blushing smile on her face. "Whew, these smoothies are starting to get to me," she said, trying to break the ice and figure out my feelings about seeing them in bed together. With the straw between her teeth, she smiled and apologized. I chuckled and said "No problem, I shouldn't have walked in," as I reached in my pocket for the key to my room.

Her expression changed and Janet said, "No wait, I should have told you." "I was only waiting for the right time," Janet said, looking directly into my eyes with a look of fear of my disapproval. "No, no, no," I reassured her. "It's ok, I'm the one that should be apologizing." "I shouldn't have walked in like that."

Janet explained that she was going to tell me later on at the nightclub. "I was going to invite you to celebrate with us tonight and tell you then," Janet explained. Janet was standing there in her robe and my suite was right across the hallway of her room. She grabbed my hand and said "Get dressed, come with us to the club, we won't be there long and on the way there I'll catch you up on the info I got today, ok?" 'I'm going to text you the address to the club, meet us around a hour or so."

It was about 7 pm and I was still pumped from my experience at the monument, so I agreed. "Hey, I'm happy for you, ya know?" I reassured Janet. Janet was still holding my hand, thanked me and kissed me on the cheek. "Get dressed, Janet said and turned away to enter her room. I smiled and started to turn away myself. Suddenly I blurted out, "Hey, how long?" "Janet replied, "How long, me and Adore or how long I've known?" "Both I guess," was my inquisitive reply. "We've been together for eight years, friends since I was twelve and I've always known." She smiled again. "Get dressed," Janet said, raising her voice. Janet walked into her room and closed the door.

I was fumbling with the hotel key to my room when someone opened it from the inside. The door swung open and I looked up to see Lisa standing there with a smile on her face. "Well hello, handsome," Lisa said. "Forgive me for the intrusion." I wanted to surprise you, so I told the lady at the front desk I was your wife and forgot my key," Lisa added. "She was only trying to be helpful so don't be upset with her ok?" I smiled and gave Lisa a big hug. "No, no, porky, I'm happy to see you." "How have you been?" We called Lisa Porky when she was a little girl and lived in the projects. Not because she was fat, but because she loved to eat.

"Homie told me you were in D.C. on business and I thought maybe we could take a flight back to Tennessee together." "Sure, no problem," I said. "I'm with my boss, Janet and I would love for you to meet her." We're meeting up later at some secret spot, she knows about here in D.C., but she hasn't given me any details yet." "Would you like to come with us?" I asked Lisa, trying not to notice how fine she was looking from being physically fit and trained in the Airforce. Lisa had taken full advantage of being in an old friend's hotel room and had helped herself to a shower and gotten comfortable in her sports bra and gym shorts that rested low on her hips and hung low, just past her knees. Her hair was still wet and she was drying her long spiral curls with a towel as she moved around the room and talked to me. She rested herself on the couch. I wanted to take a shower as well while she waited and helped herself to a glass of wine.

I excused myself from the living room area of the suite Lisa was sitting in. "I'm gonna get ready for tonight, would you like something to snack on?" I can order up something before we leave." "No," Lisa said, "I'm good, go ahead, you look tired." 'A hot shower can do wonders, I'll just relax a bit and get ready to go when you get dressed." "Cool," I replied, and gathered my things and rapidly walked to the bathroom in the other room. I closed the door behind me with relief from Lisa's attractive appearance. She was looking absolutely amazing and it felt good to see her again. I took a deep breath and looked in the mirror. As soon as I looked into my reflection, a flash of light and the sound of a 45 automatic exploded in my mind. It startled me and once again, experiences from my past haunted me.

I tried desperately to wipe the vision away. I lifted my head as I was holding on to the sink and shook my head. Lisa was here and I had to get it together. I jumped in the shower. As I was getting out, I could hear Lisa playing music. I dried off and put my shirt and dress pants on. Lisa didn't hear me coming out of the shower and I smiled as I watched her dancing to an old school song by War, "The World Is a Ghetto." 'I see ya," still got the moves huh?" Lisa laughed when she heard me and said "Never that, you're the one with two left feet." She continued dancing towards me playfully and begged me to join. "Come on, come on," she said with a smile on her face. I stood there and kept my cool but my body wanted to show off some moves for her.

I just bounced my head slowly and watched her move seductively as she got closer. When she was close enough, she hugged me and said it's good to see you again." She felt good close to me, and she smelled amazing. "Good to see you too," I said as I was fighting every urge to kiss her. We danced to the music holding each other for a moment and she could tell something was weighing heavily on my mind. Never missing a beat, she rubbed her fingers through my dreads and rested her face on my chest. Her hair was still damp and smelled deliciously shampooed and conditioned. We released each other as the music ended and looked into each other's eyes for a moment, happy to be in each other's company again after so long. She knew me well and asked what was wrong.

I held her hand and we walked to the couch. We both sat next to each other. Before I could speak, she patted the edge of the couch between her legs and said, "Come over here, sit down." She wanted me to sit on the floor and in my mind she was going to braid my dreads or grease my scalp the way she used to long ago. Lisa had a good playlist going and the mood was a relaxing one between old friends. Both feeling tingly inside but dare to make the first move. I sat on the floor between her legs and she took off my shirt and pulled back my dreads in a ponytail. She took a sip of wine and handed me her glass so that I could have some too. Music playing softly, she asked me to relax and I willingly melted at her request. Finally, for the second time today, I could breathe easily. I exhaled and let go of my fears. "I can't get it out of my head," I said. "I know, it's hard for me too." "There was nothing we could do, love." "It wasn't your fault." I told her about Janet's father sending his well-dressed thugs to threaten me about what they knew.

She didn't get upset at all and calmed me with her words. "I wouldn't worry about it," It was not your fault," she said as she slowly cut my dreads. The music, her voice, and the mood prevented me from being startled. Without a word, I relaxed more into her as she cut more off one by one. Each cut seemed to release the pain. Each cut with slow and easy music allowed me to exhale with ease more and more. I was her humble servant and she could do as she pleased. I'm not sure why she had scissors available and I didn't care. As she was approaching the last few dreads to cut off, my soul felt like the weight of a thousand woes were lifted off of me. Damn near brought tears to my eyes, but I was too cool to allow her to see that. She was cutting my dreads off, as if to prepare me for a new chapter in my life. To assimilate me into the corporate world, yet hold on to what my dreads represented in my soul. It was as if Lisa knew, like my mother did, when I was a child. I would be facing adversity again. My dreads were a spiritual journey. They represented my strength and culture. Now I had to use what I had learned to further my quest in helping others. Not just for the mentally disabled and minorities, but also strive to obtain justice and equality for all.

At that moment, another beautiful song connected our minds, body and soul together. Now, "Ghetto Love" by Jaheim was playing. "Now, there's the man I know. " Lisa said softly as I stood up to face her. "How does it feel," she asked. I replied, "You have no idea how wonderful it feels." She smiled. "Now let me line you up my guy," she said as she stood up, pushed me down on the couch and kneeled in front of me. She turned on her yoni clippers to complete the new me. I grabbed her wrist, 'Wait, are those clean," I said jokingly. "Boy, don't play, it's squeaky clean." "I just used them in the shower so it's a little wet though," she said, raising her eyebrows in a flirtatious way. "You better be glad I'm blessing your head with them." "Not many get the satisfaction," she said smiling, as she started my line up. Before she lined me up, Lisa danced around singing the Charmin commercial song. "Yep, I'm chamin clean, cause my hiney is clean." I laughed. "Girl, you so silly." I said, shaking my head and amused, that she was still the same, as she was, as a kid.

I bowed my head and let her work. Our eyes met as Jaheim was setting the mood. Suddenly, we kissed passionately and everything we felt long ago came out. She climbed on top of me sitting in my lap. We kissed and fondled each other vigorously, and then it was over. We both realized we had crossed the line. She leaned her head into my shoulder and we both gathered ourselves. Still straddling my lap, we embraced each other for a moment resisting feelings from long ago. "You're a good man," Lisa said softly and asked if Lieko and I would be getting back together."

"I honestly don't know," I replied. "There's a lot to be worked out." "I miss all of us together as a family but she's such a damn fighter and can't be compromised with." I have to hear her argue and debate with someone about Donald Trump every damn day and how Kylin's life is in danger more than before since racist are getting more bold.' "Especially if he's elected. "Sounds like she is awake." "I completely understand her concerns," Lisa said. "Yeah, me too, but she's completely obsessed with the issue." "She's deleted all of her white friends on Facebook who supported Trump, some of them have been good friends with her forever." "Kylin can't hang with his white friends at school without a lecture and we are not having a normal sex life. "Doing things as a family is nonexistent because she's so upset and she consistently looks for a fight." "You guys have a beautiful family and the both of you want the best for them." Lisa said, removing herself from on top of me.

"So, has there been anyone else in your life." Lisa asked, reluctantly. I could tell that she was a little disappointed, that I hadn't reached out to her sooner. I replied, "Hell no!" "Women these days don't want to be women anymore." "I refuse to be a coward like my father." I added. What do you mean, women, don't want to be women anymore?" Lisa asked. "Don't get me wrong." I explained. "There is nothing I like more than a beautiful, independent, woman of color." "But these days, women get independence confused with being controlling and disrespectful to their man." "I love my kids, and no woman, is ever going to tell me, that I can't have anything to do with my kids, because they think I may still be having sex with the mother." "I will never let any child of mine feel unwanted, regardless of what a woman thinks about it."

"Well, it's not just the women." "Men, don't want to be men, as well." Lisa, replied. "Sounds like you've had a bad experience with the wrong kind of woman, but there are good women out there." Lisa, added. "Yeah, I know, but the ones I know, want to tell me that my kids are grown, and that I should just move on if I'm in a bad relationship." I explained further. "I understand fully, what they are trying to say, but, If, I'm going to move on, the woman I chose to be with, must understand that my kids will forever be my kids, regardless of how old they are." "I need a healthy relationship with them, in my life." "I would treat her kids as if they were my own, and I expect the same in return." "If I can't co-parent with my kids mother, then so be it, but my home is always open to my kids, regardless if I'm with another woman or not." "She has to be willing to love my kids because family is important to me and I want them to be happy for me and respect whomever she may be."

I continued with my rant. "Mom, always kept the house clean and food on the table, even though she worked her ass off for us." "You knew my mom, Lisa, and she always said that even though she was an advocate for women's rights, she still wanted to be treated like a lady and carried herself like a queen." "These days you see women posting selfies of themselves with make up on and beautiful hair, but in the background the bathroom and bedroom is a mess." "Mom, didn't play about her house being messed up." "It was always clean," I added.

"Yeah, it was," Lisa said. "I miss her." "Why she loved your father, I have no clue, but why, she never dated anyone after that, was sad to me." "She was a beautiful, kind, hard working woman." "I don't know either Lisa," but I had to let my feelings about that go, a long time ago." "I honestly wanted to hurt that man." "I was having some real, evil thoughts about doing something to him Lisa." "But my kids are my world and I couldn't allow myself to ruin my life over his bullshit."

"Long story, short, Lisa, if a woman, isn't about family, mine and hers, I can't deal with her." "I understand Greg, you're a rare, and good man." "I just want you to be happy." Lisa, said. "You gotta get yourself together, Greg and don't let your relationship with Lieko, destroy you." "Talk to her." "If the both of you can't come to some common ground, then move on Greg." "I know how much you love your kids, and I feel that they know your character and will still come around and love you." "You've been an awesome father." I shook my head and said, "Sometimes, I don't know Lisa." I've made mistakes and I regret them." Lisa, replied. "We all do Greg." "As parents, we make mistakes, that's just life."

"But, I personally know that you have been amazing as a father, and your kids know it too." "Don't be so hard on yourself and sacrifice your happiness, because you're afraid that your kids will see you like your father." "You are nothing, like him." "If you still love Lieko, talk to her." "If she can't get her shit together, and you as well, then maybe leaving is best." " I'm sure you have your faults too, but it is good women out there that would love to have you." "Not every woman is nasty and controlling." Lisa explained. "Besides, you can get your ass in there and cook and clean too!" Lisa said jokingly. "You know my momma and yours too, had us in the kitchen busting dem suds every day." I chuckled, remembering the days we damn near had to make sure the entire house was clean before we could go outside or have company on the weekends. During the week we had daily chores to do after homework and before going to bed. "I don't mind helping Lisa, you know that." "But I'm not gonna be the man and the woman in the house, hell it's about compromise and principalities in this shit, ya hear me!" We both laughed. I sighed at the thought of losing my family and opening up to someone else.

"I don't know Lisa." Lisa stopped me and asked, "Do you still believe in love?" I sighed. "I'm not sure anymore Lisa, do you?" Lisa smiled. "Of course I do, but you have to understand it can easily get obscured by difficult situations." "What do you mean, I asked. Lisa explained. "Greg, to me love is kind of like our justice system here in America." "There are federal laws to protect the people and state laws to protect its citizens." "Agreeably one of the most perfectly designed justice systems in the world, right?" "Maybe, I said, curious about the direction she was going with this analogy. Lisa further gave her theory. "Of course we know too well how minorities and people without enough resources end up with the short end of the stick when it comes to justice." "Love is like the justice system that's designed to work beautifully for us all." "But both are only as good as the people controlling it you know." I chuckled. "So you're saying ain't no romance without finance?" Lisa smiled and replied, "Damn right." She giggled. "No, seriously Greg, they're both a reflection of us, so maybe you and Lieko should communicate about the real issues." "Love is not the problem."

"Should it matter that you have different approaches to family matters and political issues?" Lisa, added. "At the end of the day, family is what's important." "The both of you are on the same team, don't let differences take the goal away," Lisa caringly advised.

"You're right Lisa," I said, "I only wish it was that simple, you have no idea what I deal with." I must admit that It was stupid of me, thinking that if Kylin, kept his respectful way of talking with people and remained calm, he would be ok if he was stopped by the police, but after that guy got killed cooperating with police, I misjudged the fairness in this world. "I'm afraid for his life too. "That's something white people have no idea about." "I wish there was something I could do and make a difference in this world." "There is always somebody getting killed or put in jail every day." I've gotten to the point where I can't watch or hear the news because it's always our black asses dying out here." Lisa looked at me and said, "Baby there is something you can do." "What ever happened to your dream?" "Remember when we were younger, you always talked about opening up your own community center so that people like us could have somewhere to go, have fun and learn skills during the summer?" Lisa added, "I don't think anyone can fix all the problems in the world over night, but what we can do is our small, little part each day."

"I don't know Lisa." I said confused and feeling helpless. Minimum wages, keeps people in poverty." "That poverty keeps them in low-income communities." "Those communities are environments mixed with hard working decent people that eventually are affected by crime and drugs out of despair of the struggle of getting out of the trap of America's crimes against those before them and the continuous crimes of ignoring and denying the pain of it all." Lisa held my hand with understanding as we both silently remembered that deadly night. Without saying anything to each other for a brief moment, we both knew what each other was thinking about.

"Man, it is crazy Lisa." I added, breaking the silence. "Being black in America means living without our own resources and culture, yet, denied the privilege of fighting for justice without being murdered, killed or criminalized. "Look how they treated Kap." I added. "The boy kneeled to make a moral stand against injustice and police brutality in America, and they made it out to be a stand against the flag and veterans." "Shit, the way they ignore what's really going on is insane. Let's not even talk about what the fuck happened to Martin Luther King and Malcom X, fighting for equal rights." "I just don't know Lisa." I added. "I think it's time we stop asking America, especially white America for anything and take control over our own money, and invest with our own people.

'Amen," Lisa said smiling. When you're ready, count me in babe." "You just start with your family first and then work on saving your community." Lisa said while getting dressed. "Come on, let me meet this Janet you've been talking about. "What time are we supposed to be meeting them, at the club?" "An hour ago," I said, putting my shirt back on. "You will like her." "She's a good friend and good to others." I was enlightened by Lisa's compassion and understanding of the past that haunted me and my need to change things for people in the hood. I was thankful for her friendship. Without her rational way of communicating with me I'm sure I would have lost my mind. I was hurting inside over losing my family and being blamed for not spending enough time with them.

I had placed all of the nurturing responsibilities on my wife. I was so much like my mother. Providing was my way of showing I care. My wife and my daughter wouldn't allow the provider role alone. They demanded more communication, touch and time I desperately tried to shortly divide between family, community, and my career. It wasn't working and my priorities were off by a long shot. I often felt that my daughter only cared about her mother. It caused me to resent her mother because I felt that Lieko was poisoning my daughters mind against me.

Again I was wrong. I realized after they were gone that all my daughter wanted was for me to listen to her point of view. Growing up my mother didn't allow kids in grown folk's business and neither did I. I felt that one day when my daughter was older she would understand why mom and dad argued. Sadly, from the time I let go by from her early teen years to her young adult years she was searching for understanding without my communication. She only had one view of what was happening and that view was seeing her mother cry.

My daughter didn't hate me. She only wanted to see a smile on her mama's face. Her mom took the time to talk to her and I didnt. Regardless of whether I agreed with how her mom explained the situation, it was my responsibility to help her mom explain or at least tried to do so on my own. I had placed myself in the position of the bad guy. It wasn't her mother's fault nor my daughter's fault. It was all on me. I had realized too late how believing in the old ways of keeping kids out of grown folks' business without communicating could cause any child some unwanted issues in their life.

CHAPTER NINE

PARKING LOT PIMPING

Visiting the MLK monument was an awakening, yet there was a horrible feeling inside of me not yet confronted and resolved. Janet's father felt that I influenced her to speak at a gay rights rally against him and he had threaten to bring up a gun that had my finger prints on it at the scene of a crime if I didn't convince her to cancel her attendance. He felt that if his daughter spoke out against his campaign, it would surely end his chances of re-election. Mayor Hope didn't have proof that I had committed a crime in my early teens, only that I was questioned by the police about why my fingerprints were on a weapon that killed Shank dog, the nephew of the man who Fat pimping beat up for shooting Lisa's brother Eugene. No one knew what really happened that evening long ago except Lisa and me. The only other two people who knew, one died that night and the other one died later on in prison fighting off gang members.

After Fat pimping knocked out all of the man's teeth and nearly beat him to death for shooting Eugene in the head. Six years had gone by and Fat pimping was barely recovering from seeing his friend murdered that day. He was a little more talkative and every now and then he was able to smile.

Fat pimping had a job working at the Shelby County Corrections Department and it helped him to be able to advise young men to stay out of trouble and get their life together.

While working there, a troubled teenager arrived who recognized fat pimping. The young man was the nephew of the man who murdered Eugene. His street name was "Shank Dog" in the streets and he definitely did not like Fat pimping and although fat pimping tried to offer an explanation and counsel Shank Dog, the continuous disruptions at the county jail, caused Fat pimping to request a transfer.

During that time, Lisa and I were well into our later teens. We both still did a lot of walking around the neighborhood but if I had to go any further, my mother trusted me with the car. This particular evening, we heard about a party in the basement at T.R. White Sportsplex center. As kids, all the kids would go there to swim for fifty cents during the summer. The party started at 9pm and it was close by so I asked Lisa if she would like to go by there and see if we could manage to sneak in since we were not yet old enough to attend. The party was for 21 year old adults and older, and normally my friends and I would go even if we couldn't get in. Sometimes we would succeed and sometimes not, but each time we would always run into other teens we knew in the area who couldn't get in as well. This was also fun because we would all gather up money and get something to drink. We would chill in the parking lot just joking around and talking to females. Sometimes one of us would score big with the hottest female walking by and other times one of us would get embarrassed and bomb out. If that happened, all of the friends watching would get a huge laugh at your expense. We called it parking lot pimping.

That particular evening, I didn't want to hang with the fellows and took the opportunity to spend a little time with Lisa. To me, no parking lot pimping and any girl I may run into was as special as Homie's sister Lisa. We still hadn't officially dated each other and we were still stealing moments with each other that ended with a kiss. Lisa and I walked together and talked about plans that each one of us had for the future. It was just getting dark and we were in no hurry to get the party. The night was calm and the universe seemed to shine down on us like a loving spot light in the sky. She bumped into me a few times on purpose but she claimed it was always a mistake. I enjoyed it although I'd complain each time. "Boy you know I'm clumsy." Lisa would say with a smile on her face. I smiled each time, knowing she was flirting the whole time. The butterflies in my stomach finally went away the more we talked and laughed with each other. The party was only about three miles away from where we lived, yet the stars on that night and my hopes to get a kiss on the way made it seem like we walked forever.

I was disappointed to see the people and the cars in front of the building. I was so wrapped up in Lisa's eyes that I hadn't noticed how close we were to our destination. My chance of getting a kiss had passed. "Looks like everyone is having a good time." Lisa said, while softly grabbing my hand. She stopped and turned towards me. "My brothers are probably here soooo, I may have to ride home with them." She said almost as if she was expecting me to say something. In a split second, before I could think of something to say, she pulled me closer and we both stole that moment to kiss each other. She smiled when it was over and we headed toward the parking lot. I saw a few of my friends and so did she. We both got involved in our own separate group of friends. My boys were questioning me about Lisa and I could see that Lisa and her girlfriends shared little secrets that made them smile and look occasionally over at us.

I didn't see her brothers anywhere and I was hoping I wouldn't, just in case I'd get a chance to walk home with Lisa. My boys had a cooler filled with beer and offered me one. We leaned against the car and joked about each other as a few of them tried to catch a girl's attention with what they thought were cool pick- up lines. Of course, that didn't work as well as they had anticipated. Fat pimping noticed us and came over before going to the door to pay his way into the party.

Fat pimping was a little more talkative now, but still not the same as he used to be before his friend, Eugene was killed. "Be careful out here with this beer." He smiled. "I see you young fools ain't having any luck with the ladies tonight." Fat pimping was just as smooth with the ladies as Eugene was. He teased us and said that we had no mackin' skills. We all laughed at ourselves and hoped he'd put us up on some game. Fat pimping noticed a pretty girl walk by and told us that he would rap with us later. He pulled me to the side. "Young blood, I know you ain't out here mackin'." "I see Lisa over there." "The both of you can't stop looking at each other." "Don't blow it." Fat pimping said walking away.

He then stopped and turned around. He pulled his keys out of his pockets and gave them to me. "Look here," He said. "If you get a chance, wait until your boys are not around and you and Lisa go spend some private time in my car." I was happy, not only because he was trying to help me, but because I thought he was going to let me drive his car. It was a 1967 Chevy and I couldn't wait to get behind the wheel. He saw the excitement in my facial expression and said "Don't fucking drive my car, just sit in it, lil

Snow. "I won't be inside long, but if I do, once you and Lisa are through, hold on to my keys until I come out." I was hurt but still happy at the same time. Fat Pimping went inside and I walked back over to my boys and waited for my opportunity to invite Lisa to a little private time inside Fat pimping's ride. I took a big swallow of beer to build my courage up.

A few of my friends were scattering away, talking to different girls and I could see that Lisa's friends were being hounded by other boys, so I walked over as cool as I could and whispered in her ear. She agreed, and we walked over to the car. We got in and decided to get in the back seat so that we were not easily seen by people walking by. I reached over the front seat and turned the radio on. "Greg, is that a beer in your hand?" Lisa asked, pretending to be concerned about me drinking." I think she was just nervous since it seemed to her that this time, our stolen kisses may turn into something else. "Yeaaaa." I said, trying to be cool. I offered her some. "I'm gonna tell Byron you're out here drinking." Lisa said, now smiling, letting me know she was just teasing. She would always threaten to tell my big brother Byron when I was getting a little too mannish with her.

Everyone else called my brother Snow and called me lil Snow. Lisa called us by our first names. "It's good, here take a sip." I said, hoping she would. Lisa replied. "No, I don't want any." "Thanks anyway." "Ok, more for me." "You're just afraid if you drink some, you probably won't be able to keep your hands off of mack daddy." She laughed and said, "Boy please, you ain't no mack. To my surprise, she asked for the beer and took a bigger gulp than I did. "Damn." I said, teasing her. I guess you got your big girl panties on, huh?" She took another gulp of beer and threw the can out the window. "Keep on talking shit, and they won't be coming off." She got more comfortable and held my hand. "Well," She said. "Stop wasting time, mack daddy." We both smiled and started kissing each other like we never had before. This time, it felt different. It felt real. There was nothing stolen about this kiss. This time, something mystical and seductive was going on.

We caressed each other and touched places on each other's body, that we only wondered about before. We were in the back seat of a 1967 Chevy at night. We had enough room to lay down kissing, comfortably, without anyone seeing us. No, it wasn't stolen. This moment was given to us by the universe. But the universe had a way of flipping the script at any given moment.

We heard people running in the parking lot and we looked around trying to figure out what was wrong. We saw Fat pimping' running towards the car. I got out of the back seat to meet him. Fat pimpin' yelled "Give me the keys!" I rushed to get the keys out of my pocket. Pop, Pop, Pop! Gunfire rang out and Fat, pimpin' grabbed the keys and then ordered me into the car. We both ducked our heads, once inside the car as Fat pimpin' hit the gas pedal. He then noticed Lisa in the back seat laying down, hands over her head and scared. "Oh shit!" Fat pimpin' said as he drove quickly out of the parking lot. Everyone was ducking, running away or getting in their cars to speed away from the scene.

Fat pimpin' looked in the rear view mirror and asked Lisa to calm down and assured her shed be ok. He noticed a car following him quickly from behind and took a sudden turn down an alley. The car knocked over several trash cans as he dodged other obstacles in the alley. The car behind us was right behind us, showing no signs of slowing down or giving up. "Lisa screamed, "What the fuck is going on!" "Ya'll gotta get the fuck out of this car!" Fat pimpin' said with desperation in his voice. I was silent and stunned with fear. My eyes were wide opened and the chaos around us prevented me from being able to utter another word. As Fat pimpin' twisted and turned each alley way, trying to get away, we both kept looking over our shoulder for any chance of losing the car behind us driving like the speed demon of death to catch us. Fat pimpin' needed one chance of letting us jump out the car. He was trying to get us away from whoever was shooting at him. Suddenly, the car behind hit a dumpster and the chance to flee was taken immediately. Fat pimpin' made a quick turn out of sight of the car trying to free itself from the crash. Fat pimpin' reached over me and opened the door. "Get out and hide!" Fat pimpin' shouted. I jumped out and grabbed the door handle to the back seat and pulled Lisa out, who was crying and afraid. We took cover underneath an old truck parked close by.

Fat pimpin' quickly drove further up the dark alley. Laying underneath the truck, we heard the car chasing him speeding around the corner behind him. Pop, Pop, Pop! Gun shots again rang out and we heard another crash as the car behind him roared past us. I could see that Fat pimping had wrecked his vehicle and was trying to run away to safety but he was trapped. It was a dead in. The man driving the car behind him got out and said "I got yo ass now!" He fired some more at Fat pimpin'. I recognized his voice and positioned myself to see if I was right. Lisa covered her mouth and I held her close to me as I peeked to see. It was Shank dog, the nephew of the man who Fat pimpin" had brutally beaten up for shooting Eugene.

Fat pimpin' tried to break open a door in the building in the alley but shots fired at him gave him no chance but to duck and jump back into his car. Fat pimpin' then put his car in reverse and backed up quickly toward Shank dog. Shank dog continued firing and jumped out of the way as Fat pimpin' hit Shank dog's car. Both cars crashed into the truck we were hiding under. Lisa tried to hold in her scream but to no avail. Shank dog heard Lisa and turned to see where the scream came from. Fat pimpin' ran over the top of his vehicle and jumped on the back of Shank dog to protect us. They fought fiercely and then a single shot from Shank dog injured Fat, pimpin and he fell to the ground. A gun, Fat, pimpin' had strapped to his waist, fell into the street and spun under the truck in front of me. The barrel ended up stopping and pointing directly toward the center of my eyes. Shocked and relieved it didn't fire, Lisa screamed and I looked toward Fat pimping', who was slumped over. Fat pimpin' shook his head as if to say no, as I reached for the gun. Shank dog kneeled to see who was under the truck and pointed his gun at us. Fat pimpin somehow threw himself at Shank dog and Shank dog turned and fired at Fat Pimpin' again. Lisa screamed again and I was frightened but out of that fear, survival instinct kicked in to protect us. Shank dog kneeled again to get us. As soon as I saw his face, I closed my eyes and fired the weapon.

Lisa and I climbed from underneath the truck and Fat pimping' was still alive and fighting to breathe. Shank dog was not moving and blood was everywhere. We couldn't see his face. The sound of sirens were getting close and Fat pimping struggled strength to tell us to get the fuck out of there. We didn't want to leave him but he insisted. Run! Fat pimping' said. I put my hand on his shoulder and told him to hold on. He grabbed the gun out of my hand and Lisa and I ran away hoping Fat pimping' would make it.

I didn't murder anyone. It was self-defense and Fat pinpin' took the charge. He survived his wounds and told the police he had killed Shank dog because Shank dog was trying to kill him. The police secretly questioned me on why my fingerprints showed up on the weapon as well. I told him that fat, pimpin' had let me sit in his car until he came out of the club. I told them that I found his gun in the glove department and held it shortly before putting it back before Fat, pimpin' came out. I told them that I listened to the radio and then left the keys in the ignition when I saw people running in the parking lot. I further explained that I saw Fat Pimpin' get in the car and drive off with Shank dog firing his weapon in the parking lot and was speeding after Fat Pimpin'. I made no mention of Lisa at all. I visited him often and he made me promise to never speak of it again to him or anyone else. He wanted us to live our lives and be successful and made me promise to go to college and get out of the hood. The last time I visited him, he mentioned that Shank dog's uncle was causing him some problems with gang members in prison. Shortly after, I was informed that Fat pimping' lost his life in a dispute with another inmate. Ehommie and I talked about how much the hood had changed since we were little kids after Fat Pimping's death.

Or perhaps, it hadn't changed at all. Maybe it was only our innocence we had lost and we were now aware of all the pain, suffering and death that was around us from the start. As kids, we made the best of our lives with fun and games. As teens we chased girls, played sports and made fun of each other while drinking a beer or two. I guess we were trying to escape the images on television about the hood and hold on to the good times in the hood news reporters never talked about or recorded. Poverty's high risk of ending up in the valley of death was always close by. Fat Pimping and Eugene's life had a huge impact on us all. After a long heartfelt conversation Euhommie and I promised each other that day sitting on the steps in the hood that although we walk through the valley of death, we would live our best life. Nothing would stop us and we would never give up. I made good on my promise to get out of the hood, but that night in that dark alley, haunted me for the rest of my life. Now Mr. Anderson was using it against me to keep me away from the mayor's daughter Janet, and ruin my career.

CHAPTER TEN

POWER OF THE MEDIA

Lisa and I decided to call Janet and meet up with them at the nightclub in D.C. Lisa finished up her hair and make- up while I called Janet to get directions. Janet answered the phone. "Hey sunshine." Janet said excitedly. "You finally decided to join the celebration?" "I can't wait to tell you about the meeting with the attorney." "Mr. Anderson is gonna stop his bullshit once and for all or feel my wrath." Janet said, feeling powerful. Janet asked if I was on the way to meet her. I told her about Lisa dropping by to see me and fly back to Memphis with us. Janet was even more excited. "Great, I finally get, the chance to meet her." Janet texted me the address to join her and Adore' to celebrate our confirmation that Mr. Anderson could not prevent our clients from living anywhere they wanted and stop his aggressive methods showing his disapproval towards them living in his suburban community.

Lisa and I put the address in the GPS of her car rental and drove to the nightclub. On the way there I received a phone call from my oldest son Chris from a previous relationship before Lieko. I was glad to hear from him because I was trying to reach him before leaving Memphis to see if he would be available to stay at my home and be there when his younger brother returned home from his college visits. Chris explained that he had been working overtime and hadn't had a chance to return my phone calls until now. "Aye pops, is everything ok?" Chris told me that he recently saw that he had numerous missed calls from Lieko. He wanted to check with me first because he knew that Lieko and I hadn't been getting along lately. "Yeah man, everything is cooler than a fan as far as I know Chris. I'll call her shortly to see what's up." I asked Chris how he was doing and asked if he'd be coming home to visit us in Memphis. "I'm actually headed that way now." Chris explained. "Have you talked to your brother, Chris?" I asked. Chris replied, "Who, Kylin?" "No, Reshad." I explained. "Yeah, he's still working on his music." "He said that he would be down for Thanksgiving" "Chris added. "Ok, cool," I said. "I'll see you in a couple of days, when we get back from D.C." 'Alright, bet," Chris said and hung up the phone.

After hanging up the phone, I noticed that Lieko had been calling and sent several messages. Reluctantly, I started to open the messages, but at that moment we arrived at the nightclub. I should've checked anyway but I didn't want to argue or ruin my mood being that this was supposed to be a celebration. I decided to call her after Janet gave me details about the case. It was the only reason we were in D.C. in the first place. I'd have to deal with Lieko's accusations later. I had realized why she was so worried about Kylin's safety and any other person of color well-being, regardless if they were doing something wrong or not. Rather they lived in a low-income neighborhood or wealthy one. Lisa had further helped me realize that Lieko and I had the same concerns, just different methods and way of dealing with it. Like Sasha had explained. Martin Luther King and Malcom X cared about justice for all, they had different ways of dealing with it. The media highlighted those differences as a way to divide. Those two together would have been unstoppable and they knew it.

Lieko and I both loved the kids but all the hype about white people becoming bolder in their disapproval of the election of Obama and Make America Great Again antics, had caused her some real concerns about the safety of young black adults. Police brutality issues and Kylin attending private school made Lieko fear that our son would be jaded to the real world and how the color of his skin would endanger him regardless of his well-mannered attitude and white friends. The 2016 presidential campaign was causing turmoil among people and suddenly voting for republicans meant you were racist and voting democrat meant you were against what supremacists suggested what Make America Great again actually meant.

The media instigated beliefs that Make America Great Again, meaning a time when Anglo-Saxons forced their culture on minorities by any means necessary and any attempt to change or dispute standards set by them, most likely ended with some form of cruelty or even death without being held accountable. This was evident in each case of officers taking an observation of skin color and putting aggressive, criminal meaning behind it and using that biased belief to get away with unethical treatment. A false assumption about people of color constructed by evil and greed, was so deeply rooted in the minds of America, which made it easy to believe that a large white adult, equipped with a bullet proof vest, a Billy club, a stun gun, and a firearm was less threatening than an unarmed kid, teen or young adult simply because of skin color. Lieko and I fought constantly about how to make our kids aware of this problem in today's society.

To her, I sounded like a sellout teaching the kids to just behave and do as the police asked. To me, she sounded like an irrational militant teaching them that it is their legal right to ask why they were pulled over and that it was their right to exercise and to expect the same treatment as any white person being pulled over or questioned. I was afraid that asking questions would be taken as uncooperative and resisting. Resisting gets beaten, shot or jail time rather you're doing something wrong or not in our community. She wanted them to know their rights and exercise those rights regardless of the situation. We both were right and knew the horrible reality that people of color endured in the past and today's society. The sad thing is that we have to fear those who are supposed to protect us, or even mention the possibility of harm by the hands of the law due to perceptions of what the color of skin means in the minds of white American culture.

It was devastating to have had to incorporate being pulled over by the police to our kids along with the birds and the bees, future plans, accomplishments and goals. That one potentially deadly factor is one of the extra weights carried by minorities. The denial of its existence by a so called dominant race and refusal to care about the dangers of being a minority in America causes murderous outcomes to be overlooked or played down simply by the belief that a skin color makes a person a criminal, more dangerous or more aggressive than another race. The conversations about it and how to handle it, greatly strained our marriage. She felt strongly that if minorities weren't granted reparations that we should claim the sea's that slaves were shipped across on traveling to the United States. She suggested that black people could build their wealth from the trade of products and resources from one country to another, if anyone used the burial passageway of our ancestors.. "If they continue to deny us reparations, then we must claim the seas," she would say.

Lieko and I both agreed that It was how our language, power in numbers, culture, economic status and families were divided and destroyed. Yet, I knew in my heart that building the strength of family units in our communities was one important way of building it all back. I wanted to build it back and Lieko insisted that black people should stop asking and take it back.

Despite our efforts, the differences in opinion on how to guide and protect our children in a country dominantly ruled by white males complicated our marriage. My time away from home protecting the rights of the mentally disabled further added to our problems. Although she knew my time away was for a good cause, she felt that my dedication to time spent at home with family was not where it should've been on my list of priorities. My old fashion way of thinking about the roles of a man and a woman didn't help matters with my wife and daughter at all. I learned the hard way that black women had been doubly oppressed by slavery and by the expectations in a male dominated world. Neither one of them was going to be defined by those expectations. I had double trouble on my hands for even suggesting the idea of a woman's submission to a man's preconstructed requirement of what's considered to be lady-like in or outside of the home.

We both were fearful and lost our focus on a family unit, worrying about the ugliness that the 2016 election campaign was causing among a society trying to get beyond the past and believe in "yes we can." Now "yes we can," and the beautiful message it carried among a diverse nation was being scrutinized and criminalized by "make America great again." The love of our children and protecting them, was one thing we agreed on and that should have been enough to hold on but the arguments tore us apart. I was anxious about getting the celebration over with and calling Lieko with my new insight on things concerning our lives together, as family. I thought surely, this would decrease any chances of arguing with her.

We noticed that Janet was outside near Adore's rental. Janet noticed us and waved her hand in the air. She was excited and smiling. Luckily, we got a parking space close by. We got out of the car and Janet was already hurrying towards us. "Oh my God!" "I'm so glad you guys came." Janet said while giving me a huge hug and looking anxiously at Lisa. "Wassup, Janet? I asked. "I see you already got the party started." I pointed at the cup in her hand. Janet said, "oh this?" "No, this is the last of my smoothies for today." She added. "I'm trying to get in at least four a day. "Taste it." "They're amazing and it keeps the extra pounds off." Janet said, while patting my stomach and smiling. "Don't start, Miss Smoothie, queen. I said. " Men don't worry about a little extra weight." "It's just a little extra playground for the ladies." Janet chuckled. "Yeah, right." She said, noticing Lisa's heels. I introduced them to each other. "Janet, this is my good friend Lisa." "Lisa, this is my other good friend Janet."

"Oh my God, girl, I love those shoes." Janet said and hugged Lisa. I'm so glad to meet you. "How do you put up with this one? Lisa replied. "Thank you." "That color looks amazing on you." " "He can be a handful, but I love him. Janet replied. "He thinks he's cute don't he?" Lisa laughed and gladly instigated Janet teasing me. Lisa laughed and said, "I know right?" "If they took the word sexy out of the dictionary, he'd put his picture in replace of it." They both laughed, as I stood there entertained and annoyed at the same time. I was glad that they were connecting so well. I interrupted. "Ladies, I can hear you, ya know?" "I'm standing right here with my fine ass." Janet smiled and changed the subject. "Well, welcome to Club Panda, let's celebrate!" "I need at least one strong drink because I can't get Adore to understand that I'm ready to start a family." "Kids?" I asked. "Yes," she said. "I'll talk to you later about that," Janet sighed and changed the subject again. "Greg, I can't wait to get back and tell my client's they won't be bothered by any protestors, anymore." I'm happy for you Janet." "I can't wait either." I wasn't able to fully enjoy Janet's excitement, because I knew her father and his thug associates were trying to ruin my life and my friendship with Janet. For now, I'd spare her the news of it all until after we get back to Memphis.

    I placed my hands on both of their lower backs and we all started towards the entrance of Club Panda. "Let's do this." Janet said, "Wait, and let me put this empty smoothie cup away. She put it back into the car. We continued to the door. The inside of the night club was amazing. The attention to detail was phenomenal but not overbearing. It was spacious with three levels. The diversity of the people there, gave me a great feeling. I love to see people from all different backgrounds, communicating and having a good time with each other.

    There was a huge bar with an aquarium behind it, which had to be at least twenty feet long. Tropical fish in all different colors seemed to be gracefully dancing as if they were a part of the entertainment. The ocean blue water complimented the blue and white laser lights flickering, twisting and turning throughout the club. There were plenty of seating arrangements, all seemed to be VIP status on each level of the club. Near the dance floor was another bar and stage for live bands. The D.J was above the stage on the second level. He looked down at the people on the dance floor as he kept them happy and dancing to his arrangement of hype music. You could see all levels of the club, but you had to take the elevator to reach each level. Janet escorted us to the elevators that reached the second level where Adore was waiting at their table. To my surprise, I looked up towards the ceiling and noticed that it was a see through roof and I could see women swimming in a pool on the rooftop of the club.

We got on the elevator and I couldn't help but to show how ecstatic I was. 'Damn, I love this place Janet," I said. "You've been holding out." "How long have you known about this place?" I asked. I was inquisitive about everything I saw inside and wanted to know more. Especially that giant aquarium, and Janet knew I had a fascination for fish tanks. "I knew you'd love it." Janet said. Adore and I have been coming here for a few years when we both get a chance to. At that moment the elevator door opened to the second level. Adore was sitting nearby and waved at us to hurry over. She was texting on her cell phone. She looked up and said, "Come on, come on people." "I've already got shots of tequila waiting.

We all placed ourselves at the table. The seats were soft and comfortable. Almost at home on the couch kind of feeling, yet you're at the club and can order drinks and food. All the ladies were looking beautiful and I was glad to be accompanying them. Janet introduced Lisa to Adore as we made ourselves comfortable. "You already met my handsome friend." "This is his home girl Lisa." "Hello, Lisa, you look lovely." Adore said as she put her arm around Janet at the table. We all grabbed our shot glasses and I said, "To the most intelligent and amazing beautiful ladies in the club tonight." Janet replied before we took the shots to the head. "Shit, in the world!" She said smiling and Lisa and Adore both responded. "What you said!" They all laughed and I corrected myself. "In the world." I said, twisting my lips to the side as if to yeah right. We all took our drinks simultaneously.

The D.J. went old school and played Snoop Dog and Dr. Dre's Gin & Juice. "Heeeeeey!" They all said and started dancing in their seats. A female waitress came over and I ordered another round of tequila shots. The waitress was gorgeous, and gave me a flirtatious smile. At that moment all the ladies chimed in on the catchy part of Gin & Juice. "Laid back, with my mind on my money and my money on my mind!" They excitedly said leaning back, pumping and pointing their fingers at the waitress. The waitress chuckled. "What's the occasion?" She said. Lisa said, "Just celebrating our last days in the U.S." "If Trump gets elected, we're all moving to Canada. "I know that's right, book me a flight too." The waitress said giggling. 'Would you guys like to order something to eat?" Adore told us that the cheddar cheese, bacon and jalapeno fries were amazing and that we should try them.

The waitress suggested that we try the rib & shrimp appetizer platter because it came with a basket of cheddar cheese fries. "Bet." Lisa said. I nodded to the waitress that her suggestion would be fine. "Ok, great." The waitress said. She smiled at me again and said, "I'll be right back with your tequila shots." Again, the ladies leaned back in anticipation of their favorite part of the song. "Laid back, with my mind on my money and my money on my mind!" they all yelled and laughed with each other. Girl, we better have some fun, because Trump is going to have our asses picking cotton with his ku, klux, klan ass." "I will be damn!" I said. "Adore said, "Shit, your light skin ass, don't have to worry about it." "He's gonna have you in the house serving buttermilk biscuits and shit." "Shid, light skin or dark skin, we're all the same." I'm not serving anything but these size thirteen shoes in his ass." "What are you gonna do?" I asked Adore. "You can pass for white and Janet is white." "Are ya'll gonna be cracking the whip, or are you gonna stick with the brothers and sista's?"

Adore laughed. "Honestly, I'm for all my people." Black, white, or whatever." I won't be cracking a whip or picking cotton for anybody." She explained. "My mother is white and my dad is black, so I'll be moving to Canada as well, but I don't believe Trump would do anything like that. "Are you voting for Trump? I asked. "I'm not voting for Hilary." Adore said and explained herself. "If you ask me, Hilary isn't any better, so I'd rather have someone who knows business matters well and do something about this economy. "Wait, wait, wait, and hold up." I said. "First of all, Trump is a wealthy man, but he has had several business failures, and I'm surprised that a lot of women refuse to vote for her." "I would have assumed that all women would stick together and vote for a female president." "Especially since Trump is bragging on groping women." I added with anticipation of all the ladies thoughts on this issue. "Just like people assume that all republicans are racist." Adore said. "This racist shit and division of the races, is just what's highlighted by the media." "People are making a big deal out of nothing." "I'm not racist." She added.

"That's right baby." Janet said in her Adore defense. "Not all republicans are racist, but you gotta admit, all racist support Trump. " They all laughed. "I know that's right girl." Lisa said. "Look, I don't believe he really groped anyone, besides, isn't that the way it is with men of power?" Adore asked jokingly. "Hell nawh!" "That's the way wealthy men see it." And it has been allowed too long." Lisa said. "Women are not taking being objected to sexual abuse and harassment at work anymore." "You better ask

Tarana Burke." They all gave each other, high- five. "That's just another example of how bold white privileged men has gotten lately." Lisa added. The waitress came by with the next round of tequila shots. Once again, the waitress was just in time to enjoy the ladies enjoying another song. Rihanna's song Work was playing and all the girls jumped up and were playfully twerking. "Work, work, work, work, work, you see me do the dirt, dirt, dirt, dirt, dirt!" They all sang and danced together. The waitress even threw a few dance moves, as she placed the tequila shots on the table. We all took our shots to the head. Janet took her shot and said "Ok, guys, I gotta use the ladies room." Lisa said, "Great, me to." "I'll go with you." They both hurried off to the little girl's room.

Adore looked at me and inquisitively asked, "So, I take it that you're voting for Hillary Clinton?" "No, not at all." "Actually I'm not voting for either one." I added. "She looked perplexed by my answer and jokingly said, "Now that's just dumb." "Especially since people fought and died for your right to vote." "Not to vote is like not playing the lottery." "You have to be in it to win it." She said while looking at the people dancing on the lower floor. "I guess I'm rebellious like that." I said jokingly. "Adore shook her head. "Not voting is not rebellion, it's a surrender." I laughed and was enticed by the conversation. Adore was pretty cool and intelligent. I was beginning to understand why Janet loved her.

I offered my opinion to further the conversation as everyone was enjoying themselves and dancing to good music. "Why should I be forced to vote for the lesser of two evils, when we all can exercise our right not to vote collectively, until minorities' issues with equality and injustice are taken seriously?" "Of course, two or three people, or even a group of people not voting won't make a difference." "But all of us together will." "We have to stand together." I added. Adore replied. If you don't want to vote democrat or republican, just write your candidate in." "That's a useless option, if not enough people vote for that same candidate." I further attempted to make my point. "We all have to do so in unity." "Besides, both democratic and republican parties are the same." "Their agendas are concurrent at the end of the day, just dressed up differently." I added. "Adore shook her head and said, "look, just vote, it's the only way to make a difference." I could see in her eyes that she had the same fighting spirit as Janet, and I knew her wheels were turning rapidly. She wanted to hold back her thoughts but tequila shots and her opinion being challenged, was too much to handle. She couldn't help it and I knew more was coming. All I had to do was wait for it.

The waitress brought our food to the table. "Enjoy your meal." "Will there be anything else I can help you guys with?" "Thank you," I said. "Not right now, we're waiting on the rest of the too live crew to get back." The waitress smiled and said, "Ok, I'll be back to check on you." "Thanks." Adore and I both said simultaneously. Adore took a sample of the food. "Oh my god, this is delicious." She was pleased with the food and wiped her mouth and fingers. I thought to myself, here it comes and I waited anxiously. After a few good smacks of the lips, she continued. "Look, if I get poor service from a restaurant, I don't stop eating, I just don't go back to that restaurant and go somewhere, where my needs are met." Adore said excitedly, making her point. After taking a fork full of cheese fries, I said, "Got damn, you're right." "They are delicious, but it's not enough for me alone to write a candidate in, or go to another restaurant that meets my needs." "I, me, a few, in a world of billions won't work." "It must be, we, us and everyone that will get real results." "Besides, comparing a dislike for service in a restaurant, is not a fair comparison when it comes to injustice." I said, smiling and ready for Adore's response. She replied, "I understand that you are speaking in a collective manner, however, action always trumps inaction my friend." "The issues minorities have are due to inaction and poor leadership." She suggested.

I immediately jumped on it. "Exactly, speaking of trumping and poor leadership, Hillary and Trump are white leaders." "How can we depend on them to solve issues for brown people?" "And why should we be forced to do so?" I asked Adore. "Food for thought." I said, loving every moment I spent getting to know Adore while Janet and Lisa were in the restroom. "Why doesn't Kaepernick have a position in the NFL?" "The answer?" I said rhetorically. "Because he and only a few others kneeled for injustice in America." "So, the owners were able to threaten them with fines and retracting from playing a number of games, or possibly not playing in the NFL at all." If the entire players of the NFL, kneeled together in awareness for injustice among minorities in America, the outcome would have been a completely different story." "Billions of dollars lost, would've been at stake and the message would have been taken and dealt with realistically instead of just targeting Kap." Adore continued, enjoying her meal and listened carefully.

"I don't know anything about football, but I do agree that Kaepernick's position had nothing to do with a stand against the flag or veterans." She sighed. "I'll drink to that." I said, and we both took Janet and Lisa's shots of tequila. Adore laughed. "We'll order them some more." Adore said, adjusting her dress. "I do know this about football." Adore expressed her position again. "You can't score without being in the game." I chuckled. "You're right, you also can't score, without the team." Adore laughed. "Hell, I tell you what, just vote for your damn self, Greg."

We both laughed and looked around for Janet and Lisa, wondering what was taking them so long. I noticed that she was starting to get a little uncomfortable with the political conversation. I touched her on her shoulder and said "Adore, don't take this shit too seriously. "We can't get caught up in this bullshit." "Shit, it is what it is, the leaning tree ain't always the one that falls. "The leaning tree ain't always the one that falls?" She laughed. "What does that mean?" 'We all got our issues, but no matter how much you try to hold us down, one day, it may be you that fall and the leaning tree continues to grow." She chuckled again. "I gotta steal that one and put that in my bank of swag." "I smiled and said, "What do you know about swag?" Adore got up and posed. "Nigga, you see this swag and all this fabulousness!" She said jokingly, and feeling herself.

She was indeed beautiful, and full of intelligent swagger, I must admit. In my opinion, Adore was a classy, intelligent woman, that didn't have to be loud and aggressive to get her opinion heard or taken seriously. She could be intelligently aggressive, and in control with words of intellectual, wisdom. The "Me too" movement was all about empowerment of women. They use poetic vocabulary, and refuse to be subjected to any sexual ideas, beliefs or behavior that causes them to be victims of abuse. I admired the movement and I admired Janet's lover and friend.

Meanwhile, Janet burst into one of Club Panda's ladies bathrooms, with Lisa close behind. Janet looked frantically, to see if anyone else was in the bathroom. Once she discovered no one else was present, Lisa heard a loud release of air. Lisa looked shocked and amused at the same time. Lisa had a slight smile of curiosity. "Did you just?" before Lisa could finish her question, Janet said hysterically, "Oh my god!" Janet said, holding her stomach. "Girl, those damn smoothies gotta a bitch gassy!" "Lisa laughed. "Awh, hell nawh!" Lisa said while going into one of the bathroom stalls. "You keep your funky ass over there." "I thought you had to use the bathroom, not blow it up." "Whew!" Janet said, rubbing her stomach. "I had to get somewhere by myself." "I didn't know you were coming with me, but don't worry, my shit smell like unicorns and roses." Janet said jokingly. "The hell!" Lisa said coming out of the bathroom stall. Lisa and Janet both touched up their make-up and hair quickly. "Let's get out of here before someone comes in. "I don't want anybody looking at me like I just dropped a massive load in the club." Lisa said, as they both hurried out of the ladies room. They walked out of the bathroom together.

Still giggling, Janet said, before getting on the elevator, to get back to the second floor. "Damn, Lisa, I don't think I'm going to make it the rest of the night, if this keeps up." The elevator door opened. "Are you ok?" Lisa asked Janet. "Yeah, I think so," Janet replied, rubbing her stomach again. ""I feel better, but if this." Before Janet could finish speaking, the door of the elevator opened again, and two handsome gentlemen walked inside with them. At the moment the elevator started up, Janet's eyes widened, and she looked at Lisa as if to say oh my god. Lisa whispered in Janet's ear. "Spread your cheeks apart." "What?" Janet said, confused. Lisa smiled and whispered in her ear again. "Spread your booty cheeks apart and it won't make a sound." Desperate not to be embarrassed in front of the two mem, Janet, reluctantly did as Lisa had suggested. She grinned as she thought to herself. How would she know something like that. With no time to ask questions, Janet was eager to release the huge air bubble rumbling around in her stomach.

Janet pretended that she was adjusting her hair and clothes in an attempt to ease her way to her buttocks. Women are always adjusting their attire, so she hoped it would work. Janet and Lisa were both standing behind the two gentlemen, so it wasn't two obvious in the tight, enclosed area. Janet felt the gas bubble getting worse, so she had to act fast. Janet rubbed the back of her skirt and cuffed both cheeks. She quickly spread them apart, and to her relief, a silent rush of air came out. The look on her face was one of sudden relief, satisfaction and then fear that it would smell. Janet looked at Lisa and Lisa was smiling and playfully covering her nose and mouth. The two gentlemen were unaware of what was going on. The door of the elevator opened and they all got off. Janet and Lisa laughed again. "Oh my god, I can't believe that worked," Janet said. "We got to tell them that we will be leaving soon." Janet said. At that moment, the D.J. played the calling sound of the beginning of the club's famous hula-hoop contest.

"Panda – Panda – Panda- Panda." "Alright, ladies, you know what time it is!" He shouted. "Oh shit. Janet said. "Wait, I got to do this before we go." "What?" Lisa said, surprised by what Janet said. "Come on, I can win this." "I was waiting on this before you guys got here." "I can use this money to throw my client's, a celebration party." It won't take long." "Girl, I got skills!" Janet said boastfully. "That ain't all you got," Lisa said, following Janet to the stage. They hurried their way through the crowd, while the Panda – Panda, sounded and excited everyone in the club. Seven ladies, including Janet entered the contest and were proudly standing on stage. I noticed Janet and couldn't believe it.

Look, its Janet!" I interrupted Adore, enjoying her meal and dancing to the Panda call. Adore didn't look surprised at all. "Awwh shit." "Yeah, she's great at this." Adore said. "We always played this game." "She is amazing." Adore added. "I don't know about that, those are black girls, she's up against. I said, doubting Janet's chances of winning. "No, just wait and see," Adore said. We both sat up in anticipation, for the contest to begin. Adore and I could see the stage perfectly, from where we were sitting. Once again, "Panda – Panda – Panda," rang out over the club and flashing lights enticed the mood of the crowd. "Alright ladies, you know the rules!" the D.J. said. "There are none, other than, never let your hula, hoops drop. "You can drop it, like it's hot, but the hula- hoop, better not." "Do what you want to do and work those hips." "Just don't touch the hula- hoop with your hands." "The last person still standing at the end of the song, wins a thousand dollar cash reward." Everyone cheered and the entire "Panda song, began.

Almost immediately, one of the girls hula, hoop fell to the floor and she was escorted off of the stage. Janet and the others continued showing off and working what their momma gave them. "Panda – Panda – Panda!" The music continued as the crowd cheered on. Two more contestants, hula – hoops fell to the floor. I was pleasantly surprised by Janet's moves. "Damn," I said to myself, as Janet was out doing these fine ass black girls. I couldn't believe it. Hula- hoop is supposed to be black girls shit." I thought to myself. "Go white girl, go white girl." The end of the "Panda" song was nearing, as one more contestant hula – hoop fell to the floor. At the end of the song, it was only Janet and two other beautiful ladies, still standing. They celebrated with each other and waved their hula – hoops over their heads, still working their hips in glory. The crowd applauded their shills.

"Alright, alright," the D.J. said. "Looks like we are going to go at it another round." "Let's hear for the ladies," he said. The crowd applauded again. "Panda – Panda – Panda," rang out again. "This time, we're going to throw in a little twist." The crowd cheered, as the D.J. explained. Lisa was standing right by the stage, applauding her new friend. Lisa was impressed as well, as Janet pointed at her as if to say, "See, I told you." They smiled at each other while the D.J. explained the second round. "OK, ladies, we see that you have dropped it, like its hot skills." Now we're going to see if you can drop it and take shots, without letting the hula – hoops drop to the floor. Staff members placed shots on the floor in front of Janet and the last two ladies. The crowd applauded and cheered. "Are we ready ladies?" The D.J. said. The ladies danced in anticipation and the crowd cheered on.

The flashing lights and the music began. "Panda – Panda – Panda!" Janet and the other two started showing all their hula – hoop moves again. Each one of them took a shot while working their hips. Each one seemed as though they were not going to let the others out maneuver them and win the thousand dollar prize. About the middle of the "Panda song, the two other girls tried to drop down and pick up their shots. Their hula – hoops hit each other and fell to the floor. Janet was still doing her thing and loving it. "Don't stop," the D.J. said. "You make it to the end of the song and take your last shot, we're going to add five hundred more dollars to the prize. The crowd cheered Janet on. Janet continued showing off and looking at Lisa occasionally. Janet knew she had this one in the bag and she became more excited, knowing she had great news for her clients and with this easy money, she was going to throw them a huge celebration party. No more protests from neighbors, she thought to herself and smiled.

Right before the end of the song, Janet was picking up her last shot. She drank it and kept swirling her hips, while the hula – hoop seemed to dance around her hips naturally. Janet looked at Lisa standing below in front of the stage and raised her hands as if to say "Yes, I made it." "I won five hundred more dollars." Once Lisa caught Janet's eye contact again, Lisa smiled at Janet and pinched her nose. Janet's concentration broke and her hula – hoop fell to the floor, right before the end of the song. Janet laughed and said "You bitch." Janet pointed at Lisa, knowing that Lisa was jokingly referring to her gassy stomach on the elevator, and as if to say, "Girl you stink." Still, Janet was happy with the thousand dollar prize, as the crowd cheered and the D.J. gave her the money. "What's your name?" The D.J. asked. "Janet," she said and again everyone applauded. "Congratulations Janet." "How about that?" The D.J. said. "White, girl has some skills. A few of the club staff members helped Janet off the stage where Lisa was waiting.

Adore and I were applauding as well. At that moment, I felt my phone vibrate again. I answered it, while no music was playing and people were still clapping for Janet. "Hello," I said. "Where the fuck you been!" "Kylin's friend is in trouble!" "We've been trying to reach you!" Lieko was furious and scolded me for ignoring her calls. "Wait, what?" "Who's in trouble?" "Where is Kylin?" I asked. "They're at the hospital and Drake has been shot!" Lieko cried out. "What the fuck?" I said, stunned and feeling awful I hadn't answered earlier. Is everything ok? Adore asked. I shook my head no, and asked her to hold on for a minute.

"Is Kylin OK?" "What happened?" I asked Lieko. "Kylin was supposed to be staying at Homie's house until I got back." Lieko responded. "Yeah, they went looking for him and there was some protest downtown where people were fighting and Homie's ass was too busy protecting them damn Ku Klux Klan mutha fucka's. "What the…, look, I'll be on the first flight back, Asap!" I said, confused by her accusation. "I'm on my way as we speak." Lieko replied. "I told Kylin to stay close to Drake at the hospital and if he has to leave to go home and wait for me." "Ok, is Makayla with you?" I asked, concerned that Makayla was worried about her brother. Lieko informed me that Makayla was worried but knew Kylin was ok. Lieko told me that Makayla would be on a later flight to Memphis after she helped her friend Mee-Yon pack, before she left to find her uncle, whom she hadn't seen or heard from since he defected to South Korea.

"Kylin doesn't want to go over to Euhommie's house." She further explained. "That's fine." "I'm about to call him now." "Call who?" Lieko, said with an upset tone." "I told you, Homie's ass is in deep shit." "It's all over the news." "They set his club on fire for protecting those damn white folks, instead of protecting his own damn people." "Now Drake in the hospital, fighting for his fucking life!" "Look, babe, I don't know what's going on and I don't have time to argue." "I'll call you back." "I gotta call Kylin." I replied.

Janet and Lisa had arrived at the table. Adore informed them that something was wrong. I hung up the phone and told Lisa to call her brother. She knew me well, and could tell by my face that something was seriously wrong. "Oh my god," Lisa said and immediately pulled her cell phone out. I placed my hand on her shoulder and assured her that her brother was fine, but there were some complications with his club and protesters.

Lisa called her brother. Janet pulled me to the side and I placed my hand on her back and guided her out of the club, so that I could fully explain the situation. Lisa and Adore followed. We hurried outside and I explained to Janet that my son's friend was seriously hurt and we had to leave D.C immediately.

It was a quiet flight home. We all arrived in Memphis the following early morning, just before 3 am. Lisa went to see her brother, Euhommie and I headed towards the hospital. Janet wanted to ride with me, but I insisted that she get some rest and then go see the clients at the beginning of the work shift. Janet called Adore and let her know that we had a safe flight. I arrived at the hospital and saw my son sitting with the parents of Drake Seals. Kylin noticed me coming up the hallway and came towards me. I could see, from the expression on his face, that he was worried and sad. Without saying a word, we embraced each other. "Dad, they shot him." Kylin sobbed. "I'm sorry son." "You gotta be strong for him." I added as I continued to console him and we both walked towards Mr. and Mrs. Seals. Kylin followed me, still defending Drake's character. "Dad, you know Drake, he didn't do anything to deserve this." "I know son," I said approaching Drake's parents.

I hugged Mrs. Seals and asked how Drake was doing. "My baby, my baby." Mrs. Seals said. "Why did they have to shoot him?" "He didn't do anything," Mrs. Seals said. She was unable to stand for long, because her emotions were too overwhelming. Mr. Seals assisted his wife, as we both helped her back into her seat. Mrs. Seals continued sobbing and I asked my son to go get her some tissues and something to drink. "Why, lord, why?" Mrs. Seals cried. Mr. Seals pulled me to the side. He informed me of the condition of his beloved son and football star. "He is stable for now." Mr. Seals said.

"But they're afraid that if they remove the bullet, he may not be able to walk again." "Jesus, please help him," I said. Mr. Seals was a man of faith, and suggested that all we had to do was pray, and be strong for Drake. After a long, heartfelt prayer, the doctors informed us that Drake needed rest and that we should go home and pray for better results later on, after Drake has had time to recuperate. Drake's parents insisted that I take Kylin home and said that they would be there overnight.

On the way home, kylin expressed how he didn't know how he would feel towards my best friend after what happened to Drake. He further explained how confused he was to witness his wealthy friends engage in drug activity, while the police officers there were friends of the parents, and allowed it to continue, while another friend of his career was destroyed over a single blunt. I felt bad for him and was saddened that I couldn't provide any explanation that would satisfy his confusion and pain. How could I tell him what was so painfully true about being black in America, without crushing his spirit, hopes and dreams? I felt that this discussion would be better with his mom and me together. "It will be ok son." I said with uncertainty. "Get some rest and we will talk tomorrow." "The important thing right now is that we keep our focus on Drake getting through this son." I added.

We pulled up in the driveway of our home, around 4am. I could see Lieko's Infinity in the garage as the door went up. It was spotless as usual. Her tires were glistening from whatever product she used on her tires. Her parents owned a detailing shop and a few convenient stores. She learned how to detail cars, working with them. They all kept their cars immaculate. Leiko cleaned her vehicle better than anyone else could do for her. Kylin and I got out of the car and started towards the garage door entrance. Lieko opened the door before I could put my key in. She hugged Kylin and suggested he get some sleep. "Are you ok, son? She asked. "Yes, he replied as she rubbed his back. "Go on upstairs and get some sleep." "I'll have breakfast ready in a few hours. As I was taking my luggage out of the trunk, I noticed that Kylin hadn't gotten a chance to take his things inside. So, I gathered both our belongings and placed them inside by the garage door.

Lieko saw what I was doing. "I told him to go on to the hospital, and Evan drove his car home after I met them at the hospital." "Is Evan here?" I asked. "No, I took him home, his parents were worried." She explained. Lieko was already showered and wearing her usual silk or satin gown, I never knew the difference. She always slept in comfortable, but seductive attire. Her legs were long and the short gown perfectly showcased her model type, physique. I sat on the couch in the entertainment room and put my head down.

"What an awful night." I said, silently to myself. I was rubbing my head with both hands, with my head down, trying to make sense of it all. I heard Lieko, sitting in the recliner near-by. I looked up and she was just looking at me. I could tell that she desperately wanted to say something jazzy, as usual. Normally, that look would irritate me, but they say that absence makes the heart grow fonder, and in that moment, I remembered how cute that look used to be to me. She was always the jealous, feisty type. I once welcomed the challenge but over the years, her accusations and militant parenting methods, wore my patience thin. I was used to rational, calm intelligence, like Lisa. Lisa and I, compared to Lieko and I, would've definitely meant the difference between stress and peace. Yet, opposites, oftentimes, attract. One thing for sure. There was never a dull moment, good or bad with Lieko.

Still hesitant, I asked, "What is it?" Sitting with her long legs crossed and no expression on her beautiful face, I could tell that she was trying to contain her witty, spiteful remarks. "So, you cut your dreads?" She said calmly. I was a little shocked by her opening statement. "Yes." I said. "I just got tired of them." She switched legs and crossed them the other way. She leaned to the side, more comfortably and placed her arm on the armrest of the recliner. She played in her long hair with the other hand. "Looks good." She replied. I wondered what was next, trying to ignore the smell of cocoa butter. The ceiling fan was slowly circulating the cocoa butter she used to keep her skin soft and wrinkle free. The perfume she was wearing complimented it nicely.

She came with it. "Kylin is old enough to stay here by himself, if you're going to be out with your little snow bunny." "He doesn't need to be over at Homie's house while you're away." "Don't start, not tonight." I pleaded. "Don't worry, I just need you to understand that I'm serious." "If you hadn't told him to look for homie, he wouldn't have been downtown in that mess." She explained. "Wait, I know you're not blaming me for what happened?" "There is no way I could have known that would happen." I said, feeling the familiar tension between us. "I keep telling you that these white people, has gotten bold out here since that Donald Trump, mutha fucka, been running for president, and I don't feel comfortable with my son running around with his white friends," Lieko was speaking calmly, although she was furious about me not taking her concerns as serious as she thought I should. I had learned that her concerns were a bit irrational, but valid. It was enlightening to me to see that she, herself, was trying to make an adjustment in her approach in matters, involving our marriage and kids, "They are good boys, Lieko." I reassured her. She explained that she knew that they were, and how much she loved Evan and the rest of the boys. She was close to Evan's mother and they often talked about the way racist people were acting during the presidential campaign. They both were concerned about all of the boy's safety. "I understand where you're coming from Lieko." "I've realized a lot, since we last spoke." I explained. "You were right about so much babe. She slightly smiled and awaited more information. I continued, without the detail. "I just wanted to believe that this world had changed so much, especially after the election of Barack Obama." "Damn, I'm gonna miss them," She sighed. "I hope Hilary wins," I said. "Shit, she ain't no better, but I'm going to vote for her." Lieko said.

"Wow," I said. "I'm shocked that more women are not excited about a female president." "To me, it further represents the forward movement in this society to get past the labels and have equal opportunities and justice for all." "Bull shit, not with Hilary." "She is smart, but I don't think she will make much difference in minority communities." Lieko further explained. "I just don't want that bastard, Donald Trump in office." I wanted to talk to her about my thoughts on voting for the lesser of two evils, but I didn't have the energy for debate. Besides, I had a slight headache and I chose to keep my thoughts to myself, especially since she was being so calm and considerate. But Lieko was never one to let me off the hook that easily.

"So, are you still with that not voting shit?" She asked. I sat up again to explain. "'Look, I am only voting to participate in what they call the popular vote, but even if my vote counts towards the majority of votes for her, it doesn't guarantee that she will be elected president." "Regardless of how anyone votes, your vote doesn't matter, because this is not a one man, one direct vote for the person you choose." "It's only one man, one vote for your local candidates." "The presidential vote doesn't work that way. "You are actually voting for representatives to vote for you and there is no law that they have to vote for the candidate that won the popular, majority vote."

"What do you mean?" Lieko calmly asked. "Baby, it's in the constitution, that the election of the president is based on the electoral college system." "That means that only about five hundred or so people actually vote for the president." "Those people are people, chosen to represent each state." "Most of the time, they already know how your state is going to vote." "For example, "we live in a red state, with not much influence on the presidential campaign, like California, New York or Florida." "Those states have double the amount of representatives that vote on our behalf."

"That's why you always see Trump and Hilary, campaigning in those states or swing states, which have the capability to swing either way." "The little over five hundred people, that are our representatives, are not obligated by law to vote republican or democratic, regardless of how many people vote in each state, for republican or the democratic candidate." "With that being said, my love and beautiful, militant queen, the only true and fair way to vote for your president, is to abolish the Electoral College system and use the one man, one vote system, like it is for your local governor, mayor or sheriff. "Baby, you're only voting for which group of people, actually takes part in electing the president." "The kicker is, you have no connection, active or legal ties to those people, so they do what they want to do." "They are not legally obligated to vote the way the popular vote suggests that they should." I further explained that "The only way for us to truly make a difference is to establish our own political party for minorities and use the one man one vote system to turn all red states blue."

I was growing tired of the conversation, and didn't want to discourage her efforts in the community. What she was doing was important and beneficial in making people aware of how to intelligently, continue to strive for equality and justice, regardless of their race or social status. I asked if we could talk more about it later. Surprisingly, Lieko, enlightened and more aware than before. I knew she would take this information and run with it.

It was a nice change in demeanor. I was rubbing my head again and Lieko asked, "Are you ok?" I responded, still rubbing my head, "Yeah, just a lot has happened and I'm trying to relieve this tension." "I got a slight headache." She came over to the couch and sat down beside me. "Here, let me help." She placed her arm around my shoulder and pulled me close to lay in her lap. My god, she smells so good, I thought to myself. She began to rub my head and softly started singing one of our favorite songs to me. "I'm an ever rolling wheel, without a destination real." I smiled and she continued singing softly and seductively. "I'm an ever spinning top, whirling around till I drop." "Oh but what am I to do, my mind is in a whirlpool." "Give me a little hope, one small thing to cling to." She rubbed my head gently with one hand and tapped on my shoulder three times, as if we both could hear the music. She had a sultry, singing voice and she continued singing and soothing my pain. "You got me going in circles." "Oh round and round I go." "You got me going in circles." "Oh round and round I go." We both sang together, the next verse. "I'm spun out over you." We kissed like we hadn't in a long time. Afterwards, she hummed the words and I fell asleep.

A few hours later, I woke up on the couch with a blanket over me. I could smell breakfast and I could hear Kylin and his mother talking in the kitchen. I folded the blanket and walked into the kitchen. To my surprise, Makayla and my oldest son Chris were sitting at the table. She had made it home, while I was sleeping. I was so pleased to have my family all at the breakfast table again. I swear, I saw golden stars and glitter in the sun rays, coming through the window and shining down on the bacon, eggs and fruit bowl, Lieko and my daughter, had prepared. "Hey baby girl." I said while squeezing her tightly. "Dad, I can't breathe." Makayla said, smiling. I was so happy. With everything going on, seeing my family together brought some joy among the traumatic events happening in our city. I looked over at Kylin. "Are you ok, son? "He replied. "Yeah, dad, I'm good. Chris gave him a manly hug and patted Kylin's shoulder. "Yeah pops, we got this."

Makayla, immediately expressed her concerns. "What the fuck!" She changed her tone, when her mother gave her the side eye. "I mean, what in the world is going on in Memphis?" She continued. "I know one thing, Drake better not die, or it's gonna be more riots around here, and a lot of people are gonna get hurt." "Rioting won't change anything Makayla." "They don't care if we protest peacefully." "They still view us as savages." Lieko explained. "America is mentally fucked." Makayla, quickly gave her opinion. "We can change the way we look and talk just so we can get a job and put food on the table, but if you wear the wrong thing or be in the wrong place, as a black person, we still get murdered in the streets."

"It's not right, Makayla added. "It shouldn't matter how we look or talk." "Why can't we be ourselves and still be viewed as human beings?" "If I wear my afro puffs and a hoodie, don't I have the freedom to do so without a fucked up image in somebody's head that means I'm a criminal, who doesn't deserve to live?" "Aint no bad or good black people out here." "We are all human." "It's bad and good inside of everyone, no matter what color you are. "It's their own damn, mental fear of black empowerment, is why we can't get justice." "Hell, we even fear and kill each, other, because of the brain fuck, white, America has done to human beings." Once Makayla got going, even a side eye from her mother, couldn't stop her.

"Amen, baby girl." I said, looking at her proudly and knowing that I myself had recently reflected on my own separate view of black people, according to the way they dressed and behaved. I had lost my connection as to why human beings, of any race, especially minorities, would respond to oppression, injustice and poverty, not acquired by choice, but forced to live with the consequences of America's fear of retaliation. Makayla and her mom were right on point. The more we conform to a certain way of appearance and speaking, the more we help those that justify injustice to minorities, simply because of the way they look. In order to survive and hope not to be a victim of injustice, we change our normal way of communicating with family and friends, in order to be viewed as the not so bad black people, instead of the misrepresentation of violent, aggressive black people.

"Why did you cut your dreads off, dad?" Makayla asked. "That's what I'm talking about." "What's wrong with the way our hair naturally grows from our scalp?" "Why do we have to change for them, just to feel more safe and accepted?" "Makayla!" Her mother tried to stop her. "No, that's ok." I said, realizing the point Makayla was trying to make. "Baby, girl, my dreads were a spiritual process for me to be more in tune with who I am as an individual." "Now that I'm more connected with who I am and my own personal view of my role in society, and not theirs, I'm ready to use their view of me as a Trojan horse." "You and your mom can help, by turning this red state blue, if your mom decides to stay." Her mother looked at me and smiled. "So, you've decided to vote?" "Most definitely, I said. But not the way you think." I replied. Until the election of the president depends directly on one man, one vote, I won't be participating, but I am voting for my local representatives." "Your influence with minorities, can help get as many of us out to the poles and vote for the Democratic Party locally, right here in our city, where your vote actually makes a difference." "One man, one vote." "The way it should be when voting for the president," I added.

"I suggest we all embrace the way we dress and deliberately, go out to vote. When they see us speaking intelligently, wearing all blue, with our natural hair styles, we can break the image in their minds, that a style of dress or skin color justifies their injustice." "Why blue?" I asked, sensing that my baby girl was catching on. She proudly replied. "To symbolize that no matter our differences in skin color, we all stand to turn our red state blue." I smiled. We all blessed the food and ate breakfast together. After eating, Kylin, and I volunteered to wash the dishes and clean the table. Makayla and her mother went to the entertainment room. They were not in the room long before I heard Lieko, yell out to me. "Come here baby!" "You need to see this!" Kylin continued washing the dishes, as I went to investigate. Makayla received a phone call, as I entered the room.

The reporter was outside of Mayor Hope's campaign site. Mr. Hope was announcing his withdrawal from the election. He stated that with the help of his wife, they decided that it was not worth winning the election, if the community is divided by racist opinions, constructed in order to put him back in office. They asked him why, and he said that he had decided that he could not morally stand by the way the people in his community and the country were being politically manipulated. "The way social media tools are being used to manipulate and target voters, in my opinion, is invasive and immoral." Mr. Hope added. Everyone could hear the roaring of a motorcycle nearby when they asked Mr. Hope what he meant by his statement, he denied comment and said that if he couldn't do anything about it from the inside, he would do something about it from the outside, with the help of his community. I smiled, in awe of his stand.

Mr. Hope was a hero again. Sadly, after, the news went to the communities, confusion about what happened the night before. Minorities were outraged and were demanding that my friend, Chief Bond, be terminated. "Oh my God, why?" I said to myself. At that moment, the news showed a short clip of the chaos, the night before. Then, they showed a reporter mentioning the events that led to the shooting of my son's friend, Drake and a clip of Chief Bond saying, some people need to be in jail. It was totally out of context and the minority community took that statement as though Chief Bond only cared about protecting a supremacist group. They felt as though he had no empathy about what happened to Drake.

They were only reacting from the way the media reported it. They did not understand that Chief Bond was trying to protect everyone from harm. He was not protecting, only the supremacist group, supporting Trump. The news station showed live footage of Chief Bond and his sister Lisa, leaving his home. His home had been vandalized and threats were being made towards him. They blamed Chief Bond for the shooting of Kylin's friend, Drake. The power of the media can be damaging to innocent lives, if not handled with care. I felt awful for him and immediately tried to reach Homie and Lisa, but I received no response from either one of them.

CHAPTER ELEVEN

JUST LOVE

Meanwhile, Officer Byson was home on paid suspension, eating a peanut butter and jelly sandwich, watching the events unfold on television. He did not seem concerned that he had shot an innocent teenager, or that he would lose his job. His justification for shooting the teenager was that Drake took two steps towards him after he told him to freeze. In Officer Bryson's opinion, he felt threatened, although Drake was unarmed, and Officer Bryson was the one with the weapon. A perfect example of stand-your ground laws gone wrong. Bryson's girlfriend was in the bedroom packing her things and angrily slamming things around. Bryson heard the commotion. He went to the bedroom to investigate and saw her putting her clothes into a suitcase.

"Where are you going," he asked. "Anywhere away from you," she said. "You shot that poor child." "I supported your career, but not for this." She added. "I had to protect myself baby, you don't know these people." He pleaded. "These people?" She was disappointed in his response. "Drake is a good boy." I've met him and his parents at the football games." "You have no right to judge them." "Drake wouldn't hurt anyone," she said, rushing past Bryson towards the front door of their apartment. "That's where you're wrong." "They are drug infested savages!" Bryson yelled trying to stop her. "Get your hands off of me," she cried. "You better pray to God that child lives." "I don't ever want to see your face again!" She said as she ran out the door and got into her vehicle. Bryson watched as she drove away. He hurriedly closed the door in fear that someone would see him and be confronted for what he had done. The city of Memphis was about to explode with anger and pain.

"Fuck!" I yelled out loud. "What the Fuck is going on around here!" The pride I felt at the monument of Martin Luther King Jr., quickly, got depleted by the actions of the media and the people, who didn't consider or know all the facts. In one second, a good man was crucified and a manipulative, political man, was now a hero. "Oh my God, No!" "I'm so sorry!" I heard Makayla say while talking on the phone. Kylin normally stays to himself, and doesn't place himself in the middle of his parent's issues, but when he heard his sister cry out, he did, as he always has, and came in, and tried to console her. We all asked her what was wrong.

"No, no, no," Makayla cried. "Ok, just come home and call me, as soon as you get here." Makayla hung up the phone and hugged her mother. "What is it?" Lieko, asked. Makayla sobbing, replied. "He killed himself." "She got there too late." Makayla cried. "Who, baby girl? Her mother asked, as Kylin and I stood there, waiting for answers. "Mee-Yon's uncle." "He jumped off a bridge, and killed himself!" We all hugged Makayla. "Baby girl, we're sorry for your friend." "We are here for her and her family." I tried to console her. "No, dad, you don't understand." Makayla pleaded. "Mee-Yon has been looking for him forever." She has been searching for him from the time he defected to South Korea." Makayla continued crying for her friend. "Sit down, Makayla." Kylin said, as he allowed her to lay on his shoulder, sitting on the couch. I felt awful for them both, my friend and my community. I wondered if anyone in this world was truly happy. I realized that it was not just the poor or minorities, who struggle with the true well-being of life. It was people all over the world. The quality of life is not valued, over money and power. People all over the world were paying the high cost of living on free land.

The common people, who were hard working, tax paying citizens, loved being Americans, but were worn out and imincely dissatisfied with their old, ancient, biased, vague and selective contract with the government, in distributing, protection, justice, equality and the real meaning of the pursuit of happiness for all. Not just in America, but people all over the world, young and old, could feel that there was something unnatural about society. Yet they could not exactly explain it. Mee-Yon's uncle felt this unexplainable misconnection with decency in the world. The growing rate of suicide amoung the young and the old were clear evidence in the need for serious reformation of the constitution and comapassion among human beings everywhere. It wasn't just poor black people having an uncandid rise in the number of suicide. People everywhere of all ethnicities were slipping into that dark grey hole of enslavement.

The division of the races did not completely exist. No one really cared about racism anymore. It was a marketing plan targeted towards voters for a profitable gain. Taxpayer's were too tired of trying to make an honest living for themselves to be racist. Police brutality and the profit from created and controlled poverty, existed mainly in minority communities, but citizens everywhere, black or white, were quickly becoming tortured grey souls. They were feeling like robotic consumers. They were preyed upon and manipulated for the greater good of wealthy decision makers and laws that were of a selective range.

Mee-Yon's uncle was old and living alone with other older people in South Korea, ignored and feeling useless, in a world that values money and power. Character and family values had no place in a world moving too fast, to slow down for morality, family bonds and decent humanity. Mee-Yon's uncle jumped off of the Mapo Bridge, in Seoul Korea, like others do, young and old. A bridge, so, famously known as The Bridge of Death. It was becoming abundantly clear that the lack of decency in the world was not being handled and addressed properly by those in the position to make a difference.

I finally received a phone call from Chief Bond. He was at the station. I could hear the disappointment and frustration in his voice. The media had misrepresented his statements and minorities in the community were gathering themselves at the police station, demanding justice for Drake. They blamed Chief Bond and Officer Bryson. Chief Bond had no idea that Mr. Anderson had paid someone in the editing news room to deliberately destroy his character. Mr. Anderson had a vendetta against Chief Bond and I because of our connection with Mayor Hope's daughter Janet and his love for him. Janets decision to speak against her father at a gay rights event, had nothing to do with our influence. Yet, Mr. Anderson, concocted a plan to destroy us if we did not convince her to stay away from us and the gay rights events that would drastically decrease Mr. Hopes chances of re-election. Mayor Hope had dropped out of the race and had distanced himself from Mr. Anderson. Mayor Hope's attempts to overturn gay rights laws were political power moves. Mayor Hope was not being true to himself and his struggle with his own confusion he felt with his sexual identity.

His own deception to his wife and thirst for power had caused him not to have a strong enough bond with his wife and daughter to had known that his daughter herself was gay and his was wife feeling alone and unloved. It caused her to undergo constant body changing surgery, to feel better about herself. He never noticed her attempts to gain his approval. Mr. Anderson was taking advantage of a confused married man and hoped to steal him away from his family and live a life with money, power and control, the way he himself was controlling Dora. Mr. Anderson had grown tired of punishing Dora and hoped to get rid of her once and for all and have the chance at real love again. He hadn't loved any man again like he loved Mayor Hope, since his teenage love killed himself.

Now, Mr. Anderson was losing his chance to have Mayor Hope as his lover and connection to more power. It looked as though it was going to be trouble in downtown Memphis once again and Mr. Anderson smiled as he watched the crowd shout for Chief Bonds resignation. Chef Bond informed me that Lisa was safe and gave me her location. Surprisingly, Lisa was staying at my sister's house and Angela welcomed her old friend and vowed to protect her.

As the crowd grew larger, haunting winds swirled around while more stations were gathering. Chief Bond was doing everything he could to prevent anyone from getting hurt. The crowd grew more in numbers and they held signs that called for justice for Drake as reporters filmed the crowd and asked questions. Traffic was being blocked by so many people walking towards the downtown police station holding signs and expressing their concerns for Shake and Bake Drake's life and their disapproval of the justice system. Officer Bryson was not fired and was home on paid suspension. People at home watching the events unfold on television were fearful of more destruction of the downtown area and more violence.

Chief Bond denied a phone call to the station from Mayor Hope. He instead got in touch with Drake's parents and asked if Drake's condition had improved. Drake's parents agreed to come down to the station and give a statement on Drake's condition publically to reporters and ask that the concerned citizens of Memphis stay calm and pray for their son. It was getting later in the evening before Drake's parents arrived at the station. There were more news stations and the protesters were flooding the streets of Memphis. Tactical units were preparing to take control of the crowd, but they were reluctantly holding off because the situation was being broadly covered in world news.

Tanks, weapons and tear gas were being gathered and officers formed a barrier in front of the station. In a city where the poverty rate suggests that if you see a child walking down the street, there is a 50 percent chance that that child lived in a less than desirable environment, like many states in America, we could not afford to allow political differences, influence a war between the police and minorities. The norm, in the minds of Americans, was that situations like these are nothing more than watching minorities get brutalized as entertainment. The purpose of standing for justice would be seen across the world as violent people that needed to be controlled. How deeply rooted in racism, that in America, a stand for justice is seen as a stand against the police and the United States.

Chief Bond's efforts of protecting the protestors were deteriorating more and more under the pressure of higher officials who were not connected to the community in order to understand that the crowd was not a threat. Drake's parents arrived and Chief Bond assisted them to a place they could speak to reporters and the protestors and be heard clearly. Chief Bond stayed away from being seen by protestors or reporters. He knew they had a false perception of his statement and intentions the night before. He didn't want the people in his community to show any signs of aggression. He knew if they saw him they would possibly be coerced by reporters to ask questions or show that they were displeased. He hoped that Drake's parents could help with their concerns about their son and keep the event peaceful.

Drake's mother spoke to the crowd while reporters covered the announcement. Her husband stood by her side and held her close as she told everyone to pray for her son. She also pleaded that they pray for the city of Memphis to continue to show their concern in a peaceful way. She told them that her son's condition had not changed but he was in stable condition and fighting for his life. She asked that they embrace each other and close their eyes as her husband gave a few words of encouragement. The crowd listened eagerly and all joined hands and bowed their heads as Drake's father prayed for peace for the community and life for their son. As the community joined together in prayer, Mayor Hope arrived and joined Drake's parents.

The mayor was now favorable and relatable now that he had withdrawn from the re-election due to political differences that were not in favor of minorities, gay rights and the common people interest in the city of Memphis. They showed their support for his return and someone in the crowd handed him a blue tee-shirt that had the words turn this red state blue on it. It was Makayla and her mother. The mayor held the tee-shirt up and asked them to join him and Drake's parents on stage.

The crowd applauded. Lieko spoke and talked about minorities embracing their cultures without fear of being judged or perceived to hate other cultures and against the

American flag. Her speech was powerful and inspiring. Lieko gave examples of white privilege that made white people watching on television aware that they were not aware of just how deep rooted their denial is and how unconsciously they benefit from it and judge others accordingly. Lieko also talked about the one man one vote voting system and turning a red state blue. She ended with minorities needing to establish their own political party and working together with other cultures to amend to abolish the electoral college.

She explained what basic human rights was and how they should be implemented in the lives of every human being without prejudice and discrimination. Her words danced together and came out like poetic songs of love as she mentioned the right to be free from discrimination, free from cruel treatment and punishment and the right to be free to own property and not be denied it. She spoke about minimum wages and the right to have favorable conditions at work and to be protected against unemployment. Lieko spoke about police brutality in such a way that even the police officers in tactical gear understood that her words were meant for them as well. Their uniforms did not separate them from being human beings .

Her words were clear and powerful. They were words of unity and the freedom to be empowered culturally as a means to be empowered in a more humanitarian way that was justifiably filled with equality and social justice for all American citizens. She spoke about the quality of life and well-being of all human beings. "Until we view ourselves as human, instead of black, white, blue, mee-too or me and you, we will not be able to separate the injustice associated with the social groups we identify with." Lieko said. "Yes, we all love our culture, but we do not and must not hate another culture and use those differences to judge or inflict punishment, poverty and pain among them." She added. As my son and I watched Lieko speak, I thought to myself, she should be the fucking president or at least run for a political position. If women only knew their true power, they would rule this world. And what a beautiful world it would be, run by teachers of love. Especially one with melanin who was connected to the sun and the universe.

She spoke highly of the mayor's moral decision to withdraw from his re-election. She then asked him to reconsider. Everyone applauded. The energy among the protestors was turning into a magical connection with each other. The haunting winds and the eerie presence faded away. Everyone understood what was happening and tears of pain and joy showed the world that they were human beings in pursuit of justice and equality for all. Other cultures at home watching the event on television were touched by the unity and the motivational speech and prayers given by Drake's parents, the mayor and Makayla's influential mother Lieko. Even a few of the men and women in tactical attire began to weep as her words made them aware that those few bad officers that used skin color as a justifiable means to kill first, were a few officers too many." It has to stop at this very moment and in our lifetime," She said. Some of them broke the barrier between them and the protestors and stood with the citizens as they took off their helmets. It was a beautiful site to see.

From out of nowhere, a group of teenagers chanted "Don't judge, just love!" It was the high school football team Drake played for. They made their way through the crowd and in front of the stage where reporters were filming. "Don't judge, just love!" They continued to chant as the people of Memphis of all races left their homes to be a part of something incredibly life changing and humanitarian. Kylin also watching his mother's speech on television was touched and admired the football players efforts in a peaceful stand for justice for his friend Drake.

Kylin jumped into my old truck with the big wooden barbeque grill hitched to it and cranked it up. "Hold up son, we're going too," I said. My sons and I drove to the area where the basketball players were chanting "Don't judge, just love." Kylin made his way near them and Kylin and Chris fired up the grill. Before anyone realized what was going on, the police officers as if reading their minds pulled out their grill's as well and the magic of Memphis filled the scene with that old Memphis barbeque love. Everyone joined in unity and the smell and flavor of Memphis style ribs circled the crowd with joy. Someone turned on music and the once feared protest turned into a celebration for justice in honor of shake and bake Drake. They understood Lieko and Makayla's message. It was time to vote only for local representatives. One man one vote. The only true voting system and turn this red state blue. Memphis would send a message to the world that we must amend to abolish the presidential electoral college voting system. I made my way close to Chief Bond.

I was worried about him. He loved his community and it saddened me to see him withdrawn and hanging in the background so that the people he loved and protected would not see him. I gave him a plate of memphis style ribs. "Thanks bro," he said with a smile. "Are you ok, my guy?" I asked. Hommie didn't answer immediately, as he was enjoying his ribs. He chewed the rest of the tasty meat while nodding his head in satisfaction. "Although I walk through the valley of death." Homie said, knowing i knew the rest of the statement. As young teens we had promised that no matter how hard things become in life, even in the valley of death, we would not give up. He was letting me know that he was ok. "Dig that." I said in acknowledgement. "We must live our best life." We both turned our attention to the magical miracle of unity that was happening memphis style right before our very eyes. Once again, I was proud of Memphis and the never give up attitude of its citizens.

Janet was watching the event on television at her client's home. She had picked them up from the hotel and had taken them home to celebrate. She used the money she had won to throw them a huge coming home party. Janet heard the roaring of a motorcycle and looked out the window to see why it seemed so close to the home of her clients. Janet didn't see anyone and continued watching the news.. She noticed that the drawing Jasper had evidently dropped in the yard while getting in the van, before rushing away to the hotel was picked up by one of the football players who lived in that community.

"Jasper!" Janet called out to him in excitement. "Look!" Jasper smiled adorably and proudly to see his sign. His sign JUST LOVE joined together with the signs of the football player's signs, Don't judge, just love. Janet was proud of her father once again and was eager to talk to him. She thanked the staff for their time and patience while taking care of the clients at the hotel. Janet hugged everyone and asked them to continue to celebrate while she left to go see her father. As Janet was getting into her car, she felt a powerful force knock her off of her feet. She fell unconscious, as she could feel her body being thrown into a vehicle.

CHAPTER TWELVE

SHRINE OF THE LIES

Mr. Anderson was drinking heavily and staring at a picture of Todd. Todd, his lover as a teenager, hung himself in jail, after being accused of raping Dora as a child. Dora knew nothing about her husband, as far as his connection with the traumatic event that altered the rest of her life. "My beautiful boy," he said softly, touching the face of the picture of Todd. Mr. Anderson, holding a gun and drinking scotch, directly out of the bottle, was blasting, "Take Me To Church", by Hozier, in his penthouse downtown. He came through the door of his penthouse and assumed that Miss Melanie Bautista was attending to his twelve year old, artistic son that his wife didn't know was alive. He hadn't gone to his home with his wife to check on her. He was heartbroken over Mr. Hope's decision to stay with his family and withdraw from his re-election run. Mr. Anderson sat behind his desk in his room, thinking of the loss of his first love Todd. Now, he was losing Nicolas Hope. The guilt of torturing Dora and faking his son's death was eating at his soul. He desperately wanted revenge and evil thoughts erupted in his drunken mind, to make Mr. Hope pay for dropping out of the election, and ruining their plans, for a prosperous, new beginning together.

He drank and drank more of the scotch. Mr. Anderson, indulged himself with cocaine. He snorted two lines of the white powder, until he was irrational in his thinking and passed out. He fell out of the chair, onto the floor. There, he slept, until the heat and sweat from too much cocaine and alcohol, woke him up. He struggled to get to his feet.

Wondering why he hadn't heard anything from Melanie or his son. He stumbled to the locked door of his master bedroom. There, in the hallway, unconscious and bleeding from the back of her head, was Melanie.

Mr. Anderson hurried to her side on the floor. He checked for a pulse, and was relieved that she was alive. Mr. Anderson called out for his son, while holding Melanie and trying to wake her. Hurting and confused, Melanie struggled to say, "She took him." "Who?" "Who took him?" Anderson asked. "Your wife attacked me." "She took your son." "Dora?" Mr. Anderson asked, realizing that somehow, Dora had discovered his secret. She knew he was alive and the dreadful consequences, she would enforce, on the both of them. He feared for their son's life. Mr. Anderson, then noticed a broken picture frame near Miss Bautista. It was a picture of the big white house Mr. Anderson and his wife purchased when they first moved to Memphis, located deep in the woods. Mr. Anderson knew then, Dora had left the photo on purpose. Anderson knew she would take the boy there. Anderson had abused and manipulated Dora's mental state there, in the woods, and kept their son's life a secret.

Detective Oswald, knocked at the door. Mr. Anderson pulled his shirt off and put it under Melanie's head. "Wait here Melanie, don't move," he said. He looked through the peephole and saw a man holding his badge in front of it. "Mr. Anderson," Oswald said, knocking at the door. Mr. Anderson opened the door frantically. "Help, me." "My wife attacked Melanie and has taken my son." Detective Oswald, called for an ambulance, as Miss Bautista, explained what happened to Oswald. Concerned about her injuries, Oswald did not tell Mr. Anderson that he already knew that he had faked their son's death. Oswald was originally there to question Anderson about it. Instead, he asked

Mr. Anderson, if he had reason to believe that Dora would hurt the child. "In her mental state, yes." "I'm afraid she will do something awful to him." Anderson explained. "Do you have any idea where she might have taken him?" Oswald asked, Anderson. "I have no clue, if she hasn't taken him to our home." "Please, we have to find them." Anderson pleaded.

Anderson was so focused on trying to deflect detective Oswald's attention to their home an hour and a half away, in the opposite direction of the house in the woods, he hadn't wondered how Oswald knew where to find the penthouse, and why he was there. Oswald called officers and instructed them to go to the home of Mr. and Mrs. Anderson. "Give me a description of your son." Oswald asked Anderson. Mr. Anderson gave a description and explained that he was autistic. Oswald gave the information to the officers. Oswald and Anderson waited for the ambulance.

After the ambulance arrived, they took care of Miss Bautista's injuries. They carefully loaded her into the ambulance and headed toward the hospital. Mr. Anderson told her that she would be ok and that he would make sure that she got the best of care. Detective Oswald gave Mr. Anderson his card and asked him to call him if he felt he needed to shed some light on the situation concerning his son's disappearance. Mr. Anderson agreed, eager to get rid of the detective. Mr. Anderson knew exactly where and why she had taken him. He was furious and immediately called for his driver to be down stairs in five minutes.

Mr. Anderson gathered his things and got on the elevator to meet his driver downstairs. While in the elevator, Mr. Anderson yelled while he was alone. "Fuck!" He gathered his composure and waited for the elevator door to open. The door opened to the parking garage and Wilbert rushed in on Mr. Anderson. Wilbert had Mr. Anderson pinned up against the back of the elevator. As the elevator door closed Mr. Anderson calmly said, "So, what is this?" "You know damn well what this is." "You stay the fuck away from my son!" Wilbert said, confident he could handle Mr. Anderson. Always well dressed, cool, calm and collected, Mr. Anderson, in a smooth voice, asked Wilbert to release him. "You want to take your hands away from around my throat so we can talk about this?"

Wilbert had grabbed Mr. Anderson by his collar and his fist were forcibly against Mr. Anderson's throat. Wilbert let go, but then pushed Mr. Anderson as hard as he could after he released him. Mr. Anderson, calmly fixed his clothes while keeping eye contact with Wilbert. "I don't need your son man." "There are plenty of young men like your son without a father at home to raise them." "While you're away, pleasuring yourself with that cheap instagram whore of yours, I'm helping your son pay the bills at home." Mr. Anderson said insultingly. "I raise my fucking son and we don't need your fucking drug money!" "I'm not gonna tell your bitch ass again to stay away from him!" "If I find out." Before Wilbert could finish talking, Mr. Aderson quickly chopped Wilbert in the throat after distracting him by adjusting his tie and his calm demeanor.

"Find out what?" "That young black boys are killing themselves?" "Or the ones that are not, we are paying somebody black to kill them so we can continue to erase your race all along blaming and criminalizing boys like your son with a father who isn't there like you?" "Regardless,"I don't need your son." Mr. Anderson said while forcibly holding Wilbert in a choke hold. "Don't you worry, you and your son will get what's coming to you." "In the meantime uneducated black boys come a dime a dozen in the streets." Mr. Anderson added.

"Fuck you!" Wilbert said while struggling to break himself free. To Wilbert's surprise, he had underestimated the strength and the military training Mr. Anderson had. "Easy, big fella," Mr. Anderson said. "You listen and listen good." "Come near me again, and not only will I make sure your poor neglected hard working wife loses her home, I'll fucking cut your heart out and feed it to your son before I put a bullet in his head." "Like I said, this is nothing personal, it's big business." "And black men are plentiful just waiting for us to put the drugs in their hands." Mr. Anderson boasted. "We supply the drugs, they sell it, and then we arrest their dumb asses, take the drugs and put the drugs right back in the streets for another uneducated fool with daddy issues, trying to fill the shoes of a nonexistent father like you." Wilbert tried desperately to free himself again.

"I'll fucking kill you!" Wilbert said, while trying to catch his breath as Mr. Anderson applied more pressure to his throat. Mr. Anderson pushed Wilbert into the elevator wall and then slammed his Wilbert's head into it. As Wilbert fell to the floor, Mr. Anderson told him not to worry. "Rather your son ends up in jail or working for me, I still profit from it, while you remain irrelevant in his life." Mr. Anderson then kicked Wilbert in the face and Wilbert lost consciousness. The elevator door opened as if magically waiting for the powerful Mr. Anderson. He stepped over Wilbert and walked out adjusting his clothes again. There was a roaring sound of a motorcycle and Mr. Anderson turned to see where it came from. He didn't see anyone so Mr. Anderson quickly got into his car and hurried away towards the old white house deep in the woods. He knew the photo on the floor was a message from his wife Dora.

He dialed Dora's cell phone. As soon as she said hello, Mr. Anderson yelled at her.. Something he always did behind closed doors. He hated her and married her to punish her for the rest of her life. He now knew Dora was getting closer to the truth about their son and why she has lived a tortured life at the hands of the man she thought would love and take care of her. "What have you done you crazy bitch!" Mr. Anderson reluctantly asked in fear that Dora had done something horrible to their son. Dora's mental state was even worse now, since that day in the woods and a traumatic encounter with an older teenaged boy named Todd.

Mr. Anderson feared that the police would find out that it was his dirty money that paid someone to run over Mr. Mark Wardlow and his wife while they were jogging that day. His manipulation and lies were catching up with Bob. He's teenage lover Todd had hung himself while being detained by police for supposedly sexually abusing a young Dora. No one knew about their secret and Bob stayed away from socializing with the teenagers in the community. Bob was a loner and he was jealous and warned Todd several times about hanging with a group of so-called friends who didn't respect him. Mr. Anderson now feared that his son's life was in danger and his plan to punish Dora for the rest of her life was coming to a traumatic end. Ironically, Mr. Anderson was speeding to the first house he introduced Dora to her unknowing beginning of the rest of her life being beaten, drugged, and mentally manipulated. The shrine of his lies was about to come crumbling down.

Dora yelled at her husband when he asked her what she had done. "You shut the fuck up Dora!" "No Dora, he's your son." "Don't hurt him." Dora's mental state was causing her to have conversations with herself out loud in different voices as if trying to control her thoughts and actions. Mr. Anderson was used to her talking to herself in response to a question, but she had never been this out of control. He could tell that she must have been spitting her medication out he had been giving her. "You crazy bitch if you hurt him, i'm going to." Before Mr. Anderson could finish what he was saying, Dora interrupted. "There is nothing you can do to me you haven't already done!" Dora continued. "I'm already dead inside and you're going to die with me." "Shut the fuck up Dora!" "You just be quiet!" Dora said aloud to herself. Dora was repeating Mr. Anderson's voice in her head from years of mental abuse.

"You crazy bitch!" Dora said to herself in a loud, deeper tone.. "You're not crazy Dora." "He's just fucking with your head Dora." Dora said in a softer voice trying to control herself. Mr. Anderson could tell there was no use trying to talk to her on the phone. He had to get to that big old house in the woods, and get there fast. Dora threw her cell phone after Mr. Anderson hung up the phone. She started pacing back and forth in the downstairs den. The lights were dim with a little bit of sunlight coming through. The den had a log cabin look and feel to it. There were deer heads on the wall and a fireplace. The floors were of wood and you could hear the pounding of her feet as she paced back and forth talking to herself. Dora had a stocky build and had the strength of two men. "Mary, Mary," she repeated to herself as she would stop occasionally and look at her son. Although they hadn't seen each other for years, somehow the boy was not frightened. He knew she was his mother. The boy just watched her as she frantically walked to each side of the room in front of him.

"Marry, Mary," Dora said again as she started to pace the floor again. "You shut the fuck up Dora!" She yelled. "You just be quiet!" Dora yelled to herself. "Mary, Mary, she said in a softer tone, remembering the story told to her in the woods as a child and how the devil would take his revenge. "They're just fucking with your head Dora." "He's your son." Dora said, trying to control her thoughts of hurting the son of the devil. "You crazy bitch!" Dora screamed while pacing the floor. Her screams and the pounding of her feet woke Janet, who was drugged and sitting with her back against a wooden column in the den. Janet's hands were tied to the pole.

Janet, still feeling groggy, and trying to figure out where she was, noticed Dora talking to herself. Janet then realized that she was tied to a pole. She struggled to get free. "Untie me she said," irritated and confused. "There, there, precious." "Don't worry your pretty little head." Dora replied. "I won't hurt you." Dora explained. "Then Dora ranted again. "You shut the fuck up Dora, you crazy bitch!" Janet watched Dora in fear for her safety. Then Janet noticed the boy sitting across from her in a chair. Janet noticed that the boy didn't seem afraid, in fact, he had no expression on his face at all. However, he was rocking back and forth ferociously and seemed concerned about her. Highly skilled in her field working with the mentally disabled, Janet could tell that Dora had some issues right away. Dora was not just a victim of physical abuse, like Janet originally thought, she was also very sick. Janet did not let the fact that she was tied up and didn't know why or where she was, affect her rational and crisis prevention skills. "Mrs. Anderson, are you ok?" Janet calmly said. "Can you free me hands so I can help you?" Janet pleaded in a comforting voice.

"They're trying to trick you Dora," Dora ranted while pacing the floor. She was beginning to sweat and picked up a fire poker from near the fireplace. "You just be quiet," Dora screamed as she slammed the rod in the palm of her hand. Janet made eye contact with the boy and told him everything would be ok." "That's right dear child, as long as she stays out of my business, I can make that bastard pay for what he's done." Dora said while playing with the boy's hair. "How can I help Mrs. Anderson?" "Has someone harmed you?" Janet asked, making sure she didn't show aggression towards Dora. "You can help by staying out of my business like I asked you to." "I don't need your help." "If he goes to jail, how can I make him suffer, for all he's done to me?" Janet realized what Dora was talking about when she visited Anderson's home and alerted the police that there might be some physical abuse in Anderson's home.

In Dora's mind, by kidnapping Janet, she would not interfere with her plans to make Mr. Anderson pay for his evil lies, deception and abuse. But Dora still did not know the full extent of the reasons Mr. Anderson was mentally manipulating and abusing her. "He's the devil!" Dora yelled as she approached Janet with the poker in her hand. Dora raised the poker over Janet's head as though she was going to strike her. "No, no Dora, that's not good." Janet said, trying desperately to hide her fear, but the tears in Janet's eyes clearly concerned the boy rocking in the chair, although Dora's mental state was not allowing her to manage her thinking and behavior. "Please calm down Mrs. Anderson and let me help you." Janet pleaded with Dora and became more annoyed because her wrists were tied and the pain from the rope brought more tears to her eyes. "You go to your room and shut the fuck up!" Dora screamed while standing over Janet and lowering the poker to the top of Janet's head. "I don't know Dora, they're trying to trick you." Dora said calmly to herself while turning away from Janet and walking away. The boy jumped up and hid behind the curtains.

"Come here!" Dora yelled at the boy. The boy started to cry. "You're the devil's son!" Dora yelled as she rushed across the room towards the now frightened child. "No!" Janet screamed trying so hard to get her wrist out of the rope, they began to bleed.. As Janet screamed the boy suddenly yelled out "mom, stop!" This startled Dora and she stopped immediately. Dora, fixated herself on the look in the child's eyes. The word mom, coming from the child, connected with Dora's soul. "That's ok Dora." It will be ok," Janet said, sobbing and understanding that she was witnessing that loving bond between a child and his mother that no matter what the situation is or how bad things can get, love has no boundaries. "Let's get out of here Dora." Janet said calmly." "Untie me and let us help you." The boy held Dora's hand and they both hugged each other and walked together to free Janet. Dora dropped the fire poker to the floor and kneeled down to cut the ropes. Dora then heard the speeding sound of a car coming down the long narrow dirt road.

Dora stood up quickly and ran to the window. "Here comes the devil." Dora said and grabbed the shotgun that was in the gun case. "Don't go out there!" Janet yelled but Dora's eyes were different now. She had the look of pain, sorrow and revenge. Hate took over and Dora ignored Janet's plea. Mrs. Anderson ran out onto the front porch and began to fire at the car speeding towards the old house with clouds of dirt wind swirling behind the quickly approaching vehicle. "You crazy bitch!" Mr. Anderson yelled as he swung the car side to side trying to avoid the buckshots. The boy started to scream and Janet worked desperately to break the ropes that were partially cut by Dora.

The ropes shredded apart as Janet forcefully pulled her wrist away. Bleeding, scared and burning with pain, Janet rushed to the other side of the room on her knees, to comfort the screaming child. "Shhh," she said. "Everything will be ok. They could still hear the buckshots and Janet and the boy looked out of the window. There at the top of the steps on the porch, Dora steadied her aim and fired again at the swerving car. This time the windshield of Mr. Anderson's car exploded and he crashed into a huge tree stump that sent him and the vehicle flying sideways through the air. The car landed with the wheels facing the smoke filled sky. Dora's eyes widened in excitement as she cautiously approached the car. Still pointing the loaded rifle at the car, she slowly looked for Mr. Anderson's body. How ironic, Dora thought to herself with a fearful smirk on her face. You son of a bitch. You told me that my son died in a car crash and now you will die right here, right now in the flames of your own vehicle of death. Dora bent over carefully to see if she could see Mr. Anderson through the smoke on the passenger side. The roof of the car was caved in too much and she had to go around the vehicle to look in from the other side. The flames coming from the back of the car were getting bigger and the heat was getting too hot for Dora to bare much longer. No matter what, she had to see his body lifeless but she had to move fast.

    Dora rushed to the other side, almost falling down when her knee buckled from stepping in a small trench in the grass. She prevented the fall by bracing herself on the busted up, front end of the upside down, smoking car. Dora gathered herself quickly and started around to the driver's side, while attempting to return the rifle back into defensive position. Out of nowhere Mr. Anderson appeared, bloodied, scorched and mad as hell. "You crazy bitch!" Mr. Anderson said, slapping her to the ground. This time Dora meant business and it was going to take more than a slap to control her like he has in the past.

Janet watched with fear and struggled to regain full control over her body. She hugged the child as they watched on the hardwood floors, helplessly through the window.

With the swiftness and the adrenaline of a fight to the death. Dora tried to reach the rifle that had fallen a few feet away from her. Mr. Anderson kicked the rifle away and stomped Dora's hand. Dora screamed and turned over on her back and kicked Mr. Anderson in his groin area. Mr. Anderson grunted in pain and fell to his knees. The flames were getting bigger and the heat made the blood, dirt and sweat on Dora's face burn her eyes. She got up quickly and smashed Mr. Anderson in the face with a rock she had grabbed from the ground. Dora tried to get to the rifle again. Limping she hurried as fast as she could. By then Mr. Anderson, still in pain from being kicked in the nuts, had gotten to his feet and was catching up to his insane wife Dora. Mr. Anderson ripped the tie from his neck and pulled off his singed dress shirt to reveal the tee shirt underneath. He had lost his cool and no longer gave a damn about the neatness of his clothes. "Im gonna fucking kill you," Mr. Anderson said just as he was reaching out for the back of Dora's head. Luckily, Dora saw an axe in one of the tree stumps, grabbed it and turned around, swinging the axe at Mr. Anderson as hard as she could.

Mr. Anderson ducked the axe and tackeled Dora to the ground. It knocked the wind out of Dora's lungs. Before she could catch her breath, her torturer was straddling her and slapping her face. "Oh my god." Janet said holding the scared child. Janet was hoping Dora would win the fight. Janet now knew, Dora needed help and Mr. Anderson was more horrible and dangerous than she thought. Right before Dora lost consciousness, Mr. Anderson stopped slapping his wife. "No, no, no." "Don't pass out now." "I want you to enjoy this as much as I am my love." Mr. Anderson said, getting to his feet and dragging Dora's body by one of her legs away from the burning car towards the big old house in the woods. The burning vehicle exploded and the force of it slammed Mr. Anderson to the ground just as he was getting nearer to the front of the old house.

Janet knew she had to do something, so she instructed the child to run and hide. Janet struggled to her feet and grabbed the fire poker. Mr. Anderson got back on his feet and was dragging Dora up the steps. The explosion and Dora's head hitting the steps woke her. She frantically started kicking again. Dora's power caused Mr. Anderson to fall through the wooden rails of the steps. Dora quickly grabbed one of the wooden pieces and hit Mr. Anderson as he was attempting to get up and grab her. Dora ran up the steps with Mr. Anderson chasing close behind. Dora got inside the house and tried to close the door behind her but Mr. Anderson was too fast and stopped the door with his upper body and shoulder. Dora screamed and slammed his head repeatedly with the door. "You fucking bitch!" Mr. Anderson yelled as he used every muscle in his body to force the door open. Dora fell backwards on the wood floor. Dora turned quickly to her stomach, scrambling to get up. She started running down the short hallway, where she left Janet tied up in the den. "Where's my son!" Mr. Anderson yelled as Dora ran inside the den area.

Dora screamed when she saw Janet about to hit her with the fire poker. Janet was hiding near the doorway waiting to strike Mr. Anderson. When she saw it was Dora, she lowered the poker and Dora slammed the entrance way door to the den. Dora frantically locked the door and backed away from the door. "Mary, Mary," Dora softly repeated to herself. "The devil is here." Dora then realized that Janet was free and they both stared at each other. Dora made a quick dart towards Janet and Janet raised the fire poker. "Dora, let me help you." "Please don't do this." Janet said. "Dora, don't do this," Dora repeated Janet's words to herself. Dora turned away from Janet looking for her son. "What have you done to him?" "Where is he?" Dora screamed, turning back to face Janet holding the poker. Calm down Mrs. Anderson," Janet pleaded with Dora, not wanting to hit her with the poker.

"He's safe Mrs. Anderson." Janet said. "You just shut the fuck up you crazy bitch," Dora yelled and darted towards Janet again. Janet screamed and suddenly there was a crash at the door. Mr. Anderson had gone back outside and picked up the axe. He repeatedly sliced through the door with the sharp iron piece of medal. Dora backed away forgetting about Janet. "Mary, Mary," Dora whispered to herself. "The devil is here." It didn't take but a couple of more slams to the door with the axe to make a big enough hole for Mr. Anderson to see inside. He looked through the hole at Dora, scared and talking to herself. "I'm going to fucking kill you!" Mr. Anderson said while reaching in to unlock the door. Standing to the side of the door, Janet smashed Mr. Anderson's hand as he was reaching in. "Fuck!" "Son of a bitch," Mr. Anderson yelled, grabbing his hand in pain and wondering who hit him. He cautiously stood back some. Just a few more inches away to avoid getting hit and looked inside. To his surprise, he saw Janet. He gave a devilish smile. "Oh yes, I am going to enjoy this." Mr. Anderson boasted while winking his eye at Janet. "Welcome to the party babe." Dora was still talking to herself and backing further away. Mr. Anderson stepped back and snarled loudly, as he kicked the shattered door down.

Still groggy, Janet tried to defend herself with the poker. Mr. Anderson, blocked her swing with it and spun around behind Janet. Dora turned away and started running up the stairs as Janet struggled with the side headlock Mr. Anderson had her in. "Come here, you crazy bitch!" Mr. Anderson yelled as the boy came out from hiding and started hitting his dad and crying. The child kept hitting his dad's sides and back while Mr. Anderson held Janet and comforted his son. "It's ok son, it's ok," Mr. Anderson said while hugging his child with his free arm. Dora heard the boy defending Janet and came back down the stairs. As much as Dora's traumatic experience in the woods as a child had convinced her that mentally disabled children were the spawn of the devil, she had connected with her son and wanted him to be safe. "Henry." Dora called her son's name for the first time in years.

Henry had gathered himself and Mr. Anderson told Dora to come over. "Come join the party," Mr. Anderson demanded from Dora. Mr. Anderson pushed Janet down on the couch as he grabbed Dora when she came near them. Mr. Anderson picked up the pieces of rope from the floor and tied Janet and Dora's hands behind their backs. "Go to your room and do a puzzle for your mother son." Mr. Anderson instructed Henry. 'She'd be happy to see what you can do." Henry went upstairs as Janet and Dora nodded their heads at him in agreement. They both wanted Henry in a less hostile place. Mr. Anderson took his cell phone out and started taking pictures of Janet. Janet looked at him in confusion and tried to kick the phone out of his hand. Mr. Anderson laughed and said "This is going to be good." "Let's see how Daddy is going to like this." "Smile for daddy," he smirked as Janet struggled with tears in her eyes. Mr. Anderson sent the photo to the mayor with a text that read, come to the old house in deer heaven and do not contact the police or Janet dies. The mayor received the photo and his heart dropped into his stomach. The mayor ran away from the people celebrating unity and justice and threw up.

I noticed that the mayor was in distress and asked if he was ok? We didn't have a good relationship, being that he wanted me to have nothing to do with his daughter. Yet I was concerned for his well being. With his hands shaking he showed me a text message with the photo of Janet horrified, tied up with tears in her eyes. "Oh my God, where is she?" "Who sent this to you!" I demanded. I turned to show Homie. "No!" The mayor pleaded, he will kill her if I get the police involved. "He's killed before and he won't think twice to kill again," the mayor explained. Homie noticed that there was something wrong. "What's going on," Homie asked as the mayor stood there trembling. I showed Homie the photo. The mayor reached for the phone to stop me and I asked him to trust me. "Don't worry, we got this." "I love her too." "Let us handle this, please."

We all rushed away from the crowd and headed to the police office of Chief of police Bond. Before we reached his office, detective Olswald called us to his desk. There, he showed us the recording taken from the Starbucks across from the street where Chief Bond's bar was set on fire. It was a clear recorded close up of Dora. Mr. Anderson's wife. Detective Olswald also informed Homie that Dora had also kidnapped their son who was supposedly dead. "We believe Dora is at the house they own located on Devil's point." Detective Olswald explained that they found a letter at Anderson's residence demanding that her husband come to that house immediately. It was all beginning to add up. The mayor also told Detective Olswald and Chief Bond about Mr. Anderson's confession to him that he was involved in the plan to murder Mark Wardlow & his wife. They all put together a plan to rescue Janet and the child. They didn't know that Dora would be there as well. Officer Bond gave me an earpiece so that we could secretly communicate with each other. I would drive Mr. Anderson down Devil's Point road disguised as his Limo driver. Devil point road was a long curvy dirt road through the woods, saturated with deers. They called that area deer heaven. It was without a doubt a scary road to travel, especially at night.

It was getting close to dawn by now and we had to act fast. The mayor and I would approach the big haunted looking wood house from the only entrance as a distraction, while Homie & officers would be airlifted over the wooded area in the back of the house, near the lake. I got Lieko's attention. "Hey I gotta go." "Janet is in trouble," I explained. I'll meet you back at the house." "What the fuck?" "Seriously, you're leaving your family again for that bitch?" Lieko harshly reminded me of what happened to Kylin's friend Drake the last time I was with Janet. "Look, I can't explain right now babe." "I gotta go," I said trying to leave without Lieko making a scene. "Ok, you go ahead and leave your family again, worrying about her ass." "Don't worry about rushing home." "We won't be there." I hesitated and looked at her for a second wanting to explain but time did not allow it, so I just hurried away. Again, my inability to give all those I loved all my time cursed me as a father. I learned how to parent from my mother. She was a provider and that's all she knew or had time to give. I wanted so badly to secure the bond my wife and I had reestablished but a child and Janet's life was in danger and I hoped that Lieko would understand later.

Mr. Anderson couldn't have asked for anything better than Janet being at the wrong place at the right time. Bob wanted revenge on the mayor for deciding to stay with his wife and dropping out of the re-election. Mr. Anderson was furious and scorned. Now his secrets were catching up to him and the police would be discovering that he had misinformed them soon. Instead of fleeing, Mr. Anderson wanted to make sure that Janet knew about their affair and perhaps kill them all once Mr. Hope arrived. He then would take his son and plan his escape. "Let us go you fucking bastard!" Janet cried. "No, no, no sweetheart." Not until your father arrives." "We've got some interesting news for you." "If things go well, we'll all be one big happy family." Mr. Anderson said with a devilish grin again.

"As for you, Dora, my sweet insane wife, you will no longer exist in this cruel world my love." "Think of it as a courtesy for ruining my beautiful Todd's life. "Todd?" Mrs Anderson asked. "Oh yes, beautiful, sweet loving Todd." "A boy filled with hopes, dreams and so much potential." "His body was lean and strong." "His smile would light up the room." "He loved me and I loved him tremendously." Mr. Anderson explained while Dora and Janet listened in confusion. "His only weakness was his need to be accepted by friends that mistreated him and had no respect for him." "You remember those assholes in the woods, don't you Dora?" Dora's eyes widened as she started to put two and two together. "You remember my beautiful innocent Todd, don't you? "You accused him of doing something awful to you." "Something he couldn't have been capable of because he was in love with me." Mr. Anderson explained. "You took him away from me and he ended his sweet beautiful life." "That's why I've been slowly taking you away from you." "Bastard!" Dora yelled at him trying to break free.

"Settle down you crazy fool, it will all be over soon." Mr. Anderson said, rubbing Dora's hair. "Imagine my surprise when you walked into my office sniffling like a spoiled rotten little child, claiming that you were so damaged as a kid. "I knew it was

Todd that sent you to me." "Todd wanted justice and he knew I'd make you suffer." "Fuck you!" Dora screamed. "I know what happened to me." "You can go to hell with your beautiful Todd for all that I care!" "You shut the fuck up Dora!" Dora said to herself. "That's right Dora, Mr. Anderson said. "You shut the fuck up." "On second thought, you yell and scream all you want to." "Killing you is more satisfying that way when I bash your fucking skull in!" Mr. Anderson screamed while grabbing Dora by the throat. "No!" Janet pleaded tied up and sitting across from Dora on the other couch.

Janet jumped to her feet and charged at Mr. Anderson with her hands tied behind her back to stop him from choking Dora. With one swift motion, Mr. Anderson back-handed slapped Janet. She fell to the floor. Dora screamed at him to leave Janet alone. Irritated by their attempts to attack him, Mr. Anderson forcefully guided them to the wooden column in the den, where Janet was originally tied to. He binded them both together. It was getting close to dark and the fire from the car outside was slowly spreading among the trees nearby. Mr. Anderson could see the flicker of flames through the window now that the sun was going down. Before he could do anything about the flames, his cell phone rang. "We're here, The mayor said mistakenly. "I told you not to bring anyone." Bob scolded. I was worried. "It's just the limo driver," the mayor explained. We're at the gate. Mr. Anderson had locked the gate behind him about a mile down from the house. "Wait there." Bob instructed. "I'll be there shortly. "Where's my daughter?" The mayor asked. "I want to talk to her." :Dad!" Janet yelled knowing her father was on the phone.

"Shut up!" Bob angrily yelled at Janet. "It all could've been so easy, but daddy had to mess it up." "Please don't hurt her," the Mayor asked Bob. "I'm here." Janet listened, afraid and wondering why Mr. Anderson had so much hatred towards her father. "I only wanted to love you baby girl, like I loved your father." Bob said getting his M-16 weapon out of the locked case. The rifle was not enough for the damage Bob wanted to do if he encountered any problems outside. He rubbed Janet's head, wiping tears from her face. "Todd was taken from me and now Nick." "I'm not going to let that happen without a fight." Bob said softly, as if heartbroken, unaware that all was lost. Nickalos had told the police everything about the murder of Mark Wardlow and he also feared that Janet and his wife would find out about his sexual curiosity for men. Mr. Bob Anderson specifically.

The mayor was risking it all to save his daughter. In Bob's mind, he only wanted to convince the mayor to leave his family and live his life with him by any means necessary. Janet was beginning to realize that she and her father shared a common secret life and felt awful for her mother. Janet wished that she had been open and honest about her sexual preference to her parents. She wondered if she had done so, would she and her father be in this horrible situation. Mr. Anderson walked outside to confront his lover armed with a deadly weapon as Janet and Dora feared for everyone's life.

While outside Mr. Anderson signaled for his men to come out from hiding. He had called his trained ex-military thugs to protect him after sending the photo of Janet to the mayor. All of them were riding four wheelers and dressed in camouflage gear. They were heavily armed. Mr. Anderson climbed on the back of one of the four wheelers and instructed the other one to watch the perimeter of the house. Sitting in the front seat of the limo, I saw them coming down the bumpy dirt road aligned with the giant trees on each side.

The sun was getting low. Barely light outside, I hoped that the dusk along with the tinted windows would not allow Mr. Anderson to recognize me. I tilted my black, limo hat down further not to reveal my face. I noticed the flicker of flames and smoke in the distance behind them. Not knowing it was Anderson's car in flames, I began to think this was a bad idea and hoped that Chief Bond and officers were already making their way to the back of the house. "We got movement my guy." "It's Mr. Anderson and someone with a weapon strapped across his back." "Where are you?" I said, worried that the earpiece would be working properly. "You miss me?" "Homie replied jokingly and chuckled." "With that ugly mug of yours, hell no, but we could use your assistance sweetheart." "Homie laughed and said, "That's not good pillow talk, sexy." "But don't you worry, I'm coming home for dinner right now." "We're near the lake behind the house as we speak." "Janet must be inside, stall them as long as you can." "I have back up coming your way." "Cool, I love you too." I said, watching Mr. Anderson carefully. "You know I think you're cute but not that cute." "But I'm gonna save your ass this time," Homie added, while instructing the helicopter operator to lower him down near the lake. "Shit bruh, don't do me no favors," I said.

We didn't figure on Mr. Anderson having his men with him in our haste to rescue Janet and the child. Mr. Anderson got off of the four wheeler and walked towards the gate to unlock it. His M-16 automatic weapon was strapped over his shoulders and pointed towards the sky. After opening the gate he motioned for us to follow them back to the house.

We followed the four wheeler slowly, as we wondered what was on fire.in the distance. The whole scene had an eerie spell about it. The slow approaching darkness, the smoke and flames among the tall trees made the hair on the back of my neck stand up. I felt a sense of a ghostly dejavu. Something about this seemed terrorizing and familiar. Something unsettling provoked the turmoil inside of me. As we followed, the four wheeler drifted back and Mr. Anderson and the driver rolled up on each side of the limo, checking the inside first to see the mayor in the back. Then they drove around to check to see who was driving.

"Dear God, please," I said to myself, hoping he didn't recognize me. They drove ahead again and suddenly stopped halfway up the road. Mr. Anderson jumped off the back of the four wheeler and pointed the M-16 towards us. "Get out the car now," he demanded. The driver of the four Wheeler turned and drove to the back of the limo and demanded that the mayor get out of the limo as well. He ordered the mayor to walk to the other side beside me. "Well, look what we have here, Anderson said standing in front of me. Although my hands were raised, he struck me in the face with the butt end of his weapon. I fell to the ground on one knee.

Trying to get up, we all heard a roaring sound quickly approaching. As soon as Anderson and his armed associate turned towards the sound, Jermaine brilliantly performed a life saving motorcycle stunt to free us..As Jermaine got close enough to our assailants, he stopped on the dime with the front wheel of his motorcycle and spun around with the rear wheel in the air and hit both Anderson and the other man in the chest. The fiercely spinning tire seemed to cut and burn through the skin of each one of them as they flew backwards in the brush of the nearby trees. I jumped on the back of Jermaine's motorcycle and the mayor got in the limo and we all raced away towards the house just ahead to save Janet and the child. Within seconds we heard gunfire and knew they were shooting to kill. Our assailants were firing and trying to catch us on the four wheeler we'd left behind.

I felt a firearm at Jermaine's waist and removed it to defend us. More shots were fired at us as we desperately tried to avoid being hit. The shade from the tall trees, the speed we were going and the lowering of the sun helped cover us from the rapid fire of ammo. The mayor was caught off guard by a deer that suddenly ran across in front of him.. He veered off to the side of the narrow dirt road and crashed into the woods. Jermaine spun around sideways to see if the mayor was ok. Anderson got off the four wheeler near the crash before we could do anything about the mayor. As soon as Anderson jumped off, the driver of the four wheeler continued towards us and fired at us again. Jermaine quickly detoured off the dirt road leaving a cloud of dust behind. Jermaine carefully navigated through the thick of the trees as the four wheeler, followed with deadly intentions. Jermaine took a trail approaching a hill as I fired back trying to hold on at the same time. Before we knew it, the hill ended and we were airborne.

It must have been pure instinct for me to do what I did next. It was not something I would do normally in any situation. While in the air I let go of Jermaine and allowed myself to float away from the motorcycle. I went from a floating sitting position and twisted my body around towards the man on the four wheeler who was now airborne himself. I twisted my body around, still in the air with my body in a prone position pointing Jermaine's firearm directly at the enemy behind. I fired one single shot and managed to hit him in the shoulder as we both fell to the ground. I slammed into the ground hard and tumbled several feet more. The air left my body as I rolled quickly to the left and escaped the growling , four wheeler that almost crashed on top of me. I could hear the sirens of the police cars approaching in the distance, Chief Bond had summoned to help us.

Jermaine helped me to my feet as we both looked at the dead man laying in the brush nearby. I was badly shaken up and still had troubled breathing. It felt like my ribs were crushed. Jermaine was ok and he desperately tried to help me catch my breath and help me get back to the road. "No, go help the mayor!" I demanded of Jermaine. "The police are on the way!" "I can make it to the road and they will see me!" "Are you sure Mr. Snowden?" Jermaine asked. "Yeah, man." "Go!" "Get the hell out of here!" I yelled feeling the pain in my chest and ribs. Jermaine put his helmet back on and picked up his motorcycle. He fired his monster of a machine up and spun off towards the road. The motorcycle's roar was loud and had a purpose. It growled with a vengeance as Jermaine heroically willed his monster to catch up to and save the mayor from Mr. Anderson. The roar faded as I struggled to reach the edge of the road.

I could hear the sirens getting closer. "Aye man, are you there?" I said, checking my earpiece. Officer Bond did not reply. "Double 07?" I called out to Homie again, trying to joke and lighten the horrible situation we all were in. I always called him double 07 when I wanted to tease him, since we were kids. Still, there was no reply and I worried that something had gone terribly wrong. "If you can hear me, just hold on my guy." "The police and I are coming to save you and Janet;'s ass." I laughed deliriously, feeling faint but still limping to the road. I could hear the sirens getting louder and I could see the road. The heat became suddenly intense as the road seemed to appear and disappear while I struggled to reach the edge in time to flag officers down for help and inform them of the mayor and his daughter being in grave danger.

And then there was silence. I felt no pain and visions of millions of ants crawling all over my body startled me. I yelled as I tried to shake them away. I could not get to my feet. The more I shook, the more the ants attacked and overpowered me. They needed me to survive yet they were eating away at the labor of my soul. I was a necessity, yet expendable at the same time. Much like minorities and essential workers today. I remembered how as a child I admired their orderly work ethics to keep the queen alive. I found myself in the position of the government desperately struggling to survive and protect the wealthy from COVID-19. Like the queen it would either be them or myself that would survive and I was not willing to die. Not today I thought to myself.

Kicking my legs violently and trying to wipe them from my eyes, they suddenly disappeared. Still laying there, a man stood over me with a gun pointed at my face. Before I could react, he fired. Everything went into red. Nothing but red in my eyes and I could barely see an image of a man walking towards me again. I wondered if I was dead. I frantically crawled backwards, trying to get away. "No! "Get away from me!" I yelled. All at once the blood red color I was struggling to see through, went away in a flash. The image of the man walking calmly towards me became clearer to me. It was my brother Byron. Slowly he approached me smiling with a gun in his hand. Why, I wondered. Half way in front of me another smaller image joined him. Byron gave the weapon to the smaller image and the small boy walked the rest of the way closer to me as Byron stood there smiling.

I was confused and awkwardly stunned that the little boy standing in front of me looked like me at the age I took a man's life. Holding the weapon the child was shaking with fear. Without a doubt, I was sadly looking at myself and confronting the pain I'd carried inside from that deadly day forward. "It wasn't your fault." I said to him softly. "You're going to grow up and be a wonderful father." "It's ok, just let it go," I assured him as I gently removed the weapon that he was holding so tightly pressed against his chest. I smiled as I noticed how tiny I was back then and wanted to hug all of his sorrows away. He looked frightened, so I reached out my hand to comfort him. Still sitting, I got myself in a kneeling position to console myself as a scared little boy. I reached my hand out again. The boy just looked down at it as he wepted. Suddenly, he looked up and yelled like thunder. "Wake up!" I woke up to the sound of police car sirens passing by. "No, no, no, wait!" I yelled, waving my arms around as painful as it was, as I finally reached the road. The last car flew by as I fell to my knees behind it, coughing from the dust the police car left behind.

    I jumped to my feet again, and began running up the road towards the big old house. I could still hear the sirens and I could see flames up ahead. It was getting a little darker but I could still see a little light coming in from the top of the tall trees that aligned each side of this road, this scene, while getting this familiar feeling I'd somehow experienced this before. I felt an uncomfortable wind that raised the hairs on the back of my neck as I ran further and faster to escape this haunting wind, towards the danger that was just ahead. I was running away from a deja vu that had a grasp on my soul, towards a scary uncertainty of what was to be discovered ahead. With no time to think or look back, I knew I had to continue to run faster. I was needed just up the road and I wasn't going to let them or myself down. Faster I ran ignoring the pain. Getting there to save them was my only objective.

CHAPTER THIRTEEN

MARY'S REVENGE

Chief Bond and a tactical officer, fought the force of the wind hurling downward over them as the helicopter flew away. They rushed to the thick of the woods, just close enough to the lake behind the big old wooded ,white house where Janet was being held captive. They both moved swiftly and approached the back of the house near the lake. The trees were tall and thick which did not allow much light to get through. It made it easier for Chief Bond and his officer to move closer in silence. The light that was able to shine though, danced in the ripples of the lake. Bond noticed the dim light glistening from the lake but had no time to admire its beauty. He was on a dangerous mission to save Janet. Normally, Chief Bond didn't go out in the field with his officers but this was personal. It was his friend in trouble and he had lost the respect of his community over a statement taken out of context on the news. He had nothing to lose but what was truly important in his life. The love and safety of his family and friends. This he could not allow.

As they reached the back entrance Chief Bond noticed one of Mr. Anderson's men posted in position to fire upon anyone attempting to come past the perimeter of the lake. "Hold up." Bond said to his officer, pointing in the direction of the man aiming a rifle, unaware that he had been made. Bond aimed his weapon towards the rifleman as he started his slow crawl towards him. Bond didn't want to fire his weapon. He needed to capture him. The noise from the weapon would alert anyone inside the home possibly guarding Janet. His officer maneuvered tactically right behind Bond. Just as Bond was in the best position to make his move on the rifleman, Bond felt the hard steel of a weapon being held to the back of his head.

"That's right," "You know what time it is." The officer assisting Chief Bond said. "Aye man, are you there?" Bond heard me through his earpiece but he could not respond. The rifleman had lured Chief Bond into a trap with the assistance of Mr. Anderson's paid informant on the police force. The officer motioned for Bond to move forward toward the back of the big house as the rifleman met them with a smirk on his face. Chief Bond held his hands up and behind his head in disbelief one of his men was dirty. Bond noticed that the water in the lake looked as though it had started to boil and rumble over. It seemed angry and looked as though it was reacting to a severe thunderstorm but it was not raining at all. Bond felt it was disturbing for the beauty of the dim light on the lake to now be rumbling with an intense sense of knowing something was horribly unsettling and unnatural. " Hands raised and behind his head, Bond walked up the steps unto the deck with both armed men behind him. As one of the armed men opened the back door, Chief Bond could hear screams and yelling inside of the house.

As I was frantically trying to reach the house and Chief Bond was being held at gunpoint Janet and Dora were struggling to free themselves. Dora yelled, "I'm not your possession!" "God help me do what needs to be done!" she added. Dora wildly tossed her body around violently. Shaking her head in disbelief she couldn't free herself from the ropes around her wrists."I'm going to kill you, you son of a bitch! " Dora screamed. "Just shut the fuck up bitch!" Dora demanded of herself in her much deeper voice. "Janet once again attempted to calm Dora down although Janet was worried that the situation they were in was only going to get worse if someone didn't intervene soon. Janet of course was trying her best to manipulate the ropes as best she could to get them to loosen.

"Janet noticed the boy sitting on the top steps watching them. He looked frightened as Dora continued to violently scream out angry thoughts in different voices in her head. Janet used her head to motion for the scared child to come down the stairs and help them untie the ropes. Dora was breathing heavily and exhausted from her rageful attempts to break away from the pole they were bound to. It wasn't the most logical thing to do but in order to gather more strength she began to bang the back of her head against the wooden pole rapidly. "No!" Janet begged. Suddenly Dora's head fell into her chest and she was deadly silent. The child started down the steps as Janet tried to get Dora to wake up or show any sign that she was alright. "Dora?" Janet said, hoping for a response.

All the lights on the wall exploded and the chandelier burst into flames as Dora threw her head backwards with one loud pound against the pole again. Dora's eyes were wide and looking upwards toward the ceiling. She took a huge gasp for air. Chief Bond and the men guiding him towards the room Janet and Dora were in, ducked as the lights in the hallway released sparks and glass over them. The sound of Dora's head hitting the wood troubled the child and he ran back up the stairs as the chandelier hit the floor. Janet screamed. Dora's head slowly moved downward and to the side facing the windows. Her mouth was open and there was no blinking of her eyes. A different look of fear came over her face as Dora noticed the image of the kinky haired woman again. Maraciously, she stood there watching through the glass. She then began to move purposely to her right, walking outside the bay windows. The woman was fixated on Dora as Dora could not stop looking at this haunting image of herself as well. As she slowly walked a slight thundering sound surrounded the house. Rumbling clouds started to cover the sky and the ripples in the lake became more angry than before.

Still keeping eye contact with the female image, Dora's head moved slowly, seemingly controlled by the woman outside who appeared in each window making her way towards the front door of the house. "Mary, Mary," Dora whispered as the inside lights flickered. The lights went out as Dora took a deep breath in fear that Mary was about to enter the front door. There was a single loud bang on the door as the lights came back on. The door swung open and Dora could see that it was not Mary, but it was another frightening sight. Mr. Anderson forcefully pushed the mayor down the short hallway into the room where Dora and Janet were still tied to the wooden pole.

As Mr. Anderson pushed the mayor in front of Janet, he yelled. "Tell her or you all die!" As the mayor fell to the floor he looked at his daughter with tears in her eyes. "Sugar plum, it's going to be ok," he said. "Dad!" Janet said, noticing that Mr. Anderson had been assaulting her father. At that moment the two men holding Chief Bond at gunpoint entered the room from the other side of the huge house. Mr. Anderson pointed his weapon at Bond. ""Who dies first is up to you Mr. Mayor." "Tell her now or I will choose for you!" The mayor moved closer to his daughter on the floor and hugged her tightly. "Please Bob, we can work this out." The mayor pleaded. "I don't have time for fucking games anymore Mr. Mayor!" Anderson said. "You want to play games?" Okay, we'll play games!" Anderson yelled.

"Let's see who dies first." Anderson pointed his weapon at each hostage in the room." "Eeny meeny miny moe." Anderson's weapon ended up facing Dora's head at the end of his countdown. "Just fucking do it!" Dora yelled as the mayor interrupted. "Okay, wait one moment!" With one arm holding Janet and the other arm raised to stop Mr. Anderson from killing anyone else, the mayor adjusted himself in a kneeling position in front of his daughter as if begging her to understand what he was about to say. Dora began struggling and screaming at her husband again. "You son of a bitch!" "Haven't you destroyed enough lives?" "Go ahead and just kill me." "Let them go!" Dora demanded of Mr. Anderson. "You shut the fuck up bitch!" Mr. Anderson said as he slapped her with the back of his hand. Dora's head fell downward in pain.

The loud roar of Jermaine's monstrous motorcycle came up the stairs and burst into the room. Unable to stop himself, Jermaine and his bike slid to the side and fell to the floor in the room. Bond sprung into action taking full advantage of the sudden distraction. He threw a hard elbow to one of his assailants and knocked him out while disarming the weapon from the other man holding the gun behind him. Mr. Anderson aimed at Chief Bond as Bond rushed toward him. Anderson fired and hit Bond in the shoulder. Bond's momentum was enough to get going and Bond tackled Anderson to the floor. Again the house lights flickered and a thunderous sound came from the skies outside the big house. The young boy ran down the stairs and loosened the ropes enough so that Janet and Dora could free themselves while Anderson and Bond fought. The mayor frantically helped the boy free his daughter as she cried.

The hallway lights exploded again and the sparks fell to the floor and started to burn the wood floors. Something phenomenal was happening. A supernatural force was making its presence known and it was evident that she was not pleased with the evils of humanity. The fire reached the room near the two men Bond had knocked out. The fire singed their clothing and they both woke up in pain. Still they attempted to protect Mr.

Anderson who was now taking advantage of Bond's injury while they inflicted brutal bodily harm on each other. Bond saw the room filling up with smoke and struggled to get Anderson's weapon as the other two men came rushing towards them. Just in the nick of time Bond grabbed the weapon and swiftly rolled over and fired at the two men, killing them instantly.

Anderson saw Dora run up the stairs with their son and he quickly ran up the stairs after them. After firing two deadly shots, Bond turned his weapon towards Anderson, but he had escaped during the distraction while the lights flickered angrily and the smoke from the flames filled the room. Bond yelled across the room at Jermaine who was injured and stunned himself to get Janet out of the house. "Get the hell out of here!" Bond demanded. Chief Homie Bond started up the stairs after Mr. Anderson. Abeam fell from the ceiling nearby and toppled over Bond, trapping him as Jermaine helped everyone else flee the burning house. Jermaine assisted Janet out of the front entrance as they could hear police car sirens pulling up quickly outside. It was a frightening scene to the police as they pulled up. Flames violently took over the house, while the vehicle burned outside as Jermaine assisted the mayor and Janet to safety.

Everyone outside noticed the thunderous white and gray flickering clouds that were swirling above the big old house. The clouds hovered above the rooftop while the rest of the sky appeared to be normal. Lightning flickered within the darkness of the storm above. The officers were frozen in their admiration of the scene although the howling clouds presented itself to be a dangerous site to see. The wind blew at their clothing as if to say stay away. Janet hugged her father tightly while Jermaine stood there with his mouth wide open, looking up at the sky. Inside the house the crimes against humanity continued to unfold itself.

The mother of the earth warned us to protect the natural resources and used them for good. She warned us that racism would cripple minds, hearts and souls. She told us to love each other equally or the demons of social and economic injustice would destroy us. She was furious about police brutality and the lack of morality in the world. She was not pleased with the political manipulation and warned us that the laws were to protect and care for us all and not just for those who were seen as acceptable by way of wealth or color of their skin. We didn't listen and now mother nature was presenting herself to rectify the sins against humanity. Society had reached an unpleasant state of mind and lacked empathy.

We were warned that it was only our experiences that made us different, not the color of our skin or the paper in our pockets. Mother Mary was furious that we had allowed our beliefs about each other, to cause so much pain among us. She was neither good or evil, yet she possessed the power to inflict them both on those who broke her laws or obeyed them. The greater good for the land and those who cherished it as equals would prevail. With one look in your eyes she had the power to read your soul and do with it as she pleased in order to make certain that the people of the land be victorious in justice and peace among us all.

Inside the big house the flames were spreading fast. The house upstairs was filling up with smoke as Dora followed her son into one of the bedrooms. Anderson hurried right behind them but Dora slammed the door before he could get in the room. She turned toward her son and demanded that he get down on the floor as Anderson banged at the door. Dora covered her son's mouth with a pillow case and noticed that he was pointing at a square door in the wall of his bedroom. Dora opened the door and could see that it was a laundry chute that had been turned into a slide that led to the outside of the house. She nodded her head yes and helped him inside the chute while covering his mouth, protecting him from the smoke. The boy quickly glided through the smoke down the chute to safety. Janet saw him pop out and ran to get him away from the house. Janet cried as she smothered him with hugs, kisses and comfort. The boy turned to see if Dora was close behind.

Just as Dora was trying to get into the chute, Anderson's body came forcefully through the door. He fell on the floor and Janet picked a lamp up and slammed it over his head. Dora ran out of the room into the smoke filled hallway. Anderson, yelling at her, was close on her tail. Just across the hallway a few doors up, Dora attempted to enter another room. Anderson grabbed her from behind as she fell to the floor. She frantically kicked and screamed at him to get away from her. The violent kicks of survival forced Anderson back against the wall. He grabbed his groin and was choking from the smoke. It was just enough time for Dora to enter the other bedroom. She slammed the door behind her again. Just as she turned away from the door, all her pain and suffering hit her in her chest like a wrecking ball as she gasped for air to breathe. She suddenly realized she had entered the bedroom where she was sexually, physically and verbally abused by her husband as he was once again trying to force his way through the door.

Dora stood there and could not move as forgotten memories of Anderson, sexally abusing her tied body on the bed, were flashing away in her head. They pierced her mind and her soul like death by a million stabbing knives. She stood there not bothered by the banging on the door anymore. She was not bothered by the smoke or the spreading fire. She was captured in her torture she had endured and and terrified by the realization that her husband had deliberately kept her on drugs to erase his horrible acts of vengeance on her his loss of Todd. Anderson intended to torture her over and over again while manulating her already fragile mind.

As Anderson was yelling at her through the door, Dora's frightened, sad eyes suddenly became aware of the kinky haired woman who looked exactly like Dora standing right in front of her with fire in her eyes. "Mary, Mary," Dora whispered as the Fire in Mary's eyes lowered into a bluish, watery glow. In that very moment The bangiang t the door stopped and Mr. Anderson burst through the door pointing his weapon at Dora. Dora turned towards Mr. Anderson. Anderson could not see the ghostly figure of hurricane Mary but Dora knew she was there and could feel her powerful presence. "Die bitch!" Anderson fired his weapon with hate in his eyes. A bullet entered Dora's heart and came out of her back straight into Mary's heart who was standing behind Dora strangely welcoming the traffic events unfolding before them. As the bullet entered their hearts simultaneously the floor underneath them broke open from the fire. They both fell through as Dora closed her eyes and Mary wrapped her arms around Dora as they fell through into the flames. They dropped quickly to the bottom of the hissing flames. They both miraculously did not burn or hit the floor.

They found themselves turning slowly inside a glowing supernatural force field until Dora and Mary united together as one powerful being. The bullet wound healed. She opened her fiery eyes and willed the lake behind the house to respond to her demands. The lake magically floated away from the land and formed a gigantic tidal wave that looked as if it was a fifty foot sea monster sent from hurricane bitch i'm going to drown your ass.

Above them Bond again swiftly came through the door and tackled Anderson as he was firing at Dora. Chief Bond and Anderson both fell through the window and landed hard on the outside deck. The deck collapsed from the force of the two men and they fell further to the ground as glass fell on top of them. Janet screamed and held the boy tightly to prevent him from seeing what she figured to be the death of them both. I was just reaching the back of the police cars drastically out of breath and could see Bond and Mr. Anderson breaking through the upstairs window. I heard Janet scream and was terrified that I had reached them too late. I rushed through a few officers and heard them calling for the fire department to respond immediately. Before I could get past them all one of the officers grabbed me and said, "Hey, where are you going boy."

"Wait a minute, you don't understand," I replied as I could now see Janet standing with her father along with Jermaine and a child. I could see other officers pulling my friend and Mr. Anderson away from the flames. "My God, please don't be dead," said trying to get the officer to release me. "I know them, he's my friend." "I have to help him!" I struggled to get away from the officer who was pulling at my clothes and attempting to restrain me. "I said dont move boy!" The officer said while another white officer came over to help him restrain me. The Mayor noticed me and what was going on. "Hey, let him go! The Mayor yelled. The officers either didn't hear the mayor or didn't care. Before I knew it I was struck in the ribs by one officer and thrown to the ground by the other. The both of them were hitting and kicking me as I desperately tried to explain I was not a threat to them. I covered myself the best as I could while the blows to my body and face continued. Just as the other officers were coming to stop the beating or join in, a thunderous sound rang out. Everyone outside the burning house looked toward the rumbling coming from inside the house while the two officers repeatedly struck me with the clubs.

Mary closed her flaming eyes and the lake fell over the big burning house. The house hissed as the flames went t. Inside the force field the powerful being opened her eyes again. With fire in her eyes violently reacted as if she was being beaten by a million billy clubs, sticks, stones and fists. Each blow she felt from those that had been beaten four hundred years ago. She felt the pain and saw the faces of those inflicting the pain. Angry, hateful faces and evil grins and laughter rang in her head as her body seemed to bruise with each bloww from long ago. She screamed in such a sorrowful and hurtful way that the forcefield exploded around her and sent flaming fragments of the big house away into the sky.

I felt a presence inside of me as she screamed. She took over my eyes and could see for herself that the two officers violently trying to enforce their will on me were the same police officers that were using excessive force on a young black teenage boy as Dory fled the fire she had started at Bond's night club. It angered her and I felt her presence leave my body as she inflicted all the pain of four hundred years of beatings on the officers. She willed her power into their souls and allowed them to see and feel all the pain of minorities. The officers cried out of horror and shame. Their bones broke with each blow from long ago. The pain and cries was too terrifying for them to bear. They both fell to their knees holding their ears to try and stop the sound of tortured souls. They then felt the flesh tear from their backs and the sound of howling whips breaking through the sound barriers of time. No longer able to withstand the pain, the two officers laid there motionless in the dirt.

The fire cooled in Queen Mary's eyes, still standing in the center of what used to be the house Dora suffered from the shrine of Anderson's lies. With the thunderous clouds swirling in the sky above her, Mary took a deep breath of relief. The other officers could not believe what they were witnessing and stood there with an eerie silent understanding why Queen Mary did not make them suffer the wrath of Long ago.

The battered officer's laying on the ground slowly started to move again as the rain pummeled and crashed down on top of them.. At once the punishment of the thunderous rains stopped. The two men were coughing up blood and trying to get their feet. That seemed to anger Mary and she decided that they hadn't suffered enough. With the dark clouds rumbling above her she stood there in the center of what was left of the house that once enslaved her soul. Smoke circled around her feet from the smoldering rubbish as she willed her powers upon us mere mortals. Our biggest sin as human beings had been the illusion of control and the arrogance to judge others. The wind snarled and hurled tiny, burning and flickering debris around us like a pissed off tornado.

I rushed to Janet's side and helped Janet and her father cover the child's eyes and console him. Mary was about thirty feet away but she covered that distance with three steps towards the two crooked officers. As they were about to stand up from a kneeling position trying to recover from the four hundred years of pain Queen Mary had inflicted on them, Mary, now with the use and combined with Dora's tortured soul, suddenly appeared before the two officers. With the twist of her wrist the officers grabbed their throats wrenching and gasping for air as both of their bodies violently got yanked into the air. They kicked and pulled at a rope around their necks that no one could see.

As frightened as the other officers were witnessing the invisible, deadly rope strangling the two corrupt policemen suspended in thin air, some of them felt an urgent duty to protect their fellow officers. Several of them pulled their weapons and fired them at Mary. Janet screamed as chief Bond was regaining consciousness and could see through the howling wind the two men kicking in the air while the other policemen emptied their weapons with panic fire. Bond and the rest of us could only see dashes of dark smoke swiftly moving around the distraught policemen. Mary evaded bullets with the speed of light. The stunned men found themselves disarmed as Mary appeared again in front of the officers. Her flaming eyes cooled and all of the empty firearms dropped to her feet. Queen Mary released a loud roar of annoyance as she dropped the two strangling men as well. The officers cried in shame while the other cops knew immediately and understood that she was warning them that she meant no harm to them. What was meant for the two sniffling policemen to endure had been done and Mary turned away from them.

As for the rest of the officers of the law they had been decent human beings and although they knew of the two officers' repeated misconduct, Queen Mary spared them this time and it was clear that it would be this time only if they continued to turn a blind eye to brutality by misguided cops. She then swiftly turned her head at the sound of Mr. Anderson's fear as he fled into the woods. Mr. Anderson couldn't believe his eyes when he saw the power of Mother Nature but he knew for sure in the pit of his gut that he had helped create the forces of revenge and corrective actions that were about to come down upon himself and the entire human race.

Queen Mary the mother of this earth was not pleased with how we'd been treating each other and she was infuriated by the inequality and injustice in the world. She was disgusted by the separation of human beings by economic and social differences. Mr. Anderson was one those people who preyed upon desperate people in desperate situations for his own selfish and evil gain of power and wealth. Mary, Mother of Nature could feel the anguish of the oppressed and the mental and physical abuse boiling from Dora's soul inside of her. Mary felt Dora's energy and heard Dora's voice. "Let's get that son of a bitch!" Thunder erupted and lightning struck the ground in front of Mr. Anderson as he ran like a rabbit through the woods ducking and dodging each lightning bolt that hit the ground in every direction he tried to flee.

The owls in the path of the trees Anderson scattered about in fear focused their wise old knowing eyes on Mr. Anderson as he hollered and screamed "Fuck you bitch!," after each bolt of flashing power exploded just beyond him causing him to pursue a different escape route. Queen Mary could see Anderson's body heat through the eyes of each wise old owl that could hear and see Anderson rustling hurriedly through the dark of the night. He scampered through the trees trying to avoid each bolt of fiery thrusted down in his path. Suddenly Mary appeared in front of Anderson and he stopped dad in his tracks. She made a shoving gesture with her arms and her powerful energy forced Anderson backwards. His body flew backwards in the air and slammed into a tree. Anderson groaned in pain. "Dora please, don't," he pleaded. "You shut the fuck up bitch," Dora's voice snarled. Anderson looked up at her. Terrified at the sound of Dora's voice and the sight of Dora's body possessed with powers he could not understand , Anderson quickly tried to get up and escape. With her hands she ejected bolts of lightning to each side of his legs. Anderson groaned and yelled out of desperation. He was trapped with his back against the tree.

"Who the hell are you!," Anderson cried. "Mary, Mary she said with a piercing whisper of pain that made Anderson's ears bleed. The vines from the dirt around Anderson began to crawl around him. They twisted and tangled themselves around Anderson's limbs as he moaned and cried for them to stop. The more he struggled to free himself the tighter the vines twisted though his clothing into his flesh. Mary moved herself over him. She stood over Anderson almost as if she was floating. "What do you want from me!" Anderson yelled in pain as the dirty, twisted vines that entangled him sliced deeper into his veins.

"You took Todd away from me!" "He died alone and afraid because of your lies!" "Who are you to judge me you crazy bitch," Anderson pleaded as the ground underneath him rumbled and the dirt, sticks and pebbles vibrated in the air angrily. Mary with Dora inside her soul released a roar of discomforting sorrow into Anderson's face. Shift swiftly grabbed his throat and exhaled Dora's memory of that awful night into Anderson's lungs. Anderson's eyes widened and his pupils began to swell. A sudden silence surrounded him and he was now standing in the woods alone.

But these woods were different he thought to himself. They were strangely familiar. He realized that somehow he'd found himself in the trails of the woods he and Todd had shared so many loving walks together. There was no one after him and for a moment he wondered if he'd died from Mary's death lock around his throat. He rubbed his throat and checked his arms and legs. There were no bruises. He took a deep breath of relief. He was thankful that at least, if he was dead he was now in a place where he'd experienced love and happiness.

As suddenly as he felt a sense of peace he saw little Dora running towards him. her scared little body whipped through his like a rush of cold wind. He heard her pounding heartbeat and felt her fear of whatever was after her. Anderson turned and watched the small child run away though the woods. He then felt another thrust of cold wind enter through his back and out his chest as fast as it came. Although this time it was a bigger presence Anderson knew it was his beautiful Todd chasing after tiny little Dora. Anderson then realized that he was witnessing what happened that night he lost the love of his life. He hurried after them to see what transpired in those woods long ago. As he caught up to the sounds of whimpering and rustling of fallen leaves, Anderson felt portrayal and a feeling of revulsion when he saw them. Never in his darkest hour Anderson could've imagined Todd doing such a degrading and horrible thing to a child.

"Todd, no," Anderson pleaded as he lunged out to stop him. His hand quickly went through Todd's shoulders like a jet through the fog. Anderson felt the grip around his neck again and the pain in his limbs started to singe his blood. He grunting to fight for air he was sucked away back against the tree with Mary snarling in his face. Her eyes filled with flames Mary's head was the only recognizable human looking form. The rest of her body turned into smoke and wrapped around Anderson's body like a snake seeking to strangle the life out of his prey. Grimacing, Anderson's eyes widened as he felt the smoke circling around him turn into flames. Mary made the symptoms of a horrible and deadly virus spread and appear all over his body.

He screamed louder and louder from the extreme pain. Fire burned inside him as he screamed. "Dora please," he yelled. 'Shut the fuck up bitch!" Mary snarled and ripped her burning flames from inside him outwards as his body exploded into burning pieces of flesh. Her eyes cooled and she was back into her human form.

The officers were assisting paramedics with getting Bond, Jermaine, Janet and the child looked over for injuries. They all heard Mr. Anderson's screams but didn't dare try to intervene. The few officers that did try were instructed by the mayor not to go after the super being that had taken over Dora's body. The mayor told officers about Anderson's crimes and forbade them to help. The mayor knew that somehow what they had experienced that night was something beyond their understanding and Anderson would never be seen again. The little boy was standing by Janet's side while her wounds were being bandaged. He was whimpering and Janet was holding his hand. That's when they saw Dora or whatever she had become again.

She slowly walked out of the woods towards her son. No one was afraid. She was calm and there were no flames in her eyes and she was smiling as she reached out her hand and placed one hand on his shoulder and the other one on Janet's shoulder as well. She spoke to the both of them without moving her lips. A green glow traveled from her hands and formed a glowing shield around the three of them. The mayor and I stood close by watching in awe of the beautiful site. We could tell that she was pleased with Janet and something amazing was happening . Inside the shield they all smiled at each other and nodded their heads in agreement about a conversation which we could not hear. The glow, the shield and Dora vanished. Janet hugged the child and we moved closer. Janet and the boy still grinning with joy looked over at us.

'Are you guys ok," the mayor asked. "Jannet with tears of joy replied "Yes, everything is perfect." "Isn't that right little man?" To everyone's surprise the boy spoke fluently. Whatever ailments that caused his autism was gone and he would now be raised, loved and taken care of by Janet. We had witnessed a miracle but Janet knew that Queen Mary was not was not pleased with us as a society and her work was not done. Queen Mary was disgusted by the division of the races and the way we'd all been treating each other. Janet knew in heart that the world would hear from Mary again or feel Mother Nature's corrective actions once more. We all knew we had experienced something extraordinary as we all gathered in our vehicles, bandaged our wounds and drove away. Something much bigger than the human race had made it clear that our actions would no longer go without accountability.

Months later I opened a center for the youth equipped with parent support programs and credit repair education teams. I hired professionals and students of positive psychology to educate teachers and parents how important it was to be careful not to damage a child's moral and mental development by focusing only on good grades academically. Instead educators at the center looked for each person's strength in character or skill and used that to build a sense of belongingness and self worth. Janet's father was re-elected and he gladly collaborated with people who wanted to help provide food and equipment for all the physical activities during the summer programs.

Sady, at the ribbon cutting of the community center my family was there in support but I had to watch them walk away and get in the car to leave Memphis. My heart dropped as I stood there while the Mayor was speaking. My first thought was to run after them. I had gotten caught up again with something else other than them. I had not yet gotten a chance to apologize to my daughter and let her know I understood and loved her dearly. I knew all Lieko wanted from me was to try to prioritize my time. I had not yet gotten a chance to speak with her about my intentions to better my efforts in family bonding.

My mother could cuss you out and make you feel loved at the same time while providing for the family. I had learned the hard way that what looked innocent and admirable on my mother, did not look good on me as a man. I was a provider like my mother. I learned to work hard for my family but that wasn't enough. My daugther and my wife required more than just being a provider. And when I raised my voice it wasn't seen as I saw my mother. To me mom was tired and only venting. My family saw me as threatning because I was a man. They required me to be a good listner, a caregiver and spend quality time with them.

I had failed in all those areas because I had learned my parenting from a struggling single mother who had no time other than to be a provider. Her law was the law and there was nothing anyone could say about it. "I pay the damn cost to be the boss," she would say. She was the mother and the father. I hated my father because he wasn't there for us and my dreams of bashing in his corsps was only a symbol of my struggle with myself. It wasn't my father I hated. I hated that I didn't know how give my family what they needed from me other than just paying the bills. I learned that my mom paid the cost and paid her dues honorably. As a man what was good for her was partially good for me. I had know excuse. I wasn't raising a family on my on. I paid the cost to have an opinion and that was it. As far as paying my dues. I had let my family down and now they were leaving me again while I was standing in glory fighting for another cause at the opening of the community center.

My cell phone vibrated in my pocket. It was Kylin. "Dad, are you ok?, he asked. "No, son I've made so many mistakes and I just need time to fix things." "Dad, don't worry, I'm proud of you and I understand." Before I could reply Kylin assured me that they would be back home for Christmas. "Are you sure my guy?" I whispered trying not to be too loud as the mayer was speaking. "Yes, dad." "I got it from a reliable source." At that moment I heard my daughter and Lieko in the background. "We are proud of you!" "See ya Christmas!" "I love you son." "Thank you for calling," I said with tears in my eyes. "Love you too," Kylin said. "See ya soon." I was at the mercy of time again and I felt that I was losing them again. All I could do was wait and pray. I was relieved to see my oldest son Chris in the crowd smiling and pointing at Reshaud standing next to him. I couldn't wait until the opening ceremony was over and me and my two older boys could go out for dinner and catch up.

I'm not sure if he ever told Janet or his wife the true nature of his relationship with Mr. Anderson but he was definitely a changed man. The community respected him again and the mayor and his daughter were closer than before.

Shake and Bake Drake recovered miraculously and helped with the coaching of the kids basketball team. Drake swears a woman in his dreams spoke to him and her touch released him from a lengthy coma. Janet and I smiled at each other when Drake described her. My good friend recovered from his injuries as well and retired from being Chief of police. Bond and I became business partners and opened the youth center together. To our dismay the day after, Donald Trump won the election. Adore and Janet married and adopted Dora's son. As for the rookie officer who shot and almost killed basketball star Shake and Bake Drake, he was not fired from the police force. He was also never the same again.

Those who lived in his neighborhood say that he was visited nightly by a ghostly spirit. They could hear his screams in the middle of the night. Some say that they could see him standing in front of his bathroom mirror yelling and screaming for the torture to end. Right before the 2016 election, he was found in his bathroom tub in an apparent suiccide attempt and was committed to a mental facility. He still resides there and still claims that black crows eat at his eyes and soul every night.

The election was a shocking disappointment to the brown communities and the common people of the United States. Once again we as citizens of the United States were shown that we must amend to abolish the presidential electoral college voting system and not be governed only by the wealthy elite. The division of the races grew worse than before. Janet and I knew that the next four to eight years would be lessons taught by Queen Mary that we as human beings and how we treat each other would surely lead to our destruction.

The founder of positive Psychology, Martin Seligman had once suggested that in order to have a more humanitarian society we must stop focusing on economic, political and social gain. If we do not, we as a society are headed for chaos. Now Queen Mary would show us in drastic ways that the choice would be ours. That choice would be to stand together peacefully despite our differences, and survive, or continue to believe that our differences justify our thinking and behavior towards each other and die.

After Trump's victory Queen Mary knew that she would infantrate the white house and further divide them as well with her powers. As leaders they would have to learn the errors of their cognitive distance between them and the common people who depended on their guidance and protection. But first, she visited Dora's home who was a part of her powerful presence among this land. She walked towards the home through the fields of flowers where she used to play. The flowers were dead and came alive behind her as she walked past. Mary smiled gently allowing her fingertips to brush over the happily dancing flowers swaying to her return.

Just ahead was the old water well that had been sealed since Dora was a child. Dora's mother was standing in Dora's bedroom window where she would often see her daughter looking out the window over the well awaiting her father. She saw what looked like her daughter walking towards the well and noticed the land come alive with vibrant colors of flowers in the field. At first she smiled but then Mary stopped at the well. Dora's mother knew instantly that the secrets behind her Dora's father's disappearance were being discovered by this powerful being standing by the well sobbing. Her nightmares were now real. The beautiful flowers turned dark and Queen Mary looked up at Dora's mother with fire in her eyes. Dora's mother with fear in her eyes backed away from the window. What happened after that no one knows. The house is now boarded up and abandoned. No one dares go to the house and Queen Mary continues to seek out those who commit crimes against humanity.

Made in the USA
Middletown, DE
28 January 2021